MY NAME IS STRAMER

MY NAME
IS STRAMER

MY NAME IS STRAMER

MIKOŁAJ ŁOZIŃSKI

TRANSLATED BY
ANTONIA LLOYD-JONES

UNCORRECTED PROOF
PUSHKIN PRESS

Pushkin Press
Somerset House, Strand
London WC2R 1LA

The right of Mikołaj Łoziński to be identified as the author of this Work has been asserted by him in accordance with the Copyright, Designs & Patents Act 1988

Original text © Copyright by Mikołaj Łoziński, 2019
All rights reserved
Published by arrangement with Wydawnictwo Literackie, Cracow
English translation © 2025 Antonia Lloyd-Jones

My Name is Stramer was first published as *Stramer* by Wydawnictwo Literackie in Cracow, 2019

First published by Pushkin Press in 2025

This publication has been supported by the ©POLAND Translation Program

ISBN 13: 978-1-80533-213-8

All rights reserved. No part of this publication may be reproduced, stored in a retrieval system or transmitted in any form or by any means, electronic, mechanical, photocopying, recording or otherwise, without prior permission in writing from Pushkin Press

A CIP catalogue record for this title is available from the British Library

The authorised representative in the EEA is eucomply OÜ, Pärnu mnt. 139b-14, 11317, Tallinn, Estonia, hello@eucompliancepartner.com, +33757690241

Designed and typeset by Tetragon, London
Printed and bound in the United Kingdom by Clays Ltd, Elcograf S.p.A.

Pushkin Press is committed to a sustainable future for our business, our readers and our planet. This book is made from paper from forests that support responsible forestry.

www.pushkinpress.com

1 3 5 7 9 8 6 4 2

MY NAME IS STRAMER

MY NAME
IS STRAMER

TRANSLATOR'S NOTE

This novel is set in the city of Tarnów, in south-eastern Poland. Most of the action takes place in the interwar period and during the Second World War. Here are a few historical facts that the reader might find useful.

Before the First World War Poland had been wiped off the map for 123 years by the neighbouring empires. Tarnów was in the province of Galicia, part of Austria-Hungary. In this period the Poles fought hard for their independence, staging several insurgencies that were crushed. During the First World War, the independence movement leader Józef Piłsudski formed the Polish Legions within the Austro-Hungarian army. A number of Polish Jews fought as legionaries and supported Polish independence.

Within the Second Polish Republic, as interwar Poland was known, Jews represented about 10% of the population (or roughly 3.5 million in 1939). Their status ranged across society and they had a vibrant culture. Yiddish was gradually replaced by Polish as the language spoken by ever more assimilated, educated young Jews in the major cities. But anti-Semitism, always present, intensified in this period. Many Jews sympathized with or took part in the Zionist, socialist or communist movements, and were involved in illegal activities for which they risked imprisonment.

When the Second World War broke out, under the terms of the Ribbentrop-Molotov Pact Germany invaded Poland from the west and the Soviet Union invaded it from the east. Poland was overpowered and occupied in a matter of days. Much of Galicia, including the city of Lwów, was annexed by the Soviet Union. In the occupied "General Government", as the Nazis renamed what was left of Poland, the Jews were forced to live in ghettos before being deported to labour camps or death camps. Desperate Jews changed their identities, surviving by acquiring false documents, known as "Aryan papers". Many Polish Jews escaped east to the comparative safety of the now Soviet part of the country, but had to flee further east in 1942 when Germany attacked the Soviet Union.

For my father

For my father

I

NATHAN

It was for Rywka that he had come back from America. His story was that he'd thought about her every day for four whole years, until finally he'd bought a ticket for the ship home. He never told how he'd come back without a cent, and had even had to borrow the money for the ticket from his older brother. But he still liked to throw American words into conversation that nobody else in the family understood.

He brought back a leather belt with a brass buckle. A farewell gift from his brother for the return journey to Poland. They had embraced on the New York quay and never seen each other again. Examining the successive use of the belt holes showed how his figure had changed over the years. Nathan himself couldn't believe how slim he had once been.

Like his father and grandfather, he resembled a wrestler. An old wrestler. Broad shoulders, almost no neck and a chest that was thrown forwards, like a rooster's. He was proud of the fact that in town they called him "Boss".

Asked in the street how things were, he'd reply: "Good, but not hopeless."

He'd tip his hat and walk on.

Every few months a letter came from New York. Ben would write that unfortunately he must postpone his trip to Tarnów. He couldn't leave his stationery store right now. The school year was starting, and he had too many orders. He'd had to fire a dishonest employee, but he hadn't yet found a new, trustworthy one to replace her. The Christian holiday of Christmas was approaching, a time for present giving, and "it's not just Jews who buy from us!" His wife had been unwell again. The crisis had begun, and if he were to leave the store now he'd have nothing to return to America for. But he missed home, and was planning to come next year. He couldn't wait to meet Rywka and their sons and daughters.

"As parents you know best what they need, so buy it as a gift from me," he'd write.

Tucked into the letter written on company paper (BEN STRAMER GENERAL MERCHANDISE, 33 Grand St, NY) and folded in three he'd include some green banknotes. He always wrapped them in purple tissue paper to make it impossible to see what was inside. Every time the tissue paper stained the banknotes, which came out of the envelope green-and-purple, so Rywka had to wash them carefully, then dry them above the kitchen stove.

Nathan only ever gave the children the American stamps from the envelopes. He put away the dollars.

"I work non-stop, so I've no time to earn money," he'd explain to his wife.

And he waited. Waited, waited and waited. For a good business opportunity to come along. A chance that would change the life of the Stramer family. Take them out of their one-room flat with a small kitchen on the ground floor at the very end of Goldhammer Street, pick them up and put them down on the top floor of a town house with stained-glass windows on the stairwells, in a smart Polish-Jewish district, best of all near a stop on the tramline of which Tarnów was so proud. In one of those spacious apartments with lots of rooms and high ceilings, a toilet and a bathroom with running water, electric lighting and a flowery balcony.

There was a brief period when it looked as if it would come true. He had just bought a whole wagonload of rosin at a cheap price. He was told it was used by violinists to grease their bows. How was he to know there were so few violinists in Tarnów? Finally he bought a fiddle and a bow himself, and told Salek, who according to Rywka had lovely long fingers, to play it.

Despite the fact that Nathan had never been to the philharmonic or the opera, in his mind's eye he could already see his seven-year-old son there – on the Kraków stage, or even in Vienna. Rywka too found it easy to imagine him in a little tailcoat, with a bow tie and a storm of curly hair. By contrast with his brothers, he didn't like fighting or getting dirty.

"Here you are," said Nathan, handing him the instrument. "A famous violinist has never done harm to any family."

And he knew how much could be earned from selling tickets.

But nothing came of this either.

He did in fact send Salek to a Polish woman for violin lessons a couple of times. But did he actually get there? Every time they had visitors, and Nathan asked Salek to give "a little concert", the boy wriggled out of it. Until six months on, Nathan stopped asking, and simply ordered him to "go fetch your violin this instant".

After the performance Nathan had nothing to say.

Only once the visitors had gone did he twist his head on his almost non-existent neck and say in English: "Goddammit!"

Nobody understood, so he added: "That's money down the drain."

That evening, for the first time instead of grabbing his belt, he grabbed the bow. At least it'd come in useful! And indeed it did. He didn't have to strike at all hard for Salek to make noises similar to the ones that shortly before, during his "little concert", the child had extracted from his violin.

At work too, behind the till at the Jewish butcher's, Nathan waited for the business opportunity of a lifetime. As a result, in a fervour of ideas, plans and minutely calculated future profits, he sometimes gave the customers the wrong change.

"Shit," he'd say in English, if at the end of the day there was money missing from the till.

But occasionally there was too much money. Then he didn't say a word, just discreetly put the difference in his trouser pocket.

"I've got children," he thought to himself.

When the time finally came, he felt like running home from work. On the way he did the shopping. At home he never sat still for an instant. He helped Rywka to prepare the food. During supper he would ask the children how things were at school. But then he hadn't the patience to listen. At least he inquired, thought Rywka. Then he would ask her to sit down and rest. He would gather the plates, roll up his shirt sleeves and do the dishes in a bowl.

Only when he'd finished, and the children were asleep, would he remove his rolled-up dollars from the metal bedpost.

"I've got a feeling this time it's going to work out. This is going to be it."

Rywka didn't answer. But Nathan knew what she was thinking: Why didn't it occur to you last time to examine at least one of those candles properly?

He hadn't wanted to lose time, he was afraid other buyers would beat him to it, someone would offer a higher price. But his greatest fear was that the seller, who had come here all the way from Kolomyia, would find out how much candles cost in Tarnów, and would realize he was selling his for a song. Nathan had to act quickly. An opportunity like this would never be repeated. Candles four times cheaper than from the famous Jewish "Little Bee" factory, which supplied all the churches in Tarnów! Maybe even in Kraków too. So he'd heard, but he didn't know if it was true or just advertising. Anyway, he had also heard that the owner, Mr Szpilman, gave the socialists money on the quiet. But that in turn could be disinformation put about by the factory's competitors.

When the moment came to pay, Nathan had even felt like a cheat. Maybe he should have tossed in a bit more for the wretched salesman from Kolomyia, or at least invited him for lunch? But at once that feeling had given way to regret that the man had no more goods for sale. So maybe it wasn't worth it after all.

That was Nathan's unspoken answer to the question Rywka hadn't asked him.

They sat facing each other at their slightly wobbly kitchen table; the floor was uneven and the little wedge must have fallen out from under the table leg. As usual Nathan was trying to push it back in place with his shoe. That didn't work, so he leaned down, found the wedge and replaced it. Next morning, when it grew light, he'd finally clean and glue it on, he decided.

They both knew none of his explanations would convince her, which must have been why they were communicating without words. Or perhaps they simply didn't want to wake the children? They were just looking at each other, but even so, it briefly occurred to Nathan that in Rywka's bright eyes, instead of the single small candle that was burning on the table, he could see the thousand he had bought without wicks.

So what, if as soon as he realized he had run to the station and spent his last coins on a platform ticket? The train carrying the salesman and Nathan's purple-tinged dollars had long since left for Kolomyia. For ages Nathan stood among the people on the platform, repeating incomprehensible American words before going home to admit to Rywka what had happened. That night, although the window was closed, on Goldhammer Street his children could be heard crying.

Then he went to bed, and didn't get up and go to work for a week. At the butcher's Rywka said the same thing she had told the children: "Nathan has gastritis."

This time it'll be different, said the look on his face now.

It made no impression on Rywka that once again his eyes were sparkling, as in the days when she had first met him. Sometimes she merely wondered where he got his energy that constantly came and went in waves. Once she actually asked him.

"I brought it back from America," he said.

That had made her think of the sea, which he had told her about on his return to Tarnów. It too was tossed by waves, it ebbed and flowed. But unlike her, it rarely kept still.

"You caught it on the sea, more likely," she said, smiling.

In any case she definitely preferred his stories about the sea and the big ships to the ones about New York. They calmed her. She liked to think of them as she fell asleep.

RYWKA

Nathan had often promised to take her to the seaside, but that was before the wedding and the children. So far, the furthest she had ever been was to Kraków.

Of course in her youth she'd been offered the chance to leave for America. What girl wasn't asked if she wanted to go? A pleasant man with greying hair and a signet ring on his little finger had approached her in the street. A Jew, of course. He'd introduced himself as an entrepreneur, the owner of a flourishing factory in Nebraska, and "first and foremost, an inconsolable widower who has come back to Europe in search of love".

This search had taken him as far as her parents. But Rywka's father had threatened to go to the police. Not without reason was Galicia known as "Scandalicia" in those days. Everyone knew what these invitations were really about and what sort of girl these men were really looking for. Yet two of her friends from Nisko, Nesa Schnur and Lila Flaum, had decided to go. Or perhaps their parents had encouraged them, and had pushed them out of the house? She'd heard that they ended up in Argentina or Brazil. She never saw them again.

In Nisko the story was that the procurers referred to pretty girls as "silver teaspoons", "bales of silk" or "rugs from Smyrna". The less charming ones were "barrels of flour", and the ugly ones were "sacks of potatoes". She hadn't forgotten those definitions, probably because the girls used to call each other those names. And she'd wondered which category they'd put her in.

She'd realized she was too small to be a silver teaspoon. But she did have dark rims to her light eyes, thick black hair and a slender waist. So she wasn't a barrel of flour, and certainly not a sack of potatoes.

Now, on Goldhammer Street, those days seemed unreal. She'd married, moved to Tarnów, and had her children. So much had changed in her life. But had things changed in the outside world too? She used to hear about procurers dealing in "tender flesh". And not that many years had gone by. She still found herself accidentally starting the year on her letters with the number 18, as if she couldn't quite adapt to the twentieth century.

Maybe that was because she rarely read the newspaper. Who'd have the time with six children?

In fact she had given birth seven times. Their first son, Kuba, had been born too soon, with no eyelashes or fingernails. She'd reproached herself for needlessly helping Nathan to paint and furnish their first flat while she was pregnant, a place even smaller than their home on Goldhammer Street. Once she had slipped and fallen outside the entrance. She should have stayed in bed. Anyway, it didn't matter anymore.

It had been winter, and they'd wrapped him in the warmest quilt they had, but it was no good. He'd lived less than three weeks. It had felt so unnatural to arrange her own child's funeral, to walk in the snow behind her own son's coffin. She'd forced herself to shed tears. She couldn't do it, and had shielded her face with her hands so others wouldn't see that she wasn't weeping.

The little coffin hadn't been expensive, but even so they'd spent every penny they had on it. They'd buried Kuba below the cemetery wall.

In the night after the funeral she was woken by stifled weeping. She'd cuddled up to Nathan, and only then burst into tears herself.

She didn't know if Nathan missed their baby too. She didn't know if he too was afraid Rywka would never fall pregnant again, like his sister-in-law Pepi, who had also given birth prematurely before leaving for America; she and the child had gone to hospital, but Pepi had come home alone. From what Nathan said, this loss had determined their departure. On the other hand it was a known fact that in America they had the best doctors for that sort of thing.

But in their letters in neat script on company paper Ben and Pepi never mentioned a pregnancy or a child. It was in the letters that sailed in the opposite direction (perhaps they passed each other somewhere in the middle of the ocean, thought Rywka) that in his nervous handwriting Nathan informed his brother of the arrival in the world of each of the Stramer children, and wrote about their siblings. Maybe that was the reason why they had never made the trip to Tarnów, despite being their closest relatives. And yet never once did they forget to put money in the envelope with their letters.

It was easier for Rywka to understand this than for Nathan. Because what if it had been the other way around? What if we had remained childless, and instead of dollars, news of a succession of American nephews and nieces had sailed here from across the ocean? How would we have felt?

So she thought about Ben and Pepi with sympathy. And whenever she thought of them, she was reminded of Kuba.

"The first child is for God," Nathan had once said.

"Don't talk like a rabbi," she'd replied.

Which of them would he have been like? Would he have been like their eldest, Rudek, who never sought their advice about anything at all, and spent day after day running around town? What did he actually do, and where did he get the money he furtively gave her for the household?

She could only guess.

RUDEK

One Sunday Nathan happened to spot him among a band of Polish and Jewish adolescents who were fooling around, following a regiment of Austrian soldiers as they marched along the main streets of Tarnów in close-fitting dress uniforms. Possibly to mark the first anniversary of the death of Emperor Franz Joseph, because there was a band playing a march as well. That was what Nathan had gone to see. Or in fact to take a look at the violinist. At the time he was still predicting a musical career for Salek, and had only just bought him the second-hand Höfner violin. And he wanted to know what a real violinist looked like. But why couldn't he see him anywhere?

Like everyone else, he stared at the drum major conducting the band, at his white staff with the brass ball at one end. Now the ball went up, now it came down, now it spun on its own axis, and as a finale it went flying into the air.

I wonder how much he's paid for that, thought Nathan and he froze in anticipation: maybe at least once the drum major would fail to catch his ornamental staff?

That would have been less of a surprise than running into Rudek here. At first he couldn't believe his son and the other boys were picking up dog-ends from the ground, and making rude faces and gestures at the soldiers. And on top of that, bawling to the whole of Sobieski Square:

At Austerlitz and at Ulm, at Ulm as well
We got it up the arse, the French sent us to hell.

Nathan happened to know this song from his own youth. He started pushing his way through towards Rudek.

We Austrians are always top of the class
At being sent to hell and getting it up the arse.

He wasn't going to let his son sing the next verse. He pulled him out of the crowd by the collar. And in sight of everyone he thrashed him with the American belt. Without interrupting their march, a couple of the Austrian soldiers with curled moustaches turned away, but some of them held up their pince-nez.

Nathan threaded his belt through his trouser loops and asked: "Will we ever do better than under Emperor Franz Joseph?"

And added: "If I ever see you with a cigarette in your mouth again I'll tear your lungs out along with it."

That had been less than a year ago, but it had plainly taken effect, because lately Rudek was to be seen every day of the week by the wall of the army barracks on the other side of Goldhammer Street where the Austrian garrison was stationed, never with a cigarette in his mouth, only in his pockets.

For a week he'd been taking Salek there with him after school. Did Rudek look much older, or Salek much younger than he really was? Or perhaps the brothers gave that impression by contrast. The tall, broad-shouldered lad in the flat cap and plus fours leaning over the small, thin boy – squeezed into a tight school uniform with a high collar, really still a child.

Anyway, they were more than thirty centimetres apart in height, and a year-and-a-half in age. Salek didn't play football, neither on the right wing, in a blue shirt and white shorts, as Rudek did for Samson Tarnów, nor in any other position for any other team. He didn't play any games at all. He hadn't learned how to whistle through his fingers or how to spit properly. He got his uniform wet whenever they drank lemonade from the bottle together outside the shop. And worst of all, he still got piss on his trouser legs under the tree, although Rudek had showed him how to avoid that several times.

"You could shake it for two weeks and a drop would still land in your trousers anyway," he'd lectured him. "But not *on* your trousers."

It was the same thing with boxing and wrestling. Rudek told Salek to practice on his younger brothers, Hesio and Nusek, but without much success either. Finally he had just about taught him one single blow – forehead against nose. This resulted in Hesio's shirt being stained with blood, and a taste of their father's belt for all three of them.

Anyway, whenever someone picked on him, Salek would just fiercely clench his fists and spin his arms around.

Though he wasn't in any danger, because everyone knew whose brother he was – that made Rudek feel warm inside. But he did his best to prepare Salek in case someone tried to hit him in another district where they didn't know. He was to say he knew Omega, Zachar or Bänder. There was no one in Tarnów who didn't shudder at the thought of them.

"Nobody will touch you."

He didn't admit to Salek that he didn't know them either. Did anyone else need to be aware of that?

What everyone did know was that if they weren't in prison at the time, Omega, Zachar and Bänder were to be found every night in the company of the prostitutes outside Hotel Polski on Dworcowa Street near the station. But everyone preferred to avoid encountering them. Apparently they weren't afraid of anyone.

As if accidentally, they'd elbow other people, push pedestrians off the pavement and knock off their headgear – school caps, flat caps, hats, skull caps and Hasidic Jews' fur shtreimels all landed in the mud and puddles, which after even light rain were all over the place at any time of year.

And that was just the start of it. Then these knife-wielding bandits would wait for a reaction. Would the victim dare to make the slightest comment, if only expressed by a mere glance, the tiniest gesture of dissatisfaction, visible in the dark to them alone?

"You're a tough guy, eh?"

And at once they'd go so close to him that he could tell what they'd had to eat and drink that day at the station's third-class buffet.

Of the three, only Dawid Bänder didn't punch his victims immediately. First he played with his knife. And that was what people feared the most, because Bänder was unpredictable. He might let a man go free, and suddenly stick his knife in the next one.

"Want to be circumcised, tough guy?" he reportedly asked the terrified Prince Roman Sanguszko, whose car had broken down at night near the station.

Rudek was aware of the gravity of this encounter. At school they'd been taught that the Sanguszko family were the former owners of Tarnów, and on the street they'd learned that Bänder was the grandson of Idele Muc, the legendary ringleader of Tarnów's criminals. And as Rudek was one of the most attentive students at both these places, he realized that the descendants of the most powerful men in the city had come face to face with each other.

"Want to be circumcised, tough guy?" Rudek and his brothers had re-enacted this scene over and over again for a laugh in the yard on Goldhammer Street.

"Anything but that! Show mercy to royalty!" Salek would plead in the role of Sanguszko, shielding himself with his hands and fainting against the wall of the wooden outhouse.

SALEK

He'd spotted it at the theatre. Rudek had given him a standing ticket as a birthday present. The show was *Samson and Delilah*, directed by Dante Baranowski, who was also the male lead. During the performance, in the chilly, half-empty Falcon Hall,

Salek couldn't focus on the actors rushing about the stage, alternately roaring with anger, weeping or fainting. In Delilah he immediately recognized Jadwiga Geron, the elegant wife of his high-school Polish teacher, to whom he bowed in the school corridors. Should he bow to her now, as usual, at least discreetly from afar? He didn't want to offend her. Nor did he know if he was entitled to sit down, though more than half the red seats were unoccupied. Whom should he ask? Apart from that, he spent the whole time wondering if Dante Baranowski had really been born with that name.

Perhaps in the past he too had been an ordinary Salek or Jurek. And only as an adult, to appear on posters and perform on stage, first he'd had to change his name to one that sounded more artistic. It made him think of Goldhammer Street, which when they had first moved there was still called Zdrojowa Street.

And how would it sound: Dante Stramer?

After the performance Rudek was waiting outside the Falcon building.

"Rudek, why is Baranowski called Dante?" asked Salek on the way home.

"It's just that his mother was Italian, and Dante is a typical Italian name."

How did he manage to know everyone, and to know so much about them? Salek looked up at his brother in admiration.

But he could impress Rudek too.

He had soon gained popularity at the high school, during a break in the very first year, when at the sight of Father Wątorek, who taught Catholic religion, and Izaak Bleiweiss, who taught Jewish religion, walking arm in arm across the uneven courtyard, he had quipped to his classmates: "There goes the Old Testament, arm in arm with the New."

Though some of them claimed a boy in one of the senior classes had thought of it, Rudek didn't believe them. After all, their friend Romek Brandstaetter, a pupil at the same high school, was an unassailable witness to the fact that Salek said it first.

The joke had soon spread throughout the rowdy courtyard and the brick school building. The bolder pupils began shouting it in the direction of the religion teachers.

"Do you hear that, Mr Bleiweiss?" asked Wątorek eventually.

And Bleiweiss replied: "How could I not have heard it, Father Wątorek?"

After school various rumours went round about them. For example, it was whispered that they were fond of walking arm in arm because neither of them had a wife.

Salek didn't listen or take notes in Jewish religion lessons. He did his maths homework, wrote essays for the Polish class, and prepared for the private tuition he gave after school. And once he had finished, he gazed out of the window at the people walking past in the street. He thought about the fact that he too would walk down it after lessons, and those who saw him through the window then would simply see a boy walking along the street. There was nothing unusual or odd about it, and he had no idea why he kept returning to the thought that soon he'd be for others the person they were for him now.

He also watched the rubbish bin at the junction on the other side of the street. He counted how many people leaned over and put a hand inside it between the first and second bell. Right now it was number four – though less than fifteen minutes had passed since the bell rang – an old woman, sweeping aside the rubbish, probably in search of leftover food. Before her there'd been a boy, his age at most, who had rapidly picked up some bent dog-ends and put them in his coat pocket. Rooks flew down to the bin too, not only making the most noise and mess, but also ruining the reputation of others, because they threw the rubbish out onto the pavement. But Salek was unable to count them.

These days he thought the Hebrew alphabet looked sad and gloomy. He associated it with the poorest part of Tarnów, the old Jewish district. The letters hung down like sidelocks, or beards, or the trailing black coats of the residents of Grabówka that always had muddy tails.

Even so, he knew everything Bleiweiss taught them. Once upon a time it had been interesting, and he'd liked it – fairy tales for the three-year-old boy he was when his father first took him by the hand to the cheder. Not the one nearest to home, where Rudek had gone the year before, but much further away. Salek's legs ached as he almost ran to keep up with his father. He failed to notice the kerb and fell over, onto his hands, but he also stained his trousers, and worse yet, they tore at the knee.

"Goddammit!" cried his father, yanking him to his feet.

Salek burst into tears; he didn't want to go to the cheder anymore.

"You'll go to the one near home."

A year earlier Rudek had come running home from there in a frenzy, determined never to go back. It had taken his mother ages to get him to tell her what had happened. Only when she promised not to repeat it to anyone did Rudek finally say that the melamed not only tugged their ears and beat them with a cane for reciting the Hebrew words badly. He had told him to strip naked and stand in the corner of the room, and the other children were to come up and spit in his face. That was when he'd run away.

"Why did he tell you to do that?" she asked.

"Because I didn't believe the Jews crossed the Red Sea without getting wet."

In silence, Salek followed his father. All day at the cheder he kept a hand on his knee, and along with the others repeated after the melamed passages from the Torah.

In fact the old teacher did not raise a hand to the children or even his voice, but to all questions and doubts he always had the same invariable answer: "You silly child, that's what's written in the Pentateuch."

Salek heard the same thing when after a year of studying in this damp room, which was at the same time the melamed's entire accommodation, he had dared to ask his first question, carefully prepared for many days: "When God saw the children sitting on the wall and laughing at the prophet Elisha's bald head as he walked underneath, why did He send two enraged she-bears from the forest to tear forty-two children to pieces?"

It was Rudek who finally explained to him that you simply had to respect your father and both grandfathers, even though under their hats they were bald.

Anyway, luckily God did not repeat anything as cruel at the cheder. Just like the melamed, He kept quiet at the sight of the oldest boys who calmly played cards under the table, a buttons game or slapsies. He was equally unmoved when they stood behind the teacher and pretended to be dancing a waltz with him, or, blocking their noses with disgust, with two fingers they removed his old, darned long johns and socks from his wardrobe, or imitated a dog that had mistaken the old melamed for a bitch.

Maybe it was just that the melamed was far from the power, piety and clear-mindedness of the Prophet Elisha, thought Salek. Or maybe that he wasn't bald – there was long, matted white hair protruding from under his yarmulka.

II

NUSEK

As they said in Tarnów, "the further from Grabówka, the cleaner the air". Nusek only breathed with his ears there. The smell of that district was like a reminder of the outhouse on Goldhammer Street, or overnight from Friday to Saturday, when for ages the children couldn't sleep after eating too much cholent at the Sabbath supper.

"MOF?" Salek or Hesio would ask now and then.

"OOM," Rudek would answer them.

"No!" Rena would shout if she was still awake. "I won't let you. Go outside."

At night the two-room flat on Goldhammer Street changed into a bedroom. Three beds took up the whole of the main room, and the fourth occupied the kitchen. The chairs and table stood in the middle – it was important to remember them, especially after dark, on the way to the outhouse. But almost every time Nusek stumbled or at least bumped into something.

Rywka did her best to make sure each child had as much space as possible. She had decided that her tallest and eldest son, Rudek, would share a bed with the youngest, Nusek, next to them were Salek with Hesio who wasn't much smaller, and a little way off, behind a screen, slept the girls, Rena and the last-born, Wela. Only Suchard the dog and Milka the cat chose for themselves at whose feet they would spend the night.

"What does MOF mean?" asked Nusek. "What does MOF mean?" he repeated, as if he thought Rudek hadn't heard.

"You're about to get a sense of it for yourself."

"Why won't you ever tell me anything? Why?"

"For the public good. Go to sleep."

"Just tell me, what's MOF?"

"Ministry of Finance."

"But is that really true?"

"Yes. Go and ask at the bank."

Nusek wondered why his older brothers never took him seriously. How many times had he begged them to take him to the barracks with them? It was a waste of breath.

It couldn't still be to do with that silly story about a bow, could it? All the more since he did everything Rudek told him to. He meant well, the best proof that he was making an effort – trying too hard even.

Nusek closed his eyes, but he couldn't sleep. He could hear his father's steady snoring, Salek mumbling something in his sleep, and the creaking of the bed as Rudek turned over and laid his head on their shared pillow.

He could feel his warm breath on his face.

Why do I always have the least of everything?, he thought.

Room in bed, the pillow, and even the quilt, which Rudek pulls off me every night?

"Are you asleep?" he heard Hesio say.

He opened his eyes.

"What is it?"

"Do you want to know what MOF and OOM mean?"

"Yes. Tell me."

"Will you fetch the firewood and coal from the shed in the yard for me for a week?"

Nusek still couldn't get to sleep, but now it was for a different reason. Once in a while he cast an approving glance at Rudek, sleeping beside him with his mouth open. Maybe he really did deserve the entire shared pillow, and even the quilt? Nusek felt like laughing at the very thought of MOF and OOM. The crafty creatures! Like this they could say it at school in front of the teachers, or at home in front of their parents. He would never have come up with that. It took someone like Rudek or Salek to think of it. That you only had to call something by a new name – and it was sorted.

"This head wasn't made for wearing a cap," as their father would say when he was cooking up a new business idea.

But the saying didn't suit his father, and not only because Nusek had never seen him in a cap. Usually on his way out of the house he alternately took one of two crumpled old hats from the rack.

The saying was definitely more suited to the head that lay on the pillow beside Nusek.

Once again he was reminded of various situations in which he had heard them say MOF and OOM. He had suspected they were very rude swearwords, or a secret code to do with trading cigarettes, or with girls, or at least communism. Now it made him giggle, because it sounded so refined: MOF meant "May One Fart?" And OOM was "Once, One May".

He fell asleep smiling. As ever, he tried to catch the moment when he nodded off, and as ever, at the last second he failed to do so.

RYWKA

At night some of them dreamed the same thing. And Rywka was also almost certain they sometimes had the same dream simultaneously. Evidently there are individual and shared dreams, she thought, like graves at the cemetery, hotel rooms or cabins on the ships Nathan had told her about.

She could have sworn she once heard the children playing football together in their sleep.

"Pass it to me," asked Nusek.

"Hesio, to you," said Rudek. "Shoot into the top right corner."

"Goal!" cried Salek.

Rywka waited to hear what would come next, but there was just silence.

"Nathan," she said, cuddling up to her husband and kissing him on his broad nape, "you won't believe what I heard."

"All the children in all the squares and yards in Tarnów are playing it," said Nathan with his eyes closed, "and it's no reason for you to go waking me up at once."

He knew what he was saying. The day before, he'd seen a headline on the front page of the newspaper at the kiosk:

"Ball-kicking epidemic spreads alarmingly in our city". It was especially hard for him to read the final word through the dirty window. Unlike the first three words, the large, broad letters of which had drawn him to the kiosk.

As usual he didn't buy the newspaper, but tried to read at least a few lines on the spot.

> *There's no yard in our city where a dozen brats, kikes or wastrels haven't started kicking a ball around in the mud, whatever the weather. We're just afraid the ladies will take up kicking – that will be the end of the world.*

Maybe he rarely washes the window on purpose, thought Nathan, casting a look of respect at the toothless old salesman, so people won't read the papers for free.

You don't understand!, Rywka had wanted to shout. They're playing in their sleep!

But instead of that she said: "I'm sorry. Have a good sleep."

Next morning she'd forgotten about it. She had to send them all off. To work, to school, to the cheder. After dark she had already laid out the clean clothes they were to put on. She lit the kitchen stove and laid the table with a plate for each person, on which she put an evenly cut slice of buttered wholemeal bread, and then she poured them chicory coffee. As head of the family Nathan had the right to a roll for breakfast as well.

"Daddy, lend me your roll," said Nusek. "I'll give it straight back to you as soon as I've eaten it."

At first Nusek didn't know what they were laughing at. It took him a while to join in with them, and then he laughed the loudest, as if to make up for the time it had taken him to understand his own joke.

"I'll give it straight back to you as soon as I've eaten it," he repeated proudly, pointing at himself. "I'm wiser than I thought."

Before they left, Rywka washed the children's faces, straightened their collars and combed their hair.

Saying goodbye in the doorway, first she stood on tiptoes before Rudek, then bent her legs at the knees, and gradually went lower and lower as she stopped in turn before Salek, Rena and Hesio, on her way down to Nusek and Wela, before whom she squatted.

"You're descending like a New York elevator," said Nathan, who had promised not to repeat that anymore, but once again couldn't stop himself.

Rywka always kissed the children in the same spot. Her favourite. It was where the brow ended and the nose began. She didn't know what it was called, but to her it was the "saddle".

The same every morning. Thanks to this – as she kept telling herself and Nathan – there's no time to get bored. These mornings had became an ingrained habit for her. Sometimes only while eating her own slice of bread or washing the dishes did she realize that Nathan and the children had already left. As if someone else had woken them that day, and made sure they put on warm underpants, drank their coffee and left home on time.

III

NATHAN

"I BOUGHT IT," announced Nathan in the doorway, as proud as if he meant the Tarnów Fertilizer Plant, not a dresser from the neighbour on the second floor who was selling off the last of his furniture before leaving for America.

"For peanuts," he added after closing the door.

That was probably what he liked most about the dresser. And he sent Rudek, Salek and Hesio straight upstairs to fetch it.

"What about Nusek?" asked Hesio.

"Too small for a porter."

Rudek came down the stairs first. As fast as if he were carrying the dresser by himself, not with Salek and Hesio, who could hardly keep up with him, gripping its little oak feet tighter and tighter to stop the thing from falling on top of their brother.

After they'd bumped into the wall for the third time, adopting the manner of Anszel Koszcz, Rudek said: "Gentlemen... What am I paying you for?"

Salek asked if they could take a short break for him to tie his shoelace. Three steps later, when Rudek put the dresser down on the first floor, his hands were shaking.

Anszel, the tallest and most broad-shouldered of all the Tarnów porters, was their informal boss. He could probably have carried an even heavier piece of furniture on his own without problems or helpers. Not so long ago Rudek had watched him loitering at Pilzno Gate in search of work, slowly circling the market stalls at a patient pace.

Like the Earth around the Sun, thought Rudek.

Indeed, Anszel hardly stopped at all. If the porters wanted to talk to him, they had to walk alongside, circling in his orbit. He was the man they turned to for everything. He was their supreme authority, against which there was no right of appeal on earth, at least the uneven, muddy earth by Pilzno Gate.

Although with a black patch on his left eye and a rope cast over his shoulder he looked like the sort of pirate their father tried to scare them with, Anszel kept order. He always spoke calmly, with a smile even, but everyone knew what would happen to a porter who stole a parcel, for instance, or – God forbid – to a client who didn't pay for their services. Rudek had often seen Anszel taking swift action to pull the metal shaft from his handcart.

So how had he lost an eye? There were plenty of versions of that story. Anszel himself must have long forgotten how it really happened, and that was why he gave a different account every time he told it.

"There are probably more versions than listeners," Rudek explained to his brothers. "Some people have heard a different one each time."

The version Rudek liked best was the heroic one. Years ago, on a Saturday in July some hooligans had surrounded the Jewish district. They had attacked people and broken into the shops, which were closed for the Sabbath. They must have done some planning, because as well as sticks and bits of metal they had sacks for the goods they stole.

"As their bad luck would have it," said Anszel, without ceasing to circle among the stalls, "they also attacked the porters' families coming out of the synagogue on Rybny Square."

Anszel's people had set off at speed for Pilzno Gate, where for the holiday they always left their carts tied to one long chain. There they removed the metal shafts from them to use as weapons. The porters were joined by some Jewish labourers, armed with crowbars and planks. And at their head went Anszel.

"We drove them out of the district. We smashed the carts they tried to escape in and set the horses free. We got everything back. I was the only one to lose something," Anszel would say, pointing at the black patch.

"But you saved the city from a pogrom," came the reply with unwavering admiration, possibly because the nearest cities and towns had not been as fortunate.

"They got a light rap on the knuckles." Every time this memory was revived, Anszel would modestly shrug his shoulders – as broad as the dresser the three Stramer brothers were struggling to carry from the second to the ground floor.

At school Salek heard a less heroic version. Before repeating it to him, his pal from the senior class asked Salek to be discreet. Earlier on, the pal had been asked to be discreet by his father, who had himself been bound to silence by one of Tarnów's rope dealers.

"I'm not telling anyone but you," Anszel was reported to have said in a hushed tone to this trustworthy man, who was walking beside him.

Before becoming a porter Anszel had spent a couple of years in prison after catching his wife with her lover. But it wasn't clear if he'd lost the eye during his time inside or in his victorious fight against the lover, whom he killed.

Salek had heard yet another description of the incident from Hesio, a version that didn't mention prison at all.

"It seems that while fast asleep Anszel was knifed by a jealous husband, who came home earlier than usual from his job at the slaughterhouse and found him in his wife's arms."

For a while, the thought of a bloodbath that involved sticking a butcher's knife in Anszel's eye silenced the rowdy yard on Goldhammer Street.

In fact Nathan, having overheard their conversation through the open ground-floor window, claimed at supper that he had a memory from his youth of the time Anszel got drunk and crashed his bike. He had fallen into a ditch, where he must have impaled himself on something – a dry twig, a bit of wire, or a piece of broken glass. Next day he had woken up covered in blood, with one eye missing, and couldn't remember a thing.

What impressed the children most about this story was the fact that their father knew Anszel in person.

"I've met plenty like him in my life," said Nathan dismissively.

He took the opportunity to show the children the Jewish porter's punch. He called Hesio over and suddenly shoved him away by throwing out his belly. Little Hesio went flying against the wall, where luckily they had not yet positioned the elegant dresser with prominent horse's heads, but even so tears came to his eyes. When Salek timidly protested that the porters at Pilzno Gate and on Rybny Square were too skinny to punch anyone that way, without casting him a glance, Nathan merely shook his head.

"In America," he added quietly, to himself.

"I mean the way Jewish porters punch in America," he repeated aloud, as if he realized that to the rest of the family it wasn't at all obvious that the real porters, craftsmen, tradesmen and the entire pot-bellied crowd were over there, where his brother Ben had stayed. Amid really tall houses with real elevators. Really wide, long streets with sidewalks, full of real stores and cafés with customers who paid for everything with the most real dollars on earth.

"Even the sky is higher over there," he had once let slip.

Sometimes it occurred to Rywka that Nathan hadn't come back from there at all. She suspected that he often imagined how his life would have turned out on the other side of the ocean. And that to him it was more real than their life in Tarnów, which as a result he neglected.

Gently but carefully she wiped the carved wooden columns topped with horse's heads. The sophisticated oak dresser didn't match the rest of their furniture: the bench Nathan had knocked together from three pine boards, the chest with four drawers that barely opened, the eternally wobbly table or the wardrobe standing beside it with the broken back wall. It didn't suit their cramped, ground-floor apartment, or rather the apartment didn't suit it.

Who would Nathan be if he hadn't returned but had stayed there with his brother? If his brother had been more insistent? Or if that day on the quay he had changed his mind and said:

I'm not boarding the ship after all. I'll sell my ticket on to someone here and now, and make a profit on it.

Nathan could see his real life, full of success. In America success is worth striving for. Even the folks in Żabno had heard of New York. But what did success mean in Tarnów?

"I made a fortune in Tarnów."

"Where?"

At best someone in Bochnia or Dąbrowa might have heard of it, but the news would never have crossed the Dunajec, Biała or San rivers.

So was it worth trying at all, he thought, as he lay in bed for days on end, crushed by each of his failed business ventures.

When Rywka asked if he was getting up he'd reply: "No. I'm ill."

When she asked if she should fetch the doctor he said: "No. There's nothing wrong with me."

And with his eyes closed he'd turn to face the wall, but he rarely managed to return to the American dream she had interrupted.

Once he dreamed that their cramped apartment on the ground floor was really on the top, thirty-third floor of a skyscraper on Goldhammer Street, with a view of the whole of New York.

Brother, he read in letters from Ben, *over here we say that failure is the best opportunity to start afresh, this time more wisely.*

These words improved Nathan's mood almost as much as the other contents of the envelope. Once Rywka had left the house to go shopping, he'd even get to his feet for a while to hide the rolled-up dollars in the bed leg.

He always left the envelope with the stamps for the children.

Anyway, the letters from Ben were the first thing Nathan decided to keep in the elegant dresser. Only after that did he put his comb bearing the initials NS in it, and his engraved Statue of Liberty. Rywka could remember him combing his hair with it for a few years after his return.

"I wonder whether I'll go grey or bald first?" he used to say in those days.

It turned out to be the second. Secretly he bought himself Dr Drall's hair-restoring lotion. But despite its one-hundred-per-cent reliability, confirmed enthusiastically on the label by *both eminent scientists and laymen*, the medicine did not work on him.

In America he'd have saved his head of hair. He'd have got better lotion, more effective, or at least cheaper. He was sure of it.

Later on, he used the comb for his beard and whiskers. But finally, at Rywka's request he started shaving them off. She had delicate skin on her face and neck, and his strong stubble left red marks on her.

Next to the comb, on the same shelf in the dresser, Rywka put a metal candlestick. Her dowry had included gold and silver candlesticks too, but they had been sold long ago to pay for the burial of Kuba, their first child. Nathan put a battered prayerbook into the dresser too, a keepsake from his father. He had also inherited his father's tefillin, which he put on once a year on Yom Kippur. Every time the children laughed at him. But what could he do? They knew that on that day it was unseemly to reach for his belt.

For the same reason, as they walked past him they'd quietly croon:

Bong bang bing, bong bang bing.

And nothing more, but that was enough, because Nathan knew the song well.

The rabbi did a miraculous thing.
He fell in the water while he was high,
And yet his beard stayed nice and dry.

All this made him become confused about whether he should strap the little leather box full of lines from the Torah to his left arm first or to his sweaty brow.

Yet he had sailed to America as a devout sixteen-year-old in a yarmulka, with ginger sidelocks falling on his cheeks. The first night on board he couldn't sleep. He had never slept on a bunk bed before, let alone on water. He was afraid he'd fall off. He was afraid the ship would sink. "There was a storm raging," he told the story afterwards. "We almost drowned". But in fact it was he, not the sea, that was restless.

Why had his brother told him to take the top bunk? He didn't realize until the middle of the night, when the first passengers began to be attacked by sea sickness, the results of which were felt by those sleeping underneath them.

Thanks, brother, he had thought.

In third class they weren't served kosher food. What's more, he must have taken his tallit and tefillin out of his case five times – at the very start of the journey. And yet he had felt all right, he never had a hint of sea sickness. Two weeks later when they sailed into New York, Nathan disembarked with his yarmulka, but no longer on his head, just in his pocket.

Shortly after that he had had to answer the immigration officer's questions.

"Do you have a job fixed up in America?"

"No," he said, shaking his head like all those who didn't want to go straight back home on the same ship.

His brother had also warned him that at the medical inspection they'd examine his eyes. But he hadn't said they'd do it with a metal crochet hook, and that it'd be very unpleasant. In the box marked profession they described him as: *workman*.

Ben had greeted him in clothing completely unlike the gaberdine in which he had left Tarnów ten years earlier. Grey trousers, an open grey jacket, a black waistcoat, a white shirt and a black bowler hat, from under which he had no sidelocks protruding.

Nathan had immediately understood that America had smiled on his brother.

IV

RUDEK

For years it had been generally accepted that winter in Tarnów did not necessarily start with the onset of December or the first snow. Both its beginning and end were marked by something, or rather someone else. Despite bitter cold, the city did not acknowledge the change of season until the Hungarian roast chestnut seller appeared on Sobieski Square.

"He's arrived," people would tell each other.

And then, breathing clouds of steam, they would queue to buy his chestnuts, which he cooked on a round cast-iron stove.

The newspapers would report that the black-haired, black-eyed, black-bearded Hungarian with the unpronounceable and even more unspellable name had arrived, as every year, from the faraway city of Pécs, situated near the border of Hungary and Croatia. He knew only a few words of Polish: "zloty", "God bless you" and "your good health". He hadn't yet managed to learn more, but he promised to make progress this time.

Except that Rudek had heard with his own ears that the Hungarian also knew some Yiddish words, a good many too.

"You thieves, I'll get my hands on you!" he had shouted after Rudek and his pals, with no trace of a Hungarian accent.

As it hadn't occurred to them to wear gloves, they burned their fingers and dropped some of the chestnuts on the way.

But it had all started the day before, during the Hanukkah dinner, when their father said: "I never saw a Hungarian like that one in America."

As he hovered by the festively laid kitchen table, to which Rywka was bringing the dishes, he tried to calculate how much profit chestnuts could bring.

Now and then he shoved under Rywka's nose the calculations he'd made with a pencil on a greasy piece of paper. But she never had time to read it before he took it away, made corrections, crossed things out and added others, then offered it to her again.

While making these calculations he never stopped talking either. He was quite sure the newspaper reports announcing the arrival of the Hungarian were really paid advertisements – what's more, placed not at the back, in the advertising section, but on the front page, among the regional news, making it far more effective.

"I never read anything like that in *The Jewish Daily Forward*".

"Would you finally sit down," said Rywka.

At the centre of the table she set down a chicken fried in honey and garlic. According to family tradition, she cut off the rump and put it on Nathan's plate for him to cut into five equal pieces. One he kept for himself, and he distributed the rest to his sons according to seniority. Nusek smiled at his piece, despite having just put the rest of his siblings off this titbit. He'd told his sisters, Rena and Wela, how lucky they were to be born girls. He'd rather be a girl so he wouldn't have to eat it. In detail, making the relevant noises, he had told them what came out of the rump earlier. But the worst thing, he said, scowling, was that often it hadn't all come out, so you could taste it in your mouth.

Nathan had just speared his golden-fried chunk on his fork and was ceremonially holding it in the air, as if to remind them that the custom of sharing this choice morsel among father and sons was inherited from his father, their grandfather.

"Dad, will you buy me some chestnuts?" asked Nusek at that very moment.

Perhaps he was hoping to imagine a different taste while eating his piece of rump.

"The chestnuts are dead," replied Nathan, without lowering his fork.

"But the Hungarian has arrived."

"The Hungarian is dead."

"What do you mean? I saw him last night on Sobieski Square."

"Sobieski Square is dead."

"What?"

"While your father is eating," said Nathan, pointing his fork at Nusek, "everything is dead."

And indeed, for a moment the whole table was silent, if not dead.

Nusek had already opened his mouth to reply.

"But Dad, you're not eating yet," he began, when Rudek leaned close to his ear and whispered: "Shut up."

Another word and it could end in the American belt.

Rywka glanced at her husband. Brought up strictly by her own parents, she often said that strictness was either unnecessary, or unhelpful. Nathan lowered his fork.

Then he raised it again, but this time to his mouth. At this sign the others could start eating too.

Soon they were all pointing their forks at each other's plates and spearing something for themselves. Bits of white meat went flying past in the air, breast, thigh, wing, neck or crisply fried skin.

Salek did not fully understand why in Tarnów they called it "Jewish ping-pong". "Your one and only national sport". Although perhaps it was thanks to this tradition of swapping food that Tarnów produced so many excellent players? After all, at real ping-pong too the best competitors were the Samson Tarnów team.

They had won not only against Maccabi or the local non-Jewish teams, but had also brought home victory from Bochnia, and lately from Kraków itself. And Samson's children's section, meaning Salek's young schoolmates, such as little Emilek Schiff or Klein, who were described as "not much taller than the table", sometimes beat the adult competitors.

Rudek had taken Salek to one of the matches. And had taken the opportunity to explain that the professionals never say "ping-pong".

"If you want them to take you seriously, always say 'table tennis'."

All right, but how would this sound: "Jewish table tennis"?

Salek had noticed that at the wobbly table only Rywka hadn't immediately started eating. Maybe she was less hungry, as she'd been sampling the food while cooking? Or perhaps she was lost in thought, or was gazing at the children.

Rudek leaned towards Nusek again.

"They haven't got any cash right now. I'll get you the chestnuts," he said.

And next day that was how Rudek had learned that the Hungarian knew more than just Hungarian.

By the time he had run to Goldhammer Street his cheeks were red from the cold and his hands were red from the scalding chestnuts, but the chestnuts were already cold.

Not without reason was the winter in Tarnów said to have no equal. Some of the devout Jews from Grabówka had icicles forming on their frosted beards.

In the yard he whistled with his fingers. Leaning his back and right leg against the coal shed, he waited for volunteers.

"Want a chestnut?" he said, holding one out to Nusek, who was the first to stop before him.

"Where did you get them?" asked Rena.

"Where do you think?! From the Hungarian."

Each person got two chestnuts. He watched them peeling off the brown skins. Taking care that nothing was wasted. Now and then they cast Rudek grateful glances, or discreetly peeped to see how many the others had already eaten.

"A miniature feast," said Hesio, his voice shaking with cold.

And Rudek was reminded of what their father had said the day before. It occurred to him that now they looked like the best advertisement for the Hungarian and his chestnuts. And a free one, too. The only thing missing was the caption: *Despite the wind and snow, the frozen Stramer siblings are relishing their stone-cold chestnuts.*

But somehow he didn't feel like laughing.

It was Salek who improved his mood.

"Rudek, why do they sell them hot?" he asked, trying not to let his teeth chatter as he spoke. "When they're far better cold?"

"Better go home," said Rudek, laying a hand on his shoulder, "so you don't catch a chill."

A few weeks later, after they'd won a football match, Daniel, son of the deputy mayor, invited Rudek to his family home. He lived on Goldhammer Street too, but at the other end of the street, the opposite end in every respect, in a house graced by bay windows. In his bedroom he proudly turned the pages of an album full of adverts for throat pastilles, glued to black paper. Each advert was a short real-life story, with the invariable moral that one should take Fay's lozenges. The children from the local homes where the newspapers were read every day had entire collections of them.

"This one's very rare," said Daniel. "Nobody at school has it."

"Automobile trouble is a minor evil," he read aloud to Rudek, "compared with the complaints to be suffered by catching cold, especially while travelling by car. That's why one should always take along a box of Fay's genuine lozenges…"

Rudek smiled, but he wasn't really listening. He was focusing on not unduly staring around the large, bright room with a balcony, in which as well as a honey-coloured children's desk with a little lock and key, the low table at which they were sitting, a carved wardrobe with a mirror and a globe, there was also a bed. Just one.

Daniel was the master of an entire bed – Rudek tried not to think about it.

He also turned his gaze from the dark corridor, along which stretched seven more rooms.

"It's a pretty long walk," said Daniel half-heartedly, as if repeating something his father had said.

Daniel's room, the sitting room, his parents' bedroom, a dining room, his father's study, a bathroom and a separate lavatory, a cloakroom, a small room for Jagna the maid, and one more room, the name of which Rudek couldn't remember.

In that case, he wondered, how many rooms did the mayor of Tarnów's apartment have? At least ten or twelve. Rudek imagined how long a walk that must be. It wasn't appropriate for the mayor to have fewer rooms than his Jewish deputy. Rudek knew that for many years in Tarnów they had elected a Polish mayor and a Jewish deputy mayor.

He was reminded of what his father always said after having to see to something at the town hall.

"Sticky fingers!" he'd scream about the municipal officials as soon as he got home. "I don't think they won their fortunes on the lottery," he'd say, nodding his head, still in his hat, as if agreeing with himself, then add: "And definitely not by slaving away like the Jews in Egypt who built the pyramids."

Only once he had got all this out of his system could he remove his hat and shoes, hang up his coat and move on to what he had and had not been able to settle at the town hall.

"What's the most money you've ever held in your hand?" the deputy mayor's son asked Rudek.

"What about you?" he replied, to be on the safe side.

"Ten thousand. Dad gave it me to hold when I was at his office. They were just putting it in the safe. What about you?"

Rudek couldn't begin to imagine such wealth. All those banknotes! How did Daniel manage to hold them without spilling them?

"The same amount," said Rudek, knowing he couldn't say any less, but nor he did like swaggering.

"Where did you get it?" asked Daniel.

"From my uncle in America," was the first thing that came into Rudek's head. "From New York."

As a parting gift the deputy mayor's son handed Rudek a neatly cut-out newspaper advert for Fay's lozenges, evidently a spare copy. As he descended the tall stairwell decorated with colourful stained glass he read it.

Yesterday's session of the Sejm provides the best proof that a great deal can be achieved with a simple remedy. Member of Parliament Mehlmeier was to deliver a major speech on behalf of his political party, but unfortunately woke up with an extremely sore throat. At once he sent out to the local pharmacy for a box of Fay's genuine mineral lozenges, took some in hot milk, and brought the rest with him to the session. And you all know what he spoke about. The speech was a political event, but only Fay's genuine Soden lozenges made it possible.

On the way home, Rudek thought Goldhammer Street seemed different. In fact, Wałowa and Mickiewicz Streets had changed too. Was less than an hour with the deputy mayor's son enough for the world outside not to be the same any longer? Rudek recoiled onto the pavement to avoid being hit by an ox cart; the farmer returning from market can't have noticed him in the darkness, and Rudek shook a fist at him. Was that what his father meant when he said Goldhammer was nothing more than a small back street in a provincial town? The closer to home, the more Rudek felt it.

Or was it because dusk had fallen during his visit, but the gas lamps hadn't been lit yet? Was the lamplighter with the long pole drunk again?

NATHAN

Before Salek could try to repeat the advertisement brought home by his older brother without looking at the page, first he read it through twice in silence. Then he handed it to Rudek to check if he had recited all the words correctly.

He had.

Among Salek's various talents, this skill had prompted first the melamed, and four years later the high-school teacher of Judaism to persuade Nathan to send his son to the yeshiva.

"They say he'll become a rabbi," he told Rywka once the children were asleep.

"Do you want a son who spends all day sweating over the scriptures, while his wife has to sell fish at the market to support the household?" she asked.

It was true that in the past he had imagined Salek slogging, though certainly not over the Torah in a damp, half-empty synagogue, but over musical notes, and then performing in a concert hall packed to the last ticketed seat.

"And now, Rudek," said Salek, "turn the paper over."

On the back of the advertisement there was an item of foreign news cut out with scissors.

"...the curability of cancer," began Salek from memory. "A Belgian doctor whose name is so far being kept confidential, gave a lecture at the Brussels academy in which he elucidated a radical way of treating cancer. According to his method, after three days of quite simple self-treatment, the cancerous formation petrifies, and the organism excretes it of its own accord."

What was the date of this newspaper? Was it today's, a week or a year old? Had this method already reached Tarnów, or was it yet to arrive? Not even Rudek, now looking at Salek with approval, had any idea.

There was no point in asking their father. He probably hadn't a clue. Besides, they were deliberately whispering in the kitchen to avoid waking him. It would be interesting to know if in some distant country a remedy had been discovered by now for his recurring illness. But was he really asleep at the moment, or did he just have his eyes closed? For two days the curtains in the room had been drawn around the clock. Usually his gastritis – infallibly diagnosed by Rywka every time it occurred – did not last for more than a week. Unlike ordinary gastritis, it had no visible symptoms, nor did it ever infect the rest of the family.

Rywka looked after the patient. She brought him food in bed, sent the children shopping at the market, and made sure Nathan could recover in peace.

Even Suchard barked more quietly, and for hours Milka the cat lay beside him on the bed.

The children found it hard to believe that this was their father, lying in bed during the day. Especially the youngest, Nusek and Wela, who felt like lying down next to Milka and cuddling up to their father. Asked if he was feeling any better, Nathan would reply so curtly and quietly that they weren't sure if he had said "yes" or "no". Indeed, it was hard to believe that the person lying there motionless, with his face turned to the wall, was the man who hardly sat down for more than a few seconds, but ran about the flat, gesticulating wildly, and never let any family member get a word in edgeways.

Was this defenceless version of their father, hiding under the quilt, the man capable of wielding his American belt and screaming the length of Goldhammer Street?

Every time it seemed impossible.

But such was the force of the gastritis.

Nathan only got up to go to the outhouse. In his underclothes, unshaven, he went into the yard. The children could see the net curtains twitching in the neighbours' windows.

A week later, when Rywka let light and fresh air into the flat, and Nathan got out of bed fit and well, the children were as pleased as if it were to their credit too.

Their joy did not last long. After a day or two it would turn out it wasn't the mild, defenceless father of whom they had taken such loving care that had got up, but the old one.

They could tell that once again they had let themselves be taken in. Once again they had been cheated by the man who was always cheated in business.

Rywka too was sorry that along with his illness Nathan shed his gentle, understanding attitude towards the children.

Once again they heard American swearwords, once again at the sight of him Milka the cat leaped through the window into the yard.

45

V

WELA

ONE DAY, the terrified Milka fled further than usual.
Wela looked for her everywhere – under the wooden carpet-beating frame, around the outhouse, in the gateway, even behind the coal shed and the woodpile, where her older brothers smoked cigarettes. For the first time she went out into the street alone.

"Milka!" she called. "Come back!"

But the cat couldn't leave her four newly born children. That evening Wela and Rena prepared a bed for them by the stove, put down a bowl of milk and left the window ajar. Next morning Wela woke first, before their mother, and ran on tiptoes to the kitchen. But Milka hadn't come back for the night. Her kittens were asleep, snuggling up to Suchard's belly.

The dog looked after them for four days, until finally Milka returned. Wela told everyone proudly that the babies hadn't run straight to their mother. First they had looked inquiringly at Suchard. She had invented this final fact, because she herself was upset with the cat.

"Mama would never abandon us like that," she said.

"But why do you think Milka has a piece of string around her neck?" asked Rena. "Someone must have caught her and tied her up. But she bit through the string and escaped."

Wela went to cuddle the cat. Under her chin the fur had been rubbed away and was sticky with blood. She tore free when Wela tried gently to touch her there.

"But why did someone tie her up?" she asked her older sister once they were in bed, ready to go to sleep.

"Because they were unkind. Go to sleep."

Who was unkind? Next day Wela watched the street through the kitchen window. Who could it be? Maybe Mr Barabasz, the tall man who owned the house, and came once a month for his money? He always minded his head as he crossed the threshold, because once he had hit it hard. Last time she had heard him telling her parents they hadn't arranged to keep animals, and threatening to put up the rent.

"What?" her father had tried to joke. "Soon the rent will be even bigger than you are."

Wela thought everyone seemed suspicious. The salesman rushing to his exotic fruit shop on the corner of Goldhammer and Wałowa Streets. Not so odd, but he never replied when she said good day. Did he still remember that when she was very small and had been passing his shop with her mama on their way to the market, she had accidentally touched a peach and he had told Rywka to pay for it?

At any rate she hadn't forgotten the voice pursuing them: "The way they bring up their children…"

Could anyone have kidnapped Milka? Mrs Fluffy, who walked about the yard with her dog? It was to escape this dachshund, who even in summer wore a blue sleeveless sweater hand-knitted by his mistress, that Milka had run up a tree. While he growled and barked helplessly at the bottom, until Suchard chased him away.

Now Wela noticed that Mrs Fluffy always went about in the same things too: black stockings worn through at the heels, a black knee-length skirt, and a blue cardigan buttoned up to the top.

"That stinking old madwoman and her flea-ridden mongrel," her father said of her.

"Nathan, stop," begged her mother.

"Haven't you heard her jabbering away to it?" said Nathan, then stooped and put on a squeaky voice. "Oh Fluffy, look what lovely weather. Fluffy, empty your bowels. What shall we have for dinner, Fluffy? Fluffy, do you remember when the Archduke Ferdinand was assassinated? Now Fluffy, we don't eat poo. Oh Fluffy, what will become of us? Oh Fluffy…"

"And what harm does that do you?" Rywka interrupted him. "Let her be. She has nobody else."

"She might wash herself from time to time. That's all."

The fact that Mrs Fluffy doesn't wash and jabbers to her dog is nothing, thought Nusek. After all, he himself occasionally wriggled out of the nightly bath in the wash basin. He'd get into bed and pretend to be asleep. And sometimes he too complained of his lot to Suchard – every time the dog looked Nusek in the eyes with understanding.

The secret Hesio had betrayed to him was definitely worth the price of a week fetching water from the well instead of him.

Now Nusek had repeated it to Wela too: Mrs Fluffy was married to her dachshund, and that was how she got her name.

For their honeymoon, the bride and groom had decided to take the train to Lwów. But they were ejected at the first stop in Dębica, because Fluffy didn't have a ticket. And when they got up from their seats, his one turned out to be wet.

"Hesio, why do they hide the fact?" asked Nusek.

"It's simple, but how can I explain it to you?" said Hesio, and thought for a while. "Because it's a mismatch."

"Nusek, is that true?" asked Wela, who had never heard of anything like it.

"It's the sacred truth. I've seen Fluffy and Mrs Fluffy eating buckwheat for dinner from the same bowl. And they sleep together in bed too," added Nusek, convulsed with laughter.

Wela, who shared her bed with Rena, saw nothing strange about that.

"One day you'll understand," he said mysteriously.

Was it about billing and cooing? That was from the song about three pigeons, black, white and red, that Rena had brought home from school. The black and white pigeons lived happily in a single nest until the day came when the black one had to fly off to work, because he was a carrier pigeon. Then the white one was visited by a "red caller".

> *What do we learn from this little tale?*
> *Stay in your dwelling without fail.*
> *When wife stays at home and husband's out,*
> *Billing and cooing can come about.*

When Wela asked what it meant, she was told: "You're too small."

"For billing and cooing?"

What was it about that question that made Rena almost splutter laughing? And why couldn't all three pigeons in the song simply live together in a single nest, since we can, and there are eight of us, not counting Milka and Suchard?

"They'd be warmer," said Wela.

"Stop it," said Rena, waving a hand at her sister not to say any more, "or I'll wet the bed."

RENA

Maybe Rena brought the song about pigeons home from Strzelecki Park? Not long ago she'd been there for the first time with her girlfriends from school. She had spent the previous evening first devotedly, though not entirely selflessly helping her mother to fry white cheese with egg yolk and caraway seed (the mere smell made her feel sick), then begging her mother to let her go to the park after school.

"What will you girls do there?"

"Feed the squirrels."

"Is that so?!"

"Mama, everyone goes there now, please."

Next day, all the wooden benches really were occupied. One could finally tell that the winter was over. What's more, a week ago the Hungarian had packed up his stove and left. The town no longer smelled of the petroleum jelly the parents rubbed on their children's frozen hands and cheeks. And some of the boys were even going out in knee-length trousers.

But who looks round at boys in short trousers?

Nor were Rena and her two classmates interested in the buds that the smartly dressed ladies were showing each other.

Anyway, in Rena's view those women in long dresses and wide-brimmed hats, with a swinging step and an alluring look, had not come to Strzelecki Park for the sake of a few immature weeds either.

"After all, where and to whom are they to show themselves in those glad rags of theirs?" she said. "To the servants at home?"

And to whom were she and her friends to show themselves at a girl's high school? The old janitor?

Rena, Gizella and Marysia discreetly looked at the boys walking past. They often played this game on their way home from school. Which of them would a boy coming the opposite way look straight in the eyes? The first glance didn't count. After all, almost everyone in Tarnów looked at the people they passed. Only a second glance could mean that he liked one of them. It was important to hold his attention – he mustn't avert his gaze. For every look of that kind one gained a point.

Of course they didn't count the vulgar taunts of the tipsy Tarnovia fans, who on their way to a match against Samson, the Jewish team, would shout out or sing:

The Jewish men can all get lost,
The Jewish girls can come with us.

In reply Rena would tap her forehead, though she had to admit that the two tall, blue-eyed Catholics staring at her weren't bad-looking, or were at least worth counting.

And then she knew from Rudek that Tarnovia sneakily borrowed Samson's best players for its away matches. Apparently including Heśko Schreiber himself, who always wore a tallit under his shirt with the blue Samson colours, so the string tzitzit sticking out at the bottom provoked the opposition. It crossed Rena's mind that this was a sight she'd love to see. Meaning Schreiber getting changed.

"Pure muscle," the Samson fans said of him. "He can shoot the length of the pitch with his bare foot and score a goal."

"More like across it and into his own goal," replied the Tarnovia fans, shaking their fists at him and yelling: "Heśko, hide your titiz!"

But the Samson players were far more scared of their own infuriated fans, who were merciless if they lost. And as Rudek told it, they won most of their matches out of fear of them.

"That's why lately we're the kings of the second league," he said.

Or perhaps it was really because whenever they went to play a match in Kraków, Chrzanów or Lwów they secretly borrowed players from Tarnovia too? After all, no one there knew what they looked like.

"What's odd about that? At the end of the day, a goal is a goal," explained Rudek, "regardless of ethnicity. They just have to be from Tarnów."

And so the whole of Tarnów rejoiced when their clubs won, and their citizens became famous in the world outside.

Lately, so was the son of a teacher named Mrs Sobelsohn – even the Hassidim and the Catholics were proud of his successes. She showed her pupils at the girls' high school a newspaper cutting with a picture of her son smoking a pipe and wearing thick round glasses, while standing next to Lenin.

And she added that it was definitely him, even though the caption said "Karl Radek".

Whatever, one thing was for sure: he was far from being as handsome as the football player, thought Rena. Very small, and pigeon-chested, with thin, curly hair. With those looks he hadn't had an easy life at school or in the street.

People remembered that as a child he had never been parted from his books. Even while crossing the tramlines or the roadway he never stopped reading. So one day, while walking to the yeshiva, for the third time at the same crossroads he stepped in the way of a peasant cart driving to market, and what's more he lost consciousness by hitting his head on the cobblestones; as a result his mother had transferred her beloved only child to a different school. Not Jewish, and much further off – that was true – but even so, there were no junctions of two bigger streets along the way.

That was the first time he had become famous.

If the Jews crossed the entire Red Sea without getting a foot wet, the local people joked, why can't young Sobelsohn walk two hundred metres to the yeshiva without falling under a farmer's wagon?

Or maybe that was exactly what the rabbis meant when they said that what matters more than the destination is the journey that leads there? That must have been why Mrs Sobelsohn made sure it was safe at least.

The girls usually walked as far as the corner of Wałowa and Krakowska Streets, from where each could be home in under five minutes. That was fair. They would say farewell outside a shop with a window display that always amused them: I BUY AND SELL GOOSE AND CHICKEN FEATHERS, PLUCKED AND UNPLUCKED. It was Mr Schiff's shop, and here they added up the scores.

"Twelve."

"Four."

"Five."

Gizella almost always won. She had delicate features and large blue eyes; she was taller than Marysia and Rena, and unlike them she didn't have to pad out her bra with socks. Her figure made her look at least sixteen. As a result, the real fight was for second place.

The next time they went to Strzelecki Park, something was going on at the entrance, right beside the ornate main gate. They tried to push through the small crowd to see what was making them laugh.

"Excuse me," said Gizella, clearing a path to the fence, to which someone had stuck a page torn from *Our Voice*.

"Oh, come on, girls!" said Marysia, touching Rena on the arm and casting a glance towards the fountain. "Hm, that one's nice."

On one of the benches beside the fountain Rena saw her brother Hesio, who hadn't said a word about coming here. Not to mention ask their parents' permission or help to fry the white cheese. Rena's first instinct was to turn away. After all, the spring sunshine was so glaring that she couldn't recognize her own brother. That morning when they'd left the house he hadn't been wearing those long trousers or that hairstyle. He hadn't looked as if he'd bathed in brilliantine.

"Rena!" cried Hesio, waving to them.

"Do you know him?" said Marysia, smiling.

Rena shrugged. In case Hesio got it into his head to come up to them, she turned to face the fence and fixed her gaze on the sheet of newspaper pinned there.

> *It's all for us*
>
> *Once they cowered at home, the Jewboys,*
> *Far too frightened of the goys.*
> *From Grabówka's dankest place*
> *Yiddle dared not move one pace.*
> *Now he takes his Jewish gal*
> *And canters round the whole locale.*
> *A stinking, filthy common mass,*
> *A rabble of the lowest class.*
> *And here in our Strzelecki Park*
> *The Jewish kids have found their Ark.*
> *When Israel's daughters come this way,*
> *Dressed for the beach on holiday,*
> *Marvels of nature, every one,*
> *They warm their bosoms in the sun.*
> *The Lord God made it all for us*
> *Pineapples, dates, figs and citrus.*
> *Houses and flats He made to be ours,*
> *Villas, health resorts and spas.*
> *For us He made chickens, ducks and geese –*
> *But ever in search of eggs or cheese*
> *The Jewess pokes in every nook,*
> *The Jew fills his basket by hook or by crook...*

For a long while the girls walked down a path in silence, which was eventually broken by Gizella.

"That's not about us. If only all the Jews in Tarnów looked like us, and not like those sidelock-wearing, gaberdine-clad types from Grabówka – they're such a dreadful fright… Dad says then there wouldn't be any…"

"Jews at all," Rena completed the sentence, regretting that she hadn't ripped that vile stuff off the fence instead of laughing with the others.

Now she was reminded of what her father really had once told her at bedtime about the day when all the Jews had vanished from the city, even from Strzelecki Park. They'd been afraid to leave their homes, or else they had gone away, like Mama, who a month after the Russians entered Tarnów had taken the children to her parents in Nisko. Rena was still tiny then.

"Russki motherfuckers," her father had said, puffing out his cheeks as if about to spit, but actually he was at home. "They've got it in for our lot. They beat up the Jews, robbed them and pulled out their beards, skin and all. If only I'd been here at the time… That son of a bitch, Colonel Kozlov, ordered his soldiers to pour away the alcohol from the Jewish shops. He hadn't foreseen that people would scoop it out of the gutters in mugs, pour it back into the bottles and sell it to his soldiers for eight roubles a bottle. What a gold mine. If only I hadn't been sitting in the trenches…"

"But how well the Austrian uniform matched the colour of your eyes," said Mama, leaning over Dad and whispering in his ear: "Fancy scaring the children with world war. Are you out of your mind?"

VI

WELA

RENA WAS COMING HOME from Strzelecki Park later and later. To avoid waking the caretaker, and above all not to have to pay him to open the gate, their parents left the kitchen window ajar on the street side. If Wela was already asleep, Rena quietly took an apple from the kitchen and sat down on their shared bed. She'd bite into it especially loudly. And wait. Wait for Wela to say: "Stop it. I'm asleep."

(She'd been having a very pleasant, though not kosher dream – about a delicious sausage that hung from their kitchen stove, and although they ate it every day, it grew back overnight and was whole again in time for breakfast.)

"Well, not anymore."

Now Rena could start to tell her sister what it had been like, and whom she had seen, met and kissed in Strzelecki Park.

Wela liked it when, as well as stories about soldiers and housemaids in the bushes, Rena also brought her a song or at least a little ditty from her evening outings. Like today, for instance:

> *Daddy's gone on a trip,*
> *Mummy's gone on a trip,*
> *Daddy's tripped over Mummy,*
> *And now they're doing a flip!*

Wela laughed, though not entirely sure what was so funny.

"I also heard two important things," said Rena, lowering her voice. "First of all, you have to leave a party at the best moment, never stay to the end. Got it?"

Wela nodded. Leave a party? How she'd love to go to a party one day, a real one, at the elegant Hotel Soldinger for instance. Once when she was walking past it, she peeped through a gap in the curtains and saw glamorous couples dancing. Even the men were wearing jewellery. Large rings with black stones glittered in the light of the cut-glass chandeliers. And their watches hung on golden chains. As for their moustaches… Wela had pressed her face to the window pane. Some were modest, thin as eyebrows, others were curled, pointing sharply upwards. And there were some that blended naturally into goatee beards, as neatly trimmed as the lawn outside the Hotel Soldinger. Worlds away from the long, yellow beards full of food scraps, bits of fluff and tobacco that made her feel so sick in Grabówka that she averted her gaze.

Wela had also caught sight of an elderly violinist adjusting his glasses and shifting his notes in a single, magical movement. She saw how white and perfectly ironed the tablecloths were, and the napkins rolled into cones on the plates. She saw the waiters in bow ties, their hair shining with brilliantine, even smarter than some of the guests as they danced among the tables, bearing trays of food. One of them had drawn the curtains.

But… To go to a party like that one there were insurmountable obstacles to be overcome. The appropriate costume – where on earth would you get it, if you only wore hand-me-downs from your older sister?

At times like this she hated clothes. Had they been invented just to stop her from going to parties?

And what about invitations? Were they only for the girls who went to communion in lovely white dresses and white knee-length socks?

"Listen, the second thing," said Rena, stifling her laughter and leaning close to Wela's ear. "If you're on a stripping date, always keep your vest on."

Wela's jaw dropped. She had never heard of a stripping date before. But maybe that was something for her? After all, it'd be easier to obtain a single vest than complete a whole obstacle course involving an evening gown, high-heeled shoes, white gloves, jewellery and an invitation.

Maybe there was a vest to be found on Mama's shelf in the wardrobe?

But Wela didn't ask her sister what exactly a stripping date was. And why should you stay in your vest, and not your beret, knickers or stockings? Wouldn't it be easier with nothing on?

But she didn't ask, because she knew the answer already:

"You're too small."

Or at best:

"Oh, come on…"

Instead of this Wela closed her mouth (only now had she realized it was still open), and just nodded to indicate that she understood this too.

Fenced off from their brothers and parents by a canvas screen, Wela and Rena had their own private world. In fact it was not very soundproof, because it let through their father's shouts, their brothers' crying, laughter and loud conversations, and even worse things.

Usually Rudek began in a solemn tone, as if imitating Mr Tertil, the mayor of Tarnów, or Rabbi Arak from the Old Synagogue, where the faithful gathered from all over Poland.

"MOF?"

And like a children's choir Salek and Hesio would reply:

"OOM."

To which Rena would shout at them all to get lost and drown in the outhouse.

But this time someone else answered Rudek first. From Nusek's impatient, slightly squeaky voice one could tell he'd waited a long time for this moment.

"Better PYA!"

Rudek didn't even reply.

"PYA," repeated Nusek, and after a pause, during which he was probably hoping someone would ask him what it meant, added: "And I won't send you to the bank. I'll tell you myself, Rudek."

"What are you on about?" asked Rudek.

"Plug Your Arsehole."

Wela and Rena cocked an ear to hear what would come next. What would Rudek do now? Or rather what would he do to Nusek? Was he about to thump him?

But silence fell behind the screen.

The girls were tempted to lean out to check in case Rudek had suffocated Nusek with a pillow, but right now they were as blind as Mejer the Mute.

Moments later, everyone in the room could sense that Rudek definitely hadn't plugged his arsehole.

That was his response to his youngest brother. And to distract her attention, Wela held her nose and thought about Mejer the Mute again.

He was a man who came to Goldhammer Street and knocked at their door once a month, on the dot of five in the afternoon. He stood so tall and straight that he'd have been sure to bang his head if he'd tried to come inside. But despite being blind, he never bumped into things or tripped. He'd wait on the threshold, while Mama opened the door to him with a coin ready in her hand. Not even their father refused him. Maybe because he knew Mejer would only accept one coin, the smallest. Once that had been half an Austrian kreuzer, and now it was one Polish grosz. If he got more, which was a rare event, he either gave it away, or handed back change.

"The king of the Tarnów beggars, and I never refuse a king," said their father, who never gave a penny to anyone else.

"Daddy," said Wela one time, when they passed the outstretched hand of an old woman near the town hall. "Give her something."

Nathan lost his temper, and Wela had the happy thought: how lucky our father only hits his sons.

"If I were to give money to all of them," he said, pointing at the beggars who were either sitting or lying in Żydowska and Krakowska Streets, "I'd end up like them!"

61

But he always had something for Mejer, because Mejer was different from the rest. Not just because he didn't sit in the street. Dressed in a clean shirt and jacket, holding a long stick, he went from door to door.

It was hard to believe he couldn't see, hear or speak.

RUDEK

"Isn't that too much luck for just one man?" was the usual joke in Tarnów. The Stramer brothers decided to check up. Rudek, Salek and Hesio spent half a day following Mejer along various backstreets in the new Jewish district. They didn't take Nusek with them, for why should they?

Mejer cautiously approached each door and gently moved a hand across it. If he found a mezuzah on the right doorframe he knocked, and if not, he gave up and walked on.

The brothers also saw some people hurriedly removing the mezuzah from their door at the sight of him. And others, who plainly hadn't had time to do that, but who didn't fully believe in his blindness either, extinguishing the oil lamps and pretending they weren't at home.

"It's a good thing he can't see that," said Salek.

In his thoughts he wondered whether the Catholics too had their own Mejer, who knocked only at their doors. And if so, whether at the end of the month the two beggars shared the profits half and half, because in Tarnów that would be fair.

Mejer walked indifferently past dustbins, but he never missed a house or a flat. If he was given food, he didn't take a penny. He only used his stick once, when without asking, a smartly dressed man (probably a visitor, because what would someone in a top hat and tails be doing in this part of town?) took him by the arm to help him across the street. But Mejer struck the stick hard against the cobbles and broke free of him. The smartly dressed man sprang back in surprise.

They might have gone on tramping after Mejer until nightfall, if not for a woman in high heels smoking a cigarette outside the Hotel Polski.

"The hooligans are out to get you," she said loudly.

And rapped her red fingernails against the window of the hotel restaurant.

At once a man in a peaked cap pulled low over his forehead came running out of the hotel and stopped before Mejer the Mute.

"I'll smash your gob, you pervert!" he said, taking a swing. "Your own mother won't recognize you."

There was no answer, and the woman stood in between them. There was nothing else she could do.

Mejer didn't even budge – perhaps he was waiting for a coin? Had he realized what was going on, and what the woman had saved him from? wondered the Stramer brothers as they ran off. How could he possibly have known it was a woman, and a tall, pretty, blonde one too?

"From her perfume," said Hesio, who thought he could still smell its sweet, alluring scent.

They slowed down. Rudek said it was time to go home for their Friday night supper. Salek and Hesio agreed without a word. They hadn't been as hungry and as unanimous for ages.

But where had Mejer gone? Probably towards the station, where he lived and apparently slept on a seat in the waiting room.

Rudek strode along the middle of the pavement, at a similar pace to the guy in the peaked cap. He was still thinking about Mejer the Mute and his income. How much might he earn daily, weekly, monthly and annually?

On his right walked Salek, and on his left Hesio, both of whom came up to his shoulders and were trying to keep in step with him. But not only. It was enough for Rudek to cast a glance at a colonial goods store window, to look round at a girl or stare underfoot to avoid muddying his shoes for his brothers to do exactly the same, like delayed shadows.

At home on Goldhammer Street a sublime atmosphere prevailed. Their father was lighting the Sabbath candles – one for each member of the family. Not only did he not ask where they'd been or why they hadn't taken Nusek with them, but he even hugged and kissed each of them.

"I've got jobs for you," he said.

"Where?" asked Rudek, looking round for his mother, who was turned away from them, busy cooking on the kitchen hob. He noticed she was wearing a new, white apron.

"Working for me," said Nathan.

At such moments Nathan could see how closely Rudek resembled his older brother, Ben. Dammit, he looked like the young Ben, or rather Beniamin, as he was known before he left for America.

"At the Jewish butcher's?" said Rudek, looking down at his father.

How else could he look at him, when he was already the taller? But he'd gazed at him that way earlier too. It was Ben's look. So was that confident tone, and the insolently raised left corner of the mouth. Sometimes Nathan felt as if it wasn't

Rudek whose rear end he was thrashing with the American belt, but Ben, who hadn't even tried to persuade him to stay in New York. Ben, who could never come to visit his younger brother and his family in Tarnów.

Ben, whom he couldn't reach in any other way.

"You kiddin' me?" said Nathan in English, and since nobody understood it, he explained: "I sent the butcher's to hell today."

And he showed the boys the official licence he'd received to run "an enterprise offering hot dishes, coffee, tea and billiards".

"Let's celebrate," he shouted, uncorking some red wine. "Aren't you pleased?"

The children instantly froze. They looked at the bottle of Hungarian wine, old Egri bikavér, "not some sort of sweet Tokay or other filth made of raisins", as Nathan stressed every time he told the story about it. Someone had accidentally left it by the till at the butcher's. And a week later they still hadn't come to claim it – can you imagine? Such good wine!

"Finders keepers," he'd said to himself.

Nathan had been to Abraham Reich's wine shop, next to the post office on Krakowska Street, to find out. To take a look at the prices. It cost a fortune! But they didn't buy individual bottles. Not even at half price. It was hard to believe how that shop functioned, let alone how it had kept going since 1842, as a faded sign over the entrance proudly announced.

Perhaps I'll display the foundation year in my café too, thought Nathan.

The Hungarian wine had a long wait for a special occasion. Meanwhile, on Friday evenings Nathan would open the raisin brandy. Rudek and Hesio examined the Hungarian bottle from every side. Removing the cork was out of the question. So was pushing it inside with a key or a nail. Rudek came up with a different idea.

He brought home a glass-and-metal syringe. He refused to tell any of his siblings where he'd got it from. First he threatened to inject Nusek in the arse, then he stuck the needle gently into the cork in the bottle. He managed to extract a measure of wine and squirted it into a tumbler. He did the same thing five times, until the tumbler was almost full.

"Good health to the Stramers!" said Rudek, raising the tumbler, taking a sip and passing it on.

He wanted to make sure each of the siblings had a drink, even the youngest, Wela and Nusek, because then they definitely wouldn't tell their parents.

Anyway, they wanted some.

Later they pretended to be drunk. Or maybe they really were?

Holding the empty tumbler and mimicking the neighbour from opposite, Nusek reeled around the flat, bumping into the furniture and jabbering: "But darling, I swear I haven't had a drop."

And Wela rolled about on the floor laughing.

"What about this?" said Rena, coming to and pointing at the bottle.

Rudek picked up the syringe again. He had no choice, but it took him a while to get a grip on himself and plunge the needle into a bucket. He filled the syringe with water and injected it through the cork into the bottle. And again, five times.

"This business will pay off on one condition," said their father, gesticulating by the kitchen table, while the children kept their eyes fixed on his full wine glass. "You have to stand at the bar yourself, best of all with the whole family. Then you don't count your working hours and you break even."

"Daddy, does that mean..." said Nusek, who couldn't stop himself, just as Nathan raised the glass to his lips, "does that mean you're going to pay us?"

Nusek, the youngest boy, was the most like his father. That was why Nathan wasn't angry with him for asking this impudent question, but just said mildly:

"For helping your parents? Fat chance!"

And he wagged a finger at Nusek.

Is he about to spit diluted wine at us all? thought Rena, and took a step back from the table just in case.

Will he scream at us for spoiling everything? Or strike his fist against the table and leap up so abruptly that he overturns his chair? If that's what happens, there won't be a café at all! Right before our eyes he'll crumple up the official licence, rip it to pieces and burn it in the kitchen stove.

And then make us pay for the wine, thought Rudek in alarm.

Wela was sure she could already see her father going pale at the first sip, then tottering away unsteadily to go and lie down, while Mama said: "It's gastritis."

Hesio must have been imagining the storm that was about to be unleashed, flinging shouts and American swearwords across the table, because he was looking at the open window. Perhaps there was still time to close it?

Salek could already see himself standing before his father, heroically taking all the blame and saying: "Some change water into wine, others vice versa."

The siblings would be laughing, their mother would be gazing at him with admiration, their father would forgive him and say: "If only those who changed wine into water came to a better end, son."

Nusek didn't know what would happen, but suspecting the worst, he slowly started sliding off his chair and under the table.

And then their father threw the entire glass of wine down his throat.

"Well," he said, wiping his mouth with a hand, "that's something I understand. That's the taste of good, old wine."

VII

NATHAN

THE CAFÉ THAT HE OPENED a month later was not much bigger than their flat. It was on Goldhammer Street too, but on the other side, at the presentable, top end of it. At number six.

Tea, coffee, milk and snacks – instead of a shop sign her father told Rena to inscribe that nicely in white paint, in Polish and Yiddish, between the windows of the future café. He preferred not to risk writing in Polish himself.

He bought only four little wooden tables and chairs, a used billiards table and a wooden coat stand, but even so these items took up most of the space in the café, and most of the dollars from Ben.

Nathan told himself, his wife and children that this investment would pay for itself at lightning speed. You only had to do a tour of the Tarnów cafés, you didn't even need to go inside them to understand that. Before opening his own, Nathan did just that. Those cafés were always full – it was surprising there weren't more of them. He peeped inside through the windows and smiled mysteriously. Mentally he was multiplying the number of customers by the prices of the drinks and snacks, and then by the café opening hours, the days of the week, month and year.

But the competition never sleeps. So just in case he only shared his considerations and calculations with his wife.

"What a good thing it is that some cafés can be open on public and religious holidays, when everything else is closed," he said.

"Yes. Now go to sleep," said Rywka, turning her back on him and his café. "It's the middle of the night."

Sometimes Nathan went into the fullest ones, such as the Sailcloth café on Sobieski Square, the Secession on Krakowska Street – apparently modelled on the Hawelka, the most famous café in all Galicia – or the Avenue on Wałowa Street. This last café, especially its name, was the one he liked best.

"Full up?" he checked with the waiters and looked around the interior to find the special something that was so attractive to all those people, whom he thought of by now purely as his future clients.

The wooden newspaper rack? In his café he could use it for yesterday's papers, which were given away for a pittance. Why buy today's, when tomorrow they'd be yesterday's?

Or perhaps it was the old, blind pianist? He was just as out of tune as Salek. But there was no room or money left for a piano. So maybe it was worth having the boy return to the violin – Nathan pencilled it down on the sheet of paper beside his calculations and immediately imagined his son in dark glasses.

Or was it the thick plush curtains, through which the light could barely squeeze into the Secession? Oh no! Why spend money on lamps and paraffin if the sun shines for free?

Or the fresh flowers? That was an exaggeration too – wilted flowers thrown out every couple of days were just money drowned in a vase. Wasn't it better to keep them in flowerpots?

"Just a moment, please," the waiters called after him. "There's a table free for you now."

"Too late. I'll come back another time."

As the name Avenue, which he thought had the best ring to it, was already taken (for a while he considered Fifth Avenue as well), Nathan asked Rena to climb the ladder a second time and paint above the entrance to the café: THE STRAMERS.

That was when he realized that in her white dress his daughter was actually a woman by now, and that fellows looked round at her in the street. Could Rena see that they were ogling her? Staring at her olive skin, her thick black tresses, and especially brazenly at her breasts and bum? Just as he had once gaped at Rywka, whom Rena so closely resembled. On the one hand, Nathan felt pride as he watched his older daughter up the ladder towering over the whole of Goldhammer Street, over her father and all those guys staring at her, but on the other he felt jealous too, just as he had about Rywka in the past. Instinctively he glanced through the café window at his grey-haired wife, who was leaning forward, busy at work by the small bar, and then he felt something else too, something that had a far greater effect on him.

Rywka smiled and waved at him.

If only Ben could see him now. Nathan stood straight and stuck out his belly. What would he say at the sight of his younger brother in a tie, white shirt, closed pinstriped waistcoat and open jacket, squinting in the sunlight outside his own café? He took off his hat, wiped his brow and the inside of the hat with a handkerchief, then put it back on, tilting it slightly to the left. Well, possibly his trousers could be a little better pressed, and his shoes cleaner, but Ben knew what the mud was like in Tarnów.

And what would he have said to the large white sign above the entrance? Thanks to Nathan, now their name would be famous throughout the city. I'm off to the Stramers! Let's meet at the Stramers! See you at ten as usual at the Stramers!

Maybe in a couple of years someone in a New York café would say: "This coffee's almost as good as at The Stramers." And by chance Ben would be sitting at the next table.

"What Stramers are you talking about, sir?"

"The café in Tarnów, of course."

And then Ben would learn all about his younger brother and his successes.

Nathan smiled. He could already see himself opening more cafés in the future, each to be run by a different son.

What did Ben look like by now? Funny that Nathan had never wondered about that before. In his mind, his brother always looked the same as on the New York quay, when he gave him the leather belt as a parting gift. For twenty years he hadn't moved from that quay. As immobile as the Statue of Liberty.

But why was it always his older brother who would stand immobile and watch as the younger one sailed away, became mature, responsible and worthy of fraternal trust? And why, if the younger turned to look behind him, was it only to compare himself to the older, who for some strange reason, contrary to the laws of perspective, every time he looked back from a distance, seemed bigger and bigger?

Did it mean Nathan was a small Ben?

Only now did Nathan notice that Rena had finished painting and was already putting away the bucket and the ladder.

He stood a while longer outside his café. He read the sign drying in the sunshine and peeked at the passers-by to see if they had noticed that the world had changed.

RYWKA

On the first day after opening the café they had no customers. Just like Nathan recently, everyone just peeped inside. They put their hands against the windowpanes to see what they could in the strong summer sunlight.

This bothered Nathan, who every few minutes sent one of the children outside to clean off the marks left by the non-materializing customers.

"Dad," said Nusek, "they're staring at us like fish in an aquarium!"

"Pipe down," replied his father and Rudek simultaneously.

The only person (holding a suitcase) to cross the threshold of the café took one look at the four empty tables, the six underage waiters gazing at him, the boss behind the bar and the cook leaning out of the kitchen, then turned tail and left without a word.

"What the hell's wrong?" said Nathan, who'd been expecting no less than a siege on the first day.

Now he was sorry he hadn't listened to Rywka and hadn't arranged a grand opening, with free coffee and tea.

"It's pointless," he'd told his wife the day before. "If it's given away for free, they'll think it's worthless. That's what they'll say and they won't come back again."

"If I make them good tea and coffee, they'll be back."

"Bullshit," said Nathan impatiently in his American English. "Even if they do, they won't buy anything – why would they pay for something they'd already had for free? It's like with the newspapers. Why the hell buy new ones, when…"

Rywka shrugged. He had failed to convince her, she didn't understand his arguments (after all, people had the same drinks for free at home as they ordered in cafés), but she had no desire to go on quarrelling, all the more since what he had said about the newspapers grieved her. She wouldn't give anyone yesterday's coffee or tea, would she? Not even for free.

But perhaps she had no idea. She tried to remember the last time she had been in a café. No, no, it wasn't possible. Yes, yes, it must have been before the war, because the youngest, Wela and Nusek, hadn't been born yet.

She was happy to move her pots and frying pans from home into the small kitchen behind the wooden bar. She had more space here than at home, where even so she cooked the daily meals. Now she would do it here, for which she'd brought a set of kosher dishes too.

She had one other reason to be pleased. The family would be together again. Recently not just Rudek and Rena had been vanishing off somewhere and coming home late at night through the kitchen window, but sometimes Salek too, and even Hesio.

Especially since the start of the summer vacation.

It worried her. Where did they go to all day long? What were they doing? Did they spend their time in Strzelecki Park? Or on St Marcin's Peak, where apparently the young people were meeting up now? Whenever she asked them, without looking her in the eyes, they replied that they were still giving private tuition. But school had ended a month ago, and with it the private tuition, thanks to which they paid for their own studies.

Rywka couldn't sleep until they were all home.

She decided to tell Nathan about it. But anything that wasn't to do with the café had ceased to interest him long ago.

"If you've got a problem and you worry about it," said Nathan, then fell silent, as if he'd forgotten what he wanted to say next, "you've got two problems."

"What a revelation."

Rywka knew that saying well. Nonetheless, Nathan insisted he had just invented it himself. In that case, by what miracle had half Tarnów been repeating it for years? Her father often used to console her with it when she was a little girl in Nisko.

Sometimes, when Nathan was so insistent, and in that unassailable tone of his, it was as if he thought he was a rabbi or a tzaddik. In fact, during their engagement he had told her his family was descended from the chief rabbi of Kraków. That must be who Salek took after. She couldn't remember which rabbi it was, or perhaps Nathan had forgotten by then?

In any case, after the wedding he never mentioned it again.

She could also remember the time when, with his eyes shining, he used to say he would take her to the seaside, where together they would watch the sunset and swim in the sea, but meanwhile only the years had swum by.

Now his eyes only shone at the sight of the café. He got up early with Rywka, and had stopped having a lie-down in the middle of the day. He spent every moment at The Stramers, wearing his best jacket. Being careful not to stain it, he made his wife and children do most of the work. While he gazed in the mirror suspended above the bar and went outside to admire the sign.

On opening day he wouldn't let the children sit at the unoccupied tables, not even little Wela, because how would that look? "The customer enters, sees something like that and leaves."

Here he was first and foremost the boss, and only then a husband and father. Rywka was surprised by how suddenly this change had occurred, and how rapidly Nathan felt important, from one day to the next.

He walked up and down among the tables, talking more quietly and gesticulating less. He stopped doing the shopping for home. Only the café counted, and after all, he was its chief representative, the face and the name of it. Never mind the fact that it still hadn't had a single customer.

A few days before the opening Rywka had asked Nathan who would come to The Stramers. Customers. Who will I be cooking for? He cast her a look as if he still didn't understand. Should it be kosher or not? Nathan, who crossed the street at the mere smell of pork, looked surprised.

First he said that of course it should be kosher.

"Then everyone, Jews and Catholics, can eat at our place."

A little later he changed his mind.

"But will Catholics want to sit at a table next to Jews in gaberdines?"

They both knew the answer.

Finally he gave in.

"You decide, darling. I haven't the time right now."

And out he went to look at the sign.

"Yes and yes," said Rudek as soon as his father had gone. Rywka thought so too.

And so she'd had to buy an extra set of utensils and divide the kitchen with a curtain. Was that enough? There was no other solution. She decided on a cold buffet. Sandwiches, herrings and goose neck sausages. That was best on summer days. Of the hot dishes, just tripe for now.

RUDEK

On the first day in the café Rudek really did feel like a fish in an aquarium. Nusek was right. Mentally he had to agree with him. A fish in the sea and a fish in an aquarium were two very different things. But where on earth could Nusek have seen an aquarium? Rudek thought of the only one he had seen, at the home of Daniel, the deputy mayor's son. Languid, brightly coloured fish indifferently passed each other by, just as they were doing here, at the end of the day, among the four empty tables.

He remembered a small red fish that stood out from the others. It kept doggedly swallowing pebbles from the bottom and spitting them at the glass wall of the aquarium.

"It does that all night," said Daniel. "Dad says the noise often keeps him awake. And that can affect the future of the city. Now the elections are coming up…"

Did the small red fish believe it would eventually manage to smash the aquarium by doing that? Or was it just trying to draw attention to itself?

That was exactly what had to be done now, thought Rudek, and once the café had closed he headed for the army barracks opposite their home on Goldhammer Street. He'd been coming here for years late in the day – at times when the soldiers couldn't go out into the city anymore. He'd started when the Austrians were still stationed here.

He would shout over the high wall: "Zigaretten?"

Nowadays he asked the same question in Polish.

The Austro-Hungarian soldiers had thrown hellers and guldens over the wall, at first the Polish lancers had thrown marks, but now groszy and zloty coins, and Rudek invariably threw back cigarettes. Whole packets or single items. Twice as expensive as in the tobacco shop.

And invariably he didn't have to give any change.

He had tried to get Salek involved. Several times he took him with him to the barracks to let him see how it was done, and then he sent him on his own, but Salek came back sad, with no money or cigarettes. Perhaps he'd been too small? Instead of flying over the wall, the single cigarettes he threw had bounced off it and landed in the mud. He couldn't find them in the dark. And when he'd managed to throw a whole packet over he hadn't received any money for it. Although Rudek had explained to him that first they pay, then you throw.

"I'd rather just give private lessons," said Salek.

And Rudek had to admit that it was more of a success for him.

Lately he had taught a rabbi's son maths, history and Polish, above all how to speak Polish without an accent; as a result the boy had easily qualified for the sixth form at the gymnasium. And his father had come from the great New Synagogue to their little flat on Goldhammer Street to thank Salek in person.

"Why do some children speak Polish like Catholics while others have an accent?" he was curious to know.

Salek replied that the Jewish children who speak Polish best are the ones who never speak it at home.

"Why is that?"

Rudek was listening to them, proud of his younger brother for being able to engage a rabbi in conversation.

"Because they don't have any bad habits."

Could it be that at home the rabbi and his wife covertly spoke to their son in their clumsy Polish? Believing this would make his life easier?

"Sure," chipped in Nathan at once. "That's why in my house we only speak Yiddish!"

His father. On the way to the barracks Rudek all but shook his head. The man spoke Polish as well as he ran a café. But everything always had to be to his credit.

What was it like to be the son of a rabbi from the New Synagogue, or of the manager of the Hotel Soldinger, or the deputy mayor, for instance?

He wondered.

But he'd never exchange his mother for any other. Or his brothers and sisters.

It was a warm summer evening. Insects were crashing into the gas-powered streetlamps. Through the open windows he could hear someone practising the piano. And only the overflowing dustbins, which stank the worst in summer, reminded him that he was in Tarnów.

Rudek crossed to the other side of the street. He didn't even have to look around. Ever since the municipality had banned vehicles from speeding their way around the city, it had become safer. This applied to lorries in particular, which used to scratch the buildings and ruin the cobbles. And once or twice had driven into someone's home.

Rudek and his brothers were sorry they hadn't seen that.

Now he imagined a lorry driving into his father's café. With the first, thirsty customer inside.

He smiled.

Now he knew what he was going to do.

"Who's not afraid of losing against the billiards champion?" he shouted over the brick wall.

"What's the deal?" replied a voice from the other side.

"I'll be waiting tomorrow at The Stramers."

And as an incentive, to make sure the idea caught on, he threw across a few single cigarettes for nothing.

The following afternoon they appeared. The first customers, for whom Nathan had been looking out all day like for the Messiah. What's more, five of them at once. As a reward for his patience.

"Please come inside," Nathan welcomed them.

These Messiahs were not Jews. Four conscripts, not much older than Rudek. The fifth, evidently their superior, in a uniform with medals and a grey moustache like Piłsudski's, could have been their father, or even their grandfather. The others waited for him to sit down before doing the same.

They ordered a round of beer and tripe.

Nathan served them in person, and now and then Rywka leaned out of the kitchen with a cloth and wiped the wooden bar to a shine. She was curious to know if they liked the tripe.

Hesio and Salek changed their ashtrays. Hesio covered the

full ashtray with an empty one, and in both hands carefully carried it to the kitchen. Salek instantly put a clean one in its place.

Then the guests moved over to the billiards table. They ordered another round of beer, this time brought to them by Rena.

True to yesterday's promise, Rudek impressively outplayed each of them in turn. Only when it came to the fifth, the one with the moustache, did his run of luck suddenly come to an end, and though all his siblings, especially Wela, the littlest, had their fingers tightly crossed for him, Rudek's balls stopped falling into the pockets.

But that was the least of it. He struck the black ball so hard that it flew off the table and almost hit his opponent. It landed on the floor a few centimetres from the officer's muddy boots; with an ironical smile from under his moustache he brushed this off as the typical reckless move of a loser, a final, desperate impulse well known to him from the battlefield.

"I humbly beg your pardon, General," said Rudek.

"Let's play, boy," said the officer, looking proud rather than offended. After all, it was he who had reduced his opponent to this state. And before the eyes of the young soldiers, who had also heard him being addressed as a general.

"What's wrong with you?" said Nusek, tugging Rudek by the sleeve as soon as the five customers had gone.

"Nothing," said Rudek, shrugging.

He watched his father collecting and counting the money, including the tip the officer had left on the billiards table. He put the banknotes in his left back pocket and the coins in his front right.

"You have to know when to lose," said Rudek. "It's harder than winning."

SALEK

Just then the door opened and a sixth customer entered the café. He tripped over the threshold, but at the last moment grabbed the wooden coat stand to avoid falling. Salek instantly recognized him and said: "Good day, sir."

It was Mieczysław Zawadowski, the young Tarnów lawyer. That summer Salek and Hesio had often heard about him on St Marcin's Peak. Salek had actually seen him there once, but in the dark he hadn't noticed his pale blue eyes and backswept fair hair. It was said that he could bewitch the courtroom with his speeches. According to rumour he voluntarily defended not just the poor farmers who brought hens to his office afterwards, but also Salek and Hesio's older colleagues whom they encountered in the evenings on the Mount. He was a hero. Salek wondered how to show him that he admired him.

Rudek glanced inquiringly at Salek. He didn't go to St Marcin's Peak in the evenings and thought his brothers should keep well away from the place too.

"It's not Mount Sinai!" he once told them.

"Maybe it is? How do you know?" replied Salek.

Rudek waved a hand.

"A beer and a shot of vodka," said Zawadowski, loosening his tie.

He gazed steadily through the window at two droshkies

standing there. Did they have a new stop here? Or had the drivers just stopped to have a chat?

"A beer and a shot of vodka," repeated Salek to his parents at the bar, and added in a quieter tone: "It's the lawyer."

"Who?" asked Nusek loudly, whose head only just came up to the wooden bar.

Salek kicked him on the ankle.

Zawadowski was still looking out of the window at the droshky drivers.

Nathan brought a tray with the order to his table.

"It's an honour to host you," he said. "I am the owner."

Zawadowski turned to face Nathan and looked around the café, as if he hadn't quite realized where he was. His eyes only stopped on the tumbler and the shot glass.

"Many thanks," he said, and downed the vodka.

"Cheers," said Nathan.

"And to save you a trip, I'd like the same again, please."

"Yes, sir."

"I make my best speeches after it," he said, raising his hands as proof, as though he were already in court.

Standing at the bar, Salek and Hesio watched their father's and the lawyer's gestures in an effort to interpret the topic of conversation. Political trials? Class inequalities? The army firing on the Tarnów workers?

After his fourth vodka and his third beer, Zawadowski ordered coffee, then confidently stood up and without a word headed for the exit. Along the way he threw on his coat and bowed to the Stramers in farewell.

"What about the bill?" called Rudek, when Zawadowski already had one foot on the pavement. "There's ten zlotys owing."

Zawadowski came back inside and started searching his pockets, but Rudek could see that he was doing it more for them than for himself, with no certainty of actually finding anything. Finally he shook his head.

"I've forgotten my wallet."

"Sir," said Nathan, standing between him and the door, "until you pay, you can't leave."

Zawadowski glanced at his watch.

"I'll be late for the hearing."

He sat at a table. He took a fountain pen from his inner coat pocket and wrote something on a napkin.

Then he folded it in four and addressed it in bold letters:

LAW OFFICE

ZAWADOWSKI & FRANCOZ

5 LWOWSKA STREET

"The cabby will take it to my associate," he said, handing the napkin to Nathan, "and come back with the money."

Nathan passed the letter to Rudek, who went outside to the droshky drivers. As he crossed the street, he discreetly pressed the napkin to his shirt, to avoid tearing it and so no one inside the café could see him unfolding it.

He liked Zawadowski's sprawling handwriting.

Leoś, buy me out. 10 zlotys.

Rudek quickly folded the napkin.

Meanwhile Salek was watching Zawadowski, feeling awkward for his father, who was standing over him like a guard.

Anyone might accidentally forget something. Salek imagined explaining that to his father. Especially someone with so many important things to think about. And besides, he worked for free, so where would he get money from? Was his father incapable of understanding that not everyone worked purely for money?

His father would never understand that. Though on the other hand he didn't pay his own children for being waiters.

Once at home over supper Salek and Hesio had tried to talk about social classes. About the rich and the poor. From ancient Egypt, where slaves toiled to build the pyramids, to today's Tarnów, where the workers toiled in the factories. Nothing had changed. One man still had eight rooms to live in on his own, while others had to share a single room between eight. But you would only have to...

"The young always think the world starts with them," Nathan had cut him short.

And the old that it ends with them, thought Salek now, as he looked at his father.

A slave who doesn't even know he's a slave. And here he is, keeping his defender captive – the man who fights in court for justice for people like him.

He should forgive him the stupid ten zlotys. What is ten zlotys, anyway? Five hours of private tuition.

All the more since something was starting to happen. Very recently, not far from their home on Goldhammer Street, the army had fired at the striking railway workers. They'd heard the shots. Nusek and Wela had hidden under the table in fear. And on the way back from school Hesio had seen the five murdered workers. They were lying in the mud.

On St Marcin's Peak people were saying that this was the best proof that the spectre of communism was hovering over Europe. The ruling class was reacting nervously, resorting to violence out of fear, because they knew what was coming to them. Inevitably. It was simply dialectics.

Like many others they often heard on the Mount, this was a word that neither Salek nor Hesio understood. But they were ashamed to ask. After all, they had only been going there for a few weeks, from the start of the school holidays. They wouldn't even admit their ignorance to each other.

On the Mount, as they listened to the lectures in the darkness, they thought that there in the sky, softly backlit by the moon, they could already see this spectre, of which so much was being said and which was so greatly anticipated.

Maybe Rudek isn't right, thought Salek. Perhaps this really is Mount Sinai? Some of the speakers had grey beards like rabbis, but they were dressed completely differently. Open-topped shirts, often coloured and collarless. And they addressed the audience differently too, as comrades. And sometimes, forgetting themselves: "Do you understand, you little punks?"

If they couldn't find a word in Polish, they spoke in Russian or Yiddish.

When Hesio suggested to a breathless old fellow who had just climbed up the Mount that he should rest a while before starting to make his speech, the man replied: "You fool, I'll be making a speech at your funeral."

And indeed, after that he spoke for three hours non-stop and without notes about the internal and external threats the Soviet Union must fight against.

And apparently Karl Radek himself would be coming from Moscow soon.

Rena came out of the kitchen wiping her wet hands on her skirt, which changed on the hips from grey to black. Everyone was still waiting for the droshky driver to bring the money. She glanced at Zawadowski, and soon after returned from the kitchen with her hair combed, carrying a glass of water that she put before him on the table.

Nathan cast her an icy look.

She'd been going to the Mount too, but with her girlfriends. And in the darkness she pretended not to see her brothers. But it was impossible not to look at the tall, handsome Zawadowski.

Soon after, the cabby arrived, with a business envelope containing twenty zlotys and a letter, which the lawyer quickly read, crumpled up and threw into the ashtray. But then he removed it again and put it in his inner coat pocket.

"Thank you for the water," he said on his way out.

VIII

NUSEK

Nusek followed Salek and Hesio about the café like a shadow as they served the customers. A very attentive shadow. Whenever they took a short break and stood by the wooden bar to talk, he was there too, raising his head to listen.

Never speaking and hardly moving, he caught individual words and waited for them to talk in abbreviations again. Then he either laughed out loud or winked knowingly to show that he understood what they were talking about.

He couldn't immediately guess what these new words meant.

Only when he heard them again at bedtime, and soon after smelled the same thing as everyone else in the room, did it finally dawn on him. He realized that his brothers were plainly bored with MOF, or had given it up for some other reason, maybe because it wasn't such a mystery to outsiders anymore, so they'd decided to replace it with new abbreviations: CPP and CWPP. This time Nusek deciphered them on his own, without Hesio's help.

CPP – meaning Cheeser Permitted Please?

He coped in the same way with the more elegant form that until recently they had used more often, CWPP: Cutting Wind Permitted Please?

But why, next morning when he proudly told them he knew all about CPP and CWPP, did they pretend to have no idea what he was talking about?

NATHAN

Each day brought new customers to The Stramers café. Nevertheless, Nathan was not fully satisfied. He hadn't expected this.

Rena helped her mother in the kitchen, taking on the kosher part, but she didn't have much to do, because although most of the customers were Jews, as Nathan put it, they were the kind who think they're Poles.

Rudek, Salek and Hesio kept carrying trays to and fro among the tables. According to Rywka as she stroked their heads, Wela and Nusek were "mascots and walking advertisements for the café", but in Nathan's view they just got under everyone's feet. Most of all his, as he was constantly going in and out of the café.

"Goddammit," he said whenever he went outside to wonder what next.

But it was one thing to leave someone else's café, ostentatiously slamming the door on your way out, never to return again, and quite another to leave his own, from which there was no escape.

As soon as he looked at the four tables, Nathan knew where

he had made his mistake. But could he squeeze a fifth one in? He'd have to throw out the billiards table. But even if he did, what would that add?

Nothing.

In anger he felt like spitting on the ground. But why spit on the pavement outside his own café? That was pointless too.

How was he to know that people would spend so much time sitting in a café? For hours they chatted away or said nothing. They gazed at each other or out of the window. They smoked cigarettes or snorted snuff. They played chess or cards. They did some writing or reading. They laughed out loud or nodded off with their heads on the tables.

While time went by.

And only one thing didn't change: they went on and on and on sitting there.

New people came in, they'd be sure to order sandwiches, tripe and beer, followed by apple pie and coffee. But so what, when they went straight back out because all the tables were occupied? They'd go and spend their money at his competitors'.

On the whole, these days the customers at other cafés seemed to him far better than his own.

Don't mine have anywhere to go? Don't they have anything better to do? he thought. Some honest work? Families to feed? Children missing them at home, or parents needing their care? Or, just like him, did they have nothing but his café?

In fact he could live with it, but why did they order so little?

Were these the famous "coffee-shop campers"? Half a day over a single cup?

And how carefully they avoided the waiter's eye by staring into space.

But what wouldn't they do to keep a cup on the table that the waiter couldn't clear away because it wasn't quite empty?

"Something else for you, sir?" (Either you place an order, or so long, bye bye.)

"No, thank you, I've still got some." (Leave me be.)

"I can recommend our delicious tripe." (At least order some bread and butter.)

"Maybe once I've finished my coffee?" (I'm not leaving a groszy more here.)

"Or perhaps you'd like some apple pie with cinnamon?" (In that case, get out.)

"No, thank you." (Get out yourself, I'm not budging.)

And so on, for days at a time, weeks – how much longer?

There were moments when he wanted to drop it all and go to Oświęcim, straight to Zofia Biesiadecka's travel agency, where they had the cheapest tickets for the liners to America and Canada.

Nathan couldn't stop thinking about it, not even after work. The whole house was asleep by now, but he was still in the kitchen, swaying as if at sea as he leaned his elbows on the ever more uncomfortable, wobbly table. The wooden wedge that sat under the table leg had vanished long ago. Someone must have tossed it into the oven by mistake. Right now he had too much else on his mind and no time to deal with it.

It was lucky that at least he'd had a letter from Ben recently. Before reading it, Nathan had run to the exchange bureau. But they'd refused the purple-stained banknotes; he'd forgotten about the wretched tissue paper. That night Rywka washed and dried the dollars, and first thing in the morning Nathan exchanged them at a different bureau.

There were so many of them in the city. Fancy not having noticed that before. And they all had a fixed rate: 5.25 zlotys to the dollar. At once he imagined himself standing before an exchange bureau with a sign above the door that read: "Stramer's".

Nathan and the table keeled dangerously to the right.

He still hadn't written to tell Ben about the café he'd opened thanks to his donation. His dream was for this information to reach his brother by itself. But now there was nothing left to boast about. Before he found out it had opened, he'd hear that it had closed.

What was to be done?

Nathan keeled to the left. At the last moment he grabbed hold of the table and put his foot in place of the missing wedge.

Soon after, he smiled to himself.

He only had to think of Ben, and at once he had an idea.

Nathan went to bed feeling calmer.

In the morning he went to the shed. He came out with a saw and some sandpaper under his arm. He walked indifferently past the kitchen table, at which the rest of the family were finishing their breakfast.

He can't have heard Nusek asking: "Dad, what are you doing?" Because he didn't answer.

At the café Nathan didn't stop to remove his hat or his best jacket. There was still an hour to go before opening. In fact Rywka would arrive before then with the youngest two, but the older children would only come after school and the private lessons they were giving at the flat, now that it was empty during the day.

He knelt at the table closest to the window, where the regular "campers" usually sat, ruining his mood and his business. Time to put an end to that. He reached for the saw, but stopped himself. Someone might see him from the street.

He carried four of the Thonet chairs into the back room, into the kosher area behind the curtain, to be on the safe side. He turned them upside down and took a good look at them. Bentwood, with woven seats and rounded back rests. Solid Austrian workmanship. Whatever else, he had made a good deal by buying them along with the tables from the Sailcloth café. They were getting rid of their old furniture, because the new owner wanted everything to be modern.

Being careful not to break them, he sawed a centimetre off both front legs of the first chair. He tried sitting on it. Yes, that should be enough. He slightly shortened two legs on each of the other three as well, and rubbed them with sandpaper.

He put the chairs back in place at the table nearest the window.

Before sitting down at the next table, he tossed his hat onto it, and thought to himself, not for the first time that day: this head wasn't made for wearing a cap.

From there he examined his handiwork. Fine craftsmanship. At first glance the chairs looked no different from the rest. He opened the door to Rywka, who had brought the shopping in two wicker baskets, but to avoid jinxing his luck he didn't say a word. He just gave her a hug, and helped to carry the shopping into the back room.

"Why is it so dusty here?" she said, pointing at the floor.

Nathan shrugged and instinctively brushed the dust off his jacket sleeves.

He'd set the trap. Now he just had to wait for his poor regulars to fall into it.

As if to spite him, this morning they didn't appear. Nathan stood on the pavement outside the café, looking out for them. Maybe they sensed something? He took the opportunity to try to catch a little of the September sun, to keep a touch of his summer tan, which Rywka liked so much.

He felt relief when at about noon, squinting into the distance, he saw the familiar stooping figure of his most regular customer. He was coming this way, carrying a stack of documents, two books and some newspapers in both hands.

You can still read? thought Nathan. Wasn't it enough yesterday?

At home lately he'd also been upset by the sight of his sons, Salek and Hesio, sitting over their books each night. It was the new fashion. He'd rather they were still kicking a ball like Rudek. But what could he do, when now it seemed even the god-fearing yeshiva pupils, in yarmulkas and sidelocks, went about Tarnów with serious expressions on their faces and prayer books under their arms, but inside, under the religious covers, they had books by that Marx guy.

And despite having the same outward appearance as in Nathan's day, now they were different on the inside.

So at least it was said in Grabówka.

And was it true that at the synagogue the pupils rocked steadily over the holy books, while actually muttering lines by Marx or Lenin or whoever to themselves?

At any rate that was what his sons did at home.

"Some people work for the family," he told them. "Others for a pair of glasses."

And if they didn't react or pretended not to hear, he put out the lamp.

"Waste of paraffin."

He rightly imagined that in the darkness they'd raise their eyes.

"We're self-improving," Hesio told him once.

"Self what? More like self…" he replied, then instantly fell silent, and began to laugh, but controlled himself in front of his daughters.

"Leave them alone," said Rywka.

That boy's sure to be self-improving, or rather, as Nathan put it in his thoughts, self-abusing. Under his watchful eye the oblivious regular customer had now spread out his papers on the table by the window. He'd been pleased to see that particular seat was free and he'd have plenty of light. He didn't know that straight after opening Nathan had carefully placed a card on it marked RESERVED, which he had removed just before the regular came in.

"Good day, what can I get you, sir?" asked Nathan as usual.

The regular surveyed the café, as if trying to find the answer to this difficult question in its modest interior. Or maybe he was wondering whether there was anything cheaper than a cup of coffee for twenty groszys.

"A small black coffee, please."

After placing his order he immersed himself in his texts. He never tore his eyes from them, not even when Nathan put down the cup before him.

Actually it would have been enough to sprinkle something into it to be rid of him, for good and all. Poison instead of a trap. But that wasn't the point.

Standing by the bar, from the corner of his eye Nathan watched as the regular battled with his chair. He dug his feet into the floor and squirmed on the woven seat, but he couldn't stop sliding off. He interrupted his reading, stood up briefly and pushed back the chair, but moments later the same thing happened again.

In spite of all he did not surrender, but with the tenacity of an American cowboy mounted each of the other chairs, all of which eventually threw him off too.

Giving up, he looked around the café, as if trying to understand whether there was something wrong with it, or with him. He glanced inquiringly at Nathan, who for the first time in ages gave him a friendly smile.

That must have tipped the balance, because the regular picked up his things, carefully counted out twenty groszys, put it down and threw on his jacket. He came close to forgetting about his coffee but, already nearing the door, he remembered it. He turned back and, to be on the safe side, drank it without sitting down.

"Bye bye," Nathan bid him farewell.

He glanced incredulously at his watch, and then admiringly at his own reflection in the mirror above the bar.

Well, well, he thought, he held out on the sawn-off chairs for less than twenty minutes. Will anyone persist for longer? Maybe the customers who were just entering the café.

Time began to pass more quickly. Nathan couldn't keep up with looking at his watch, the regular customers kept changing as one replaced another, and all day nobody sat out more than half an hour at that table.

For the first time ever the table by the window earned its keep, bringing more profit than the other three.

That evening Nathan went outside and stood proudly in the street before the window marked "The Stramers". As on the day the café had opened.

Rywka and the children had already gone home, and Goldhammer Street looked deserted, as if nothing were left in it but Nathan and the lighted lamps.

He let out a deep sigh. Even the Tarnów dustbins stank less than usual.

For once he wasn't bothered by the sickles, hammers and graffiti about the proletariat that someone had been scrawling in red paint on the buildings recently. Though they should finally be painted over, better yet the son-of-a-bitch should be caught and made to paint them over.

Nathan was full of good ideas today.

He imagined writing a letter to Ben: not only did I get rid of the campers, I made money out of them. And from across the ocean an enthusiastic reply would come, full of banknotes.

Dear Nathan,

Pepi and I congratulate you with all our hearts! We can't wait to be leaning on the bar at The Stramers with you, Rywka and the kids (to be on the safe side, we won't sit down!), drinking your world-famous coffee. So we're boarding the first ship to Europe.

On a wave of success and American blessings, he knew what his next step would be. Revolutionary.

That Lenin of theirs with his hammer and sickle can hide his face. All I need is a saw, he thought, before hiding himself in the depths of the café.

Late into the night the sound of sawing could be heard.

On his way home at dawn, he was sure he could smell his own private revolution in the Tarnów air. Though he slept for less than three hours, he hadn't awoken feeling so well rested for ages. As he sat in the outhouse, gazing through a cobweb in the dirty little window, he remembered his dream. He'd been playing the violin on a large stage, the first time he'd ever held a musical instrument, and although he was out of tune the sophisticated audience had given him a standing ovation.

On the way to work he could still hear the applause. He made a greater effort than usual to avoid the holes and puddles, and before crossing Mickiewicz Street he looked three times to make sure no bicycle, car or horse and cart was coming.

Not even in the wartime trenches had he taken such good care of himself.

Because today he felt unique, valuable, worth far more than ever before. Like someone with a winning lottery ticket in his pocket. Or an American prospector coming home from an expedition with a sack full of gold.

What a wonderful world, thought Nathan, breezing along in such a good mood that he was even prepared to drop a penny into a beggar's tin.

The great inventors must have felt this way before me. The man who thought up the wheel must have looked underfoot that day to avoid tripping and falling under an elephant or a camel, or into a lion's maw. This is how they must have felt, what were they called? Marconi, Radiostein or something.

Nathan Stramer's invention was the sawn-off chair leg.

And in keeping with his expectations it had worked – the whole café was wriggling on them, bringing him record profit that day.

If it goes on like this… thought Nathan, multiplying the future income in his dreams and on a sheet of paper.

Unable to restrain his imagination, he had already spent some of it on gifts. A trip to the seaside for Rywka. But she couldn't go on her own, could she? Train tickets for the whole family. Our first vacation.

But who would run the café in the meantime?

That night Nathan decided that in this situation it was high time to share his discovery with the family. But first he closed the door of the café and all the windows. Rywka and the children had to swear this conversation wouldn't get outside.

"Sit down," he began in a whisper. "What I'm about to tell you is worth more than anything you've ever heard before."

He sat down too, just in case, on the billiards table.

"Dad, have you gone crazy?" said Rudek, all but clutching his head when Nathan finished.

"You cretin!" cried Nathan, taking a swipe at his almost fully grown son. "Is that how you talk to your father?!"

But he didn't hit him. After sawing thirty-two chair legs he wasn't sure of his hand.

"Surely you're not being serious, Dad?" said Rudek, correcting himself.

He and Salek and Hesio exchanged glances. And he put a hand to his mouth to hide a smile.

Looking at Rywka's and the children's expressions, Nathan realized how other pioneers who were ahead of their time must have felt before him. He too could remember the first tram, which was said to have run over a soldier, a nursemaid and child and an old woman before it had even left the depot to drive onto the streets of Tarnów. All the great inventors had had to contend with similar misunderstanding, ill will and rejection, even on the part of their nearest and dearest.

He felt sorry for them.

For whose sake had he sawed off all those legs? Not his own. He was already at the seaside.

He'd done it for the family.

They'd thank him yet. Especially Rudek – the first-born, who one day, one sad day, would inherit the business from him. But he still had a lot ahead of him, you still have a lot to learn, son.

And you could tell at once he'd never been to America. Maybe instead of the Polish seaside he should send him to his uncle in New York? Let the boy see what the real world is like, and by the by the world will find out about Nathan Stramer's brilliant idea.

After all, over there they say: *less is more*. And here you have it: less of a chair means more money.

As long as they didn't accidentally forget whose idea it was. People in America have a short memory.

"I'm being serious," he said to his future successor, who would make his chairs famous. "Want a bet?"

Rudek shook his head.

"Afraid you'll lose?"

"No," said Rudek. "I never bet."

"Why not?" asked Salek at once.

"When two people make a bet," said Rudek, "one's a cheat and the other's a fool."

"What?!" said Nathan, clenching his fists.

That little brat has crossed all the limits today. He's not going anywhere. Not even the seaside. He's staying here to mind the café.

Rywka laid a hand on her husband's arm.

"I don't understand…" They all turned towards the window, as if only now noticing that Nusek was standing there. "Why is one a cheat and the other a fool?"

"Because one knows he's right and he's cheating the other," replied Rudek.

"What if neither of them knows?"

Salek's question was stifled by Nathan's already long-suppressed outburst. American swearwords shook the café walls and window panes. Rudek got up, turned around, and at a calm pace went outside.

Like a double shadow, Salek and Hesio went after him.

"If neither knows, they're both fools," explained Rudek out on the pavement.

And as Nathan hadn't calmed down, next to emerge was Rywka, holding Wela and Nusek by the hands.

For a long time Nathan went on sitting there, or rather walking among the four empty tables, shaking his head, gesticulating and now and then saying something to himself, or maybe not to himself?

A week later it was clear to him that he'd done well not to make a bet with his son. Anyway, so what, when even without betting he had lost. In that time, day by day, he had lost customers.

Finally nobody came.

Nathan stood in the dark outside the café, and once again Goldhammer Street looked deserted, as if nothing were left in it but Nathan and the lighted lamps.

That night he was struck down by gastritis.

Rywka explained to the children that his shouting had been the first, early symptom of the illness. And that was how it should be regarded.

She left the curtains drawn.

IX

RUDEK

NUSEK COULDN'T SLEEP. It was the first time he'd slept alone in the bed. Now he had the whole quilt and pillow to himself. Rudek had gone to Kraków to study at the Jagiellonian University. He'd chosen his course at the Philosophy Faculty: classical philology. Nusek had no idea what that might be.

"You're too stupid to understand," Rudek had told him at the station before leaving.

"It's *bullshitting*," put in Nathan.

Nusek couldn't understand that either.

"It means studying nonsenses," said Nathan, laughing, once the train had moved off with Rudek aboard.

"Dad..." said Rena, grimacing and looked around the platform in the hope nobody had heard her father. "Please."

So many times the children had asked him not to distort Polish words. Better not speak Polish at all than speak it like a Jew. What was the harm in him talking Yiddish as usual?

Or English – that at least no one here at the station could understand.

Nathan just smiled at his daughter. Meaning he'd done it on purpose. Not even Rywka could always tell when Nathan was making mistakes and when he was deliberately twisting words. Sometimes she thought it was his way of trying to turn his mistakes into a joke.

But perhaps this time he was trying to amuse Rena, who was gazing sadly after the train, in which an important part of her life was going away.

Usually Rywka didn't like this sort of joke, though for other reasons than the children's.

"That's how they make fun of the Jews from Grabówka," she'd say, shaking her head.

"And so what?"

"Who are you laughing at? Think about it."

But now, on the platform, she just listened to the departing train and gazed at the steam from the locomotive.

Rudek had also left behind his two faithful shadows. Salek and Hesio ran after the train, waving to their older brother, until they stopped, out of breath, at the end of the platform.

Soon they were leaning their backs against the metal railings, talking to each other in hushed tones.

At home too they were always whispering into each other's ears.

"Comrades, go and conspire in the outhouse!" their father told them. "It's a good place. No one eavesdrops on the communists there."

But could he be sure? Since closing down the café, Nathan often stood by the open window during the day. Recently he'd heard Salek, out in the yard, telling what he'd spend the money on if he won the lottery.

"I'll keep ten per cent for myself. I'll give another ten per cent to my family. And the remaining eighty per cent to the Party."

Nathan couldn't restrain himself, and had shouted from behind the curtain for the whole yard to hear: "Then you'd better not play at all!"

Anyone who saw the Stramers coming back from the station could guess that something had ended, or at least changed. There was no wind, and the sun was shining, but they were walking home with their heads drooping.

They were plainly having trouble finding their place on the pavement. Should they walk side by side, or one after the other? They couldn't make up their minds. They were missing the element that generally took away the need to worry about such things.

Salek was trying to walk in the middle, in Rudek's usual place, but he kept bumping into his father's shoulder as Nathan battled to regain his old position.

"Don't get under my feet," he heard.

How had Rudek always managed to be in front or in the middle from the day he'd started to walk? thought Rywka, who was at the back. If Hesio, Rena or any of the other siblings had been born first would they have been like that too? Or was there another reason for it?

It's a good thing he's gone, she consoled herself.

He'd been the first in the family to get his school certificate (and with such good results! She was so proud of him), and now he was the first to go to university. And as usual the rest of them would probably follow him. She felt a pang of anguish, and bowed her head even lower to avoid thinking about it.

She tried to imagine that in Kraków Rudek would finally have a break from his siblings. In Tarnów he was always there when they needed him, which was all the time. Going away will be good for him, and it won't hurt them either.

On the platform, Rudek had shoved some money into her coat pocket, without letting Nathan notice.

He'd often come home, he'd said: what's eighty kilometres nowadays? As well as the trains, which go to Kraków every few hours, there are also going to be buses soon, running from Oak Tree Square.

At the same time Rywka drove away the thought that eventually they'd all go away, and she and Nathan would be left on their own at 20 Goldhammer Street, an old couple in a two-person apartment.

Only Wela and Nusek were still smaller than she was. But even they were a head taller than the metal plaque in the tram with the thick line and the sign to say that children under a metre travelled for free.

But as in the past, Nathan looked like the tallest again, possibly because he was wearing a hat.

"Look out!"

In the gateway Nathan turned to face the others, holding his nose as a sign that Mrs Fluffy was coming the other way. In all these years she had hardly changed, she still went about in a blue cardigan and black skirt, still holding a lead and talking to her beloved dachshund.

A few years ago Nusek had seen the dog lying in the yard, not moving, with Mrs Fluffy leaning over it.

"Get up!" she kept saying. "Your supper's going cold."

Nusek ran home.

"Fluffy's dead!" he called out, like the boys who sold newspapers in the streets. "Front-page news: Mrs Fluffy's husband's dead!"

"Her husband?" said Hesio, tapping his forehead.

"You once told me they got married."

"And you believed me?!"

Nusek burst out laughing.

Rywka was the most concerned. Next day she decided to go and see Mrs Fluffy. Nathan took a wooden peg from the clothes line and pretended to clip it on her nose.

"Breathe through your mouth at least," he advised as she was leaving.

She came back amazed. Mrs Fluffy was behaving as if nothing had happened.

"She's still going for walks with the lead in her hand," she told them, "still talking to the dog."

"And it's still not answering," said Nathan.

When she got home from the station, Rywka stopped to look at the photograph that was standing on the chest of drawers.

A week before his departure, Rudek had taken all his siblings to the newly opened photographic studio at 4 Krakowska Street. He knew the owner, Chaskiel Bronstein, from the Jewish scouts. A few years his senior, Chaskiel had been his team leader.

Now he was proudly standing on the pavement outside his own studio, as Nathan had in the days when he'd run the café.

106

"Good name," said Rudek, shaking Chaskiel's hand and casting an appreciative glance at the shop sign saying "Fotografika". "Spot on."

Chaskiel greeted each of the siblings in turn.

Rudek had told them to dress up that day.

"No holes, no patches on your knees or elbows. No stains or missing buttons. Don't worry about the colours, they don't have to match, they won't show up anyway. But comb your hair for me, and don't get your shoes dirty on the way."

The night before he had supervised them to make sure they washed their hair and cut their fingernails. He'd deliberately woken Nusek, who was probably just pretending to be asleep, because as soon as he opened his eyes, wide awake, he'd said: "Why do I always have to bathe in the water everyone else has used?"

Rudek took a comb with him, quite unnecessarily. Rena and Wela had their own hairbrush, and from what he saw in Chaskiel's shop window, these days the men and boys usually posed in caps and hats.

When Salek asked him why, Rudek briefly wondered whether to say: "Because they want to look taller". Or else: "They must be hiding something under that headgear".

Finally he just shrugged.

"It's the fashion."

His own choice was to pose with a fob watch on a chain.

"Where did you get that?" asked Hesio.

None of the siblings had ever seen it before.

"I just got it. So what?"

With a grey sheet as the backdrop, Rudek was the only one sitting down. Chaskiel placed the bamboo chair to one side, and positioned Rudek's right hand on the armrest ("Let it rest casually"), with the chain dangling from his index finger and the watch, in a round case, touching his left hand. Rudek was to hold it still at waist height.

He posed Rena, Salek and Hesio half a pace behind Rudek ("so you don't shield your brother"), and Wela and Nusek ("Drop your shoulders, I won't eat you") next to Rudek, who was still taller than they were, even though he was sitting down.

With her hair loose, in a white blouse and a black skirt below the knee, Rena looked perfect. Even so, Chaskiel spent the longest time posing her.

She simply had to stand behind Rudek, but the photographer needed to check if her hands were resting the right way on her older brother's shoulders ("Pity not to show those fingers a pianist would be proud of"), to make sure there was no shadow falling on her face ("It'd be a sin not to capture the profound look in those eyes") and consider whether to show the pendant she was wearing ("Yes, I just have to straighten it a tiny bit").

Whatever, Rena could see that today even her brothers had their gaze fixed on her, and kept casting glances at the low neckline of her blouse.

"Here we go..." said Rudek. "Keep your hands still."

"Just don't move an inch!" said Chaskiel, and hid behind a large camera on a tripod.

"You shut up and do your job."

"But you don't understand. For the models to feel relaxed, I have to talk to them." Chaskiel pulled the black hood attached to the camera over his head. "Did you know that in the old days the photographic studios had special metal supports? People used to prop the backs of their necks against them to avoid moving while the picture was being taken. It was like being in a vice – those things pinched horribly. That's why everyone looks so stiff and miserable in the old photographs. But luckily there's been some progress, and I take much kinder pictures. Now then, pay attention, no breathing and no blinking!"

After taking the picture Chaskiel removed the case containing the glass negative from the camera.

Three days later Rudek went to collect the photograph and carefully wrote on the back:

In memory of this day,
Rudolf, Rena, Salek, Hesio, Wela and Nusek Stramer

How many private lessons had he had to give to afford something like that? was Rywka's first thought when she received the photograph as a present from her son. "You'd have done better to buy yourself something," she'd said.

Her eyes had filled with tears.

"Don't worry. I'm not going to cry," she said now to Rudek in the photograph.

Finally she had time to take a proper look at him. What a handsome, well-built, modern man. Nathan said he was the spitting image of his brother Ben.

Now I'll have two Rudeks, one in Kraków, and one here on the chest of drawers.

"Mama, when I buy something for someone, two people are happy: they are, and so am I," Rudek often used to say. "But if I buy something for myself, only one person's pleased."

It was a good thing that at least he'd bought himself a watch.

Who had brought him up so well? Definitely not I, not Nathan's shouting and belt, and not the synagogue he refused to go to. The school? The street? From early childhood he'd never asked anyone for their opinion, he'd done everything by himself. And he must have brought himself up too.

His wife would be lucky.

He had never brought a girl home. And so, in spite of all, she was relieved when on Yom Kippur she happened to overhear his conversation with friends.

She had heard a knock at the door and went to open it.

"Good evening, Mrs Stramer."

"Good evening," she said to her eldest son's friends. "Come in."

"No, thank you, we just… Is Rudek in?"

Rudek threw on a jacket and went out to meet them.

Through the half-open window she smelled the cigarettes they lit behind the coal shed.

She heard what the loudest of them was saying, Daniel, the deputy mayor's son, who must have inherited his father's booming voice: "Well, we've said our prayers, we've done our fasting, now let's go whoring!"

She heard laughter.

She remembered Daniel from his childhood, or rather the beautiful pram in which his nursemaid carried him. Imported from Vienna. All Tarnów was in awe of it. It glided along on tall wheels, upholstered in blue-and-white leather, shaped like a plane that was just about to rise into the air along with the girl pushing it.

Just in case, people got out of its way, but then everyone put their heads inside, using the excuse of admiring the baby to check if the interior was just as neatly finished.

It was then that Nathan had said: "He can't walk or talk yet, but he's already the owner of three large houses in the city centre."

Rywka had mainly carried the baby Rudek in her arms. That may have been why he began to crawl so quickly and was soon walking. At less than ten months old.

Who'd have thought at the time that little Daniel, the passenger in the Viennese pram, would be a guest in their house years later.

"Are you coming with us, Rudek?" he asked now.

Rywka didn't hear the answer.

Soon after, Rudek came back into the apartment, but didn't remove his jacket.

"Salek, Hesio," he said, "we're going out!"

"What about me?" asked Nusek, and as he didn't get an answer, he tried a different way: "Where are you going?"

That did the trick.

"Why are you asking if you're not coming?" he heard at once.

Lately the brothers were always answering his questions with other questions. Usually: "But who?" Nusek would explain who he meant, and they'd go on asking "But who?"

"But I'm telling you, me, that's who!"

"But who's listening to you?"

Every time he let himself be taken in. Now he would do it to someone at school. They didn't treat him like that there, no one ignored him there, called him names or hit him. Even the older boys wouldn't have dared to take a swing at him.

At school they knew whose brother he was. That was enough for him to have peace and quiet. They knew he was the youngest of the Stramers.

To this day they could all remember how on finishing his last class Rudek had lit a cigarette in the school corridor right in front of the headmaster, at whom he had blown smoke. Or at least Nusek kept reminding his schoolmates about it.

"That was their final encounter, the final battle, the final duel between the king of the school and its headmaster. The whole school held its breath. You can ask the head. He got tears in his eyes and started to cough. It was a knockout."

His classmates listened to Nusek's stories – as he put it himself – smellbound.

Why couldn't it be like that at home too?

"Mama!" cried Nusek, running to her to complain. "They're refusing to take me with them again."

This time Rywka didn't insist they take him with them.

She couldn't share what she had heard that evening with Nathan, who often spent the holidays, and every New Year, lying in bed with gastritis.

Anyway, perhaps it was for the best?

All three, Rudek, Salek and Hesio, were past their bar mitzvah, she thought. Their sins had stopped passing on to their father, so why on earth wake him?

According to the Torah they were adults, but according to Rywka?

She left the kitchen window ajar for them.

Lying beside her husband in the darkness she imagined where Daniel had taken her sons. What were they doing now? And with whom?

When she closed her eyes, she saw them in the embraces of her friends, Nesa Schnur and Lili Flaum, whom she had last seen almost thirty years ago, before their departure for Brazil or

Argentina. She had envied them for breaking away from Nisko. She had envied them the voyage. Now she was surprised nothing had changed since then.

The more she imagined it, the more tightly she cuddled up to Nathan and kissed his broad nape.

X

HESIO

Hesio woke up with a bellyache, or rather the ache woke him. He could tell exactly where it was coming from – classroom number fourteen, on the second floor, where today at four o'clock Miss Matraszek would call him up to the blackboard.

So she had forewarned.

Why had he put it off all week and done nothing? Maybe he was hoping Rudek would come from Kraków and help him. He sometimes dropped in unexpectedly. He'd always been good at Latin, and ever since he'd started studying classical philology he kept coming up with Latin phrases that no one in the house could follow. A bit like their father with English.

"So you do take after your father," Nathan would say on these occasions. "*Like father, like son.*"

"Stramer, you should be digging ditches, not sitting at a desk," Miss Matraszek had told Hesio last week. "What sort of a name is Hersz-Cwi anyway?"

And what sort of a name is Matraszek? thought Hesio with his fists clenched under the desk. It sounds like a lizard that spreads tropical diseases.

The lizard had addressed the class: "Extremely poor, childish material."

And added as if to herself: "For obvious reasons."

His classmates had consoled Hesio with sympathetic glances, and someone had tossed him a piece of paper folded in four from Flounder in the back row: "She's probably got her period."

But can you have your period every week?

Hesio turned round to show he'd read it. Flounder was repeating the year, and was twice the size of all the other boys in the class. Every day he came to school on foot from a village outside Tarnów with his shoes slung over his shoulder. He only put them on in the city. And at school he sat in the back row, where he barely fitted by now.

The pupils were always turning round to him and giggling, while the teachers pretended not to notice what Flounder was doing under the desk.

Now and then, looking the other way, they simply said: "Flounder, trousers."

"What's that, Miss?"

"Button up your trousers!"

Lately he had confessed sadly to Hesio: "My parents want me to become a priest. But I haven't got a calling. 'It'll come with time,' they keep saying. I want to do something else."

After a nature lesson, when no one was looking, he wrote in chalk, in crooked letters, on the medical room door: *GYNAECOLOGIST (delves in ladies' pussies).*

That was what he wanted to do in life. And his dream was that one day there'd be a sign like that on the door of his consulting room, Dr Flounder's surgery. He asked Hesio to check for mistakes. There weren't any, but Hesio didn't know what to say to him.

Because he realized that Flounder saw nothing vulgar, boorish or even funny in what he had written. He simply had no other way of describing it. The thing that interested him most.

Once, at the sight of some Jews praying, he nudged Hesio and asked: "Why are they rocking to and fro like a sick man prodding a pussy?"

Whereas in Strzelecki Park, in the presence of girls, Dr Flounder, or the village gynaecologist, as they now called him in class, went red, stammered and pushed the small Hesio in front of him.

"You do the talking."

What was he to do?

Maybe Miss Matraszek wouldn't turn up? Maybe she'd fall sick? Or a miracle would happen, and like last year she'd fall over on Samson's slide by the statue of the Unknown Soldier and break her tailbone?

But for that it had to be winter, which hadn't started yet.

Maybe I just shouldn't go to Latin, thought Hesio, still lying in bed. After all, it's Friday, and we're Jews, we spend the day getting ready for the Sabbath. But that won't work anymore. It did, until the headmaster saw us playing football instead of lighting candles at home.

They shouldn't have played on the pitch next to school.

"Where their participation in lessons on Fridays and Saturdays is concerned, pupils of the Mosaic faith are guided by their own whims and caprices," claimed the headmaster at the teachers' committee meeting, as he reduced the guilty pupils' marks for conduct. "There's no need to prove what an adverse effect this trivializing of the school, of learning and the teachers has on all the pupils."

Hesio and Flounder were listening at the door of the teachers' common room.

"The same applies to the Jews' dilatory attitude – during breaks they don't speak the Polish language but talk in Yiddish. This habit must be eradicated for understandable reasons, and to prevent the resulting harm to the Polish language."

"He's getting a stiffy," whispered Flounder into Hesio's ear.

"On the other hand," the headmaster continued, "in the sphere of everyday manners I note a significant improvement. The pupils are clean. Even the Jews have clean footwear. Evidently our recommendations on hygiene were not imparted purely by way of theory but the work was based on didactic and educational principles…"

"It's stiff now," Flounder managed to comment before Hesio pulled him away from the door.

"Juszczyk's coming!"

They hid in the toilet, where thanks to the warped windows it was even colder than in the classrooms. They waited until the old janitor, Jan Juszczyk, had plodded past along the corridor. At this time of day he had finished work and was going down to his flat on the ground floor. As a result he didn't feel like peeping into the cubicles on his way.

Apart from him, only the headmaster had a flat within the school.

"Perhaps they call on each other after hours?" said Flounder.

And when they went back to the teachers' common room, he flexed his biceps as a mark of recognition that the headmaster had not yet come to a conclusion.

"The punctuality has gone up. Closing the gate at eight o'clock on several occasions has proved a good and effective means of realizing this demand. We have found that the most frequent latecomers are the Jewish pupils, who retire for the night at later hours and as a result sleep longer in the morning. The lack of clocks in some homes also contributes to this situation. Yet another sore spot."

At this point Matraszek-the-lizard pitched in: "I would like to ask Mr Wachtel to exert his influence upon the Jewish youths, who behave worse than the Catholic boys. They organize fights and write indecent words and phrases. Most of them are not making progress in their studies. And some of them refuse to sing the national anthem, 'Poland Is Not Yet Lost'. The reasons for this conduct should be properly investigated and discussed. Let us not forget that during the partitions we brought up our youth in a spirit of patriotism. Now our efforts to kindle an affection in the young for belonging to the Polish state are being hindered by destructive foreign influences, separatist ethnic ambitions and in particular communism."

"I think she's excited. She's wet," said Flounder, licking his lips.

"Yeah," whispered Hesio to his friend's protruding ear. "She's even kindled me."

In his sad tone, Wachtel began by thanking the headmaster for so efficiently settling the matter of the boys who disturbed him while taking Mosaic religion lessons.

He meant the Catholic boys, who had a free lesson then, and went into the garden to make noise and throw stones, or rather pebbles through the open classroom windows. Flounder, for example, threw them specially to land on Hesio's desk.

"Wachtel hasn't got a stiffy. Shall we go?" said Flounder, nodding towards the exit at the end of the corridor.

But Hesio shook his head, he still had hope. Maybe the Mosaic religion teacher would stand up for his pupils and come to their defence. Or at least say something inspiring.

Something like: the Lord gave, and the Lord has taken away, as he said recently in a lesson to Mordechai, whose father had died.

"I am grateful to you, Headmaster," said Wachtel meanwhile, "for treating Jews at the school on a par with the Catholics, for which you and all the teachers deserve great credit. So I too propose lower marks for conduct for the Jewish brats who ruined the school fence with paint."

You scumbag, thought Hesio.

He was sorry he hadn't listened to Flounder and left earlier. He'd rather not have heard that. And he'd also rather his friend didn't see him wiping his eyes with his jacket sleeve. He gritted his teeth, but it didn't help. Maybe Flounder would think something had fallen in his eye?

Rena and Salek didn't understand how he could be friends with someone like that. But in fact at such moments Flounder was a good friend, and anyway, they should be free of class prejudices. That's the point of communism, isn't it?

And since Rudek had left Tarnów, it didn't hurt to show up in the city now and again with someone twice as big and strong.

"But who's inferior by class?" Salek would probably ask him. "Are we, or the peasants?"

Hesio nodded to Flounder that they could go.

"You're right," he said, as they were leaving the school, past the chapel and the scout hut, where he had never been either. "He hasn't got a stiffy."

All the way home Hesio kicked everything that lay in the street. Stones, chestnuts and rubbish. He didn't even feel like going to Strzelecki Park.

You won't be able to write this down in your shitty notebook of good deeds, he thought, his mind still on the Mosaic religion teacher.

Wachtel had told his pupils to keep a notebook recording their good deeds. Every day they were to write one down. Hesio usually did it at the last moment, the night before the lesson, writing out all seven in a single go.

During the lesson they had to read them aloud.

On Monday I escorted a blind beggar across a busy street. On Tuesday I helped my younger brother to carry a bucket of coal into the house. On Wednesday I helped my mother to make fried cheese. On Thursday...

What about Thursday? He'd run out of ideas. He couldn't exactly put that he'd distributed leaflets about the city headed *Hands off the USSR!*, daubed hammers and sickles on the school fence or written on walls in red paint: *Long live communism! Long live the communist youth! Workers and peasants, only the Party fights for the welfare of the working class! Young working masses, join the Union of Communist Youth!*

He agreed with Salek that some of the slogans the older comrades told them to write were a bit long. It was a waste of paint. And there was a greater risk of being caught, because you spent longer painting.

But what about the wretched Thursday? No more good deeds were willing to occur to him, just the blind man, the coal and the fried cheese.

And the old woman (hunchbacked of course, and in a head-scarf), but last week he had already gone shopping for a sick old woman twice, and fetched her medicine from the pharmacy, as well as taking her dog for a walk.

Anyway, thanks to Hesio she was probably well again by now and didn't need his good deeds this week. But next week, who knows?

"Salek!" That evening they were sitting together by the oil lamp. "Will you do me a good deed?"

He passed the notebook to his brother, who without a second thought began to write:

On Thursday at about ten p.m. I was on my way home when I saw a girl walking along on her own. I was worried about her safety. Out of concern I went up and asked if I could escort her home.

As ever, he overdid it. He meant well – how could he have known they'd find fault with it in class?

"That's not a good deed!" said his classmates. "He wanted to chat her up! That's all. Nothing more."

"But he had to deviate from his path to help her," said Wachtel, coming to his defence at the end of the lesson, although some of the boys laughed in the break at the word "deviate".

Others asked which girl he meant, was she pretty and where could they meet her.

Hesio confirmed that she was pretty.

They also laughed at what the teacher had said just before the bell, once he had wiped the blackboard with a sponge, swept back his thinning grey hair, closed Balaban's textbook and unbuttoned his jacket, of which the pupils in the front row were instantly aware.

"What's faster?" they joked in class. "The speed of light, the speed of sound, or Wachtel's stale sweat?"

"Dear children!" Luckily Wachtel had done up his jacket. "The feast of Purim is approaching. On this holiday it's customary to send gifts to people you respect. It's called *shlach munes*. And *shlach matanot* means 'send a gift'. Tell your parents I live at 28 Wałowa Street. Have you written it down?"

"This year," Hesio told Salek that night, in their shared bed, "he can kiss my arse! We're not sending him anything."

"Oh, come on!" said Salek, waving a hand. "They wanted to fire him, like Bleiweiss, don't you understand why they made all that fuss about hygiene? He had to sacrifice something, he was fighting for his life."

"You're exaggerating!"

"You know how many unemployed there are in Tarnów. He didn't want to be number one thousand four hundred and one. Don't get upset, it's his problem, not yours."

In sum, thought Hesio, Salek had told him the same thing as Flounder: yours gets stiff, so what the fuck are you upset about?

Except that Salek never swore. And unlike Flounder, he only ever referred to girls and women as "ladies".

SALEK

Since Rudek's departure for Kraków the siblings took their troubles to Salek. It was his word they waited for, as they drank ersatz coffee each night at the kitchen table. Even their mother, kissing Salek on the forehead, had started jokingly calling him "the family rabbi".

"But everyone knows what I think about religion," he told her. "It's opium for the masses."

In fact he could honestly admit that he'd never tried opium, but he had tried religion at the cheder and the synagogue, and that had put him off opium for good, since it was the same thing.

Rywka remembered how the melamed and old Bleiweiss had pestered them. They had tried to persuade her that reading the ancient scriptures was Salek's calling. Maybe they were right, she sometimes wondered, and because of us he'd missed it.

She liked the way Salek spoke. Calmly, even more clearly than Rudek. He let each word and sentence resound.

He never swallowed the Polish endings, like Nathan and the pupils whom he tutored at home. Unsure how to decline the Polish words, they preferred to mumble them, in the hope they'd manage to blur or hide their mistakes.

So Salek usually began the first lesson with case inflections.

If during the lesson the pupil spoke to him in Yiddish, he interrupted at once and said: "We're in Poland. Forget about Yiddish."

And if it was a girl, he recited a poem to her:

Remember – whatever path your fate
May send you on towards your goal

Each is born to this estate
A human being and a Pole.

Naturally, without the slightest trace of a foreign accent, and without mentioning that the author was Tetmajer, not Stramer. In fact the names were a bit similar, he thought. Maybe it wasn't a coincidence? Maybe he'd once been called Kazimierz Przerwa-Stramer, or Salomon Przerwa-Tetmajer? That at least was how he understood the poem.

Each night he would recite whole pages of books by heart. He never did it of his own accord, but always at the request of his siblings, who usually asked for Sienkiewicz's *Trilogy* at bedtime, and only once in a while he smuggled through something from Marx.

Once the oil lamp was out on Goldhammer Street, far more happened in the ground-floor room with a kitchen than in the daytime: in between the unfolded beds the heroes of the novels came together again. There, following Wołodyjowski's duel against Bohun, he and Zagłoba formed their plan to make Skrzetuski happy. Skrzetuski conversed with Zagłoba, and Rzędzian placed the beautiful Helena in the care of Witowska, the castellan's wife.

The flat was full of Tatars, Swedes and Poles.

With her eyes closed, Rywka enjoyed listening to this too from the bed in the kitchen.

That was how she imagined the talkies, which she'd heard they were going to start screening at the Daydream cinema.

She tried to remember the title of the first movie, silent of course, they had shown for the opening. There had been posters on the advertising pillars all over town. What was it? *Apache Girl* – "a great thriller in ten acts!" Or maybe: "a super-sensational, super-action-packed drama in ten acts"? Yes, perhaps that was it, because in those days they still described everything as "super-".

But she didn't know what it was actually like. Sometimes she regretted not having found out for herself.

Maybe because the dark-haired girl on the poster, the Apache girl, looked a bit like her. Though the Apache man was the opposite of Nathan – tall and slender, with long hair like a woman's.

Why hadn't she gone to the cinema? Or to the films they showed after that either.

Since I never went to the one I really wanted to see, why go to others that I found far less appealing?

Besides, to go to the cinema you had to have the time and the money. And she was always short of one or the other, usually both at once.

Anyway, was the cinema for adults at all? These days Rywka would rather her children went there. The same went for the books they brought home from the library and from their friends. Who can afford to go to the cinema, let alone a bookshop, when they have six children?

And they could always tell her afterwards what they had seen or read. She preferred hearing it from them. And as she listened to them, she felt as if she were sitting in the cinema, or reading a book by the light of the oil lamp.

Maybe Nathan would still invite her to the Daydream cinema one day? But she felt she would rather see the sea. She couldn't remember the last time he'd taken her anywhere.

No, in fact she could remember, although it was long ago. Quite soon after opening The Stramers café, Nathan had taken her to a special football match. Someone had given him the tickets. Or maybe they'd paid him with them at the café? Who could it have been? Probably Mr Zawadowski, the lawyer.

"It's a unique match, you'll see," Nathan had enthused. "The smallest citizens of Tarnów play against the tallest. It'll be quite a show."

Like everyone else on the stands, Nathan laughed throughout the match. Although it was his first time here and he didn't know the rules. The same went for Rywka, though she couldn't understand what was so funny about some big men kicking, trampling and scoring goals against some small ones. Or stronger men beating weaker ones, like Nathan whipping the children with his belt. In any case, the players on the muddy pitch had soon stopped smiling too. And the next day Salek had told her what they'd written about the match in the newspaper: *It was well thought-out, but during the action there was not much joy because the game was played too seriously*. Rywka nodded.

At night, when Salek had finished his "reading by heart", Sienkiewicz's heroes would linger a while in the apartment, until the last of the siblings was asleep.

Now and then for a joke, or to check if they were listening carefully, Salek would suddenly recite something from memory that wasn't by Sienkiewicz or even Marx, but an item from the newspaper, for instance:

> *In this building, inaugurated in 1927, modern appliances are used: a steam-powered oven and an electric washing machine, both of which outclass similar appliances at private institutions. The tidy cells, state-of-the-art workshops, spacious corridors, lecture hall, stage, and prison chapel with a carved wooden altar make Tarnów's jail the best equipped in Poland.*

Had Salek really memorized all that to perfection, or could he have been making it up from start to finish? How could she know?

HESIO

Hesio was still wondering what to do before the Latin lesson, in case by some miracle Matraszek-the-lizard failed to break her tailbone. Go outside with wet hair? It probably wasn't possible to catch cold that quickly. At most he'd toughen himself up. Like last winter, when each morning he and his brothers had done Swedish gymnastics in the yard. They'd rubbed themselves with cold water, and done bends, squats and press-ups. Best of all in the snow.

Everyone, even Suchard the dog and Milka the cat, who never went outside in that weather, watched them in alarm.

"Why is it called Swedish gymnastics?" Nusek asked Rudek, his teeth chattering.

"This is how they exercise in Sweden."

"How do you know?"

Rudek thought for a while.

"Read *The Deluge*," he said, and rubbed himself with snow.

Hesio had read *The Deluge* recently too, but he couldn't remember any gymnastics. Unless they did gymnastics during the battles that had gone on for so long that he'd skipped a few pages. Anyway, even if the Swedes did exercises, in the end it hadn't helped them in their clash with the Polish sword.

No wonder. Kryński the history teacher had taught them that in those days the Polish knights practised pulling themselves up on bars, horses and all. Without removing their armour, of course.

They must have drunk less than the Tarnów lancers from the Fifth Mounted Rifle Regiment, who had managed to lose a horse while inebriated.

Or maybe just before the lesson Hesio should cut himself with a knife and go to the school doctor with a bleeding finger? He'd done it once before, the wound had become infected, and he still had a scar on his thumb. What did he need another scar for? Maybe he'd better do what Flounder did in lessons – Miss Matraszek certainly wouldn't call him up to the blackboard with his trousers unbuttoned. Flounder isn't as stupid as they say he is at school. He knows what he's doing.

By the way, I wonder who he imagines when he does it? Beautiful Helena from the *Trilogy*?

But what am I to do?

"Are you asleep?" said Hesio, gently nudging the snoring Salek.

Half an hour later they were on their way to school together, and Hesio no longer had a bellyache. Salek had written it all out for him in his exercise book.

"Now at least we know why we went to the cheder," he said, before they parted ways to their separate classrooms.

During the break before Latin Hesio was the only one who didn't go out into the corridor or the playground. Just in case, he shut the door. He stood before the blackboard, and in the top right corner, next to the half-erased subject for an essay left over from the Polish lesson (*To die for your fatherland is sweet, but to live for it is no less sweet*), he started to copy out in chalk the small Hebrew letters Salek had written in his exercise book.

Meantime he muttered to himself: That scumbag Wachtel would be proud of me!

וללאָנ עצידניװ עװק טאַסע טסעטאַס אמירפּ אַעראַא
טאַבעלוק עװקמאָטקער סעדיפּ עגעל עניס אַאָס עטנופס

That scumbag Wachtel would have been proud if he had understood that his pupil had transcribed Ovid phonetically into Hebrew.

Now in the lesson he simply had to stand up and, without understanding a word, read out what he himself had written.

Unless Miss Matraszek decided to wipe the board clean, but usually she didn't touch it at all, and also kept her distance from the stinky, tattered sponge and the white chalk to avoid soiling her hands and clothing.

Satisfied, Hesio sat down at his desk. From the distance of the third row – in case he had to answer from the spot – he could read it without problem too.

Cogito ergo sum, as Rudek would say. In fact, to be fair to Salek, Hesio should say: My brother thinks, therefore I am.

The bell.

At once the classroom filled and fell silent. All they could hear was the clatter of Miss Matraszek's heels. The Latin textbook and the class register landed on the oak table. The chair grated as Matraszek pulled it back before sitting down.

In this silence it seemed to Hesio as if each of his classmates were holding their breath in turn, as though each of their hearts were beating faster and faster. Or maybe it was just his?

Along with the others, his eyes followed the nail of Matraszek's index finger as, with a distinct hum, it slowly moved down the list of names. Those whom it passed gasped with relief, but the rest were still afraid to stop holding their breath, as if breathing might make her think of them.

Without a word, Miss Matraszek reached the bottom of the list. Only now did she raise her head and look around the class. While her finger slowly started climbing back up.

Several names later, it made a short stop in the vicinity of the letter W (Wakspress, Wąs, Wolf, Wrona and Wyderko held their breath again), then it passed U (Unger) and began to slow down at T (Tokarski, Tatar, Tramer, Trybulec), then finally stopped at S.

Hesio remembered Rudek's story about the time Matraszek had called a boy up to the board and he had fainted.

"Take away this body, please," she had said to the class.

There was only one other teacher whose every word and movement were as closely heeded, and who caused the pupils the same bellyache. Wearing singlets and shorts, they shivered in the gym. Jan Klimek, the PE teacher, never shut the windows, not even in winter.

"A healthy spirit in a healthy body," he often said.

Was he trying to toughen them up, or to blow away the stink of the cigarettes he smoked during lessons?

Every class began with him reminding the pupils what they weren't allowed to do.

"Don't be late, chat, fight, fail to do your exercises or carry out my orders," he'd say, turning a medicine ball in his hands. "Don't do your exercises incorrectly, or fire a bow or a small-bore gun at each other. Because otherwise…"

He firmly blew the whistle he always wore around his neck. And stared the pupils in the eyes. They knew. The whole school knew. It was said on the quiet that Klimek had learned his method during a stretch in Tarnów prison. Or even more quietly that he used to work there, and this was how he'd kept the worst bandits and degenerates in order. Some also whispered that he seemed to think he was still working at the prison.

In any case, at liberty, or at least in the school gym, no one wanted to be on the wrong end of Klimek's tongue. Even Flounder meekly did all the exercises. And was the only boy in the previous year to get A grades for physical exercise on his report. He couldn't understand why this prompted a fit of laughter among his classmates. For all the other subjects, including conduct, he had nothing but Fs.

With his hairy paws Klimek would grab a pupil by the hair, tilt his head to one side and, with the entire class watching, slowly lick his ear, inside and out.

The very thought of it made Hesio feel sick.

Like the others, he'd rather be hit across the hands with a wooden ruler or a pencil case, what they called "the whacks", write out a hundred times "I promise to behave myself in singing lessons" or even have his face wiped with a dirty sponge by Hieronim Potok, the school doctor, who when antagonized taught them hygiene that way.

"Do you know, children," Klimek would change the subject, "that beating your meat makes hair grow on your palms?"

If anyone cast a terrified glance (as Hesio had in the first lesson) while he checked their hands, Klimek threw the medicine ball at them.

"Catch!" he'd shout and blow into the whistle.

But it was usually too late. And the five-kilogram ball toppled the victim.

Klimek would laugh at his own joke, along with the rest of the pupils, amid whose forced laughter Hesio could distinguish the sincerest and loudest voice – Flounder's.

Klimek called Hesio "the village philosopher's brother".

"But you're not as much of a freak as Salomon."

By now Hesio would have preferred to be the village philosopher, the freak or especially the family rabbi.

When you have a brother, do you have to be nothing but that brother's brother? Can't you simply be yourself?

And what if you have three brothers?!

Though for the time being Rudek was studying in Kraków and Nusek was still small.

Anyone who looks at you, even that stupid gymnastics fool, in the first place sees your brother, he thought. And you too – you look in the mirror and who do you see first? First of all you see your own brother! As if it weren't enough that you have to fall asleep and wake up every morning next to him – his is the first and last face you see each day.

As if in people's eyes Salek and Hesio Stramer were conjoined, like Siamese twins.

Sometimes Hesio wanted someone to separate them.

And this in spite of the fact that the girls in Strzelecki Park would say to him: "You're quite like Salek, but you're better looking, more handsome."

So why do I always have to be his brother, but he's never mine?

Maybe I should change my surname? Hersz-Cwi Tanner, Werner, Kowalski? Perhaps a new first name would suit the new surname better – Henryk, Karol or Józef?

But it was too late for that now. Miss Matraszek stopped her reptilian claw at the level of the name Stramer.

She called him up to the board, but why did she have to stand up at the same time too, shielding it from him? Hesio had to rock from side to side to read anything off it.

"This is not the synagogue. Stand still like a human being," said Miss Matraszek, but then luckily she sat down.

XI

NUSEK

R UDEK'S DEPARTURE, his mother's sorrow and his father's run-ins with Salek were of no concern to Nusek, who didn't notice them, just as an ordinary, little person can't see what's going on high up, at the summit of power. Or so said his father.

Something else mattered. Nusek was pleased to have become king of his own bed, to have it all to himself, and that was that. At first he kept it to himself and didn't flaunt it, unsure how long his reign would last.

Maybe there's something they've overlooked, like the couple of groszys he sometimes found in the wicker shopping basket or in the pocket of his father's coat, hanging on the rack by the door.

But days went by after Rudek's departure and nothing changed. His parents didn't tell him to get out and share with Hesio or Salek, who probably wouldn't have gone for it anyway. Not because they were almost inseparable and constantly whispering to each other, but just because they believed everyone should have everything equally. They were even less likely to send him to sleep with Wela, so they definitely wouldn't give up his bed to Rena either. Nusek realized that even if they wanted to, his parents had no move to make.

The youngest, and he already has a bed to himself, he thought with pride. And he's the only one in the house. Even Mama and Daddy sleep together.

Once in a while he was sorry he couldn't consult Rudek at bedtime. Today he'd have given up the whole pillow and half the quilt to find out what his oldest brother would have done in his place.

Instead of that he'd have to use his imagination. Of course he could ask Salek or Hesio for their opinion, but it wasn't the same, especially since they'd become communists.

This year Nusek had finally reached the age of eleven and could join the shomers – the Jewish scouts. At first just the "puppies" group. He had a faded scarf and a green uniform handed down from Salek and Hesio.

In the first place, he had wanted to sign up for the Polish scouts, like his classmates, but Rudek had warned him it was only for Catholics.

"Are there girls in the shomers too?" Nusek had asked to make sure.

The first assembly, on St Marcin's Peak, with the best view of the city (the sun was reflecting off the golden cupola of the New Synagogue, all but dazzling Nusek), was led by Fredek Haber, a classmate of Salek's.

The Polish scouts turned out to be having their assembly at the same time there too.

Fredek glanced at them, presenting the first shomer commandment: a shomer is a guardian of the truth.

"That means you can always count on the word of a shomer."

To explain the second commandment – a shomer is a pioneer for the rebirth of his nation, his culture (Hebrew) and his homeland (Palestine) – Fredek went on and on, until first Nusek stopped understanding, and then listening.

His thoughts began to centre on the synagogue cupola. If you were to melt it down, how much gold would there be?

And how much could you sell it for at the jeweller's shop on Wałowa Street, where nobody ever asks where you got things from?

Apparently that was where the cast-iron cemetery crosses and zinc plaques from Tarnów's gravestones disappeared to. And afterwards the Catholics couldn't tell who was lying where.

So they'd be sure to take the gold cupola as well. And only too gladly.

Finally, with more and more glances from side to side, Fredek the scoutmaster said: "The shomer is a man of action who can work for his own living."

But up on St Marcin's Peak it felt as if two children's armies were forming without a single command. Staring hard at each other, they were closing ranks. For now they were tensing their muscles under their uniforms, clenching their fists and shooting glances.

As Fredek reached the seventh commandment – a shomer is brave, brisk and lively – they were surrounded by Polish scouts.

"Who are you?" they asked.

"Scouts," said Fredek, and after a short pause he added more quietly: "Jewish ones."

"Get out of here. This is our hill."

He started grappling with their leader. Leaning forward, they held onto each other by the arms and pushed. Sweating, in almost identical green uniforms, indistinguishable.

Meanwhile the cubs and puppies supported them.

Fredek explained the last commandment – the shomer is pure in speech, thought and deed (he does not use tobacco or alcohol and he upholds the principle of chastity) – on the way down St Marcin's Peak, with a black eye, a swollen lip and a stained, torn uniform.

What would Rudek have done in Fredek's place? wondered Nusek. Would he have ordered the retreat too?

He certainly wouldn't have grappled pointlessly. And he wouldn't have waited for the other guy to knee him in the face. Above all, he'd have hit first – that's what he always taught his brothers to do – that mattered more than muscles or the length of your arms.

And what would Salek have done? He wouldn't have fought over whose hill it was, because everyone knew it was St Marcin's. Besides, he was opposed to private property.

There was one other matter on which Nusek would have liked to consult his brother. Was he doing the right thing with the notes that Karol Szpilman, son of the Little Bee candle factory owner, kept giving him for Rena? Along with an orange or a sweet.

Nusek ate the treats while he read the notes.

What nonsense they contained! What's more, some of the sheets of paper were perfumed, enough to make you throw up, and then you had to wash your hands. It was hard to believe Karol was a friend of Rudek's.

In these notes of his he invited Rena for a walk in the marketplace. Then he complained that she didn't come. Then he apologized for complaining. Then he begged her forgiveness. Then he promised not to write anymore. Two days later he'd be asking for *just a short answer, one sentence, so I'll know you're thinking about me too, otherwise I'll go mad.*

In Nusek's view he'd already gone mad. He was always walking or riding his bike past their windows. And whenever he could, he questioned Nusek about Rena's reactions. Did she say anything after reading his note, did she smile, blush or cast a knowing glance? Had she asked about him?

"I'm hungry," Nusek would say, and at once he'd get a sweet from Karol.

He knew that for every one of Rena's smiles he'd get another.

"Maybe she asked you to tell me something?" said Karol.

Nusek shook his head.

Only once did he have a short message from Rena: don't send flowers with your letters any more.

"But why not?"

"She prefers what you sent before. It can be chocolate, too. Milka."

"But why doesn't she write back to me?"

Nusek shrugged. What was he to say? He turned the orange boiled sweet in his mouth. After all, he couldn't say she'd never received a single one of Karol's letters because he'd thrown them all in the privy. And he'd even used some of them.

It was probably the first time in his life when anyone had looked forward to hearing from him so much. He didn't have to fight to get a word in, as at home. No one interrupted him, no one outshouted him.

"She gets hay fever," he said at last, as if he hadn't understood the question.

"Poor thing."

He was given a third sweet.

What would Rudek have said to that? He'd probably have praised him. On the one hand he was getting sweets and oranges for free. And on the other...

Rena would fall about laughing if she saw that nonsense. And she'd probably read out the best bits to everyone else so they could have a laugh too. And Salek would instantly learn them by heart and then repeat them at school.

"So on the other hand you're doing Karol a favour. For a few miserable sweets you're saving him from ridicule. But now shut up and go to sleep," Nusek imagined hearing Rudek's convincing voice at bedtime.

Just in case, he preferred not to ask or even imagine what Salek or Hesio would have to say about it. Probably that reading other people's letters is abominable, and the only thing worse is not delivering them. They'd also tell him to take them to Rena. And do it instantly.

Easy to say.

They read too much. Their father was right. It did them harm. What on earth did all those books by the philosopher with Santa Claus's curly beard have to do with life?

Nothing. As much as Hanukkah with Christmas.

If only that Marx fellow didn't just wave his pen around but dropped by sometimes with a gift.

For as long as he could remember, Nusek had wanted to have a Christmas tree at home, as most of his classmates did. With baubles, colourful decorations made of glossy paper, with chains and a star on top. It could be smaller, it didn't have to be right up to the ceiling. As long as it could be seen through the window. Then Santa Claus or the Angel that visited the children in Tarnów might make a mistake and come to their house too with a sack of presents. Again and again he and Wela imagined this scene.

"How can you trust a man like that?" said Nathan, thinking of Marx of course. "You don't go to the synagogue, but you trust a guy with the beard of a rabbi?"

NATHAN

Since he'd be working as an insurance agent for the Assicurazioni Generali Trieste, Nathan knew that to inspire a person's trust and to persuade them to do something in the first place you had to be smooth-chinned and in clean shoes. According to the manager of the Tarnów branch that was the basic principle. Nothing else, least of all the arguments, ever really persuaded anyone to buy a policy.

What about books? Weren't they a waste of eyesight and time?

"You can't make chairs out of them," said Salek to provoke him.

"You could saw them shorter..." added Hesio.

They'd been taking more liberties ever since he'd had a job and was in a better mood. The problems with gastritis had abated lately too.

Now Nathan concluded these quarrels calmly with a remark he'd learned from his boss: "Just live a bit and you'll see."

And like his boss, he would wave a hand indulgently.

At Rywka's request he had stopped putting out his sons' oil lamp in the evenings. He tried to get through to them by other means.

For example, yesterday at dinner they had asked him: "Is it true that during the war you were in the same trench as the writer Ferenc Molnár and the painter Kokoschka?"

"Why's that? Are you writing a book?" replied Nathan.

Were there so few soldiers in those stinking trenches who were writing or drawing something in their sketchbooks? Better not think about it while eating. But how was he to know if that was them.

"Dad, you once said you were with them."

"Then I must have been."

And as a warning he told them about a lad from Austria, Ludwig, who even on the battlefield was never parted from his beloved book. A worse case than your young Sobelsohn. Once during an attack the book fell out of his rucksack and he went back for it amid flying bullets and soldiers' bodies.

Nathan wouldn't have believed it if he hadn't seen it for himself. Imagine risking your life for a few printed pages. You'd have to be out of your mind.

It was a miracle Ludwig had survived. They said it was because the enemy were too busy tapping their foreheads to fire at him.

Anyway, apparently he'd gone mad from all that reading long before. He'd already given his family fortune to the poor in Vienna before the war. Well, apart from the books, presumably. What's more, he'd boast of it: a palace, some mansions, some gold.

"*I wish I knew you before*," Nathan had said in turn, showing off his knowledge of English.

Unless Ludwig made up the palace, the mansions and the gold. In the trenches they were all equally in the shit, so everyone invented something. Nathan for example told them he was descended from the chief rabbi of Kraków.

Once at roll-call they were standing to attention next to each other in the back row. Ludwig had his book under his arm.

"Wittgenstein!" the general ordered him to step forward.

As he saluted, his book fell on his foot.

The general screamed at him, almost shouting himself hoarse. After the war Nathan had tried shouting like that at his children too, but without hurting his throat.

Ludwig was transferred, and soon after he was taken prisoner.

You can see for yourselves.

But did the children actually know why Nathan was telling them this?

They probably thought it was all *bullshit*, that he was kidding them. They winked at each other, and cast their father the same look as the soldiers in the unit must have cast at Ludwig.

"What was he reading?" asked Salek.

What sort of a question was that?! He hadn't understood a thing! Or he was making fun of his father on purpose. He was always asking questions about inessential details. Needlessly. Nathan had promised Rywka not to shout at them so much. Talking didn't work. He longed for his American belt.

"A book," he said, pointing at the pile on the windowsill. "One like yours."

A book is a book. Apart from the Talmud, which no one had ever read in its entirety either, they were all alike. Some bigger, some smaller. Thinner or thicker, what was the difference?

At least little Nusek kept his distance from them.

"It's a fashion that'll pass," Nathan explained to him. "As soon as you look round there'll be something new. It's like with the newspapers. It's not worth getting too accustomed. Yesterday it was the violin, today it's books, tomorrow it'll be something else."

Nusek just nodded.

What a relief. Finally a kid who didn't argue with him. And to think he only managed it the fifth time. Maybe thanks to the name? After all, Nussim is quite like Nathan. Why didn't he hit upon that at the very start, with his first son?

In America they understood that long ago, that was why they named the son after the father and just added Jr – Junior.

And that was the point!

When he was a little boy, every morning as his father shaved and polished his shoes before going to work, Nusek watched him in delight. Now too, as he packed his papers and the sandwich Rywka had made for him into his leather briefcase, thanks to his youngest son, Nathan felt like the captain of a ship setting off on a long voyage across unknown seas and lands. He forgot he was an agent knocking on door after door to press insurance policies on people.

Nusek would go on waving after him for ages through the kitchen window, as if he were standing on the quay, and Nathan were sailing away down Goldhammer Street into the great big world.

At these moments he understood the point of having children.

So he had always tried to hold back the American belt just before Nusek's little bum. So that it just touched him, nothing more. He still couldn't forgive himself for the one time he laid into him so hard, and with the violin bow too, that the little boy bawled louder than ever before or since. Yet Nathan had been really careful. Not like with his older sons, Rudek, Salek and Hesio.

It was doubly painful. Not only had Nusek felt pain, but so had Nathan, as if he'd hit himself. He'd broken the bow and gone back to the American belt. But that had only partly worked. Admittedly, Nusek didn't yell like that again, but Nathan went on hurting.

If only Nusek wouldn't bug him every winter about getting a Christmas tree.

"We're not going to ape the Catholics, are we?" Nathan had patiently explained to him. "Not to mention how much those trees cost. They grow in the woods for free, why should we have to pay for them in the city?"

Especially as that was just the beginning, because at once you had to buy something else to put under the tree. On top of that the children believed some Angel or Santa Claus bought them those presents with their own money. There was no thank you. You could forget about gratitude.

It was the same every year. Cleverly conceived. You had to give it to the Catholics, Christmas was the best business idea in the world. In a couple of days the shops earned more than they usually did in a couple of months. You could tell at once that Jesus was a Jew.

But as they rightly said in Tarnów, anything in excess was bad for you. Why did they need Easter too? Why did Christ have to die if he instantly rose from the dead again? Oh well, not everything the Catholics did was a success. That holiday needed a bit more work. It didn't entirely pay off, because nobody bought gifts for anyone.

He remembered what Ben had once told him in a letter: *All religions are as bad as each other, but the most durable human virtue is business.* It was hard for Nathan to disagree with that. Like almost everything his older brother said.

So who's doing the talking matters more than what he says, thought Nathan. Probably Ben thought so too, because a couple of times Nathan had asked him not to wrap the dollars in tissue paper any more, but Ben always knew better.

Unlike Nathan, he never listened to his brother.

Rena in turn must have noticed Rywka washing and drying the banknotes on the oven top after Ben's last letter, because she was pestering him for a gramophone again.

If Ben were in my place would he give way and buy it for her? thought Nathan. After all, they were his dollars.

One time Nathan had almost let himself be persuaded. Only halfway to the shop on Krakowska Street did it dawn on him that it was the same story as with the Christmas tree. Rena let slip that it wasn't enough to turn the handle for the gramophone to play. You had to buy records too. And each one cost money.

"That's going too far," decided Nathan on the corner of Krakowska and Nowy Świat Streets. "*I'm not a fool.* We're going home."

All the way back Rena walked half a step behind him, with tears in her eyes.

She only cried them out at home, where they soaked into her mother's kitchen apron.

"Unfortunately a pot alone is not enough to make cholent," said Rywka at supper, more to console her daughter than to convince her husband, who shrugged and replied: "Too bad."

"Dad," said Hesio, giving it another try, "you'd never have hit anyone in the war with nothing but a rifle."

"What do you know about war?" said Nathan, not noticing as Hesio rolled his eyes. "Just a belt'd be enough for you."

Satisfied, Nathan went back to his food. He was sure he'd ended the conversation there. But then Rena spoke to him, for the first time since they got home.

"I'm moving out anyway." And got up from the table.

Rywka shot her husband a glance. So he'd be in no doubt who had brought it to this. As ever when he was upset, Nathan forgot to close his mouth while eating. To Rywka he seemed alien.

She knew that once Rena made up her mind, that was it, there was no going back. A second child would be leaving home. Just six of them would be left in the room with a kitchen on Goldhammer Street. That was settled. What she didn't know was that someone else would beat Rena to it. Move out before her, or rather be taken away.

XII

HESIO

Hesio was eating his supper quietly, his thoughts occupied by what Salek called "the economics of love". Hesio was impressed by the accuracy of this term. He'd have liked to come up with something as apt, but as Salek would say with a laugh: "You're plainly better in practice than in theory". Maybe that was true? Even though he read just as much and the same books as his older brother, he remembered less of them afterwards, and definitely couldn't "read from memory".

For a while he examined Salek's head. It really was large and bulging, not just at the front but at the back too. And it was hard. He remembered Rudek teaching Salek how to headbutt.

"You grab the guy by the lapels, you tug him towards you with all your might and whack him on the nose with your forehead. You've got a head like stone, he won't get up in a hurry."

But to this day Salek couldn't force himself to hit anyone in the face, not even with his head.

Hesio instinctively ran a hand over his own head, as if trying to compare the capacity.

Size does matter. Flounder is right.

Flounder's stiffy was twenty-five centimetres long. At first Hesio didn't believe him, so in the school toilet, right before his eyes Flounder took a measurement with a wooden set square from the maths room.

He had to admit he wasn't lying. But there was something else that made an even greater impression on Hesio. His foreskin. The skin covered almost the entire twenty-five centimetres. It was the first time he'd had a close look at anyone uncircumcised.

"Who at school has a bigger one?" asked Flounder.

He was proud of having reached this impressive size through his own hard work. After all, he'd even worked on it during lessons. And he told Hesio that girls' breasts grow bigger too if they're massaged every day.

"Not bad," said Hesio, with an appreciative nod, "for a future priest. It'll stick out from under your cassock."

"The coming of the Lord is at hand…" Standing there without his underpants, Flounder began in a pious tone, but was laughing too much to continue.

It had recently occurred to him that the priest repeated this on every possible occasion. Now he sat in church just waiting for these words.

"Do you hear what they're saying?" he said, nudging Hesio, "The coming of the Lord!"

Whatever else he may have had, Flounder's head was smaller than Salek's.

You can't have everything – as Wachtel was fond of repeating during their Mosaic religion lessons.

But which of the Stramers had a head as big as Salek's? Certainly none of the siblings, not even Rudek. It was just as impressive as Rena's breasts, which Hesio stared at whenever she rose from the table in a huff.

In their field they had no equals, he mused. They're like Sienkiewicz among writers, Marx among philosophers and Matejko among painters.

Hesio was as proud of them as Flounder that day in the school toilet. Or his father in the doorway of The Stramers café. Or Mayor Tertil, who had managed to get the famous writer, Stanisław Przybyszewski, to come to Tarnów. Romek Brandstaetter, Rudek's friend from school, liked to imitate Tertil officially welcoming the rather deaf old man: "Great master!" he'd shout. "You are the motor-driven plough of Polish literature!"

But it was probably something else that was making Hesio feel so excited now.

What might Lotka Goldberg's breasts be like? He had a rendezvous with her in half an hour's time at Strzelecki Park. Perhaps she was a bit like his older sister in this regard. But not in any other. In Tarnów Rena was spoken of with respect as being touchy, and thus untouchable, while Lotka was shunned by the girls at school for having loose morals. But maybe they were simply jealous of her for being tall and buxom? They said she invited boys home on purpose and paraded before them in nothing but her bra and knickers. And even lay like that on the rug. While they sat on the sofa and could do nothing, because her parents were in the next room.

Lotka has them in her grip, thought Hesio.

Apparently she drank and smoked too.

As long as she wasn't too hungry. Hesio had agreed to meet her at the main gate. From there they were to take a walk to the Sailcloth café.

"Why don't we agree to meet at once on the spot?" Lotka had asked.

"On such a nice evening?" he had answered with a question.

He had two pieces of halva ready in his pocket. That should be enough. He'd bought them on the way home, after tutoring, with his date in mind, of course. They had cost him all the money he'd earned in the two hours he'd spent teaching Polish, almost two zlotys. At the usual place – the shop that sold colonial goods. Quite near the wall on which he'd painted a hammer and sickle in red a few nights ago.

He found it hard to believe that Lotka was the niece of Tarnów's most famous – for now, thought Hesio – communist. This kinship had just as strong an effect on Hesio as her appearance and the gossip that was spread about her. Luckily, she had no physical resemblance to Karol Radek whatsoever. But was there a spiritual likeness? wondered Hesio, smiling to himself.

Just think how much more Radek could do for the good of the cause and how much further he could go if his face were anything like his niece's. And there's her height too. That would instantly raise him to the summit of power in Moscow.

But, as Wachtel the Mosaic religion teacher so often says…

Unless his father was right after all, and it was the other way around, thought Hesio. Maybe if Radek were a bit better looking, he'd have better things to do and wouldn't be obsessed with communism.

But anyway, Radek had already done everything he could – that's to say he'd changed his name, which he'd made famous in Tarnów by falling under all those peasant carts with book in hand. Ludwig, his father's fellow soldier in the world war, couldn't be torn from his reading by bullets on the battlefield either. For people like that, books must be more real than reality.

"You know what, my uncle says that even the stockings I wear," said Lotka, stopping and showing her shapely calves in spotless white stockings, "are stained by the blood of the workers."

Thanks to this, Hesio could take a good long look at them by the light of a gas lamp.

"It's true," he confirmed, shaking his head sadly.

On the whole he agreed. And sympathized with the oppressed seamstresses. What if he were to introduce Lotka into the ranks of the Party? People would finally stop saying that only ugly girls became communists. In Tarnów every young person belonged to some sort of organization. And it was the competition, meaning the Bund, the Zionist Youth or Beitar who painted that portrait of the communist girls.

Lotka would instantly attract new members and sympathizers. Catholics too. Because as well as pretty girls, there could be more of them too. Flounder would be the first to believe in communism for a girl like that. Instead of practising onanism – Hesio smiled at his friend in his thoughts – he'd switch to communism.

But could he be sure Lotka was being serious about her stockings stained with blood? Not making fun of him?

"Not to mention other items of clothing," she added, and this time she smiled mysteriously.

They had moved away from the street lamp, and now there was a shadow across Lotka's face, so perhaps he had just thought she was smiling. As for the rest of her wardrobe, at best he could only imagine it.

Maybe that's why she undresses so often? he thought. Because she feels bad in those clothes that are defiled by exploitation?

And then he thought: has she got me in her grip already?

"Would you like some halva?" he asked, to change the subject.

She took it willingly, and immediately started to eat it. According to plan. So who is in whose grip?

The economics of love works. And halva is far more effective than chocolate, with which he began. He had found that out at his own expense. A couple of mouthfuls filled them up for ages.

"Do you know what my parents used to say when I was little?" Lotka stopped and said. "No sweets before dinner or you won't have any room left in your tummy."

Hesio felt as if he were losing control of the situation. Had she just said that for no reason, or had she seen through him?

"And do you know how I used to answer? I'd say I won't eat my dinner, or there won't be room in my tummy for dessert." Lotka began to laugh, and a little later Hesio joined in.

She's not so naïve. If she was that determined as a little girl…

She must have seen through him. Or someone had warned her. Was it one of those girls who'd taken this same walk with him, eaten the halva too, and then ordered just a small coffee at the café?

On the other hand, what's wrong with that? What's wrong with treating a girl to halva? She can always say no thank you.

But how else, with hardly any money, can you invite a girl to a café?

The end justifies the means, as he'd heard so many times at Party meetings. It was no accident that he'd hit upon this idea during one of them. After all, unlike Hegel's march of the Spirit through history, no innocent flower was trampled on the path of the economics of love.

"When I was four years old," said Hesio, deciding to change the subject and reciprocate with a story from his own childhood, "I boasted to my mother that I liked a little girl we used to play with in the yard. 'What colour are her eyes?' asked my mother, to which I replied: 'I don't know, she didn't tell me'."

All right, at least she laughed.

But what colour are her eyes, in fact?

He'd noticed that every time they spoke Lotka stopped for a while. And since in the course of their fifteen-minute walk he had managed to appreciate that Lotka never did anything without a reason, he started to wonder what it could mean. Was this her way of letting him know that the moment had come for him to kiss her? Already?

So they needn't go to the café at all. He looked inquiringly into Lotka's eyes. Green. It'd be the greatest triumph in the history of the economics of love! But it was too dark for him to decipher anything specific, apart from a playful glance.

He looked away. Safer to do it the usual way. Once in the café, he'd lay a hand on hers, as if by accident, and see if she withdrew it.

Lotka lived on Nowy Świat – "New World" – Street, as Hesio could sense in her manner and her confident tone. Her family occupied the entire first floor of a mansion near the marketplace. Hesio had never been inside, but he had often stood in the street to admire the colourful stained-glass windows above the main entrance and the ornate bay windows at the front. Which made him feel overawed.

Maybe it was because of his father, who dreamed of moving to this district when he finally made his fortune. It was his favourite place – after New York, of course.

"Just look! Look at that façade, and the flowers on the balconies. Electricity, plumbing and water from the tap. What more could you want in life? All done with future generations in mind."

Hesio had no trouble imagining Lotka's children, grandchildren and especially her attractive great-granddaughters, who in a hundred years would still be right here, squirming on the rug in nothing but their underwear before the eyes of their helpless male schoolmates.

He didn't even try to imagine his own children in the house at the far end of Goldhammer Street. The rented flat on the ground floor, as wobbly as the table and chairs in the kitchen. So full of things that you couldn't even squeeze in a rug. There were mice running across the floor and a draught from the door.

That was the old world. He'd rather see his descendants on New World Street. And himself in the company of not just Lotka's father, who bought up rabbit skins and represented a hat factory in Bielsko, but also her uncle, Karol Radek. He'd keep him safe while walking down the streets of Tarnów, discussing the similarities between the French and the October revolutions.

Dutifully wearing the light grey hat gifted by his father-in-law. A few extra centimetres wouldn't hurt. Some special leather gloves would complete the look nicely, with cut-outs on the palms, the kind car drivers wore.

So maybe our daughters and granddaughters, he thought, glancing at Lotka, will live on New World Street? But in that case without rolling around on rugs in a bourgeois manner.

Was it possible? Despite the class struggle and the imminent revolution of the proletariat? Who knows? He'd have to ask Salek.

"More halva?"

"No," said Lotka, stopping at a bench. "No, thank you."

Why doesn't she move? Why don't we keep going? Surely it's not possible…? he thought. Lotka sat down on the bench, Hesio beside her.

Yes, yes. Perhaps it was possible. He no longer needed to ask Salek for his opinion. Yes.

It was soon confirmed that Lotka was not untouchable.

All the better, he thought shortly after. We're a good match.

An hour later, when they reached the café, Hesio realized that he had declared the victory of the economics of love prematurely. Lotka had worked up an appetite, and without the slightest inhibition ordered far more than her predecessors. She ordered for Hesio too, who defended himself by saying he wasn't hungry.

At some point he stopped thinking about the bill. He knew he definitely couldn't afford it. But he wasn't going to run off, dragging Lotka after him on her high heels.

At most, like Mr Zawadowski at The Stramers café, he'd remain here as a hostage. But who was going to buy him out? To whom could he send a droshky with a request for help?

The only person he could think of was Rudek, but he'd have to wait until Saturday when Rudek would be coming to visit. Or maybe he could turn to the Party?

Just in case, Hesio ordered a cream puff and an éclair – to keep himself going before help arrived. He remembered that luckily he still had a piece of halva in his pocket.

"Indeed," said Lotka, smiling from the corners of her eyes, "you weren't hungry."

Thanks to the cream puff and the éclair Hesio had gained a bit of time to think. What else could save him? A fire, an earthquake, a whirlwind. Unfortunately, there was nothing he could do. Apart from that, he was feeling sick.

Gradually the coat racks and the neighbouring tables were emptying, while he delayed asking for the bill. Or rather his sentence. Seeing the waiter yawning, he looked away. By now they had turned off the gramophone, ostentatiously swept the floor, wiped the table tops and put the chairs up on them.

In spite of which Hesio was surprised how calm he felt. He wasn't getting upset. He was sure that somehow it would all work out as usual. That was why he was so often chosen to paint slogans on walls and stick up posters at night.

Finally the waiter started heading for their table with the bill. How would he explain himself? That was less of a problem. But what would he tell Lotka? That he'd forgotten his wallet? He could say it had been stolen, or maybe best of all, that in a moment of passion it must have fallen out of his pocket under the bench. And was probably still lying there, if no one had taken it away.

The waiter was three steps away when Hesio felt Lotka grab him by the sweaty hand under the table and put her purse into it.

Who was in whose grip?

XIII

SALEK

THE NEXT NIGHT Hesio's dream about Lotka was interrupted by knocking, or rather hammering at the door. It tore Nathan from a dream about New York (he'd been flying among the spires of skyscrapers), and Rywka from one about Brazil (or Argentina); Rena had been dreaming of Zawadowski the lawyer, Wela of the Angel that brought presents, Nusek that he had less than the others again (though less of what he couldn't remember), and Salek that the police were knocking at their door.

And they really were.

"Police!"

Old Suchard began to bark.

Nathan pulled the quilt over his head – had they added up the small change he'd embezzled from the butcher's for all those years, and then at the Assicurazioni Generali Trieste?

"Open up!"

Fancy interrupting his dream at the best moment! Hesio opened one eye. Doing that should be stamped out, or best of all prohibited by law, like anti-Semitism in the Soviet Union.

Wela burst into tears and cuddled up to Rena, who in the first instance was surprised it wasn't Zawadowski.

Salek calmly opened the wardrobe and fetched out a bundle packed with the most necessary things, prepared according to the instructions repeated at meetings. Long johns, socks, a warm sweater, a toothbrush and a self-education kit (meaning an exercise book and pencil).

No famous revolutionary had yet avoided prison. Sooner or later it was bound to happen. But he knew perfectly well why they'd come for him right now, in late April. The day before, during a meeting at Tarnów's Siła club, they'd arrested forty workers from the shoemakers' section. Maybe one of them had grassed on him?

Besides, they'd been nabbing important comrades such as Janusz Grzyb, Mojżesz Ortsman and Staszek Pisz off the street. So they were only missing him.

He had often imagined the moment of arrest. And the faces of his pals from the final year at school when they found out.

"He was asking for it," they'd say with a mixture of satisfaction and envy.

Ultimately, of the two evils it was better to sit in a prison cell than in a classroom.

With flushed cheeks and tears in their eyes, his female Party comrades would take it in turns to bring him parcels and listen to his ardent words in the courtroom.

If the going was tough, he could always make chess pieces out of bread and play against himself.

But could the Party manage without its district activist? That was his biggest worry. Who was going to fill in for him? What a pity that Hesio, still lying motionless under the quilt with his eyes closed, wasn't mature enough yet. In fact, as far as his younger brother was concerned, it'd be better for Salek to remain at liberty. So Hesio wouldn't get into bad company, or fall prey to negative influences...

But sometimes you had to sacrifice your loved ones for the good of humanity. He could see himself, sketched in pencil in the history textbooks, alongside the eternally frozen Polish insurgents, battling against the wind: survivors of the January Uprising, the November Uprising and... In this country just about every month had its heroes.

Were all thirty days in April definitely already taken, or would someone have to make room for him?

Rywka nudged Nathan a third time to get up. No effect. She glanced at the photograph on the chest of drawers – she was missing Rudek, who always knew what to do and say. He'd have been up and standing in the doorway long ago, or he'd have escaped through the yard.

"Open up! Or we'll break it down!"

Rywka went to open the door in her nightshirt.

"Is this the residence of Hersz-Cwi Stramer?" they shouted and came inside.

There were three of them.

"That's my son Hesio," she said. "What's happened?"

"Which one is he?"

"Get up," they said, standing over him. "Please come with us."

But Hesio didn't move. He couldn't. He was waiting for his erection to go down. He didn't want to let them arrest him like that. So now he was trying to forget about Lotka as fast as possible.

Meanwhile a search was in progress – the bedding, clothes, school textbooks and exercise books were landing on the floor. The policemen had no choice, even if they didn't want to, they'd have to walk on them to move between the beds that were unfolded everywhere. One of them, the youngest, was an old classmate of Rudek's, who apologized every time he trod on something.

And kept peeping across at Rena and Wela's bed.

As well as Hesio, they took away (or as they put it, "sequestered") a red flag marked CPP, three editions of the journal *Comrade*, books titled *Street Fighting* and *The ABC of Leninism* and an anthology of revolutionary poetry.

It was in this collection that Hesio had published a poem under the pseudonym Henryk Weber.

They also looked for the Tarnów local newspaper. The one in which Zawadowski the lawyer described what really went on at the town hall – who won the municipal tenders, who was granted all possible licences, and why. Recently there had been a notorious article about an accountant from the road construction department, who for years had been adding fictional workers to the payments list and collecting the money for them. Zawadowski had not held back on the names and personal remarks, so his newspaper was constantly being confiscated and closed down, and had to keep changing its name. Last week it had come out as the *Tarnów Flea*, this week it was the *Tarnów Wasp*, and next week? Maybe the *Mosquito*?

"There's no evil that does not bring good," said Nathan in Polish once the policemen had left. "At least they've taken that communist trash away and freed up a bit of space in the wardrobe."

Salek shrugged. The main thing was that they hadn't found his list of names of Tarnów communists.

He was proud he'd hidden it so well. But he couldn't remember where. So he'd been scanning the room for it during the police search, ready to follow the example of his older comrades and activists, by eating the names if necessary, rather than leaking them.

"This the best hiding place," they'd say, pointing at their skinny bellies, which had consumed many a sheet of paper before now.

"You got him into this," said Nathan, stepping across the clothes and exercise books to reach Salek's bed. "Now you get him out."

"But how…?" Salek replied in his thoughts, without even looking at his father.

Has this man ever tried to understand his own children? If they didn't resemble him in appearance, nobody would believe he was their father. They were like the thesis and the antithesis, like living proof of Marxist dialectics. Had their father ever tried to understand anyone at all, if only himself?

Had it occurred to him how Salek was feeling now? Unappreciated, outcast, unjustly not arrested. Erased from the school history textbooks.

Wasn't that how the pupils felt who competed against Salek in declamation contests, and then had to applaud him on the school stage, in front of everyone, when he won the top prize, as following his recent recital of Kornel Ujejski's poem, "The Burial of Kościuszko"?

Anyway, the moment when the police had asked: "Is this the residence of... and made a short pause to look at their notes, had reminded Salek of the moment before the ceremonial announcement of the winner. Now he was turning it in his head, this way and that, as if unable to accept defeat.

Actually, the fact that the police didn't arrest me reflects badly on the police, not on me, he was trying to persuade himself. They're just ill-informed.

But who else knew about it? How would his Party comrades take the news?

The world must have been full of these silent heroes.

Unless there had been a mistake.

Maybe they'd bring Hesio straight back and say that all your Jewish names are alike, and of course they meant Salomon Stramer.

"On reviewing his activities there has been a decision to arrest him immediately," the policemen would announce, and warn: "Watch out! Apparently he's dangerous if confronted."

Now he could even feel the pleasant chill of the handcuffs tightening on his wrists.

This thought only consoled him briefly. From political prisoner he had once again become an ordinary sixth-former. Quite undeservedly, he was free, sitting on the bed, entirely his from now on, instead of enjoying captivity on a prison bunk, in the select company of robbers – pickpockets and horse thieves.

Anyway, conditions in those two places were not far apart. Apparently in winter criminals came from all over the country to let themselves be caught in Tarnów, because the local jail was the most modern and comfortable in Poland.

"Now you get him out," repeated his father.

Since their departure his mother had been standing in her nightshirt in the open doorway. Maybe she too was waiting for them to come back and say they'd arrested Hesio by mistake. Women whose husbands had left for America were known as "American widows", she was thinking. What about a mother whose child had been locked in prison?

Why do they need all this politics? She had wanted to ask Salek and Hesio this question several times before now, but didn't dare. After all, she had never asked Rudek where he got the money he gave her for the house.

Nathan came up to her.

"I've heard that the revolution consumes its own children," he said. "But why does it have to consume ours too?"

XIV

RUDEK

ON THE LAST DAY OF APRIL Rudek arrived by the evening train from Kraków. Rywka burst into tears as she greeted him with a hug.

Every time he came home, Tarnów seemed smaller. The houses weren't as tall, the streets were narrower, and the flat on Goldhammer Street was even more cramped. But now for the first time he also had to bow lower to embrace his mother.

He gave perfunctory answers to the questions asked by the friends he met on his way from the station, for fear of needlessly stirring their envy.

He was careful not to say at every step: "But in Kraków we…"

After all, he knew the joke: What do the people of Tarnów say about the Cracovians? They say they're snooty, they think they have all the answers and that they're really someone. And what do the Cracovians say about people from Tarnów? Nothing.

The first of May was sunny. Early that morning Rudek went to the Daydream cinema and bought tickets. For all the siblings, apart of course from Hesio, and also Salek, because he knew he wouldn't be able to persuade him to join them.

Wela, Rena, Nusek and Rudek sat side by side in the fifth row. As the lovers, Ellen and Timothy, whispered to each other tenderly against a tropical background, a march going past the cinema drowned out their declarations of love.

Rudek noticed that Rena was gazing longingly at the screen and at the door by turns.

"Free the political prisoners!" they were chanting.

Rudek nudged Rena's arm and held out some Milka chocolate in her direction. Without tearing their eyes from the screen, Nusek and Wela presented their hands for a piece each too.

Would the beautiful Ellen accept Timothy's proposal on the upper deck of the ocean liner?

Wela was afraid to breathe out. How she'd love to sail away on a long voyage one day. Sleep in a single cabin with a bathroom the size of their flat. See foreign lands, and enjoy love and romance on the sunny deck of a ship, surrounded by handsome sailors.

She longed to see Ellen in a snow-white dress with a veil.

In his bow tie, Timothy was so handsome that in Ellen's place she wouldn't have hesitated a moment longer.

The cinema auditorium was filled by the voice of Adam Ciołkosz, leader of Tarnów's socialists.

"Comrades!" he shouted the answer to Timothy's proposal. "Even the weather is on our side today!"

"Shut up!" yelled Rudek.

Was Ellen weeping with joy because she'd accepted, or with sorrow because she'd refused?

The Stramer siblings exchanged glances, but none of them knew.

"After the film I'm going to ask for our money back," said Rudek, trying to console them. "Or at least free tickets for the next screening."

He glanced towards the shouts coming from behind the door. At least Hesio was safe – in prison, but what about Salek?

Nusek held out a hand for another bit of chocolate. Rudek pretended not to see in the darkness.

SALEK

Because of the arrests, Salek and his comrades had been unable to organize their own, communist march. So they were demonstrating alongside the socialists and the Bund. Anyway, they had almost failed to get here at all. They had run up at the last moment when the march was already on the move. Their shirts were torn and blood-stained, their flags ripped, and some of them had black eyes.

On their way to the demonstration they had been waylaid by members of the Zionist youth movement. It began with insults and threats to throw each other out of their native Tarnów, where they went to the same schools, lived on the same streets and played in the same courtyards.

"What's keeping you here?" cried the Zionists. "Sod off to the Soviets!"

"And you sod off to Palestine! Go bust a gut in a kibbutz!"

Then there was some pushing and shoving. And finally fists and sticks.

As usual, Salek stayed out of the fighting. He could feel his knees trembling. He was probably just as afraid of hitting as of being hit. Someone punched him on the back of the head, but his skull was so hard that he barely felt it. Nevertheless, he turned around and gazed into the brown eyes of his assailant (the son of kind Dr Gramada), with the same ironic look he cast at the "kosher patrols" – the groups of young Orthodox lads who went out hunting for Jews eating ham sandwiches.

He shook his head: it was pointless.

But for some people any reason is good enough to let fly with your fists.

"Let's not fight each other," Salek had said, trying to calm the situation.

He hadn't failed to be arrested just to be late for the demonstration now.

He managed to convince his comrades, but not the Zionists, who outnumbered them.

As he and his friends were running off, it occurred to him that all these young people will be like their fathers and grandfathers in a few years' time. They'll still be quarrelling, but in a civilized way, within Tarnów's dozens of Jewish organizations and social circles. They'll be debating and arguing from dawn to dusk on every possible matter: from translation of the Torah, via the price of tram tickets until the coming of the Messiah.

Each of them had to have the last word, that was why this had been going on for so long and would never end.

"I'm right!"

"No, I'm right!"

"You always have to be right!"

"No, it's you that always has to be right!"

And so the millennia go by.

No matter that it wouldn't lead anywhere and nothing would be left of it, because for each person the one and only thing that counted was what he was about to say. No matter that his spectacle frame was glued together, his fingernails needed cutting and there was a lottery ticket sticking out of his dirty shirt pocket. And his children were waiting at home, hungry.

What mattered was to have your say before someone else took the chance away from you. And to hold on to it for as long as possible.

A bit like in football.

That was how Salek saw it now.

And the Catholics probably take an even dimmer view of us, he thought.

There was just one chance to break free of this and do something together for everyone.

That was why he was demonstrating today. Tomorrow they'd probably write in the newspapers: *It's a long time since Tarnów saw such crowds.*

A good thing the general strike has been declared, he thought.

At the head of the march went the cyclists, then a brass band, the socialist standards and a whole sea of proletarians.

Salek was on first-name terms with many of the workers. He greeted them with a nod.

He stared at the cloud of dust that rose from under the demonstrators' feet.

They'll march by, the dust will settle, they'll go back to work and it'll be the same as before again. What's to be done for this cloud, instead of settling, to rise even higher, permeate people's consciousness and fall from it one day as revolutionary rain?

Salek sneezed.

Far ahead, rippling on the surface of the crowd he could see Zawadowski's light, round hat. By contrast with Salek, Zawadowski was one of the most senior demonstrators. It was hard to push through to him, but luckily Salek could keep sight of him on the horizon, like a lighthouse.

"Work and bread!" shouted the demonstrators.

Now they had turned from Wałowa Street into Krakowska, on the way to the railway station.

Salek didn't count how many people trod on his feet or how many people he trod on. But he finally managed to catch up with Zawadowski. He reached out a hand and gently tugged at the lawyer's coat sleeve to get his attention.

"Excuse me, Mr Zawadowski…" said Salek, looking up, dazzled by the sun. "My name is…"

"Hello, Salek!" Zawadowski interrupted him. "What happened to you?"

At first Salek couldn't understand. Zawadowski had to point out to him that his shirt was torn, and his collar was hanging by a thread.

"Who did that to you?" he asked. "Is that the work of the nationalists?"

"No, it's nothing." Salek waved a hand, ripped off the collar and stuffed it in his pocket. "But sir, I wanted to tell you about my…"

"Call me by my first name."

Salek shook the lawyer's large, warm hand; he must have forgotten how their father had kept him prisoner at The Stramers café by now. Or else he didn't bear grudges. Well, unless he didn't associate the name with that... And only remembered him from meetings on St Marcin's Peak.

Salek could feel his comrades' eyes on him. He was flattered that they could see him in the company of the star of the Tarnów Bar.

"Mieczysław..." If only they could hear how he was addressing him too.

"Is it about your brother Hesio?"

"Yes."

"I'm aware of the case." Zawadowski laid a hand on Salek's arm. "I've taken care of it already."

Salek was so surprised that he didn't know what to say. The less you know, the better for you, as he'd often been told. He had no idea the Party was acting so quickly and effectively in response to the arrests. It hadn't even forgotten the rank-and-file members. It must have had its own people within the police or the prison services.

"Thank you very much, sir."

"In the first place, stop calling me sir!" said Zawadowski, jokingly wagging a finger at Salek. With a handkerchief bearing the monogram MZ he wiped the sweat from under his hat.

"It's bloody hot," he said. "And all this dust is making me thirsty."

Maybe Salek should buy him a beer? But he hadn't a groszy on him.

Zawadowski glanced at his watch.

"Well, I must be off," he said. "Give my best to your sister."

He turned right and disappeared in the shade of Nowy Świat Street, leaving the proud Salek, thrilled by every word of their five-minute conversation, all alone with the crowd that had been its witness.

XV

RYWKA

IF AT ANY TIME of day or night Rywka heard a noise from outside like horse's hoofs hitting the ground, but neither approaching or moving away, as if the horse were walking on the spot, she went straight to the kitchen window.

The children called this agreed signal "clicking your tongue". Or just "the doorbell".

They could simply have knocked on the glass, but they knew their mother washed the windows every day. And maybe they were eager to have their own special method? They always did everything their own way, didn't they?

"It's not the nineteenth century anymore," they sometimes replied to their parents' advice.

Recently Rywka had woken in the night, sure she could hear "clicking". Had the students, Rudek and Salek, come home unexpectedly from Kraków? Or maybe Hesio had escaped? But there was nobody at the window.

It happened several times during the day as well.

"Why do you keep going to the window?" asked Nathan.

"It's the best thermometer," she replied. "To see how people are dressed outside."

One day she heard the "clicking", and there stood Mr Zawadowski with a bunch of roses. They'd seen each other a month earlier at his legal office, Zawadowski and Francoz, where he had announced that he would defend Hesio on a voluntary basis. Now he looked even more surprised than she was.

He probably doesn't know we live here, thought Rywka in the first instance.

But who had "clicked"? There was no one apart from Zawadowski.

Still outside the window, he took off his hat, bowed and kissed her hand. A handsome man with salt-and-pepper hair. She had just chopped the carrots and onions for vegetable soup. At around one o'clock each day five or six "lunchers", as she called them, paid for a meal at her table. She'd prepared the second course, tongue in horseradish sauce, the night before, and only had to heat it up.

She quickly withdrew her hand.

She'd cooked enough for the children and Nathan too; since losing his job at the insurance company ("Rywka, these days they only employ their own people"), Nathan was helping her by running to the market each morning for the shopping. But soup and seconds could definitely be found for the lawyer too.

"It's for me," said Rena, standing beside her mother.

She was wearing knee-high lace-up boots, a pleated black skirt and a white blouse with little tucks that Rywka had never seen before.

"I'm just coming," she said, smiling at Zawadowski.

And Rywka understood why lately Rena had been coming home through the window so happy. And why she and Wela then spent hours whispering and laughing in bed.

"He calls me Sarenka – his little doe," she'd once heard Rena say.

A week later, when her daughter packed two white blouses, two black skirts and underwear into a suitcase Rywka didn't protest. It'd be no use anyway. It was early in the morning, and Rena clearly wanted to get going before her father came back with the shopping.

"They'll be living in sin!" screamed Nathan, but at Rywka. "With his wife and children too, I suppose?! The shame of it!"

They only had Wela and Nusek left at home, each in their own bed, of course. To the youngest children it felt as if the flat had got bigger, the table in the kitchen was longer and wobblier, the wardrobe was deeper, the chest of drawers wider. As if the furniture were growing with them.

For Rywka, without Rudek, Salek, Hesio and Rena the flat on Goldhammer Street simply felt empty.

She wiped her eyes on a corner of her apron.

Lately it kept happening to her. For trifling reasons. All it took was for someone to whistle a jolly tune below the window. A seaside postcard gnawed by mice that an old Jew in a gabardine tried to press on her at the market. Wela's dress torn at the armhole. The thought of her hometown, Nisko.

Sometimes as she looked in the mirror at her long, grey hair, she caught herself thinking: Is that it? Is that all?

Only yesterday her mother in Nisko had been braiding her black curly hair into plaits. From morning to night her mother would follow her about, asking questions: What are you doing, child? Where are you going? Look out for...

Now Rywka could see her mother's glance in the mirror.

Another childhood emotion had come back to her too. Her parents would tell her to go to bed, but she'd refuse. It was a waste of time to sleep when she knew the day would never be repeated. She'd lie in bed with her eyes open. She was an only child who longed for siblings.

She had made this dream come true, but for her own children. So she did her best to leave them in peace and not torment them with questions.

She had left the family home in Nisko, just as they were now leaving their home on Goldhammer Street. Or maybe, as she thought now, she'd done it with even more determination and even more pain for her parents, without looking back. She had escaped to the city, the big city, which for her children was too small by now.

Nathan should understand that too.

For where did he see the "real life" he so often talked about? Only in New York? And where was it for the children? In Kraków? In Moscow? It was probably in a different place for each one.

And for her?

Hair goes grey everywhere, she thought.

Well, perhaps it had been happening more quickly in Tarnów of late.

Hesio was still detained in prison. On her visits it consoled her to see that he had good conditions. During the day, the political prisoners weren't locked in their cells. He was reading more than at liberty. He praised the prison library. He had learned to wash daily from head to foot with water from a single mug. As he said: the authorities take care of their enemies. Even their teeth. Once every three weeks they took him to the dentist, accompanied by a senior warden armed with a pistol of course, who in the waiting room genially advised him to give up on the communism.

But was it all the truth? Hesio was only seventeen. At liberty he never complained about anything either.

"When you're in difficulties and things get a little bit better," he'd said recently, "they instantly seem very good."

What was he talking about? Perhaps it was the joy he felt when his cellmate was transferred. The one who used Hesio's toothbrush every time Hesio went for interrogation. He didn't even try to hide the fact. Three times Hesio had come back and caught him red-handed.

The cellmate always answered his requests and threats by saying: "As a communist I'm opposed to personal property. Aren't you?"

Hesio found this more exhausting than the lengthy interrogations.

He'd lost weight.

Rywka and Lotka, his girlfriend, took parcels to the prison for him. Apart from food, in one of his letters he asked for seeds. At first they were sure it was communist secret code... But it wasn't. They were allowed to cultivate a small garden in there.

"The governor," explained Hesio when she went to visit, "was in prison himself during the partitions."

Rywka ran straight to the market for those seeds.

Recently, Rudek had come to Tarnów to talk to the judge's son. They'd gone to Wałowa Street for a beer at the restaurant adjoining the City Hotel.

Prices as high as in Kraków.

He'd let him win at billiards. After the second game and the third pint of beer Rudek learned that the most important thing was for Hesio to behave himself during the trial.

"No fooling around. Then he'll get a short sentence."

To finish the evening they each had a glass of Hungarian brandy.

"To your brother's health," said the judge's son unexpectedly. And he must have decided that was enough, because then he got up, without even pretending he'd pay for himself.

Rudek showed his mother the bill: expensive for Tarnów, but not for a judge's opinion.

Zawadowski was hopeful too. In the worst case they'd prove that Hesio belonged to an illegal organization, the Communist Party of Poland. He should be out soon. They wouldn't want to detain a minor, whose case was already the talk of the town.

These days the Stramers were known as "the communist family". Strangers kept knocking at their door from early morning. They weren't allowed to forget for an instant that their son was in prison. Nathan felt like a New York doorman. Well, with the basic difference that those guys didn't work for free.

Pilgrimages of young people kept coming to 20 Goldhammer Street to ask what to do to become a communist.

"Fall on your head," Nathan would say, shutting the door in their faces.

Some managed to wink at him conspiratorially, others handed him a piece of paper with their address. Whatever he said, they were sure he was part of the conspiracy too. After all, he'd raised his son to be a communist. They went on trying to send their greetings to Hesio through the closed door and windows.

"Get out!" shouted Nathan to the entire yard.

Maybe he should start collecting money from them for Party registration fees? But no.

They'd scare away the lunchers too.

There were already narks lurking under the windows. Even little Wela had seen Lieutenant Kania, who went after communists all over Tarnów. She'd heard them calling him "the pig's head". That was enough for her to recognize him.

"They'll set the inspectors on us," worried Rywka. "Check why we serve lunches without a licence."

Late at night they heard a knock. This time the "comrades" had gone too far. They should all be locked up. Time to deal with them!

Nathan yanked the door open, shouting: "Who the hell is…" but he broke off, for there on the threshold stood elegant Mr Szpilman, owner of the Little Bee candle factory, with a silk handkerchief in the pocket of his navy-blue jacket.

"I hope I'm not disturbing you?" he asked at the sight of Nathan holding his belt.

"Please come in. Be our guest."

"I'll only take a moment of your time."

XVI

NATHAN

THE DAY BEFORE THE TRIAL, they were all sitting at the kitchen table, as in the past. The only one missing was Hesio, for whose sake they were gathered here. As ever, they were elbowing and interrupting each other.

Rywka was making coffee. She had bad forebodings. At least so she told them later; for the time being she didn't let it show, because she had five of her beloved children at the table.

She'd baked them a cheesecake with chocolate icing.

"Keep one piece for tomorrow," she asked.

Rudek was in a new, pin-striped suit, white shirt and tie. He had come to Tarnów straight from work, which he'd left earlier than usual, and had deliberately taken the next day off too. Each morning he went to the university (he had switched to the Law and Economics Faculty), and in the afternoons he worked as a clerk at the... Rywka couldn't remember the long name. Probably only Rudek and Salek were able to repeat it: the Central Board for the Sale of Candles in Eastern

Małopolska, the Dąbrowski Basin and the South-Western Congress.

And of course Mr Szpilman knew that name – with a single phone call he had arranged for Rudek to work there, the day after he had been to see them on Goldhammer Street and announced that he helped political prisoners and their relatives.

"So in actual fact why do you do that?" Nathan had asked.

Szpilman was careful not to mention that this time his son Karol, who was in love with Rena, had asked him to do it.

"Because I can," he said. "And I'm a socialist."

The owner of a factory was a socialist? Of course Nathan had heard it before – there'd been rumours in Tarnów for ages that Szpilman was squandering the family fortune, but he wanted to make sure, because in America it would be unthinkable. There a capitalist-socialist was destined to go bankrupt.

Especially now, during the crisis, when – as Ben wrote to him in his letters – life had become dangerous, even in the best districts. People went around with their heads raised to get out of the way in time. Guys in suits kept falling out of the windows of skyscrapers after losing everything from one day to the next. It was like an Egyptian plague.

The world was changing. Even the one across the ocean.

Why don't they jump off bridges into the river Hudson? Nathan asked his brother in a letter, because he'd remembered that when he was in New York that was how they did it.

As soon as I get the opportunity I'll ask, Ben had replied.

Now Salek was reassuring his parents that they needn't be mistrustful, Szpilman knew what he was doing.

"Marx was supported financially by his friend Friedrich

Engels, whose father owned a factory, and a far bigger one than the Little Bee in Tarnów," said Salek, looking around his audience to see if his words were making the right impression.

"To hell with him," remarked Nathan in English, and since as usual nobody could understand, he translated: "Szpilman is throwing his money down the drain."

"Worse," said Rudek, smiling. "He's sending it up in smoke."

Nathan clapped his oldest son on the shoulder and felt he could just as well be acclaiming Ben, who might also calmly say something of the kind.

He rarely had such thoughts, and now, seeing the children sitting at the table, it flashed through his mind that people were never regarded in isolation. There was always someone else standing behind them, to one side, or in front. With similar hair, eyes and gestures. For as long as he could remember, his father had always compared him with Ben, in those days still Beniamin. And now here was Nathan, comparing his own children to each other and to the rest of the family.

At the same time his fingers could feel that his son's suit was made of decent, solid fabric. He'd like to have one the same. With much shorter trousers, of course, but the jacket would have to be just as broad in the shoulders.

How lucky that unlike Salek, Hesio and even Rena, at least their first-born wasn't mixed up in communism. Nathan was sure he deserved the credit for that. After all, who had given him the name Rudolf? In honour of the Habsburg family and Imperial-Royal Austria-Hungary, in honour of happy times.

But just a moment. Were they really all that good and happy? In that case why had Ben, followed by his younger brother Nathan, sailed away to America?

And why was the Austro-Hungarian monarchy referred to nowadays as an "experimental station for the end of the world"? Nathan didn't follow the conversations at table closely, but he had actually heard Salek say these words. And they had hurt his feelings.

HESIO

"Coffee?"

Rywka began to fill the mugs, while Rena and Wela carried them to the table.

They couldn't have known that at the same time Hesio was being taken from his cell for a routine visit to the dentist.

"So you'll look presentable and smile nicely in the courtroom," said the warden, patting him on the back.

At Goldhammer Street they carefully avoided conversations about the main subject of gossip in Tarnów these days, which was the wife and two children the lawyer had left for the young Jewish woman.

The sympathy and compassion of the entire city, as well as the outrage and insults, were aimed in a predictable direction.

"We just have to wait a few weeks," Zawadowski consoled Rena, "until they find themselves somebody new."

"No, that's not the point." Almost every night Rena dreamed about his abandoned family.

Last night Mrs Zawadowska had run out of a burning house. Wanting to save her, Rena had tried to put out her burning dress. But at the sight of her Zawadowski's wife had turned around and run back into the fire. Rena woke up.

Now, at home with the others, she was doing her best to think about something else. She questioned Rudek about the girl he'd been seeing in Kraków.

She wanted to know how they'd met.

"On the train to Tarnów," said Rudek. "She was in the same compartment, sitting opposite."

"And you fell in love?" asked Wela hopefully. "At first sight?"

"Well, I don't know, because she had her eyes closed, she was asleep. But six months later we met on the train again."

"And that's when it happened?"

Wela imagined her brother travelling the same route for months on end (sitting in the same seat in the same compartment) in the hope of meeting the sleeping princess again.

As the amused Rudek was kissing his sister on the head, Hesio and the warden were leaving the prison building.

"How old is she?" asked Nathan, whose first concern was actually what her father did, secondly whether there were any inherited diseases in her family, and only in third place her age.

So he'd started at the end.

"She's my age," said Rudek, and as Nathan had made a face as if he couldn't remember how old his oldest son was, added: "Twenty-four."

"I like that," said Nathan, casting a long look at Rena, who pretended not to notice.

Meanwhile, Hesio and the warder had rapidly walked to Bernardyńska Street, where the dentist's surgery was located at number sixteen.

"And what is the lucky girl's name?" asked Rywka, smiling at Rudek; she was curious to know if the girl was Jewish.

And had they gone to bed together yet?

183

"Ruth."

By the tone in which he said it, she knew: they had. Maybe she was pregnant? And that was that.

"Rudek and Ruth! Rudek and Ruth!", cried Wela in delight, all but folding her hands in a gesture she'd seen the actresses make in American movies. "Lovely."

And her mind was filled not just with the idea that they were a perfect match, but with the image of their wedding ceremony and the American party that would follow. As on the screen at the Daydream cinema, she could see herself catching the bouquet thrown backwards by the bride.

Hesio and the warder entered the villa where on the first floor the dentist received his patients.

"Is it a serious relationship?" continued Nathan, gradually clearing the way for questions about the health of Ruth's parents and her father's income.

Rudek thought for a while.

"Well, the interrogation's over," he said, got up and winked at Wela.

At the very same moment, Hesio turned around on the landing and pushed the warder, who flew down the steep stairs, shouting and cursing, while his prisoner jumped out of the window.

Less than half an hour later the police knocked at Goldhammer Street. They shoved Nathan aside in the doorway. They ran into the flat, trailing mud after them.

"Where have you hidden him?"

Nusek, until now invisible, silent, shielded by his older brothers, hid even more effectively, behind his father's chair. Wela burrowed into her mother's apron.

The policemen searched the floor for traces of blood, because despite a twisted ankle, the warder had managed to fire two shots after the runaway. They refused to say more. For the good of the investigation.

On the day of his escape Hesio walked twenty kilometres to the village of Biała.

He didn't run to avoid prompting suspicion. In the darkness no one could recognize how he was dressed. He marched briskly down the surfaced road, feeling as if something were carrying him along.

Lately in Tarnów you could be fined for walking in the roadway. Who knew? Maybe on the roads outside the city too? Better not risk it.

A good thing this autumn is warm, he kept telling himself. In winter I wouldn't manage to cross the snow in these thin shoes.

Gradually he started to relax, and it slowly dawned on him what he had actually done.

At the thought of the consequences first his neck went stiff, and then his legs began to tremble at the knees.

Have I screwed up, or what? he thought, shaking his head but walking onwards.

When would he see Lotka? His parents? His siblings?

How would they react to what he'd done? He knew that Goldhammer Street was the last place where he could show up now.

He'd have given a lot to see the face of cowardly old Wachtel when he found out how brave his pupil had turned out to be.

But in fact he'd have given even more to reverse time. Maybe he should turn around and hand himself in to the police? It's pointless, I won't erase what I've done that way. And what will my Tarnów comrades think of me?

He also felt bad about the old warder, whom in prison he'd come to like. They shared an enjoyment of political bantering. It was no accident that the warder wore a handlebar moustache in the style of Piłsudski, who was the main topic of their debates.

"He's a bloodthirsty dictator," Hesio would start by mentioning the May coup d'état and persecution of the opposition, not just the communists.

The warder let that slide. But soon he would come back to the topic with his own opinion: "He's our greatest national hero. He fought and won independence for Poland."

And as an incentive he'd add: "The marshal was a socialist in his youth as well, and he was in prison. And he has nothing to do with the Jews."

Hesio would shrug and reply: "In your place I'd shave off that moustache."

Each one stood by his heroes.

The warder always had the last word: "Do as you should, and what will be will be."

On the landing at the dentist's villa Hesio had only meant to push the old man aside to reach the open window; he hadn't expected him to fall straight down the stairs. His first instinct was to run down after him. But it was too late.

As they say at Party meetings: "Where timber's chopped, woodchips fly."

Incidentally, the dark forest surrounding the road looked a bit scary.

The warder can't have been too badly bruised. After all, he'd come outside and shouted: "Stop, or I'll shoot."

But his pistol must have jammed, because Hesio only heard the first shot after turning into a side street.

In the moonlight he could see some village buildings. Which number was this? He wasn't exactly going to go and ask the headman.

Some of his classmates could afford to go on vacation. In summer they went to the countryside with their parents. For a breath of fresh air, as their mothers put it. They'd rent a house from a peasant farmer, who for the time of their stay would move his family into the barn. For an extra fee the peasant fed the visitors and drove them to the riverside.

Sometimes the host's and the holidaymakers' children knew each other from school.

His classmates would return to the city with stories about village girls wandering among the wheat fields in nothing but headscarves. About rolling in the hay with them. But definitely not at this time of year, when the crops had already been harvested.

He wondered where Lotka's family went on holiday. Probably abroad – Berlin, Vienna, Paris. And to the Swiss resorts in winter. Hesio should run off there. Best of all with her.

But you escape to where you can, not where you'd like. Just as wanting to go on holiday isn't enough to be able to do it. Further proof of the fact that social existence determines consciousness.

He was hungry.

In the dark all the wooden cottages looked the same. There were no lights burning in any windows; the village had already gone to sleep.

"We go to bed and get up with the hens." Hesio remembered what Flounder used to say, seeing nothing comical about it, unlike their classmates, who'd answer him with: "In the city we do that with women."

So which of these cottages was home to the future priest and his family?

XVII

RYWKA

As if Rywka didn't have enough troubles, Nusek was the first of the siblings to refuse to study. Since Hesio's escape and trial he had stopped trying at all. He'd even resigned from the shomers. He still wasn't covering his own school costs – where would he get the money? Was he going to give tutorials on loitering in town with his (in Nusek's words) "bosom pal" Lolek Szpeda?!

Who is a worse influence on whom? thought Rywka. They're so restless they double before your eyes. It's an explosive mixture.

As they said themselves, Nusek and Lolek were attracted to each other like two magnets. In Rywka's view, it was more that they were dragging each other to the bottom like two stones. Or to put it another way, they acted on each other like two medicines that shouldn't be taken simultaneously. The immediate side effects were truancy and dreadful grades.

What was more, this just made them laugh like two little weasels.

And they both said studying was a waste of time.

These moments reminded Rywka how badly her three older sons were needed at home. How badly she missed them.

Salek's departure for Kraków, which she'd been fearing throughout the year before, vanished in the shadow of Hesio's arrest, escape and trial. One day she and Nathan, Rena, Wela and Nusek had simply escorted Salek and his suitcase to the train. Rywka felt calm about him. She knew Rudek would be waiting for him at the station in Kraków.

What did she feel as the train moved off? It was probably envy. She envied those who had yet to discover Salek in Kraków.

That was how he used to encourage his siblings to read the books he suggested: "I envy you the joy of discovering it."

But when exactly had he gone? The last few days, weeks and months had piled on top of each other.

She remembered how brilliantly Salek had passed his final exams. How he'd asked her if he should go away to college now. Whether she'd cope without him.

He must still have been at home when the trial took place, because he'd hugged her in the courtroom when the verdict was announced. Or maybe he'd come specially from Kraków that day? As he was led away, Hesio had turned to Salek and Rudek and called: "MOF?"

What did he mean?

And so another bed in the flat was unoccupied. She took the bedding off it, nothing more. Let it stay where it is. And wait too.

Four years will pass quickly.

On their return home from the hearing Nathan had undressed and gone to bed. He hadn't got up for several days. Whereas Rywka kept waking in the night and couldn't sleep.

She knew that now she must focus on the youngest two. On Wela, and especially Nusek; the more he needed her, the less he showed it. Or so she kept telling herself at difficult moments. It worried her that at times she ran out of patience.

For years, whenever Nathan had a row with Rudek, Salek or Hesio, she had tried to justify him by telling herself: If you have six children, can you love them all equally?

He saw it, or at least explained it to her a different way.

"Someone in the family has to take on this thankless task," he'd say, with a reverent look on his face, referring to screaming at the children and thrashing them. "In our case it fell to me."

But have I been equally fair to all of them? thought Rywka.

For is it Nusek's fault that he's different from his older brothers?

"The least blessed with something between the ears," as Rudek had once said of him in anger.

Or perhaps Nusek is trying to draw attention to himself this way?

"So what are you going to do?" asked Rywka at last. "What isn't a waste of your time?"

"We want to be electricians," said Nusek and Lolek, proudly looking at each other. "It's a profession with a future."

Nathan's reaction surprised her more than their answer. He didn't grab his belt, he didn't scream in American, he just stood there calmly and smiled.

He's plainly growing old. Or he knows something about electricity.

"I was like that too," he told Rywka, but only that night at bedtime.

Is he justifying Nusek or himself? That was her immediate response.

Because now it was just Nathan and Nusek, the only males still at home, who weren't earning. Even Wela ran about the city giving tutorials in Polish and Latin. So far, she was teaching three of her classmates. For a zloty an hour. That was a decent fee. In Tarnów the home-workers who took in sewing were paid two zlotys for a whole day's work.

XVIII

HESIO

FEELING PLEASED WITH HIMSELF, once again Hesio read the *Illustrated Daily Courier* with his picture from the trial on the front page.

It described how he'd hidden in the village of Biała at the home of a schoolmate, most probably an accomplice, a *suspect individual*, whose sudden progress in his studies had prompted the justified suspicions of his teachers at school. Once notified, the police organized a manhunt (in reality, a single policeman had turned up on a bicycle – it made Hesio smile), but the fugitive had managed to slip away to the nearby woods. Next day his luck ran out. He was recognized and caught by Lieutenant Kania at Tarnów station, just as he was boarding a train to Kraków.

The article ended with the comment: *Now the communist Hersz-Cwi Stramer will sit in prison, contemplating his foolishness.*

And indeed that was what he was doing. Why exactly had he gone to the station? He didn't even have the money for a platform ticket. He might have guessed the "pig's head" would be waiting for him there. He might just as well have gone to Goldhammer Street, to Lotka, or straight to the police station.

Did I let myself be caught on purpose? he questioned himself. And why on earth did I escape at all?

In the newspapers brought to his cell by the new warder – small and clean-shaven, with fair hair fashionably combed back – there was hardly a word about his fortnight in the village.

A pity.

There was nothing about the poverty of the illiterate peasants of Biała, or the wealth of Count Romer, his beautiful palace, garden and fish ponds.

He hummed a song he'd heard on one of the very first days, sung by Flounder's father.

The squire's ample stores
Are fuller than you think,
He'll unlock the cellar doors
And give us all a drink.

If Hesio had written the article, he'd have started with that. But history is written by the victors…

Then he'd have described the peasants' one and only entertainment. Their Sunday races after church. There was no church in Biała itself. The peasants had to drive to Brzozówka. And after Mass they raced each other down the highway to the inn. As they whipped the horses' rumps with all their might, the carts with woven wicker sides creaked and tilted dangerously on the turns, leaving a trail of dust and people screaming as they fled onto the verges.

But even more dangerous were the races that came later, from the tavern back to Biała. After dark. Barely conscious, the drivers would grab hold of the reins. The horses would trip over stones and the carts would collide. Hesio knew this from Flounder's stories. Once in winter one of the carters had had an accident and fell asleep in the snow; when he woke next morning, all his fingers were frostbitten. The horse was wiser and ran off.

Hesio slept in the barn. He knew that some people don't feel at home anywhere. His father, for instance. And that he, Hesio, was the opposite. Wherever he happened to be, he could always cope, even in prison. He liked to think of himself that way. But why was he having to prove it in a barn that stank of cow and horse shit?

They told Flounder's parents he'd come for a few days to help their son with his studies. Did they believe it? He didn't care. He just wanted to lie down and go to sleep. But on the first night the straw got into every fold of his clothes, tickling him, and the animals just the other side of the collapsing wooden fence were restless until dawn.

To get to sleep, he breathed through his mouth and tried to imagine that instead of hens running around the place, he was being visited by peasant girls with fancily braided thick blond plaits that they undid specially for him. Even more emancipated than Lotka. Simple girls, who don't know what shame is.

Somehow he couldn't imagine Lotka in the barn.

"Calm down, Kraków wasn't built in a day," he consoled himself with Rudek's new saying, which, like all the previous ones, had instantly caught on within the family.

During the day he grazed the cows and waited for Flounder to come home from school. Then in the poor kitchen, only slightly larger and – apart from the smell of damp to which he quickly grew accustomed – much the same as the one on Goldhammer Street, he really did help his friend with his lessons. And gave him spelling tests, to look authentic in the eyes of Flounder's parents, who watched with delight as in crooked letters their son wrote "burd" instead of "bird" for the umpteenth time.

Were they already imagining him in a dog collar?

With flushed cheeks and a headscarf that emphasized the blue of her eyes, Flounder's mother poured them milk. Hesio also adored the curd cheese she made in a stoneware pot and stored in the vestibule.

"Drink it while it's hot."

Then she'd cover her own mouth to show she shouldn't disturb them. Her hand was swollen from making butter with a plunger in a wooden churn.

Meanwhile Flounder's father would be sitting at the table, talking to himself aloud. "The parish scribe's getting a rival, ain't he? Flounder's son! You can see that with the naked eye. It paid off to provide for the laddie."

With every day in the village Flounder's parents reminded Hesio more and more of his own.

If I'd been born and brought up in Biała, would I be the same as their son? he wondered. Does social existence always determine consciousness?

And where were the cruel peasants hiding, the ones their grandmother in Nisko used to frighten them with when they were little? She'd told them they would come into the cities to loot the Jewish shops, beat up the Jews and slash the bellies of the pregnant Jewish women.

Holding hands, the Stramer siblings listened to this with mouths agape.

"In one case they replaced the baby with a live cat and sewed up the woman's belly."

What happened? To the woman, and to the cat? Grandma never got to the end of the story.

"Mama!" Rywka interrupted her. "That's enough!"

"But it happened, daughter."

"Long ago, and it's not true."

Next day their mother took them home to Tarnów.

Now it was hard to believe those stories.

At any rate, over two weeks in the village Hesio never met anyone like that. Unless they were hiding, just as he was? Or perhaps it was all fairy tales to frighten Jewish children?

Of course the peasants of Biała regarded him as an outsider, but how else would they look at him? No one came after him with a pitchfork.

In fact, as he soon discovered, there were three Jewish families living a quiet life in the village. One leased a tavern, another ran a shop, and the third had a small farm.

One sunny day he met the son of the third family, who with a book in his hand was grazing cows in the pasture near Hesio.

"What are you reading?" he asked in Polish, just in case.

Although the boy's hair was the colour of straw, Hesio was sure he could just as well have addressed him in Yiddish too.

But how old might he be? Ten at most.

Hesio was still of an age when he had no trouble telling precisely who was nine, who was ten, and who was eleven years old.

The boy showed him the cover of an English-Polish dictionary.

"I've got an uncle in America," he explained, as if to excuse himself.

"So have I," replied Hesio, and it occurred to him that he'd never met Ben.

Maybe he should change that and run away to find him in New York? At once he could see the disgusted faces of his Tarnów comrades.

Max Kierbel was still at junior school, but when the sun began to set and they both got up to pull out the stakes securing the cows, he proved to be not much smaller than Hesio.

His curly blond hair definitely gave him several extra centimetres.

"Hey, kid!" Hesio called after him. "You don't have anything else to read at home, do you?"

The three cows knew the way to the Flounders' farm better than Hesio did. They walked patiently ahead of him, lethargically flicking off flies with their tails. They were calm, because unlike Hesio, they knew what lay ahead of them. The evening milking, and then sleep. And the same thing again tomorrow. Hesio had only once seen them get upset.

It was when for a lark Flounder pulled them by the udders and squirted milk against the wooden walls of the barn. They had kicked with their hind legs and threateningly tossed their horns.

"Leave them alone," said Hesio.

"You don't know," said Flounder, smiling mysteriously, "what the others do to theirs."

And he demonstrated by rhythmically moving his hips.

At supper, straight after the communal prayer that Hesio recited no worse than the others by now, he began to tell them about his encounter with Max.

"Doesn't he look too much like the count?" old Flounder interrupted him with a laugh.

Hesio hadn't seen Count Romer yet. And thought it better not to show himself to him of all people. He might have heard or read something about Hesio's escape.

"Like two peas in a pod," old Flounder answered himself.

And his son illustrated with gestures under the table how this might have come about.

Hesio inevitably began looking for similarities between Flounder and his father. Was it from him that Flounder had inherited the famous twenty-five centimetres?

The very thought was enough for old Flounder to grow (a little) in his eyes. Unless this was another of the count's doings.

"Beauty of an angel, nature of a devil," as Flounder's mother said of the count.

Next day, Max brought him a book. On the cover was the word *Titanic* in large letters, a drawing of a ship and the inviting subtitle: *Not a troop of cavalleros, but in the end they died like heroes.*

"You won't destroy it?"

It was probably still lying in the barn, buried in the straw.

Now, as he sat behind bars in custody he felt like the passengers on the *Titanic*. The ones in third class. For whom there weren't enough life jackets, blankets and places in the lifeboats. They had less of a chance than the first-class passengers' dogs.

But apparently it had a pleasant aspect too. They stopped fighting. Nothing depended on them anymore. Gradually they felt blissful.

And Hesio too felt the same way now.

XIX

WELA

Like everything nowadays, school was getting more expensive; this year the fees were sixty zlotys a month. Luckily Wela was such a good pupil that she had a discount and paid (for herself, of course) half that sum.

Today after lessons she came home trembling.

Incidentally, Rywka had noticed long ago that her boys and girls came back from school in different moods. As soon as they entered the house, the boys dropped their schoolbags, cursed the teachers or their classmates, and usually told her everything without being asked. The girls, or at least Wela, were the exact opposite.

What had happened?

Rywka quietly put the water on to boil for some ersatz coffee. She knew that the fewer questions she asked, the more she'd find out. She had loathed the way her mother would bombard her with questions whenever she came home. Wela nervously sipped her coffee. Finally she began to tell her story. Chaotically and in monosyllables. At first Rywka couldn't understand what dreadful event had occurred in the Latin lesson.

"One thing at a time, Wela," she asked. "So Mania, whom you tutor, was called to the blackboard and gave the wrong answer, yes?"

Wela nodded.

"She got it all in a muddle. But before the teacher had given her an F, she told me off in front of the whole class!"

"What did she say?"

Wela took a deep breath.

"She said, 'Well, Miss Stramer,' and wagged a finger at me. 'Is that how you teach?!'"

As she spoke, Wela had tears in her eyes, and Rywka had to bite her lower lip to stop herself from smiling.

"She found no fault with herself," Wela finished.

And at once began to feel a bit better.

When she'd finished her coffee, Rywka put a few groszy in her hand to buy herself fifty grams of ham and a roll. It wasn't kosher, but it was an effective form of consolation. Wela was even more fond of ham than of Italian ice cream from Pudelski's café.

It's lucky her religious grandparents in Nisko don't know about it, thought Rywka.

"Thank you, Mama."

But in fact it was Rywka who should have thanked her, because she stopped worrying for a while, she smiled, and for the first time since Hesio's escape she actually laughed.

"Well, Miss Stramer," she repeated to herself softly as she waved to Wela through the kitchen window, already on her way down the street to the butcher's. "Is that how you teach?'

She sat down by the kitchen stove and wiped her face on her apron.

Little Salek had once asked her why people more often cry at weddings than at funerals. For years afterwards she'd proudly repeated her son's words.

They came back to her now, and made her laugh too. She couldn't stop herself. She laughed louder and louder, occasionally wiping away the tears with a corner of her apron.

XX

SALEK

IN AN OVERSIZED COAT borrowed from Rudek with the collar raised, and in an ash-grey hat with the brim turned down, Salek didn't look like a revolutionary activist. He didn't even look like a third-year philosophy student at the Jagiellonian University.

That was all right, because he was travelling as a Party district organizer.

Reflected in the windowpane, set against the escaping countryside, he looked more like his father now. At any rate, like an ordinary passenger on the train to Częstochowa who wouldn't catch the tired eyes of the early-morning travellers and conductors.

And that was the point.

So far for lectures he'd gone no further than the small town of Rybnik, but even there on leaving the station he had managed to get lost on the way to the "arrival point".

He only had to start pondering academic ontological dilemmas, considering the problems of dialectic materialism, or dreaming about Irka. And soon he'd be looking around himself, without a clue where he was.

He comforted himself that he wasn't the first to have this problem. Moses must have been bad at finding his way too, since it took him forty years to lead the Jews across the desert, which wasn't all that big on the map.

So how did Rudek manage never to get lost?

"When it comes to finding your way," he once told Salek, "you're a tabula rasa."

It was just the same in Kraków, although Salek had lived there for three years. How often he'd gone round and round the Marketplace, back and forth, passing the Cloth Hall and St Mary's Basilica, never knowing which way to leave it to reach the university, Rudek's place or Irka's parents' house.

After a couple of circuits he was no longer sure which direction he had come from either.

To make matters worse, sometimes he was being tailed by the narks – familiar to all the Kraków activists, Kapusta and Macioł.

Salek told Irka about it during one of their first conversations.

"They probably thought you were trying to lose them," she said, laughing.

Now and then in the Kraków Marketplace Salek had turned around and cast them helpless glances, causing the narks to fix their eyes on their newspapers or the nearest shop window.

"Once I was tempted to ask for their help," he admitted.

"A great idea," said Irka, adjusting Salek's round-framed glasses as they slid down his nose. "They're always happy to help communists."

And she added that in Kraków it was easiest to lose a tail between two and three in the afternoon. Because that was when the agents had their lunch break. At first he thought Irka was making fun of him again, but it soon turned out to be true.

Later on, they often broke free of the narks together, and ran, holding hands, through gateways and courtyards, or down steep, narrow alleys that Irka knew well. Not because they were "going to do a job", but they simply didn't want to be spied on while kissing on a bench in Planty Park or in the meadow next to Jordan's Park.

It was Salek's first trip to Częstochowa. Outside the window, some of the villages looked as if they'd come from nineteenth-century photographs. Wooden cottages, dishevelled peasants in dirty sheepskin coats, children in oversized boots. All he needed was Irka and her camera. What had changed since those days? The partitions had ended, Poland had regained independence, the revolution had triumphed in Russia. But in these people's lives?

Thinking about it, he always had doubts. Poland was an agricultural country, after all. The opposite of Germany, which was mostly industrial and as a result, according to Marx, "doomed" to the outbreak of socialist revolution. But in Poland it was no accident that the Party was trying to bewitch reality by writing on the flags and leaflets "Worker-Peasant Alliance".

Salek knew the time of the meeting and the address of the "arrival point" where he was to leave his things and stay the night. He also knew his talk by heart (*A common front: the current political situation as proof that only communism is capable of stopping world fascism*), and merely reminded himself of the password he was to give when they opened the door: "I bring greetings from home."

To which the host (or maybe hostess?) was to reply: "How is mother's health?"

Full-on conspiracy.

But unfortunately Salek only had to introduce himself and the questions began. He'd been through it many times. Was it you that escaped from prison? How did you trick the guards? How did you dig the tunnel? How did you manage to hide for so long at liberty?

Then the mild disappointment: Ah, so it was your brother, of course. Without noticing, they'd address him informally, as if talking to a child. Your older brother, presumably?

Salek would shake his head.

And see the revolutionary zeal fading in their eyes.

Anyway, the most incredible stories were told about Hesio, who still had a year left of his four-year sentence. Despite being in handcuffs, he'd got the better of three armed warders. While in hiding he hadn't stopped agitating – he'd read the *Communist Manifesto* aloud to the peasants working in the fields. And "by a means known only to himself" he had eluded the police dragnet that had surrounded the entire village so tightly that a pin couldn't have slipped through. Meanwhile he had disappeared like a needle in a haystack.

A hero of our times.

Every movement needs them, Salek explained it to himself. To realize that, you only had to go into the nearest church and see the fellow nailed to the cross in there.

He remembered the first time he'd seen the figure on the cross at the home of a pal from the yard. "Poor man. What happened to him?" he'd wondered.

"Rudek, is it true we did that to him?" he'd asked at bedtime.

And now the lot had fallen to their brother…

For this reason among others – thought if he were going to be entirely frank with himself, just for this one – Salek decided to adopt an alias. He had announced this at yesterday's meeting of the CPP's District Agitprop Unit, at six in the morning on Garncarska Street, where Schmaltzbach, the dentist, lived.

"That will be safer," he'd said.

Nobody questioned it and no one was surprised; some of the comrades changed their aliases on a weekly basis, and it was hard to keep up with them. They lost track of them themselves. At their meetings, Salek sometimes couldn't tell who was addressing whom.

He chose "Gustaw" from a list he'd made the day before the meeting. He had been hesitating over "Fred" or "Zygmunt".

This wasn't the game it had been on St Marcin's Peak in Tarnów.

In the jolting train to Częstochowa Salek recalled scenes from the meeting.

They had talked about intra-organizational work, about issuing new appeals and plastering the city in posters to mark the anniversary of the October Revolution. Someone suggested drawing a commemorative postcard, photographing it and then enlarging and duplicating it, but the idea was rejected for lack of resources.

Schmaltzbach the dentist (alias "Heniek"), from one week to the next an ever more nervous host, kept interrupting the others to say: "Be quieter. Walls have ears."

Irka had arrived late, in a dark-blue beret and a light overcoat. Under it she wore a simple navy-blue, knee-length dress.

The meeting was chaired by the secretary, "Majewski", who had recently returned from the Soviet Union. He alone did not sit huddled on the floor, but in the dentist's chair, gently leaning back against the mobile headrest. Now he got up and began his speech with a detailed plan for infiltrating the milieu of army officers.

"I shall apply to headquarters to assign us two clever young women for the Kraków district…"

"But not disgraced communist women," put in Perla, alias "Mańka", whom Salek often saw at the university. "And not Jewish girls!"

"We must recruit Polish women," agreed "Majewski". "So their involvement with the officers won't prompt suspicion. They'll also help to establish cells at workshops and factories producing for the army. That's essential for performing acts of sabotage if Poland were to attack the Soviet Union."

"What form would this sabotage take?" wondered the senior metalworker with a neatly trimmed white moustache who was sitting beside Salek.

"Wincenty" was a legend, a veteran of the 1905 revolution.

The story was that for years he had consistently refused promotion to master craftsman or even to foreman. So the workers at the factory would know that he couldn't be bought by anyone. That he served the revolution, not the capitalists. Not everyone believed this story – it didn't seem true to life at all.

"Wincenty" was also known for grabbing young female comrades by the knees.

"We shall contaminate the gunpowder and the lubricants used for military means of transport. We'll use a special substance that destroys the axles and bearings in a matter of days. Lorries, cars, cannon and other vehicles will be unfit for use."

"Majewski" pretended not to hear "Wincenty's" next question about the name of the substance, and added: "But if anything happens, don't worry, comrades. The Party's feelers reach all the way to general staff."

Just then Irka waved at Salek with her palm open. She was wearing his engagement ring. Salek bit his lip to stop himself from smiling.

"Majewski" was assigning the tasks. He announced that tomorrow "Gustaw" was to travel to Częstochowa to give a talk. Salek didn't immediately realize that this was aimed at him, but soon he was glancing sadly at Irka. He wouldn't be able to come to lunch at her parents' house.

Before sinking back into the dentist's chair "Majewski" addressed the tram driver, Gadomski.

"Watch out," he said, theatrically pointing a finger at him. "You're at risk of a charge of immoral conduct."

"What do you mean?!" Gadomski all but stood up from the floor. He was not much taller than Salek. He spread his hands, as if surrendering. "What for?"

He looked around the room.

Does the Party know that much about me too? thought Salek.

"For infecting your female comrades," said "Majewski".

Tears came to Gadomski's eyes and he didn't answer.

"That's your final warning," said "Majewski", wagging a finger at him again.

Last to speak was the dentist. And it was more like a whisper. He was afraid of leaks. He didn't want to lose his patients. Any loud noise in the street already made his hands shake, which greatly complicated his work and could end in tragedy. The day after the previous meeting he'd had a visit from three policemen who had asked if a murder had taken place in his dental surgery.

Of course he denied it, but he almost had a heart attack. They had poked around the surgery, and then left. "You can see for yourselves what things are coming to."

As a result, he was asking them to find a new site for future meetings.

Before leaving they held the traditional collection for the Party. Salek tossed in a zloty, Irka gave two. But the tin was different from usual. Its shape reminded both of them of the keren kayemet, meaning the tin boxes that hung in many Jewish homes. Coins were tossed into them to buy "the land once promised to Abraham by God" from its Arab owners. Maybe it simply was one of those tins, that someone had brought from home? Had they emptied out its contents beforehand?

As ever, to avoid prompting suspicion, they left one at a time, at two or three-minute intervals. Salek left before Irka and waited for her on a bench at the tram stop. He liked his new alias. And he liked himself in it too. What about Irka? Soon she was sitting beside him.

Now on the train Salek was gazing at "Gustaw's" reflection in the window. A bit like looking at a stranger, or the hero of a novel. Or maybe by now "Gustaw" was looking at Salek? he thought.

"Are you that fond of Mickiewicz?" Irka had asked yesterday at the tram stop. "So you could be Konrad too?" Gustaw, also known as Konrad, was the hero of Mickiewicz's epic drama, *Forefathers' Eve*.

He was feeling warm. He took off his hat and unbuttoned Rudek's thick coat.

Since Rudek had become a father, Salek, who had been living with him and Ruth, had moved out to avoid burdening them any longer (and to make room for the baby's cot and a nanny). Rudek had helped him to find a cheap flat in Kazimierz. Two rooms in a basement, like in a story by Orzeszkowa. He shared it with a friend of Rudek's from Tarnów, Benek Laubhart, who was visited by young women almost every night.

"How do you do it?" asked Salek, impressed.

After all, he could hear everything through the thin wall, and had to admit that Benek was a genuine success in bed.

Benek just shrugged.

"Go on, tell me..."

"I like girls and I'm not choosy," he replied. "I take whatever comes along. One day it's a princess, the next it's a dog."

That was his favourite saying. Some said: "Fortune is fickle", others said: "Some you win, some you lose", but Benek always said: "One day it's a princess, the next it's a dog".

In Kraków Benek was supported by the parents of his fiancée from Tarnów, who also paid for his share of the flat. Of course Salek knew who she was – Franka was the older sister of Lotka, Hesio's girlfriend.

Small and stooping, she wore spectacles and could have been Rudek's age. "To her and my misfortune she hasn't much in common with her younger sister," Benek complained. "But plenty in common with her famous uncle, Karol Radek."

Salek remembered hearing people say she'd grow up to be a famous pianist. But nothing of the kind had happened.

'When she sits at the piano it's better to leave the house," said Benek, blocking his ears at the mere memory.

After her final school exams, Franka's father had sent her to Vienna, to a foreign trade college. And when she finished that, he told her to go to Florence and enrol for any course at all.

"Lots of wealthy families do that," Rudek explained to Salek. "After a master's degree abroad they send their children to Italy for a while. Because in Italian the word 'master' is 'dottore'. You can check in the dictionary. For instance, all you have to do in Florence is to sign up for any college, and they'll give you a piece of paper saying you're a 'dottore'. And then you can come back to Tarnów with the academic title 'doctor'."

So these days Franka was an accountant at the firm owned by her father, who in the presence of his clients and employees never addressed her as anything but "my dear Doctor Goldberg".

"She should be glad she has a job at all," said Rudek. "Others people I know, mostly after a law degree, are happy to be invited for coffee and a cake for forty groszy."

Once a week Franka sent Benek a food parcel (which, admittedly, he readily shared with Salek).

"And that's the best thing about her," Benek told him.

"You're a swine," replied Salek.

"If you don't like it, don't eat it."

"One day it'll end badly. You'll see."

Benek shook his head. His beautiful black fringe almost fell into his eyes.

"A common swindler," Salek disdainfully described him to Irka, and did everything to make sure they never met. Why take the risk? He knew best what effect Irka had on men, and Benek on women. Tall, handsome and agreeable, not just in conversation. On top of that, lately he'd gone about in a fashionable cycling cap, a gift from his future father-in-law, who had recently added these caps to his range of goods.

"I can get one for you if you like?" he suggested.

"No, thanks."

"At half price?"

After moving to Kraków Salek had started dressing like other people to avoid standing out. Sitting in a café on every second corner there were two philosophy students just like him, two office clerks like Rudek, not to mention the Beneks, with whom Kraków was awash, as if they had come here from all over Poland.

The same could be said of the young women: half of them looked like Marlena Dietrich, and the other half like Greta Garbo. Salek couldn't take his eyes off them.

"That's probably why I keep getting lost," he excused himself to Rudek.

The women often sat on their own, smoking cigarettes by the windows of cafés and restaurants. Salek also watched them at the cabaret to which Rudek had first taken him a year ago, to see a performance by Karol, his friend from Tarnów – the son of Mr Szpilman who owned the Little Bee candle factory.

Throughout high school in Tarnów Karol had gone about sadly in pursuit of Rena. Now on the stage in Kraków he sang with an artificial smile and a fake Jewish accent that nobody in his wealthy, assimilated family had had for decades.

I don't really know what's better, thought Salek as he listened to him.

> *What does a Jew need to feel all right?*
> *A Christmas tree up to the ceiling in height,*
> *A son in good health, studious and bright,*
> *That's what a Jew needs to feel all right.*

After the performance Karol came and joined them at their table. Rudek stood him a bottle of vodka. All the way from Lwów, from Baczewski's distillery. He probably wanted to repay old Szpilman for getting him his job at the Candles Syndicate. Salek only drank three shots, because next morning he had a Party meeting. Rudek too was getting up early for work, in spite of which he drank on a par with Karol, who didn't have as strong a head as he did.

"After each performance I get to know a girl more intimately," said Karol, winking. "If I go to work, I meet girls. If I don't go, I don't. Simple."

He observed the Stramer brothers' reaction, to see what impression his new life among the Kraków bohemia made on them.

"I stand them a glass of wine, and then we take a droshky to my place," said Karol, gesticulating as if he were still on stage. "I perform four times a week, which gives me on average sixteen women a month."

The Stramer brothers exchanged glances.

"All right," said Karol, standing up suddenly, almost overturning his chair.

He stood still for a while, as if waiting for applause.

"Time for a piss," he said at last.

"Why do you think he's telling us all this?" asked Salek once they were on their own at the table. "Does he want us to report to Rena that he's gained experience?"

And he began to laugh at his own joke. He didn't have as strong a head as his older brother either.

"The things Kraków does to people…" Besides Karol, Rudek was thinking of other friends too, including Benek Laubhart.

"But at least this one has inherited his father's talent for numbers. Sixteen is no mean figure."

Karol came back less sure of himself.

He confided that after the whole business with Rena, once she'd got involved with Zawadowski, he had promised himself never to fall in love again.

The Stramer brothers nodded sympathetically, for what were they supposed to do? Rudek took the opportunity to glance at his watch.

"But instead of that I'm constantly falling in love," said Karol sadly.

They drank up their vodka and left the cabaret.

Waiting for them on the way was the continuation of Karol's monologue, punctuated by singing – first they learned that people liked him, then that they didn't like him, and finally that Karol didn't care what people felt.

With relief, they saw him all the way home.

Together they walked across night-time Kraków. (Rudek preferred to go on foot, even if he could afford a droshky.) And they felt all right in each other's company. Like in the past, when as boys they'd run about Tarnów. Now too they didn't have to say anything. They gazed in the lamplight at the fine rain and the shining cobbles as they sidestepped puddles. Over the years a great deal had changed, inside them and around them, yet they were still walking along together. And Salek still looked up to his older brother, in whose presence he never had to worry about how to find his way. This nocturnal walk was what he remembered best about the entire evening, perhaps because Rudek surprised him with a nasty question about Irka.

At daybreak Salek was woken by shouting. Hungover, Rudek was having a go at his wife. This time it was about new shoes. He was showing her how to walk to avoid wearing her heels out so quickly. She must raise her feet higher, and stop shuffling at last!

On the train, Salek smiled, having just remembered how straight after moving to Kazimierz he had naively asked Benek Laubhart why he didn't bring his fiancée to live with him in Kraków. It must have been the first day, before he'd heard what happened at night on the other side of the wall in his flatmate's bedroom.

"Why bring wood to the forest?!"

Benek left a mess everywhere. He didn't wash up after himself and rarely put things back in their place. It may have been his shirts, jackets and ties scattered all over the flat that influenced Salek's next change of style.

Of course Salek still believed, and even tried to persuade his siblings, that the important thing was what was in you, not what was on you.

"If you're interesting and progressive inside, you don't need to show it on the outside."

But evidently this rule didn't work everywhere, and definitely not in Kraków.

He started wearing shirts with open collars and brightly coloured scarves – yellow and red.

He always remembered to wear at least one colourful item. He'd adopted this principle from Benek. The only time he didn't apply it was when he was under cover for the Party.

Like Benek, he also began to smoke cigarettes.

In his second year at university he had gone to an optician's, because even by squinting in the front row at lectures, he could no longer see what the professor was writing on the board. At once he remembered his father shouting: "Stop reading, you blind moles! Do you want to end up in bloody spectacles?"

Salek hadn't been to Tarnów for almost two months, because he spent his Saturdays and Sundays with Irka, often at her parent's summer cottage outside the city. In the mornings they went for walks in the woods, then had lunch on the veranda and discussed politics with Irka's parents, and in the afternoons they lay wrapped in blankets on deck chairs, reading books and newspapers aloud to each other.

"Salek, you must know that Papa has one serious fault," she said before the whole company, with a suitably sad look on her face, at the first lunch where he met her parents. "He likes going to theatres, concerts and private views."

Yes, she knew how to amuse everyone. Most of all her father – that well-known Kraków lawyer, a socialist who looked like an aristocrat, with a wave of black hair and a moustache even thicker and longer than Piłsudski's, in whose Legions he had served during the war. That must have been when he came to resemble him so closely.

But had he looked Jewish before then? wondered Salek.

He knew that he would never look like Irka's father. As they said in Kraków, a tailcoat fits best in the third generation. What about a moustache?

He should have introduced his fiancée to his parents long ago, but something was holding him back. What?

Their parents had immediately accepted Ruth, Rudek's wife, into the family and treated her like a third daughter.

Who was Irka's father, to whom strangers bowed in the streets of Kraków, and who was his father?

Salek's main concern was for Irka to meet his mother. Irka knew what she looked like, because above the desk in his room Salek had hung a photograph of his mother that Rudek had given him the day he moved out. (Rudek had managed to drag Rywka to the photographer's studio for the first time in her life!) Benek's immediate comment had been: "Not bad, but isn't she a bit old for you?"

What would her meeting with Irka be like?

They weren't exactly going to drive up to 20 Goldhammer Street in a droshky. Was he ashamed of the poverty of his family home or of his fiancée's wealth?

And what if Irka wanted to go to the lavatory at Goldhammer Street? And realized that all his life her fiancé had been going to a stinking outhouse in the yard.

Such questions delayed his trip to Tarnów from one week to the next.

On Irka's twentieth birthday her father gave her a camera, the Rolleiflex of her dreams. Sleek, black and rectangular. She wore it around her neck in a leather case. It suited her, her black eyes and black hair, which she tucked behind her ears.

"It's my new necklace," she said.

Or else she hung the Rolleiflex over her shoulder, "like an elegant handbag".

How much did it cost? She refused to tell Salek.

Some new words appeared in their lives. Aperture, exposure time, shutter, depth of focus, film speed. For Salek there was something exciting about them.

Viewed through a lens, the world looked different. And it was entirely up to them which bit of it they'd preserve forever on one of the twelve frames.

"You're more interested in the world," Rudek once told them, "than the world is in you."

Salek got the impression that Rudek wasn't entirely pleased by his relationship with Irka. On the one hand he advised: "That's an excellent match. Brother, get married."

But on the other, now and then, when he saw them happy together, he couldn't stop himself from making nasty little comments. He'd address them as "the happy couple" and ask "How's the class struggle going?" As if trying to leave a scratch on their happiness.

Maybe it was to do with the more and more frequent quarrels he was having with his own wife? Or the property accumulated for generations by Irka's father's family, while since becoming a parent Rudek had been economizing again, and Ruth kept turning her suits and coats at home.

Irka photographed Salek sitting on a deck chair in a new white shirt with an open collar, reading Hegel's *The Phenomenology of Spirit* in the original. As a blur while playing with Bodo, her German shepherd dog. Seated on a park bench next to the camera case ("The entire composition is spoiled!"), or staring into space in her father's hat, a flat Panama with a black band.

"Smile, you're my Muse. Smile, Mona Lisa," she said, bringing the light meter close to his face. "Aperture five point six, speed one sixtieth."

Sometimes they would walk about Kraków, tearing the camera from each other's hands when both wanting to photograph something different at the same moment.

They took serious portraits of each other in profile for their student identity cards against a sheet that they hung up in her room. That was Rudek's idea.

"Don't waste money on a photographer," he'd advised.

"I'm bored with photographing Kraków," Irka had said lately. "Why don't we go to Tarnów? And take some pictures there?"

All right, he decided now on the train. This coming Saturday he'd introduce Irka to his parents.

And at once he felt calm.

Once again he mentally ran through part of today's speech. Naturally, he always spoke from memory. He had realized that was necessary long ago, at a lecture given in Tarnów by an old communist wearing pince-nez, alias "The Count", who began his talk by reading from a sheet of paper: "Comrades! As I look at you now, as I behold your noble countenances…"

That was enough for them to start laughing instead of listening to his speech about favourable conditions for revolution.

"When I get the chance I'll tell that story at table to Irka's parents," decided Salek. "Perhaps they know 'the Count', he was in the Legions too."

Irka's father still hummed songs from those days. Especially when he thought he was alone on the veranda. Did he realize he was out of tune, or was he ashamed of what had become of the Legions? The fact that the former legionaries, with whom he had fought for independence, were now political opponents and were putting each other in prison.

Nevertheless, Salek and Irka often heard singing from the veranda:

The Legions are a soldier's song,
The Legions are the madcap's fate…

"That was our version of the game you play with your illegal party," he explained to them.

And when asked why in that case he didn't become a communist, he replied: "Communism is concerned with the masses, while socialism pays attention to each individual."

Salek put his hat on his knees and rested his head against the windowpane. The train shook. Soon he was in Tarnów, in the main square, outside the town hall. Where there was usually a market. He must have been about seven or eight. He squeezed through a crowd of people, but oddly no one was selling anything. Suddenly the whole square went quiet and everyone fell to their knees. Everyone except him.

Right across the centre of the square drove a smart open carriage, with a bishop dressed in purple, or maybe even an archbishop.

But the people praying weren't looking at him, just at Salek. He could feel their hands on his arms, pulling him to the ground.

"I'm not the one who's different!" he shouted. "It's you that are all the same!"

He woke up, and was relieved to see the compartment with its steamed-up windows, and the calm faces of the passengers who must have got in while he was asleep. Had they heard him shouting?

A toothless old woman in a floral headscarf smiled at him.

The train was slowing down.

"Częstochowa?" he asked her.

"Yes," she said.

He quickly did up his coat, put on his hat and said: "Goodbye."

At the station he looked around for the nearest exit.

"Gustaw?" a man accosted him from the crowd.

Salek nodded. So they've sent someone to meet me. Maybe the Party warned them that I sometimes get lost. But the man walked on and disappeared. Salek wasn't even certain what he looked like. Was he to run after him or wait on the platform?

Soon after, two officers came up.

"You're under arrest," they said, and grabbed him by the hands.

XXI

RENA

Rena turned the handle and put on a tango. She'd been given the gramophone by Mieczysław after their last conversation about leaving Tarnów. When she had told him she couldn't stand it here any longer. In this city where everyone knew all about them, and his wife and children lived three streets away. She only had to go outside, to the market, to an International Red Aid meeting, or to her parents' flat, and she was almost always bound to run into them.

"Let's get away from here," she begged him. "We could rent a small flat in Kraków, a room with a kitchen."

Instead of that she got a gramophone. As if Mieczysław thought he could keep her here with it. With a gramophone that itself looked ready for a journey, because it was shut in a suitcase.

Mieczysław wanted to stay in Tarnów for the same reasons that made her want to leave. He wanted to be near his daughters, and she couldn't blame him for that.

"It'll pass, Sarenka, it'll be gone like yesterday's rain. You just have to wait. Things will brighten up."

But it kept on raining, and Mieczysław kept drinking, more and more.

Rena opened the wardrobe, looked at herself in the mirror on the door, and for a while she danced with her own reflection. That was the sight he desired so much. The first time he had unbuttoned her blouse and started to kiss her breasts, she had asked: "Is that it? Is that what you wanted?"

He was quite offended.

But in fact, despite his assurances, she still didn't know. Was there really more to it, from his side of things? Did he himself know?

"It'll hurt a bit," he'd warned her the first time they went to bed.

Soon after that she began to notice couples where the man was "salvage" (a term she'd heard from her friend Gizella). She'd never noticed them before, but now it was as if Tarnów were full of them.

She'd pass couples in the street and find herself wondering if the man walking arm in arm with a woman had left his wife and children for her. Who was the victim of their happiness?

"Don't be melodramatic," said Mieczysław when she told him about it.

"And why do you drink?" she replied. "You always have to finish the bottle."

"The sorrows of old Werther," he said, smiling.

On top of that, the song now playing on the gramophone was "Drunken Tango" sung by the Dana Choir. Why did music sometimes match life so idiotically?

Life will be hard again tomorrow,
At twilight mournful eyes will gaze with sorrow
Into the cruel distance far away...

Rena had decided what she'd say to Mieczysław today. Not as soon as he came home from the office, of course. Let him rest a while, let him have a beer, let them enjoy the hot dinner she was about to make.

And they'd talk about the usual things, but without touching on their relationship and without quarrelling. A safe topic. Something they both agreed with, or both disagreed with. The crisis in the country: the pre-election arrests, the law-breaking committed by the government of colonels and the dictator Piłsudski. The beating and arrest of the leader of Tarnów's socialists, Adam Ciołkosz. Mieczysław and Rena had demonstrated arm in arm for his release. That had been one of their first public outings. Had it achieved anything? Except that they'd run into Mieczysław's wife in the crowd?

Rena had felt that the other demonstrators were looking at her as though she were guilty of the imprisonment of Ciołkosz at the very least. As though they had actually gathered and were marching across the city to protest against her and her relationship with Mieczysław. Her stomach ached, she felt like crying and she would have burst into tears if not for the police, who began firing shots to disperse the demonstrators.

After supper Mieczysław would light a cigarette.

"Darling," Rena would say, looking him in the eyes. "This is senseless, even from a mathematical point of view. Three people are unhappy so that two can be happy, but even so they're not capable of it."

For now she was talking to the tarnished mirror on the wardrobe door.

"If you refuse to go away with me, I'll go alone. I'll be fine. I have Rudek and Salek in Kraków, they'll help me. I want to go to college anyway."

And at once Mieczysław would imagine the students and professors at the Jagiellonian University gazing after her.

Maybe that would persuade him to go with her.

And what would her mother advise? Rena would have liked to ask her. Go to 20 Goldhammer Street when her father was out and Nusek and Wela were at school. Sit down at the kitchen table, have a cup of chicory coffee and tell her all about it.

She'd be sure to find some time for her between cooking for the lunchers, doing the housework and taking parcels to the prison. Between worrying about Nusek, who refused to go to school, Hesio, who was in jail, and her father, who wouldn't get out of bed.

Lately at Goldhammer Street Rena hadn't dared to start the conversation. She seemed to feel there was no room for it in this cramped flat. Once full of children, now it was full of problems to do with them. She was waiting for her mother to ask her first. But while slicing the carrots Rywka cut her finger. She had never seen this happen to her mother before. Rena finished chopping the vegetables and parsley for the soup for her.

That day her mother didn't ask her any questions. Just about one thing. But it had nothing to do with her or Mieczysław.

In Rena's day, were there songs like the ones Nusek brings home from school now?

"Like what?"

"Well, you know…"

"*Billing and cooing?*" said Rena, laughing. "About the faithless pigeons?"

Rywka shook her head.

"Worse," she said, and through the window she called Nusek. He ran in from the yard with his friend, Lolek Szpeda. Rena could smell cigarettes.

"Mama, what happened to your finger?" he asked.

At Rywka's request the two boys began to sing:

They took Moishe to the army corps
Oy vey, boom!
Although there was peace, not war
Oy vey, boom!
Moishe saw a hairy vole
Oy vey, boom!
It showed him its little hole
Oy vey, boom!

And then, laughing, they started on the next song:

They sent Srulek to the war
And they strapped him to a sword…

"That's enough now," said Rywka, unable to hear more of it.

Once they had vanished behind the coal shed, her mother told her about the conscription board before which Nusek had had to appear, like every pupil in the first year at the trade school.

"Family name?"

"Stramer."

"Given name?"
"Nissen."
"Denomination?"
"Mosaic."
"Mother tongue?"
"Polish."
"Nationality?"
"Jewish."

"Excuse me, gentlemen," said the sergeant, turning to the other members of the board, seated at a table covered with a shabby green cloth. "This clashes, it doesn't add up... Mother tongue Polish, but nationality Jewish?"

The others shook their tired heads.

And changed the nationality to Polish.

Nusek didn't protest. He felt distinguished for having come out of it so well. And perhaps that was why at the end he saluted.

"Respectfully taking my leave, sir!" he said.

"You don't put a hand to an empty head," replied the sergeant.

Why should they want our Nusek to be Polish? At first Nathan dismissed it his own way: "Haven't you got bigger worries?" But then he spent the whole evening pacing from the stove to the window and back, trying to figure it out. Lately they've been saying we're all Poles, and that only religion divides us, he thought. Maybe that's the point? Hell knows. Or do they have it written in the documents that before we became Jews we were Poles? No, more likely it works the other way around.

Rena didn't know either. Besides, she had other things on her mind and no desire to think about it. When Rudek arrived in Tarnów on Saturday evening with his wife and one-year-old

Róża, he explained that it was simply to do with statistics. It was a policy of the new government, which was interested in the percentage of Poles in society being as high as possible.

"That's what I thought," said Nathan.

Rywka didn't fully understand, nor had she heard it all, because she was busy caring for her granddaughter, and whenever she was doing that the rest of the world stopped existing, not just because the baby was crying into her ear. But she looked at her eldest son in admiration. Had she ever looked at him any other way? She relaxed every time he came. Rudek always knew everything. And everyone was used to the idea that things were as he said. Even Nathan had come to terms with it by now.

XXII

RUDEK

"Your daddy was in my arms just a short time ago," said Rywka to little Róża.

Róża had stopped crying and was smiling. The whole family was in love with her. And apparently the most in love with her of all was her Kraków nanny, whom Ruth called Nanna, and whom Rywka hadn't met.

There was something about the baby that had even Nathan crawling about on the floor with her, pretending to be her dog. Rywka couldn't remember him playing like that with any of their children. Rudek found an explanation.

"It's because Róża is the most like you, Mama."

No one had made her feel so pleased for a long time.

Rywka was wondering if she should talk to Ruth. Did her daughter-in-law know that it was best for a mother to let her child try whatever she was eating? Then the baby would learn to eat everything.

But lately Ruth seemed to have changed. Not as a mother, but more as a wife. She looked at Rudek differently than before, often with a tearful gaze. And her fists were clenched. Maybe that was just her way of hiding her cuticles, chewed until they bleed? Today her hair was a mess and she wasn't wearing any make-up. Is that the look of a woman who wants to please her husband? – that's what Rywka's mother, Rudek's grandmother, would have asked at the sight of her. And that was Rywka's first thought today too.

Maybe she should talk to Ruth about that, rather than about feeding Róża, but certainly not now and not in everyone's presence. And wouldn't it be better first of all to ask Rudek if he had any objection? And at the same time find out about Salek. Why didn't he get in touch? How had the new girlfriend turned his head?

As Nathan said: Who on earth is she anyway?

And by the by, Rywka would also tell Rudek the healthiest way to feed a child so it wouldn't be too tubby, yet strong.

Anyway, Rudek was the best proof that it worked. You only had to look at him: the tallest, broadest shouldered and strongest in the family. With that healthy, olive complexion too.

He's more and more handsome as he gets older, thought Rywka.

With his hair neatly cut, scented and pomaded. Almost every time he came to Tarnów he started with a visit to the hairdresser. He said it was cheaper than in Kraków, but was that what it was about? The hairdresser was an old friend of his, the younger sister of a classmate, a girl he'd always liked.

Rudek could remember the embroidered blouse Antosia was wearing ten years ago when she came into her older brother's room and asked: "I'm not disturbing you, am I?"

She may have disturbed her brother, but not Rudek.

"What is your desire?" she asked today.

As ever, they looked each other in the eyes.

"Cut it," he usually said, "so I don't have to think about it."

He gazed at her open-necked white blouse, patterned with pink roses.

This too was a regular feature of their game, of which he'd have a dreamy memory for the rest of the day.

This time the only new element was the answer Rudek had thought up that morning on the train to Tarnów, while Róża was asleep in his arms.

"My desire?" By now he was looking up at Antosia from the barber's chair. "For it to last as long as possible."

"I'll do what's in my power," she had instantly replied. "But I can't promise much."

We understand each other well, he thought. We'd make a fine couple.

Lately he had been saying that to himself about various women worryingly often. He was aware of it. Usually at work of course, at the Candles Syndicate, in the presence of his secretary, Miss Zuzanna Lipska, with whom he went to lunch each day.

Each evening, in a sinking single bed, in a room with a kitchen and two identical black cats, she would say: "Call me Zula."

Only then did she "feel the height of bliss" and scream at the end. But that was nothing compared with her friend, who apparently could only do it to the sound of a passing train. Rudek joked that now he understood why some people build their houses by the train tracks. How did they manage before the railways were invented? Zula laughed. And what could have worked on Ruth? Rudek didn't know and was less and less interested.

After his first evening visit, Zula was delighted that the bathroom door had stopped squeaking. It only took a second and a drop of oil, but she threw herself around his neck, thanked him and was as thrilled as a child.

He left with scratches on his back. And the conviction that some women needed less to make them happy than his wife.

Is Miss Lipska pretty? he wondered on the way home. He thought so, but he didn't know. She was certainly different in every respect from the distinctive, dark, broad-hipped Ruth. They were like the negative and the positive – that's how Salek would describe them, now that he'd taken up photography, were he to ask his opinion.

Including that Lipska was the positive.

A petite, blue-eyed blonde with freckles and shapely legs. With such a typical figure and hairstyle that all over Kraków, and sometimes even in Tarnów he thought he was seeing her from afar. She wore a cross around her neck, and sparkling rings on her long fingers, like from a stall at Tarnów's Burek bazaar. Was that good or bad? A lack of taste, or thrift? For all that she had beautiful moles on her back. He was sure of it. The same went for the wrinkles around her eyes. Would he have noticed them if she hadn't told him about them herself?

"My fifty-year-old mother has fewer wrinkles. It's not fair. I told her that the other day, and she didn't even deny it! Can you imagine?"

In fact they could go to her flat during the lunch breaks too, he thought. It would even work out cheaper, because Zula could cook something now and then. But no, it was too risky.

Of course at work they still used formal terms of address.

Once at the office she greeted him with a kiss on the cheek. Was she sure no one could see them? Or perhaps on the contrary – she wanted someone to see them at last? Rudek didn't speak to her all day, and that evening he went straight home.

The next day he said that if she did it again he would smack her in the face.

He too should be more careful. Salek may have sensed something. Some time ago, when they'd walked across Kraków at night, he'd asked him about other women. It was true that a little earlier they'd seen Karol Szpilman home, completely drunk, after spending all evening boasting of his conquests. So maybe that was where Salek's question came from?

Although he knew he didn't show it, Rudek had been drunk that night too. And perhaps that was why he'd opened up to his younger brother more than he'd wanted.

"When there's a bed, it's of no significance," he had said. "But when there isn't one, there bloody well isn't one."

At first it had been a relief, as if he'd been wanting to unburden himself for ages, but he soon felt regret. On top of that it had started to rain.

"So what about Irka?" he asked. "Has she let you sleep with her yet?"

He regretted that even more. As it was, he hoped he had only said that, and not "let you fuck her" or "screw her". But unfortunately he wasn't sure.

Anyway, those communists are so prudish, thought Rudek; he imagined they copulated like nervous rabbits, without taking all their clothes off, because at any moment the Party might interrupt and summon them to a meeting, to agitation or a demonstration.

As if the Party were the wretched wife they were betraying.

They were its slaves. Couldn't someone as intelligent and well-read as his brother understand that?

He consoled himself that Salek did know how much he had drunk at the cabaret that night, even if he hadn't been staggering, gabbling and singing (or rather bawling) to the whole Marketplace like Karol Szpilman.

He had just asked his brother one question too many.

Rudek recalled what the young Szpilman had sung at the time.

In Russia of old, princes and princesses had fun,
But now the streets with bright red blood do run.

"Shut up!" people had cried from their windows.

"Cracovians!" Szpilman had shouted back. "Don't you understand? This is your new St Mary's bugle call!"

"Go to sleep, Jewboy!" Those were the politest words they heard.

"Why do people pay serious money for my performances at the cabaret," said Szpilman, genuinely surprised, "but don't want to hear me for free in their own street?"

At any rate, that evening Salek hadn't answered Rudek, and they hadn't returned to that conversation.

XXIII

SALEK

After a trial and transportation to Łomża Salek's handcuffs were removed and he was taken to the governor, who passed him, or rather tossed at him a newspaper with a red headline on the front page: *In a haze of blood: the great famine and Ryutin's trial.*

"That's what your Bolshevik paradise is like," he said. "I'd send the lot of you to Bolshevia. They'd soon deal with you there."

Then he calmly immersed himself in Salek's dossier. What might he find there?

Height 1.61 metres, lean build, hair and eyebrows black, eyes brown, nose Semitic, ears small and thick, lips protruding, face oval, lean and very swarthy, appearance dejected, teeth healthy, clean shaven, chin small and pointing forwards, speaks Polish, German and Yiddish, short-sighted, wears glasses in round horn-rimmed frames.

"Appearance dejected?" said the governor, looking up at the prisoner bent over the newspaper, as if wanting to see if it were true.

And he grimaced – hard to say.

Salek could read between the lines of the Polish newspapers that wrote about the Soviet Union. Ten years for criticizing Stalin and forced collectivization? Lies and nonsense! Typical slanderous propaganda by the Polish fascists.

But what had been proved in court against Salomon Stramer? Not much. Apart from participation in the last illegal meeting held at the dentist Schmaltzbach's there was nothing but old stuff, even an incident dating back to Tarnów – his speech at the socialists' assembly at the Workers' House on Goldhammer Street. He couldn't fail to admit it, the court had too many witnesses. A stuffy hall full of workers. No wonder, the Polish Socialist Party always offers something to eat at the end.

That was one of the first serious tasks Salek had been given. Not just delivering communist leaflets or sticking posters on walls at night anymore, but disrupting a Polish Socialist Party meeting. He was surprised how simple it was. Just like at school (he was probably the youngest person there anyway), he only had to raise a hand (he could feel it shaking) and start talking (his voice was shaking too). "The PSP's only tactic is to deliver empty opposition speeches, with no real militant action behind them!" Breathe in and out. "The PSP is an obstacle on the road to revolutionizing the workers!" Breathe in and out. "The PSP is responsible for the workers' poverty to date!"

At first the socialists tried to interrupt him. But Salek knew he couldn't allow that. It was the basic principle. Everyone knew that once you lost the floor you couldn't recover it easily.

They shouted for him to stop, saying he'd used up his time. They drowned him out with shouts of: "Go home, child", "Down with the commune", "Shut your gob, you creep, you son-of-a-bitch". They whistled and stamped. One socialist even flew at him, but the others held him back.

But hardly any of it got through to Salek. He was more bothered by something else. Out of nerves, or maybe for fear of being late, he'd forgotten to go to the privy before the assembly. And so, during his fiery speech at the Workers' House, his main focus was on the struggle against his own bladder.

"Long live the workers' and peasants' government!" he said through clenched teeth. "Long live the dictatorship of the proletariat!"

And then he ran into the yard, while the company threw themselves on the now cold pierogi.

But I'm sure you won't find those details in the court files, thought Salek, glancing at the fat, red-faced governor.

The second time he'd disrupted an assembly he'd had worse stage fright because he was performing in front of Irka. And in Kraków.

At a meeting of the All-Jewish Election Platform he had started by criticizing religion as an opium for anaesthetizing the working masses. Then he had described the nationalist movement in China as the model revolutionary movement for a regenerating class. And called on the proletariat worldwide, naturally including the Jewish one, to support it. Maybe he went on about China a bit too much (and then about the striking British miners), but he wanted Irka to be aware that she was dealing with a full-blown revolutionary with broad horizons, extending beyond Kraków, Poland and even Europe.

When he got to the fact that even the moderate Jewish parties supported capitalists, several Zionists tried to interrupt him, but just as in Tarnów, they were soon arguing among themselves. And yet others shouted at them: "Not everyone at once! This isn't a Jewish bazaar!"

So once again he had succeeded.

"You don't ply your trade as a tailor, I see?" said the governor, who had finished reading the dossier and tossed it onto the desk.

Salek looked at him in astonishment.

"So you didn't unstitch your jacket?"

"No, sir."

To steel his nerves he tried to imagine the governor sitting opposite him in nothing but his underwear.

A picture of Lenin, cut out of a newspaper and folded in half, had been found under the lining of Salomon Stramer's jacket, as well as a notebook with several aliases of Kraków comrades and a sentence that the court found particularly interesting: "Ether is flammable!" (They must have added that, because he had definitely never made any such note.) And a letter from Tarnów prison from a colleague, Markus Kohn.

In court he had testified that he had no idea how those things got there. He had only just bought the jacket at the Kraków market, and why on earth would he unstitch it? He didn't know Markus Kohn.

The governor just smiled and signalled to the warder to take the prisoner to his cell.

The Catholics make special pilgrimages to Częstochowa for this purpose. That's to say for a miracle.

Salek was finally in the place where he'd longed to be for years. Just as his father longed for New York, or Irka for Moscow.

But it was because of her that he couldn't fully enjoy his new address "behind bars".

He missed his fiancée.

"I couldn't have foreseen that miracles happen to non-believing Jews and communists as well" – that was what he'd say when she came to visit him.

She wouldn't believe what neighbours he had. She'd be jealous. He wouldn't have had the chance to meet them on the outside. They were old combatants, legendary comrades.

They'd pointedly whistle "The Internationale" as the warders turned the keys in their cell doors. Instead of getting up and standing in line before them, they'd lie on their beds, in boots, reading. They'd walk around the prison yard with their hands in their pockets, and when the warders told them off for breaking the rule that forbade talking and ordered them to keep their hands folded behind their backs, they'd respond with a shrug (without removing their hands from their pockets, of course) and rude comments such as: "He sticks to me like a pubic louse to the bollocks."

Or they'd tell the whole yard: "Don't be so full of yourself, or you'll have an accident on the outside quicker than you think."

Nonetheless, it was rare for a warder to "remove" them from the walk, and they were punished with a hard bed or twenty-four hours in solitary confinement. He'd be more likely to say in an appeasing tone: "All right, man, stop it. That's enough of your lip."

"The warders are prisoners too," the old communists explained afterwards. "But on the other side of the door. They're in between us and the governor. But just like the dentist, the barber and the bathhouse staff they can be useful. We transmit news 'to the outside' through them, you get it?"

In response to the admiring gazes of the young ones, including Salek, they'd say: "We were communists in the days when you were still in nappies."

Or more modestly: "Do a bit of time and you'll soon see."

They were personally acquainted with just about all the secular saints, from Lenin to Karol Radek, about whom Salek was particularly eager to question them, because Radek too was from Tarnów. Twenty years before him he'd walked the same streets, and looked round at the girls whose daughters Salek had gazed after twenty years later. He may even have sat in Strzelecki Park with the same book, on the same crooked bench with a view of the bust of General Bem. Throughout high school Salek had liked to imagine it that way. And he loved to think that by following in Radek's footsteps he too would get to the very top, climb the communist Mount Everest, and that one day their busts would stand alongside General Bem's in Strzelecki Park: Radek, Stramer and Bem.

For now, Salek was helping his fellow prisoners to write letters.

"Write it all just as I say."

"It won't get past the censor."

"Then write it so it will."

His cellmate "Justyn" told Salek that during the lessons he gave to the illiterate, he learned more from them than they did from him. A year's study in prison is equal to five at liberty. He had learned more in a single year than throughout his degree in linguistics. At first Salek took this with a pinch of salt, as the gushing declaration of a young activist from a wealthy bourgeois home. But he soon realized he was wrong.

At any rate, it was impossible for a petty thief or burglar, even a murderer, who had landed in jail in Łomża to be released without being class-aware and ready to combat the exploitation on which this unjust world relied.

The world that had caused them to end up in prison.

They always said they were innocent. But thanks to the communists they understood that it was true.

Doctor of law Szyja Fensterblau beat it into their heads on a daily basis:

"You could say the Poles were the Jews of tsarist Russia. And they played a key role in the entire Russian revolutionary movement, especially the October Revolution. And not just the workers, but also Poles from noble families, who prepared Feliks Dzierżyński's afternoon tea, consisting of chocolate ice cream, cake and cherry jam."

This was Fensterblau's way of checking if the prisoners were really listening and taking note of what he was saying with understanding.

Anyone who'd written down "chocolate ice cream, cake and cherry jam" had to raise a hand, and the others burst out laughing. And then they all began listening attentively again, noting down the most essential things in the lecture, because nobody wanted to be laughed at the next time.

Incidentally, why was it ice cream, jam and cake that occurred to Doctor Fensterblau? Several of the listeners exchanged meaningful glances, but discreetly – after all, they were professional conspirators. They knew that because of a stomach complaint the doctor was the only man in the entire prison to be brought special meals each day from home, delivered by a maidservant.

A communist, but he has a maidservant. Behind his back the prisoners made fun of him. Just as to begin with they joked about his name – Szyja, meaning "neck". If only it were at least "Głowa", meaning "head". Lucky it wasn't "Noga", meaning "foot"... Or when talking about him they'd make a gesture to say "he's up to his neck in it".

They only stopped when "Justyn" asked if they found the name Jesus just as funny.

"Why so?"

"Szyja and Jesus are the same name. Jesus in Yiddish is Szyja. They both come from the Hebrew Yeshua. Yeshua in Polish is Jesus, and in Yiddish it's Szyja."

In the outside world "Justyn" had apparently been a highly promising student of linguistics. And that was confirmed in prison.

Each night Salek would watch with mild envy as "Justyn" sat down to work on his notes. Every two months his old professor, Kazimierz Nitsch, a linguist from the Jagiellonian University, came to visit him. And "Justyn" would hand him a carefully penned new chapter of his study of prison slang.

Among the stories the old activists told about Karol Radek, the fact that Salek found most interesting was the least political – about the five per cent. Apparently Radek, who was obsessed with statistics, had calculated that only five per cent of humanity was capable of falling in love. And that this regular feature had been observed in every society since time began. Whether feudal, capitalist or even socialist.

And so it was important, according to Radek, to come upon one's own five per cent, and to avoid the remaining ninety-five. Here lay the key to personal happiness.

Radek had confirmed his theoretical studies through many years of practical research, which was still ongoing, having failed to find his own five per cent. This explained his numerous affairs with women.

Maybe it was the same for Hesio, Benek and Karol Szpilman? thought Salek. They're simply searching non-stop, while I'm lucky enough to have found it at once.

And for the rest of his life. He was sure of it.

He often felt as if his experiences only took on meaning when he told Irka about them. Otherwise it was like going to the cinema alone, or admiring a view on your own – you have no one to turn to and say: Look how beautiful.

So every night, last thing before sleep, he talked to her in his head, trying to tell her about his day, as interestingly as he could. And she'd smile, make fun of him and hug him.

Why hasn't she come to see me? Maybe she's been refused permission to visit?

He wished he had a photo of Irka here. Best of all the one he hadn't taken in the woods beside her parents' summer cottage. She had suggested he should photograph her naked.

"Why?" he had asked.

"I'm twenty-two years old," she said, starting to pull her dress over her head.

She wasn't wearing a bra under it.

Salek looked around. The woods were so sparse. What if someone came along the path and saw her naked among the trees? The peasants often drove their carts this way.

Irka looked so beautiful in the not-existent picture. He could bring it to memory. The setting sun was illuminating her dark hair, long neck and delicate shoulders.

"It's chilly," he said. "You'll catch cold."

"As you wish," she said, shrugging, and got dressed again.

In fact, a day later, not far from the spot, they had used a self-timer to take their favourite picture of themselves together on a checked rug. But it wasn't the same.

The prisoners often talked about the first thing they would do on leaving: "I'll smash the gob of the sucker who ratted on me." "I'll have pork chops and cabbage at the station bar." "I'll go for a beer and then to the brothel."

And on his release Salek would take a photograph of Irka naked in the woods. In three years' time.

XXIV

RYWKA

RYWKA KEPT THINKING about what the teacher had said to Wela. For a week she'd gone to bed, woken in the night and got up in the morning with it. Of course Nathan hadn't noticed a thing. And that was lucky too. You never knew what might enter his head, and she didn't want him to kick up a row at the school in his broken Polish. It would be even more unpleasant and idiotic for Wela, and the teacher would merely say: "Old Stramer is so uncouth. Like father, like daughter."

She'd use the same spiteful tone as when she'd addressed the laughing Wela a week before in class and said: "You wouldn't find life as jolly in Hitlerland, Wilhelmina."

Several of the other girls had giggled.

Everyone, even the children, knew perfectly well what she meant. They didn't have to read the *New Journal* and the *Illustrated Daily Courier*, or hear the news on the radio. They only had to listen to their parents, grandparents or teachers. Or walk about the city. The streets of Tarnów were full of the nightmares befalling the Jews in Germany.

How could a woman like that be a teacher?

Luckily Wela seemed to be gradually forgetting about it. Only Rywka was being less successful.

Maybe I should go and talk to her? she wondered in bed at night. Let's see if she has the courage to repeat it in front of me.

One night Rywka dreamed that she was shouting at the teacher. And as for you, you shiksa, you'd be sure to have fun in Hitlerland!

She woke up with a smile.

She thought of asking her elder daughter's advice. Rena should know what was best for twelve-year-old Wela. Take no notice and forget about it, or go to the school and make a fuss? That was why she'd steered their conversation towards the anti-Semitic songs Nusek was bringing home from school.

Anyway, Rywka didn't know how to help her elder daughter either. How do you advise on matters of the heart?

At best she could repeat after Nathan: "Here's some good advice. Do as you think best."

But instead she had cut her finger chopping a carrot.

And was at once reminded of something she used to tell the children whenever they did themselves harm and came running to her in tears.

"Grab hold of your ear and squeeze it."

Then they felt a pain in the ear, and for a while they forgot about the bashed knee, grazed elbow or little finger they'd banged into the door frame while running out of the house.

That helped them. So maybe she should catch hold of the smaller problems to stand in for the bigger ones.

Because how much time can one spend thinking about nothing but the fact that one wasn't allowed to send parcels to the prison more than once a fortnight?

Never yet has any mother's worrying shortened her son's sentence, as Salek wrote to her in a letter.

Instead she'd cut her finger, and was focusing on the stupid high-school teacher.

But it wasn't just about her. What was happening to people in Tarnów lately?

"It's the same in Kraków, Mama," said Rudek when he came on Saturday. "They're saying things they wouldn't have dared to think a few years ago."

As if suddenly they'd all made a deal with each other, she thought.

SALEK

Dear Parents! In a couple of days (on the 23rd of this month) it will be the first anniversary of my arrest. A whole year has passed, and you still don't know what happened after I was arrested. At two in the morning the police barged into, or rather entered our house and I was taken from you, with no regard for the financial circumstances I was leaving you in. It was a painful moment for me, I was upset at having to abandon the family against my will. Outside it was snowing. Deathly silence reigned in the city as I was taken to the police station. I thought everyone was asleep, but when I got there I found out that wasn't true…

My dears! You're sure to be curious about my life in prison. At first everything horrified me, worst of all the constant jangle of keys. But I'm used to it now, and something else bothers me: the bell for going to bed and getting up. My days go by quickly because I'm always on the go. I'd tell you more about it, but I can't because of the censorship.

My dears! Don't think being parted from you has made me forget about you. Never! I think about you just as before. I wish I could help you, but how? I long to know how life is treating you. There was a time when we could see each other, at least within the prison walls, but now unfortunately all the gates are closed to us. And so I wish I knew, dear Parents, how you're coping with the current crisis. Don't worry about me, I'm well, I'm all right. I have thick underwear and warm boots. What's the news at home? How are you, my dearest father and mother, and how is everyone at home? Have you received anything from America? Here I shall end my letter. With very best wishes, your loving son.

When Salek finished reading out the letter he'd just written for the young tailor Piotr Sowa, he realized he had tears in his eyes. He couldn't have written as openly to his own parents.

"I've got conjunctivitis," he told Sowa.

And one more thing: how would the tailor's illiterate parents read his work?

"Well," said Sowa, who probably hadn't thought of that either, because for a while he was silent. "I expect they'll go to the village headman, or the postman will help. Don't worry about it."

So far the hardest letter to write had been the latest one ordered by the cobbler Icek Grynblum.

"My sister has left our village for Warsaw," the cobbler explained. "She's living in Nalewki, and everyone knows what they do there. Write and say she's not to go whoring, understand? Or when I come out of prison I'll smash her fucking head. Write and tell her that."

Salek asked Icek to tell him more about his sister, and only started writing once he'd learned that their parents had sent her to Warsaw to find a job and help them financially.

Dear Ida,

You know what? I'm not too pleased with your partners. They seem to me unsuitable. It's very puzzling that all the people you've been dealing with seem to think the fact that you work hard and slog away is unworthy of a human being. You have to know that everywhere, especially in a place like Warsaw, there are various kinds of people whose "profession", so to speak, is making love.

It looks to me as if you're coming under their influence. And I think in these cases you've got to be careful, and you should only have more to do with any individual once you've got to know him well. Don't be too quick to believe amorous promises, because accepting them too hastily can cost you dear. I'm not writing this because I want to dictate to you what you should do. But I regard it as the duty of every good brother and friend, and since I count myself as such, I'm advising you to act as I suggest.

What's my news? I received the trousers, galoshes and sweater. Thank you very much for them – for a while I couldn't go out for walks because I had nothing to wear. I'm well, and that's the main thing! Your brother.

Salek finished reading aloud. Icek was looking down at him. He was one of the tallest prisoners in Łomża. It was hard to interpret his powerful stare. His breath was much more telling. Everyone knew that Icek occasionally liked to barter with the warders, swapping the tobacco his sister sent him for a half litre of vodka to be brought to the prison for him. He was also known for sunning his tattooed torso in the open cell window and whistling at the sight of the female prisoners in the neighbouring women's exercise yard. He was constantly being penalized for it with a hard bed.

He couldn't care less, but just told his fellow prisoners: "It's good for your back."

Icek still hadn't spoken.

Salek couldn't help thinking: Will he want to smash my fucking head in too? But instead of that, the cobbler laid a hand on his shoulder.

"Well," he said, smiling approvingly. "I told it to you nicely, eh?"

Salek just nodded – he was relieved to be still in one piece. In his thoughts he could already imagine telling Irka about it at visiting time.

"In his presence I felt like David facing Goliath. I was trying to remember the punches Rudek taught me in childhood. Or at least how to keep up my guard. But Icek suddenly gave me a warm hug and said: 'Thank you, you've expressed my words beautifully'."

That should amuse her.

XXVI

RENA

AFTER SEPARATING from Mieczysław, Rena had moved to Kraków. For the first month she had lived at Rudek's place in Podgórze.

Maybe she shouldn't have brought the gramophone with her and gone on playing the records they'd listened to together in Tarnów.

There were days when she didn't think of Mieczysław as soon as she awoke. Or not until noon, if she was busy all morning. But the moment she became aware of it she felt like crying and couldn't think of anything else for the rest of the day.

After a month Rudek had helped her to find a room in an old lady's flat, which was in Podgórze too. Mrs Radziejowska, an impoverished gentlewoman, was a bit like Mrs Fluffy, who prompted their father to hold his nose as soon as her saw her in the distance. Here he'd have done the same.

She also had a dog, and it was a dachshund too, but unlike Mrs Fluffy, who never forgot her Fluffy and took him out for regular walks, even after his death, Mrs Radziejowska often failed to take Borys out, even though he was still alive.

"They could swap places," said Rudek, "with mutual benefit. But the main thing for you is that Radziejowska has rented you a decent room at a cheap price. And in Kraków that's rare."

Rena just had to clean the flat once a week.

At college, her mind was still full of Mieczysław. Perhaps that was why she could so nonchalantly walk past the nationalists standing outside the university with anti-Semitic placards reading: WE DEMAND GHETTO BENCHES! DEATH TO JUDEO-COMMUNISM!

In Tarnów there was none of that. But in Tarnów there was no university. Though the other day Nusek had told them about problems with class photographs. The Polish children had refused to pose for a group photo with the Jewish teachers. And as a reaction the Jewish children had refused to pose with their Polish classmates.

Rena shook her head.

In her schooldays that would never have happened.

When had all this begun? She could remember her mother telling her about some anti-Semitic songs. Had she really been so wrapped up in her relationship with Mieczysław that she hadn't noticed anything?

As she had planned, Rena had enrolled in the Philosophy Faculty at the Jagiellonian University to study mathematics and nature. On the first day of the academic year she wove her long hair into two plaits and gave herself a crown braid. Mieczysław loved kissing the back of her neck. She wore lace-up, mid-calf boots, a navy-blue knee-length skirt and a sky-blue blazer. Even Rudek, on his way out to work, had stopped in the doorway. And it took him a while to say: "Are you going to a beauty contest or the inauguration lecture?"

Evidently, grief suited her. She saw shining eyes in the mirror. Her breasts had grown a little. She didn't know that was still possible after twenty.

A pity Mieczysław couldn't see that.

The university janitors called the humanities courses "communist". And it was the "communist" students who called for a boycott on attempts to introduce ghetto benches and encouraged others to sit wherever they wished.

Apparently one of the Jewish students who had obeyed them and refused to sit in the part of the hall set aside for Jews, was thrown out of the window by the nationalists during a lecture.

The professor didn't notice a thing.

Luckily it was the first floor.

Only once had someone put a fourth-class train ticket to Palestine on Rena's desk. Who did it? She turned around, but everyone behind her was intently listening to the botany lecture. She crumpled up the ticket and tossed it to the floor.

"My dear young lady," a nationalist from the All Poland Youth accosted her after classes, whom she suspected of planting the now crumpled ball of paper. "Don't come to college tomorrow, my dear."

"Why not?"

"We're going to beat up the Jewboys," he said, gesturing as if he were already waving a stick studded with razor blades. "It'll be unpleasant for you."

She cast him the coldest look she could muster.

And as she did so, she took a good look at him – nothing special. Was this the latest man, as Mrs Radziejowska put it, remembering her own youth, to be drawn to her like a moth to a candleflame? The nationalist opened his mouth, as if wanting to say more. But before he could do it, Rena turned and left.

When she got home after a long day at college, Borys and his mistress would already be asleep. So she'd tiptoe down the corridor to avoid waking them, but just in case, as experience had taught her, she never took off her boots.

She knew what she would find, despite the agreement to do the cleaning once a week. She'd start by washing the dog piss off the floor. It's not his fault, she thought. As it is, he's a good boy to spare the ottoman and the shabby Persian rug in the sitting room. But all the same, it made her feel ill. She knew that next she'd be holding her nose in the bathroom, cleaning up the dog mess in the bathtub.

Mrs Radziejowska was invariably surprised by this.

"My Borys?" she'd say to Rena at breakfast, sitting under two crossed sabres on the wall. "He would never relieve himself in the bath!"

It was a waste of time trying to explain. All the more since Mrs Radziejowska was afraid of catching cold and never opened the sitting-room windows in the morning. Rena felt sick from the stuffy air and wanted to take Borys for a walk as soon as possible.

Outside she never let him off the lead because he attacked cyclists, biting their ankles and tugging at their trouser legs.

Mrs Radziejowska claimed he never did that with her.

No wonder, thought Rena. Since you never take him out.

"No wonder," she said. "He knows who's his mistress."

And, happy with this reply, Radziejowska would throw Borys a slice of sausage from the table.

So Rena did her best to come home as late as she could. After classes at the university and two or three hours giving tutorials to high-school pupils, in the evenings she'd drop in on Rudek and Ruth.

She'd still be in time to give Róża a goodnight kiss. How quickly she'd become a little girl! Today Rena asked her if she'd rather be a child or a grown-up, and Róża said: "I want to be a child, a child, a child!"

"Why?"

"Because I don't like wrinkoldies."

Rudek should write down the funny things she said.

Rena helped Ruth to make the supper.

Then they waited in silence at the kitchen table. She remembered how in Tarnów they'd all talked on top of each other. The flat on Goldhammer Street was so full of life.

Here it was so quiet, apart from saliva being swallowed and stomachs rumbling, you could hear Ruth sticking her needle into the clothes she was darning. And Rena turning the pages of her notes. She was getting ready for the next day and trying not to think about Mieczysław. But was he trying not to think about her right now as well?

When they had first met, he had written to her in letters: *I think about you far too often, you unbearable girl!*

At the end, before she left for Kraków, they had jointly decided it would be better to part.

But was life worse for him now too?

Enough! She must concentrate on the here and now. Kraków. November 1935. A quarter to ten.

Didn't other people have bigger problems? Salek and his Irka, who had so charmed their parents when she came to

Tarnów. She'd taken their picture in the courtyard in front of the coal shed.

Apparently, at the time of her arrest in Kraków, in answer to the policemen's standard question of whether she could afford a droshky to the prison, she had said she didn't want a droshky but would rather walk through the city at bayonet point.

"For communists, going to prison is like going to paradise," Rudek told her wickedly. "She wanted to share her fortune with the passers-by."

He couldn't have known at the time that Irka would fall sick in prison.

And what about Hesio, whose Lotka had been sent to study in Vienna by her parents? And her sister-in-law, sitting opposite, hunched over her needlework? What might she be escaping in her thoughts? Watching Ruth as she cast the occasional anxious glance at the clock above the table, Rena couldn't fail to guess.

Hadn't Mieczysław's wife had just the same anxious look on her face whenever they'd run into each other?

Rudek was spending more and more time at the Candles Syndicate. They never knew when he'd be home. But they could be sure he'd be tired, irritated and hungry.

"Doesn't it bother you?" Rena had once asked.

In the middle of darning her husband's sock, Ruth's needle came to a stop.

Rena regretted her question.

After all, they both knew that Rudek would rather have been a Latin teacher, but he couldn't have kept the family or been able to help his parents, and anyway, almost all the schools were refusing to employ Jews by now.

So they both knew that wasn't what Rena was asking about.

Ruth looked at Rena; perhaps she was going to say something, but just then they heard the key turn in the front-door lock, so she shrugged and went back to her darning.

The floor creaked in the corridor and Rudek entered the kitchen at a brisk pace.

"We're swamped with work."

He loosened his tie and threw his jacket on a chair.

"How now, girls? How's Róża?"

"Don't shout so loud, you'll wake her," said Ruth.

Rudek raised his eyes and smiled at Rena, who had got up to greet her brother. He kissed her on the cheek.

RUDEK

"Is she pregnant?"

Already fast asleep, Rudek was not sure who had asked him that question. He didn't know where he was. He couldn't think what he was doing. Who was he lying next to? He tried to wake himself up, but his eyelids must have weighed a ton. Is that you, Nusek? Ruth? Zula? He managed to open his eyes. As every night, he was lying in bed with one woman, while thinking about the other.

"She's pregnant, isn't she?" said Ruth.

But he was always careful, and if he didn't have a condom he made sure he withdrew in time. He turned over onto his other side.

Lipska pregnant! Did that mean the decision had made itself? For a while he felt relief.

He'd be a father again. Another Stramer would be born. A boy or a girl?

If it weren't for Róża, he'd have taken the decision to separate and it would have been over.

He adored bringing her presents. Placing a doll on the mat, knocking at the door and hiding on the next landing down to see how pleased she was. He gave her piggy-backs around Kraków. He took her to the swimming pool, and even to Cracovia matches.

What she liked most was jumping on or off a moving tram together. He'd hold her in his arms, while she clung to him tightly and squealed. It was their secret – Róża had promised not to tell anyone about it. What could he say to her now?

He wanted a cigarette. He rarely smoked, only when he was upset; Róża had never seen him with a cigarette. Lipska smoked Egyptian ones, the most expensive kind, four zlotys a packet. On her salary! He couldn't understand it. Selling cigarettes was more profitable nowadays. He knew something about it, after all, he used to sell them to the soldiers. Nowadays he just lit one in bed occasionally and handed it to Zula, who would smoke it with her head on his chest. If she was pregnant she'd have to stop.

But hold on... How did Ruth know about the pregnancy? And before he did? Had Lipska been to see her, and told her all about their affair? She had once threatened to do that. But when could she have done it? What if she'd sent a letter? Did she imagine that after a stunt like that he'd still want to be with her?

Rudek took a deep breath and in the most casual tone possible asked his wife: "How do you know?"

"I'm a woman," she replied.

He pretended to yawn to gain a moment for thought. He was wide awake now. There was still one way out. Now, to his wife, he'd deny everything, and if Lipska wasn't lying and really was pregnant, he'd send her for a termination.

"I don't understand," he said to his wife. "Who's pregnant?"

"Well, obviously not me!" Ruth sat up in bed.

She rested her head against the wall, tucked up her legs and wrapped her arms around them. Rudek felt sorry for her. What must she be going through now because of him?

"Your sister."

Next day after work, in the sinking bed, Rudek told Zula about it.

Perhaps he should buy her a new mattress. They had worn this one out completely. In one spot the spring had come through the material and you had to be careful not to injure yourself. In another it was stained – only fit for the rubbish heap.

He'd seen a shop selling mattresses in Kazimierz – he should go and check the prices.

Zula listened to him attentively, with Miss Zuzanna Lipska's fixed blue stare, which he knew so well from the front office at the Candles Syndicate. That gaze was serious, searching, not laughing at him. That was why he spared her a few details of the previous night. Especially some of his thoughts, including the brief moment of painful disappointment, and then great relief, when he'd realized it wasn't Lipska who was pregnant.

Rudek lit a cigarette, took a drag and handed it to Zula.

She was interested in the story of Rena and Zawadowski the lawyer. She wanted to know how long their affair had been going on before they became a couple. Did she see a reflection in them of her own relationship? At any rate her cheeks flushed, followed by her small, slightly protruding ears, which he liked so much.

"I'm sorry for Rena," she said.

Rudek rarely sought anyone's advice. It must have been the first time he'd asked for Lipska's. Like Ruth, she thought he should talk to Rena without delay, as subtly as he could. In these matters you couldn't wait. And in case of need, Zula had a tried and trusted doctor.

In case of need… Rudek wouldn't forget.

Before talking to his sister he would have a chat with Salek. His next visit was due to take place in a week. All day on the train for ten minutes' conversation in the presence of a warder. Thank goodness they no longer had to talk through a bloody grille as at the beginning. At least he could give his brother a hug.

Salek was his weak point, and always had been. Rudek was fully aware of it.

His younger brother had never provoked or upset him. Unlike Nusek, who always annoyed Rudek, just by being in the vicinity. He asked stupid questions, poked his nose into other people's business and played the martyr. At Goldhammer Street Rudek sometimes used to catch Nusek, lie him on his back, pin down the boy's arms with his knees and slowly release a thick stream of saliva towards his face. Once it was almost touching Nusek's nose, as he alternately begged for mercy and kicked, Rudek would suck it back into his mouth at the last moment. Unless it was too late. He didn't always succeed.

But Salek? There was something about him that made Rudek want to help him. Maybe because he hardly ever asked for help. He was the quietest of the brothers. And he'd always sorted everything out by talking.

The warder brought him into the visiting room.

Rudek looked at his brother's gaunt, pale face as Salek stifled a cough and wiped his nose on his uniform sleeve.

"How are you feeling?" he asked.

"All right!"

At once he remembered Salek as a little boy. He'd fallen out of a tree and Rudek had led him home by the hand. There was blood pouring from his nose, he had a swollen knee and he was crying.

"How are you feeling, son?" asked their mother, bending over him.

"All right," he'd answered.

And now Rudek was helpless. The rage he had felt at the stupid communists all the way from Kraków to Łomża was gone. What really lay behind all their fine words about social justice, in defence of the disadvantaged and the minorities? They couldn't even agree with each other, they insisted on self-criticism sessions and apologized like small children, while lecturing others! And they incited the workers. Even the activists who occasionally spent the night at Rudek's place on stopovers often grumbled.

He didn't talk to anyone in the train compartment, just to his brother in his thoughts.

"You tell me, what do the communists ever manage to achieve? Apart of course from their ham-sandwich-eating campaign outside the synagogue on Yom Kippur? They just get themselves put in jail and let people insult them by calling them 'Judeo-communists'."

He must have it out with Salek at last!

But once on the spot, in Łomża, the only thing he wanted was to get him out of there. He'd left all his anger on the train. He'd even change places with his brother if he could.

He'd brought Salek the photograph of their parents that Irka took in the yard at Goldhammer Street.

"Nice light," said Salek approvingly.

Rudek nodded; he was no expert on that. Their parents were sitting on a crumbling wooden bench in front of the coal shed, looking straight at the camera. Their mother, her hair entirely white by now, was wearing a black blouse with white spots. She was smiling. Was her right eyelid drooping slightly, or did it just look like that in the picture? She had her hands on her knees. And what about their father? He looked the same as ever – his crumpled suit and the hat pulled low on his forehead had aged more than he had.

"When did you last see Irka?" asked Salek.

And Rudek had to tell him.

Two weeks earlier he'd arranged to see her father. Brodner had broad connections from the days of the Legions. Could he galvanize them to get his future son-in-law out of prison? A single phone call would probably do the trick.

Rudek had gone to the meeting in his best suit, hoping to persuade him to take action.

Was there a better address in Kraków? Not far from the Marketplace, Planty Park and the University. In an Art Nouveau house. And inside… He tried not to look around too much, just as he had once avoided looking at the home of his friend, the son of Tarnów's deputy mayor. But he noticed that even Irka's room was bigger than his living room and bedroom in Podgórze combined. Bigger than the entire flat occupied by his parents, whose picture before the tumbledown coal shed Irka's father had just handed to him.

In this interior, full of expensive modern furniture and paintings, it looked like a souvenir from the previous century.

Brodner was wearing a white shirt, a long black tie, and a lavender scent. But Rudek could have recognized him in the street merely by his gentleman's moustache, which he knew about from Salek's stories.

"What do you think, why do guys need to wear long ties?" Rudek was reminded of a question Zula asked as a joke. "But you don't have to…"

And did she know why Jews needed traditional Polish moustaches? For the same reason why some of them were no longer circumcising their sons.

They went into the sitting room and sat down on club armchairs by the fireplace. How comfortable, thought Rudek. How much rent would I have to pay for one of these chairs?

From the days when he first came to Kraków as a student, he still counted everything in terms of rent. It really was the most universal, international currency. More so than even the dollar.

Irka's father was the first to bring up the topic of Salek. It turned out that at the very start of his sentence he had written to Salek to say that he'd be happy to intercede for him where necessary. But Salek had refused.

"Please ask the prisoner if he'd be so good as to leave the prison!" said Brodner, smiling.

"They're all playing at being heroes," said Rudek.

"They think it's a game," said Brodner, nodding. "But it has serious consequences."

"I'll persuade Salek to change his mind," Rudek promised.

At the same time he didn't believe he'd be able to.

"Then of course I'll take care of it," said the lawyer. "Including the two-thousand-zloty bail."

At that moment even Brodner's moustache stopped bothering Rudek. Wasn't it better to grow a moustache and live in peace than have a revolution and turn the whole world upside down?

"I don't know how to thank you."

He'd got more than he'd expected. The opposite of the joke that had been doing the rounds in Kraków. Briefly he wondered whether to tell at least the punchline.

The parish priest is riding along in his cart, it's winter and it's snowing. He sees Moishe coming along on foot. The priest gives him a lift to the city, and on the way he says: "What about that Judas fellow, Moishe? Why did he sell the Lord Jesus for thirty pieces of silver?" To which Moishe replies: "Well, Father, he probably couldn't get more."

Instead of that he asked about Irka.

Brodner was surprised Rudek didn't know anything. Irka had fallen ill, so they'd released her from prison and put her in the hospital in Kraków. The doctors suspected severe pneumonia. In the best case.

"Over the past week her state has deteriorated," added Rudek, as he told Salek about his meeting.

Salek abruptly stood up from his chair in the visiting room.

Rudek realized that now he didn't need to convince him – Irka's illness was a sufficient argument for coming out of prison.

"The censors must have stopped her letters," said Salek, and sat down resignedly.

And he became just as sad as Brodner had been that day in his beautiful flat.

XXVII

RYWKA

ONCE AGAIN, as in the past she had all her children in the kitchen at Goldhammer Street and was watching them eat. How could she help it if that was her favourite sight?

Not so long ago they'd had trouble scrambling onto the chairs and their feet had hardly reached the floor. But now as they took their old places they barely fitted at the table. She couldn't know that this was the last time she'd have them all together.

Who had changed the most in that time? Definitely Wela and Nusek. Though Rywka didn't notice, because they were with her on a daily basis. By now they were both taller than she was, Wela had filled out, and Nusek was starting to sprout a moustache.

Luckily Hesio had put on a bit of weight. And grown into a man. Probably thanks to the horticultural school he'd attended, because after prison they'd refused to take him anywhere else. And he looked good in a shirt with the sleeves rolled up. All her sons had inherited Nathan's nice, strong forearms.

Even so, Rywka thought Salek had changed the most. Not just because like Hesio he now walked diagonally across the room when he was thinking about something. He had not changed outwardly, in appearance, or temperament, because he'd always behaved seriously and maturely from early childhood.

But inside he wasn't the same anymore. And that worried Rywka.

She didn't want him to break down. But – she wondered – did he have to go too far in the other direction? Did he have to be quite so brave, show no weakness at all and pretend nothing had happened?

She could still see Irka's visit in her mind. They had sat at the same table. Overawed, Wela had listened in silence to the adults' conversation and gazed at Irka's dress, buttoned up to the neck, navy-blue tweed with a tartan collar. They ate the apple pie their future daughter-in-law (as they thought of her) had brought from Kraków unnecessarily, because Rywka had baked a cheesecake for her arrival.

"And it's much tastier," admitted Irka.

She liked everything at their place and wanted to photograph it all. The street, the yard, the flat. Even Nathan and Rywka. She inquired what Salek had been like as a child, as a boy, and as a son. Where he'd slept, where he'd played, where he'd done his homework. When she realized it had all happened in one and the same room, she was impressed.

"I had everything at my fingertips," she said (Rywka was looking at her beautiful, slender hands and her engagement ring). "I was born in a house where there were hundreds of books on the shelves ready and waiting for me. I only had to reach out for them."

Nathan shook his head, but luckily Irka didn't know what he was thinking.

"And Salek achieved everything by himself," she added.

Unexpectedly proud of his son, Nathan nodded. As if it were to his credit.

Rywka couldn't remember exactly when Salek had started to read so much. Rudek must have brought a book home from the library, or taken his brother there. She didn't mention the cheder. Why should she? It was plain to see that Irka's family had stopped going to the synagogue long ago. Salek had brought home more and more books. Rywka remembered that at first he had only borrowed books by authors starting with A. Then starting with B, and C. Irka was utterly delighted.

"He had no one to advise him, so…" said Rywka, mildly confused.

"…he made good use of the alphabet!" said Irka, laughing.

Once he had told his mother that being in the library felt like being in a sweet shop where everything on the shelves was for free.

Rywka looked at Irka, at her long lashes and shining eyes. She understood perfectly what this girl felt for Salek and what Salek must feel for her.

He's had more luck than Rudek, she thought at the time.

But as her father, Salek's grandfather, used to say, you never know where lightning will strike.

Why had it hit them? Who knows?

That Sunday, Irka had left Rywka, Nathan and Wela in excellent moods.

"Despite all those books she grew up to be such a decent girl. And pretty. And she doesn't even wear glasses," said Nathan as they waved her goodbye at the station. "It was worth sending the boy to college."

Salek wasn't in time to say goodbye to Irka. He was only released from prison a week after her funeral.

"I'm going to Spain," he said now.

"You're exactly what they need there," said Nathan.

Even Rywka smiled at the idea of her son in a uniform with a gun. Everyone knew that of all the brothers he disliked and avoided violence the most.

But then it occurred to her that this was to do with Irka, and that Salek deliberately wanted to let himself get killed in Spain.

Who could stop him? She glanced at Rudek.

"Well, off you go," said Rudek, who also understood that it was no joke. "You'll always be my brother."

Now nobody will stop him, thought Rywka.

And a week later Salek left. How? With whom? By what route? It was all a secret that not even his older brother knew.

XXVIII

NUSEK

Long after Salek left, Nusek was still repeating those two sentences to himself: "Well, off you go. You'll always be my brother."

Others, like the teachers at school for instance, could gabble for hours and he remembered none of it. Especially when he had to take a test. The best proof of this was Nusek's grades. But sometimes when Rudek said something... He could never be a teacher. That was for sure. One of the first things Nusek learned at school was not to listen to the teachers. Lolek Szpeda helped him with it. It was no accident that they had always sat on the same bench together, but these days at the trade school.

"Can I go with you?" All his childhood Nusek had repeated this question.

Usually his brothers didn't bother to answer.

They'd disappear through the gateway, and for years he imagined all the wonderful things he was missing.

One time he called after them from the yard: "But why not?"

The question came out spontaneously. And at once he regretted it, because the best thing he could expect to hear was "For the public good."

Rudek turned around and said: "Life is not fair."

And indeed, he was right.

Every passing year simply confirmed it.

The world would definitely have been fairer if they'd taken him with them.

Ever since his brothers had left Tarnów he sometimes imagined being one of them.

Rudek, walking down Krakowska Street, these days the site of the best shops and cafés. He doesn't just know everyone, but they bow to him first. To which he replies with a slight nod.

And what if he was Hesio? He'd finally go to bed with a girl. Best of all with Lotka. And if not her, it could be some other girl in Warsaw. Hesio had good taste. He'd be sure to have found himself one there by now. At least one. He was probably canoodling with her right now on a park bench.

Yet he rarely imagined being Salek in Spain and having to fight "for your liberty and ours" against the fascists. Not that he was afraid – of what? Salek had written and said that not once had he fired his gun yet. And their father was always saying that at war the first order a soldier gets is to "dig in", and then he waits in those shitty trenches. But Nusek hated waiting. Perhaps he'd done enough waiting already before being born as the fifth of the siblings. So at least he told himself. But on the other hand, at home they were always talking about Salek and worrying about him, because for months they hadn't had a card from Barcelona signed "Salo".

Sometimes Nusek would catch himself wanting to tell his brothers about a dream he'd had. But wouldn't they keep interrupting and not let him finish telling it? A few nights ago he'd dreamed that life in Tarnów suddenly came to a halt, as if someone had stopped time. The cars, buses and trams were at a standstill. People were frozen like in photographs. Some with their wallets open at the tills in shops, or with their trousers down in the outhouse. Women in the middle of a fitting at the tailor's. Antosia the hairdresser in her bra, having just taken off her overall in the back room...

Everyone except Nusek.

He could calmly take a few banknotes from the tradesmen's tills. Just to borrow – he'd give it back by and by, when he had the money. He could kiss the girls he'd always liked, and even the ones he didn't fancy. And not one of them would smack him in the face. At the patisserie on Sobieski Square he could help himself to Italian ice cream, his favourite flavours: pistachio, vanilla and chocolate, two scoops of each, and on the way out he could rip down the sign on the door that said "No entry for Jews". Crumple it up and stuff it into the gob of the old man who owned the patisserie.

Then time began to move again, the old man started to choke, and Nusek woke up.

He only had one regret. He hadn't managed to eat the ice cream.

That day he went to the same patisserie. He stood in front of the shop window. It was just as in his dream. There was the owner, the ice cream, and the sign on the door. He didn't go inside, not because of the sign, but because he didn't have any money. After all, he had lighter colouring than any of his brothers, and in summer his hair went fair in the sunlight. These days that was his only reason for feeling better off than they were.

What sort of satisfaction do you get from not looking like who you are?

At any rate, they'd never have been let into that patisserie. Not to mention another café, which he had managed to enter not so long ago, in spite of the sign saying "NO ENTRY FOR DOGS AND JEWS". Nusek could feel the searching stare of a waiter, standing by the entrance. And so he had asked: "Why no dogs?"

The young waiter had laughed and let him go inside.

Anyway, Nusek hadn't even sat down at a table. It was the favourite café of the boys from the All-Poland Youth disciplinary guard. Why take the risk? He just waved through the window at Lolek, waiting outside, and moments later, avoiding the gaze of the young waiter, he calmly left the café. He'd made a bet with Lolek that they'd let him in. And he'd won.

At home nobody was amused by "Why no dogs". He shouldn't have boasted about it.

But how else could he have won the bet, he wondered?

His mother shook her head and shot a glance at Rudek in the group photograph of her children on the chest of drawers. Nusek knew that look well. Once again his brother would tell him off when he came from Kraków.

"So what did you win?" asked Nathan, as if in an effort to support him.

Don't ask! thought Nusek, and shrugged.

Lolek Szpeda's family was even poorer than the Stramers. So to be able to give Nusek the zloty they had bet, first Lolek had to borrow it from Nusek.

And Nusek had agreed, on condition they used the winnings to buy their favourite cake, a cream puff, and then eat half each on a bench in Strzelecki Park. After all, they were bosom pals.

Lately they argued less, and if they did, they made up with each other by turns. Just as they'd agreed.

And it worked. It stopped mattering who'd insulted whom first.

"Drop dead, you stinking Lach scum," Nusek would hurl for instance, adding as he walked away: "Now it's your turn, don't forget."

As they queued for the cream puff Nusek played with the coin he'd won, flicking it up in the air with his thumb. As they watched it spin and reflect the light, they were both reminded of the same thing. A bottle top. Instead of going to school, they'd trail about the city, loudly belching under people's windows (Lolek could belch the entire alphabet but Nusek could only get as far as "k"), using the porcelain cap from a bottle of beer they'd drunk for target practice. At some point Lolek had stopped five paces in front of Nusek and opened his mouth.

"You'll never hit it," he said.

Nusek waited for the wind to drop, then calmly aimed and…

"Ow!" cried Lolek, squatting down and clutching his face.

The pain he felt was just the herald of things to come. He knew what he'd get at home for a broken tooth.

His mother still beat Lolek with a metal coat hanger. Nusek often encountered her, because she worked as a caretaker in the next-door yard. At her place he'd had his first taste of delicious strawberry pierogi. She was nice when she was hungover.

Lolek had never seen his father. Sometimes he said he'd gone away to America. Or that he was a mountain guide in India. His mother only mentioned him when she was angry with Lolek: "You're even worse than that son of a bitch."

Nusek could remember the exact moment when he'd realized why Lolek said he was worse off than Nusek. They must have been about ten years old. His mother called Lolek over to her. She was raking up autumn leaves in the yard. In a headscarf and long skirt she looked the same as usual, but she could hardly stand upright. Her speech was slurred too. All they could understand was that she wanted them to go to the shop.

Nusek dropped his gaze to avoid looking at them. And then he saw the steady, transparent stream flowing from under her skirt onto the grass.

In Strzelecki Park all the benches were occupied. As planned, they shared the cream puff, but standing up. It took them less than a minute. Lolek's face was still covered in icing sugar. Nusek had wiped his on his jacket sleeve.

"What do you want to do after trade school?" he asked.

Lolek shrugged sadly. Just like Nusek whenever they bothered him with the same question at home. So at once he realized his mistake. Instead of "What do you want to do?" he should have asked "What can you do?" However, he didn't let it go.

"Rudek's sure to sort something out for me in Kraków," he said.

Lolek didn't answer; he was staring into his uncertain future, somewhere beyond the roofs of the Fertilizer Plant. Everyone knew how bloody hard it was to find work in Tarnów now.

"Don't worry," said Nusek, clapping Lolek on the shoulder. "I'll ask for you as well."

"Great!" said Lolek, clapping Nusek too; they always reciprocated.

Anyway, it was time for another chat with Rudek. Nusek wasn't a child anymore, wasn't too little for him to take to Kraków. Someone had to tell Rudek that.

His mother, perhaps? His father probably wouldn't listen.

There was no point in waiting for Rudek to come up with an offer. After all those years in the same bed he'd never think of his brother in need. Nusek had already heard him promise Wela, a year younger than he was, that after high-school graduation he'd find her something in Kraków.

And once again Nusek would be left behind in the Tarnów courtyard.

Well, all right. It was obvious that after school Wela would go to college. Not to Vienna, like her wealthy schoolmates. But to Kraków, like Rena.

She wanted to study medicine, which a few years ago wouldn't have been a problem, but now... Rudek had gone specially to find out.

Then he'd come to Tarnów on Saturday and explained to their parents and Wela that pharmaceutics is a good subject too, and being a pharmacist is a good profession. Pharmacies are needed everywhere, so you won't have to worry about a job.

And it was obvious. He didn't have to say that since Piłsudski's death more and more paths were closed to them. That it started with "Each to his own for his own" and "Don't buy from the Jew", and ended with smashing the Jewish shop windows and slogans such as "Jews to Madagascar!" That the powers that be wanted Poland to be like Germany or Italy. That this policy appealed to the young, who marched with torches and wanted "national revolution". That nationalism was tomorrow's tide.

Everyone was talking about it. And about the imminent war. Even Nusek knew the names Hitler, Daladier, Chamberlain and Beck by now.

Rudek told them about the two civilized-looking old gentlemen he'd overheard on the tram in Kraków.

"Well, he must be a smart fellow to have come to power!" shouted one at the top of his voice.

And the other, perhaps hard of hearing, leaned towards the first and just as loudly replied: "There must be something to his agenda if they pay him so much attention!"

Rudek was relieved to get out at his stop.

As in the tram, everyone at Goldhammer Street knew who the old gentlemen were talking about.

Nathan became serious.

"In the Talmud it says: *Woe to the seeing man who is led by the blind man.* And I say to you: Woe to the deaf who are led by the blind man."

"That's like in the joke about the two owls," said Rudek. "One says to the other, 'You're as deaf as a post!' and the other replies, 'And you're as deaf as a post!'"

He was trying to relieve the tension a bit, but they can't have understood because they didn't laugh much.

Wela reported that at school they'd been told to write an essay for their homework on "Mistletoe". Her good friend, Wilga, had stood up and begun to read: "The Jews are like mistletoe, they are a parasite that feeds on the blood of the Polish nation". And she got an A.

She had never said anything of the kind before. Wela had cried all the way home from school.

"She's probably jealous of your boyfriend," said Rywka,

hugging her daughter and stroking her hair, which nowadays Wela combed behind her ear according to the latest fashion.

Nusek thought Wela should have thicker skin. She got too upset. If he was upset by what he heard every day in the school corridors, he wouldn't have time for anything but sniffling into his handkerchief. All those Yids, Jew-friends, Jew-lovers, Jew-praisers and Jew-lickers…

But since falling in love, Wela had become oversensitive. And she never stopped talking about her feelings. Anyway, Nusek didn't like that boyfriend of hers, Max, at all.

"Why not?" asked Rudek, who hadn't seen him yet.

"Too good-looking."

"Are you jealous?" said Rudek, regarding Nusek from a height of almost one metre eighty. "I've heard that he set up a book-keeping firm, he's doing very well and also helps his family."

"They live in the countryside, so sonny boy signed up for lunches at Goldhammer Street and comes to pester us every day," said Nusek.

Maybe Rudek was right about this too? After all, they say that in all Tarnów there's no boy handsomer than Max Kierbel. Wela said that when they walked down the street together everyone looked round at them. Nusek had seen how deeply even Rena gazed into his blue eyes whenever she came from Kraków. And he'd bought Wela a bike for her birthday too. Maybe Nusek would change his opinion of Max, if he bought something for him occasionally too?

Nusek accompanied Rudek on the way to catch his train back to Kraków, and spent the whole time steering him onto the obvious subject. He told him that once he finished school he'd be looking for a job as an electrician. But these days even professional tradesmen were having a hard time finding anything. What's more, he had no bloody contacts. But he was longing to move out of home, to stop burdening their parents. Had Rudek listened to him at all? Doubtful. Maybe he'd gone deaf too by now, over there in Kraków?

Just in case, Nusek ran round his brother and repeated the same things into his other ear.

Rudek shook his head as if shooing away a buzzing mosquito. Now and then he interrupted Nusek to greet and exchange a few words with the acquaintances they passed in the street. Conversations like everyone's lately: "Hitler's bluffing. You'll see. Those German tanks are made of cardboard."

"The war will pass us by."

"Hitler will swallow Stalin and choke on him."

But it was good to be seen together in the city, to remind people whose brother he was, thought Nusek despite his anger.

Rudek even stopped at a shop selling mattresses. And without a word he went inside. Nusek was left alone in the street, unsure in the first instance what had happened.

Rudek was more interested in the children begging outside the station than in his brother's need. Lately they were everywhere. He watched them playing tiddlywinks and smoking cigarettes. He gave one little girl a few groszys.

On the platform Nusek waved goodbye to his brother, but in fact he was bidding farewell to his hopes of a better future.

He took two steps forwards. One more and… If I have to be a nobody, better I didn't exist at all. If he'd thrown himself under the train, then Rudek would have been sorry. Especially as he'd had the chance to save his younger brother's life, by finding him a job, for instance at the Candles Syndicate where he worked. Even there they needed electricians, surely?

What would the look on Rudek's face be like as he placed a pebble on Nusek's grave? If only it were possible to see that from on high....

"If you can't get the plums out of the jam jar with your hand, smash the jar" – that was all his brother had said to him.

I'm not going to convert, like Wilner, thought Nusek, as he passed the Holy Family church on Krakowska Street. What use would that be?

At school Wilner was bottom of the class, with worse grades than Nusek or even Lolek. But he had an uncle in Warsaw, a former Legionary, who had promised to get him a place at the Army Sanitary School. On condition his nephew converted. It didn't matter that he'd failed to complete secondary school. And now what? After the holidays Wilner was off to Warsaw.

As Dad said: Each follows the faith of his choice, and you can't go wading into other people's private business.

Why wading? Now Nusek shrugged.

If I wanted to go away like Wilner, I could always ask Hesio. He keeps saying that every cleric, whether Polish or Jewish, is like a cancer, but he does have a friend who's going to become a priest any day now.

Unfortunately, baptism alone wasn't enough. You had to have connections in Warsaw too.

There'd also been a lot of talk in Tarnów about the younger son of Dr Gramada from the Jewish hospital. He'd got the best results in the whole city for his final school exams. And had gone to the Gdynia Maritime School. That was his dream. He did very well in the exams, but when he undressed before the medical board, they said: "Your health isn't good enough for the navy."

When he got home, his father immediately summoned a medical board of his own. They examined the young Gramada, and unanimously declared him fit and well. They sent this statement to the minister of religious affairs and public education. A few weeks later the answer came: Ludwik Gramada has not been accepted into the Maritime School for lack of places.

As a consolation, his parents sent him to study abroad.

As a consolation, Nusek could at best go for a beer or a cream puff with Lolek.

He had just reached home, when he suddenly felt he must hide away and disappear. It wasn't late yet, but he undressed and went to bed.

"Nusek!"

Next morning his father wrenched the quilt off him. Nusek pretended he was still asleep.

"Goddammit! Get up."

Nathan shook his son.

"Leave me alone, Dad." Of all people, his father should understand. "I've got stomach ache."

"Stop fooling around."

He was more understanding about his own "gastritis".

"You must run to the marketplace."

Ten minutes later Nusek was racing so fast that he didn't notice the shopkeepers boarding up their shopfronts with plywood or sticking tape to their windows crosswise.

He could already see the long queue outside the town hall from afar. It was forming a living letter S. When he got close, he tried to find someone he knew in it. They hadn't started issuing the gas masks yet, but people were already saying there wouldn't be enough for everyone. There was no chance of queue-barging, but just in case he tried. Without success. He had to go and stand at the very end.

How could it still be so hot at the very end of August?

His shirt was sticking to his back. At home he hadn't even had time to wash his armpits.

In the queue Polish was mixed with Yiddish. What were they all gabbing about? At first he couldn't understand.

No, surely not? He'd been at the station yesterday with Rudek, hadn't he?

"A time bomb? Where?"

"In the left-luggage office."

"What?!"

"It killed twenty people."

And just a few hours after Nusek had left the station.

Showered in dust and terrified by the explosion, horses had galloped through the city, dragging overturned droshkies after them.

Who had planted it? The fascists? The communists? An engine driver or stationmaster who'd lost his job?

Everyone had a different story, and they were all pleased it wasn't their arms, legs or head that had gone flying across the station hall yesterday.

Nusek was sweating even more, despite feeling cold.

Damn, is it a sign or what, he thought, that I survived and I'm fully intact? Even if I had ended it all yesterday by throwing myself under a train, it wouldn't have been any use, because my death would have been lost among twenty others. And today people would have been talking about the victims of the time bomb, whatever.

Nusek was no longer last in the queue.

His older sister's best friend, Gizella, had come up to him. He'd often gawped at her when she came to visit Rena. But this was probably the first time she'd ever looked at him, and definitely the first time she'd been so pleased to see him.

Nusek remembered that Salek had once described Gizella as a "beautiful young lady". Whenever they passed her in the city, at the very best Lolek would say: "Nice piece of arse". What about Rudek? Since he'd had a wife and daughter he probably didn't look at other women at all. But what if he saw her? Anyway, why should he care? It didn't matter what anyone said about her, just how he was to talk to her now. He'd heard that conversation works best on women. For now, he just spluttered: "Good day", and was struck dumb.

She was still half a head taller than Nusek, although he was standing up straight and slightly on tiptoes. To be on the safe side, he pressed his arms to his body, so she wouldn't notice the wet stains under his arms.

It turned out she'd also been at the station yesterday. And she too had been lucky. All the cases in the left-luggage office had burned to ashes except for six, including hers.

"The station is surrounded now," she said. "And there are machine-gun posts on the neighbouring roofs."

Why were you storing a suitcase at the left-luggage office? he wanted to ask, but probably like Hesio, who used to keep communist leaflets there, she wouldn't have told him the truth anyway.

Before he could ask another question, two indigent young Jews in gaberdines started shouting behind them, half in Polish, half in Yiddish, that Gizella had jumped the queue. Nusek clenched his fists. They weren't at home in Grabówka. One more word and… He wanted to let fly at them.

The sidelock wearers must have got in the wrong queue.

"We're waiting for gas masks, not the Messiah!" he cried.

Gizella just smiled.

You only had to glance at them. It was Jews like them the boys at trade school laughed at. How sweaty and stinky they must be under those rags. How could the Stramers have once looked like that?

The woman queuing in front of Nusek and Gizella turned around, plainly wanting to say something too. Not much more was apparent from her face. The broad brim of her hat shielded her eyes and nose, casting a shadow down to her open mouth. She was also jiggling her foot nervously, as if wanting to kick Gizella out of the queue. With his fists still clenched, Nusek moved to protect her, just in case.

"Instead of wearing these masks, isn't it enough to wet some towels?" asked the woman in the hat. "And hold them to your face?"

"You're right," said Gizella, nodding. "It comes to the same thing."

This allowed them to move one place forwards.

"She was probably desperate to pee anyway," said Gizella.

And Nusek gazed admiringly into her blue eyes.

At this moment he wanted the queue to last until infinity. Was that what the rabbis meant when they said the journey is what counts, not the destination? Not for nothing had his father been taking him to the synagogue of late.

XXIX

SALEK

ONE OF THE FIRST DECISIONS Salek made on his return to Paris was not to call himself "Salo" anymore. It was "Justyn" who had first called him that in prison in Łomża. After that, it was the name they'd given him in Spain.

After a few weeks' intensive study of French, Salek had learned a word that sounded identical, though spelled a different way.

"Salaud" – meaning a dirty swine.

In Spain, before the unit moved on, they used to check to make sure he wasn't missing.

"Salo, are you sure you're here?" they joked, because of the time they'd forgotten about him.

That night he had lain down behind a wooden beam in a barn and immediately fallen asleep. The next morning he'd woken up feeling well rested, but found he was entirely alone.

Two years earlier he and some other volunteers had walked to the border of France and Spain near Perpignan. Crossing into Spain was surprisingly easy. The border guards pretended not to see the six foreigners carrying luggage.

On the way they'd met Roman, and they'd stayed together. He was a metalworker from Poznań, tall and broad-shouldered like Rudek, but older than them by at least ten years, already past forty. He'd left two children behind in Poland, whom he kept showing to them in a creased, fuzzy photograph. He told them how he had tried to get into Spain three times before. The last time he'd been found hidden in a wardrobe on a ship to Marseilles.

He had trained Salek and "Justyn" for war. "You don't argue with fascists. You just kill them," he said.

Two days earlier Salek and "Justyn" had arrived in Paris by train from Kraków. They were better prepared for the journey than Roman, at least outwardly, because unlike him they weren't wearing the short leather jackets with large side pockets that were fashionable among the revolutionaries. They had new blazers, Polish passports with visas stamped in them and proper suitcases that wouldn't arouse suspicion. They were also wearing round horn-rimmed spectacles. They didn't look like illegal freedom fighters on their way to take part in the Spanish civil war, violating the neutrality of democratic states.

Salek had only had one tricky moment, in Berlin. But of his own volition. He had jumped out at the station to get a cup of coffee. Gazing up at the fluttering swastikas, he had started imagining his own imminent death at the hands of the fascists. The train had almost left without him, and he'd only just managed to grab the door of the last carriage.

In Paris they knew to whom to report, and they had the address of a hotel.

Thanks to his map, "Justyn" had quickly found his bearings, so Salek didn't have to worry about how to get there.

"When do you want to be in Spain?" asked the guy in such a large cap that his ears were invisible beneath it.

There was a red poster depicting Lenin on the wall behind him.

"Yesterday!" said "Justyn", looking at Lenin.

"All right, all right," said the man in the cap.

They were to spend two nights at the hotel, then go to the Gare de Lyon to board a train to Perpignan, each wearing a navy-blue beret and with a rolled-up newspaper under their right arm – the signs by which "the right person" would recognize them, and then take care of them.

If they'd stopped in Paris a week longer, "Justyn" would probably have started to speak in French. He was always reading the shop signs, the posters and the two newspapers they bought at a kiosk for their departure. He learned the language incredibly fast.

Salek had no interest in learning it. He was sure he'd never have any further use for it.

He imagined how less than a hundred years ago Mickiewicz too had walked the streets of Paris, pining for Maryla Wereszczakówna.

> *At every hour and in every endeavour,*
> *Wherever I wept with you, wherever we did stroll,*
> *I'll be beside you everywhere and forever,*
> *For everywhere I left a part of my soul.*

But Mickiewicz could at least write his M. a letter and get an answer. What about Salek?

He remembered how they'd sat on the bench at the tram stop, and Irka had made fun of his new pseudonym, "Gustaw".

"Are you that fond of Mickiewicz? So you could be Konrad too?"

In the evenings he and "Justyn" had time to talk more seriously. They drank wine in their hotel room; they couldn't afford to go to a café.

"Justyn" said that since the Moscow trials of Zinoviev and Kamenev he couldn't understand a thing. Who could have imagined that those old revolutionaries would be demanding the death penalty for themselves and spitting on their own entire past?

"Everything we've... All our effort in prison. Bloody hell, Salo..."

Salek too had memorized Kamenev's words: *The sentence that falls on me will not be a cruel one, but proof that everything has its limits, even Soviet magnanimity. And so I spit on all the complaints about the cruelty of the sentence passed on me.*

"Justyn" suddenly began to weep. "Please don't tell anyone," he said.

"Are you joking?" They both knew what he meant.

They looked each other deep in the eyes.

"Justyn" said in a louder tone that the war in Spain would give him the opportunity to be on the right side again. The world had regained its contours and colour. There it was divided into two camps.

"Black, reactionary, fascist, on Franco's side. And bright, democratic, libertarian, on the beleaguered Spanish Republican side," added Salek, also a little louder than before.

They were lying in bed by the time Salek added that he couldn't stop thinking about Irka. He wanted to reciprocate by saying something just as personal, so "Justyn" would know that he could still trust him.

Next morning, feeling hungover, they boarded the crowded train and burst out laughing, because the first thing they saw was a large group of fellows in navy-blue berets with rolled-up newspapers under their arms.

After crossing the border from France into Spain they still felt as if they were in a slapstick comedy. On the train volunteers from all over the world had offered each other wine, brandy and liqueurs. They'd sung revolutionary songs. They'd pointed at the olive trees and orange orchards they passed. Through the open windows they'd whistled at girls and waved their red and red-and-black handkerchiefs. Salek had only ever heard about anarchists before then. At every stop along the way to the Brigade headquarters in Albacete people threw flowers and silk ribbons, and shouted: "Saludos Brigadas Internacionales!"

In their compartment Roman was the only person who didn't respond.

"What's wrong?" asked "Justyn".

Roman just shook his head.

At the station in Albacete a brass band played them a welcome march. The young communists, anarchists and socialists eyed each other closely. As soon as he heard them speak, "Justyn" told Salek where they were from – Americans and Britons, students from Oxford and Cambridge alongside illiterate metalworkers from the Czech lands and miners from Poland, Lithuanians and Latvians.

The generals were to be on familiar terms with rank-and-file men and to be paid the same wage.

Salek noticed "Justyn" discreetly wiping away a tear as he took the oath.

"We swear to fight loyally for the Spanish Republic and for democracy worldwide. We are all equal. There is no difference between workers, peasants, the lower and middle classes. Anyone who fights in our ranks is one of our fellows."

That same evening they were invited to a banquet by their Soviet comrades. Caviar, vodka and toasts, raised by comrade Kaverin: "Let's drink to victory!"

Before reaching the front, they underwent five days of training at the Karl Marx barracks.

"Why don't they teach drill?" wondered Roman, the only one of them to have done military service before now, and to have reached the rank of a reserve NCO in the Polish army.

Salek shrugged.

They were shown Goya's prints, *The Disasters of War*, so they'd be aware of what might be in store for them. Headless corpses, genitals cut off with a sabre, rape and executions. They were also warned about the terrifying new features of this war. The Italians were using flamethrowers to burn our men alive. And the German Messerschmitts were flying close to the ground to spot and fire at our positions from the air.

They were taught to aim at the head, chest and belly. But no one gave them any weapons, so Salek just wrote it all down in his notebook. Throughout the training not a single practice shot was fired. The whole time they waited for a Soviet ship that was supposed to sail in any day now with a supply of medium and light machine guns. It finally arrived on the very last day, but all it brought was food.

Soldiers returning from the front handed their weapons on to the new volunteers.

On the way they kept repeating the words of one of the British commanders of the Brigades: "This isn't a war. It's a comic opera, where the occasional accidental death occurs."

And that's exactly what happened to Roman.

On their first day at the front they were given orders to dig in and wait. Hour after hour went by monotonously. Now and then, one of the soldiers couldn't stand it any longer, and fired in the direction of the enemy, who were so far away that even by squinting through his spectacles, Salek couldn't see them.

"A scout ran past on the skyline," the eager soldier would explain.

"Premature ejaculation," was Roman's only comment, casting a glance at Salek and "Justyn".

"Ejaculatio praecox," agreed "Justyn".

Not much has changed since the days when my father was in the army, thought Salek. They say some of the weapons are from the world war anyway. And apparently someone had seen a shell with the date 1917 on it.

The soldiers wrote letters, played cards and uncorked bottle after bottle.

"I wonder if they boozed as much in the Austro-Hungarian army?" said "Justyn", smiling.

"And did they have lice hopping about on their balls?" said Roman, scratching. "Did your old man ever boast of that?"

"Oddly enough, no," said Salek, shaking his head in his tight, ill-fitting helmet.

Each of them was dressed differently. They looked as if they were from three different armies. Or from a single army of people in fancy dress, in coats that were too long and trousers that were too short, and that fell down when they walked because they were too baggy as well.

But they weren't bothered about it. After a few hours in the trenches everything was like a joke, including their motley uniforms and the stories about dud shells that flew from one frontline to the other without harming either side.

Late in the day, less than fifteen minutes after the conversation about lice, a stray bullet hit Roman. Where had it come from? They couldn't tell if someone from their own unit had fired it by accident, while trying to unblock his rifle.

Roman lay calmly on his back, with a tiny black hole in the middle of his forehead. He never got the chance to kill a single fascist.

It was the first time Salek had seen a corpse. One minute the man was there, the next he was gone.

Later he realized that never for a moment had he wanted to be in Roman's place.

In their letter to Roman's wife, he and "Justyn" wrote that he'd died a hero.

Several weeks later they were almost killed too when the German planes began to drop bombs on Barcelona.

They were on a pass, they'd been drinking all day, but had instantly sobered up when the bombing began. "Justyn" decided they had to flee to the west, towards Tibidabo mountain. He dragged Salek after him, though to Salek it made no difference. Night had already fallen and they couldn't see the way. In the narrow streets Salek kept bumping into the stone walls of houses. Now and then the earth shook. He could tell he was walking over broken pieces of furniture and random bits of metal, probably some of the empty milk cans that were lying about everywhere.

Suddenly they heard music. A small wooden door opened, and they saw a thin streak of light and smoke. They peeped inside, and there was a dance floor, full of couples, soldiers and women.

"Listen, you do as you wish," said Salek. "I don't give a damn, I'm going to stay here and dance."

If something were going to happen to him, let it happen here.

To die while dancing is better than dying on the battlefield.

At the bar they drank to Roman in the traditional way. A glass of anisette each, the sweet liqueur he'd liked so much on the train to Albacete.

"Why was he so quiet then?" asked "Justyn".

It was still bothering him.

"I don't know," said Salek.

They went onto the dance floor.

Once again the earth shook, like a powerful jolt on the Tarnów or the Krakow tram, and a *muchacha* who was dancing to "¡Ay Carmela!" fell on top of Salek.

He could feel her warmth and her calm. Half an hour later they were kissing and cuddling by the wall near the exit. There they'd found the only free corner. But even so they had to move closer to another couple, because every time someone came in, the wooden door banged into them.

In a break between kisses the girl asked who he was, what was his name and where was he from.

"I'm Salo. A Pole. From Poland."

"Very nice," she said.

She was probably drunker than he was, because a little later she asked the same questions again.

And then asked them twice more.

These breathing spaces gave Salek the chance to take a look at her. Even in high heels she was smaller than he was, with black eyes, curly hair and a vertical scar above her left eyebrow.

There was no trace left of the thick red lipstick she'd been wearing when she fell on him.

The fourth time he told her for a change that he was a Jew from Poland, and she pushed him away from her.

"It's not true!" she said, laughing.

"Why not?"

He couldn't understand her reply. "Justyn" would probably have been happy to translate, if he weren't asleep under a table.

The girl showed Salek what she meant by putting both hands on the top of her head and pointing, while slowly repeating: "Los Judios tienen cuernos."

Salek copied her gesture to give himself exactly the same horns, leaned forwards, and with a fierce look on his face mimicked a bull attacking her. And she played the role of a trampled toreador.

Was it Maria? Now he was the one who couldn't remember her name. Paloma, or Nuria? At some point they had pressed their hands together. She had short, boyish fingers. They were the only thing he didn't like about her, but they were what he remembered best.

They'd struggled with his army belt which had refused to come undone. He was ashamed of having lice.

"Are you surprised?" said "Justyn" next day. "They haven't seen any Jews here since the days of the Inquisition."

Salek often thought about that happy night. Had the girl known how much it meant to him?

He had come here to be killed in a righteous war, to sacrifice his life to a just cause, but a few months later he wasn't so sure the war was righteous or that the cause was just, or if he still wanted to die for it.

None of them understood any of those ideas anymore.

His fellow soldiers from the Brigade kept disappearing overnight, the prisons were full of anarchists, socialists and Trotskyites, and at the sight of their Soviet advisors in the cafés, the comrades lowered their voices and exchanged nervous glances, like Salek and "Justyn" that night in the Parisian hotel.

In Spain they no longer allowed themselves such open conversations. But they only had to look at each other to know what the other was thinking.

Salek knew that war is governed by its own rules, but could everyone who'd been arrested really be a spy?

Of course, there were actual spies. Like the man who latched on to them one night in Barcelona, following them from bar to bar and offering them cigarettes. As he took the packet from his inside pocket once again, they saw that he had a pistol. They searched him, and also found on him a code, some invisible ink and developer. When they pinned him down, he admitted he'd been sent by the Polish consulate in Madrid.

Or the soldier from their unit who tried to defect to the fascist side. At nightfall, he'd escaped from the trenches and, holding a white handkerchief, gone to let himself be taken captive, but he must have got confused in the dark, and two hours later he came back to his own side.

Was it necessary to arrest so many innocent men to find the few genuine menaces?

Hadn't Roman's death in a way heralded what happened later?

Censorship operated in Spain too. And better than at the prison in Łomża. He and "Justyn" had the chance to find out in person, when they were promoted from the ranks to be political commissars. It was recognized that they'd be more useful on the ideological front. They were to give lectures, organize presentations and edit a wall newspaper.

They were summoned by the Polish unit's chief political commissar. He had an office on the top floor of a modern four-storey building. And a terrace with a view of Barcelona. Despite his important post, he wore the same ordinary soldier's uniform as they did. Salek recognized him as the legendary old warrior "Wincenty", now under his own name, Sobczuk, whom he remembered sitting next to on the floor at the meetings in Kraków.

"Your tasks, comrades," said Sobczuk, lighting a cigarette, in a more serious tone than when he'd been "Wincenty", "also include reading letters. Remember, no sentiments. If you find phrasing in the letters that could be harmful to us, obliterate it."

"But…" said Salek.

"There are no 'buts'." Sobczuk started to cough, stubbed out his cigarette and threw the butt from the terrace into the street.

"Comrade," Salek tried again. "We'd rather our work involved something else…"

"Well, I like to smoke but I'd rather not cough," Sobczuk interrupted him. "Got it?"

Why on earth did we come here? thought Salek next day, as in the same building, but two floors below, they drew thick black lines through their fellow soldiers' letters.

On the other hand, they hadn't forgotten Sobczuk's final remark, spoken in the doorway: "It's a responsible task and I'm glad I have you two."

They were flattered to be trusted by "Wincenty", who in Kraków had had a reputation as one of the most honest communists. But was Sobczuk like that too?

Was he right that subjectively harmless letters might objectively prove dangerous? That even innocent criticism could provide information and arguments for the enemy? That the fascists were just waiting for love letters full of pathos?

My dearest darling Lidka,

You can imagine what happens to a man's soul when he takes part in the fight he dreamed to join for so many years. You remember how full of hope I was for victory when I left. Here my hope has increased threefold. People who like to sleep and eat well lamented over me. Such a young boy and he's off to die. Fools! What do such people know about the feeling that's called "devotion"? This sacred fire raises a man to such a level that no privations concern him. And the fascists cannot frighten him, despite being much XXXXXXXXXXXXXXXXXXXXXXXXXXX than we, the Internationalists.

You cannot imagine how happy I am. In truth, my artillery XXXXXXXXXXXXXXX XXXXXXXXXXXXXXXXXX XXXXXXXXXXXXXX

It's four thirty a.m. and I came back from sentry duty a short time ago. During my watch I missed you and thought of our Sundays, how we walked arm in arm about the Saxon Garden. I miss you very much, and at these moments I take your photograph from my pocket and gaze at you. My mind is filled with every moment of our love, our joys and our quarrels. Now there's probably a nice boy waiting for you by the gate, and perhaps he's having more luck than I did. Your daddy won't show him the door. Or maybe right now you're sitting alone at home, listening to the radio or reading a book.

Your ever loving Dawid

They wrote their own letters and cards home just as cautiously as they had at the prison in Łomża. And then they lost the desire to write at all. They only sent perfunctory messages to say *I'm well, everything's all right and no pasáran!* in letters that next day they had to read once more, because they automatically landed on their desk.

"Everywhere they're celebrating, except in our revolutionary city!" said Salek on the first of May, when in Barcelona the joint anti-fascist parade had been called off at the last minute, because the various factions couldn't come to terms on something as simple as this.

"Who's still fighting the fascists?" they said, exchanging glances over the desks heaped with letters.

Meanwhile, every day they read in the papers:

Brotherhood in arms, the fraternity of bloodshed, a sense of the common, anti-fascist cause and the fight against a common enemy have united us all into one, great big family, where there's no friction, but many bright, beautiful and sublime moments.

At this point Salek had a dream that stuck in his memory. He came onto the pitch during a football match. Looking around the players, he saw nothing but familiar faces. But he didn't know whose team he was on, because everyone was dressed differently. It was a rough match, with plenty of fouls. There was no referee. Salek got the ball, and wanted to strike or pass it, but to whom? Was he with Rudek, Roman and Franco? Or with his father, "Justyn" and Stalin? They took the ball off him before he could make up his mind. He looked for Irka on the stands. He saw Hesio in the front row and averted his gaze. He got the ball again and scored a goal. But he didn't know if it was for his team or an own goal – he still couldn't tell whose side he was on. When he woke up after the match, under his head the pillow was wet.

Then what? Next day, they asked Sobczuk to transfer them back to the front. There at least they were really fighting the fascists. He agreed.

But it was too late by now. Fewer and fewer voices sang each morning at roll call, with diminishing sincerity:

> *When the battle is fought and won,*
> *And our enemy is laid low,*
> *We shall swap bayonet and gun*
> *For workman's hammer and plough.*
> *None of our spirits will ever fade,*
> *As the fascists are crushed and die,*
> *To the front, Dąbrowski's brigade,*
> *The flag of Liberty flying high.*

They were cold, it was snowing and there wasn't enough food. On the river Ebro, their unit was hastily being withdrawn, but some documents had been left at general staff that couldn't be allowed to "fall into the clutches of the fascists".

"'Justyn'," called the commander. "Off you scoot to general staff for the papers!"

And tossed him the car keys.

"Justyn" never came back.

Salek wrote a personal, friend's farewell for the brigade newspaper. He mentioned Roman too. He'd had two good friends in Spain. He'd lost one the first day at the front, and the second when it was all over.

Next day, he didn't recognize his own text as published:

"Justyn" was killed by an enemy bullet. Though short, his life was rich – filled with learning and fighting, imbued with revolutionary passion and a great sense of patriotism and internationalism.

XXX

RÓŻA

Róża OFTEN WOKE UP in the night. She could hear her parents shouting. The sounds of someone tugging, or fetching down a suitcase from a high cupboard, then slamming the wardrobe door. Then she would run out of her room into the passage in her nightshirt to be in time before her father left the house. She'd grab him by the hand first. Then her mother.

And she'd join their hands together. She knew her crying worked on her parents like glue. And that tonight her father would stay.

Each morning she ran into their bedroom to see if they were both there.

But now it was going to end and everything was going to be different. All right, and together. Her father certainly wouldn't move out to that "blonde whore" of his now. In the compartment of the crowded train on which they had left Kraków, her parents had wept, held hands and sworn to each other that they'd always be together. Calmly, without shouting and complaining.

"The whole family should be together now," her father had said.

Maybe in Tarnów the three of them would sleep in a single bed? That's what she'd like.

Róża had tears in her eyes too, but of joy. It was the happiest day of her life. She was so pleased the war had started.

Never mind not going to school. Never mind having to leave lots of her toys at home. Never mind that they hadn't taken all their clothes and books. Even so they had three full suitcases and a bag that only just fitted on the rack in the compartment, and kept slipping off it. But where at her grandparents' place was there room for her doll's house? Nothing would happen if it waited for her a while in Kraków. Nanna would take care of it – during the war she could play with the dolls if she wanted (Róża had given her permission). Even her favourite one, which she must have left in her bed under the pillow. It would remain in good hands.

In fact Nanna was the only one she'd miss. She'd been with her since Róża was a month old. That was almost seven years. She still tasted her soup for her to make sure it wasn't too hot, so "my dear little Róża" wouldn't burn her tongue.

They wouldn't see each other for a week or two. Maybe less than that? It might not last that long, because the people in the train were saying we'll show those Germans and soon it'll all be over. We won't let them have a single button! Earlier she'd heard the same thing on the radio.

She just wondered, what did the Germans need the button for? Nobody was saying. Did they do sewing, like her mama? Then why not just give it to them and have peace and quiet?

Róża was gazing out of the window. The sun was dazzling, she had to blink and shield her eyes with a hand to look at the people the train was passing. They had bags and cases too. But from a distance they looked tiny, like toy figures. They were being overtaken by little toy cars and horses pulling carts loaded to the brim. A traffic jam had formed on a miniature bridge because one of the little cars had broken down. Unable to get through, the others were hooting at it.

The scene was just asking for a child's hand to appear from above to tidy up and put all the little figures and toys back in their places.

For now, Róża closed one eye and, through the glass, she pretended to be picking up and moving the broken car. But carefully so it didn't fall off the bridge into the water.

At the station Nanna had said that if it went on for longer, she'd drop by to see them in Tarnów. She'd hugged her again, and whispered that she'd bring her something sweet when she came. Probably doughnuts from her sister in the country. The best in the world.

Róża smiled at her own reflection in the compartment window. Didn't Nanna look like a doughnut herself – small and fat?

Especially when she stooped by the kitchen window. She'd put a cushion on the windowsill, lean her hands on it, then rest her chin on them. And watch.

She said she didn't need the radio or the newspapers to know what was going on in the world. She knew everything about everyone at first hand, without leaving the house.

Who had bought a new coat and hat. Who went off to work in the morning with his wife, and came back an hour later with another woman. Who had died and who had had a baby. Which woman was pregnant, while her husband drank vodka all day.

She said it was her cinema. This film was shown with no interval and no tickets.

Nanna also liked to knock back a shot of vodka at the window when Róża's parents were out and she was playing with her doll's house. Róża knew where she hid the bottle. In the wardrobe behind her clothes. Anyway, her parents knew that too, but they never said a word to Nanna.

Now she was looking at her parents. They were whispering to each other. Probably so that the other people in the compartment couldn't hear them. Róża couldn't hear either. For a while she thought her papa was whispering a poem to her mama. A love poem, perhaps? She knew her parents had met on a train. Later all she understood from their conversation was that Aunt Wela and Uncle Nusek were at home. But Aunt Rena and Uncle Hesio probably weren't there yet. They'd have to set up beds everywhere as in the past. And buy a car so everyone could…

Outside, something began to make such a loud noise that she couldn't hear a thing.

She turned back to the window and saw a little aeroplane. She tried to catch it between her thumb and index finger, but it seemed to realize, banked to one side and flew lower. There was a nice pattern under its wings. A second one appeared. Now they were both flying straight at the little cars, horses, carts and people on the bridge. Róża tried to point them out to her papa. And at that very moment there was nothing left of them. The tiny bridge snapped in half, the figures overturned, and the little cars, carts and horses fell into the water.

Something shook the train, and the bag fell onto their heads. Beyond the window there was nothing but a cloud of smoke.

The train braked sharply. The conductors shouted that no one could stay on board. Before she knew it, her father had picked her up, handed her to her mother, and they were first to run out of the compartment.

When they came down the rusted steps from the carriage into a field, Rudek was already there with the suitcases and bag. For the first few kilometres of their journey along the tracks he teased Róża, refusing to say how he'd done it. Only when they stopped for longer in the forest did he tell her the truth.

"That's not fair!"

"Why so?"

"I wanted to jump out of the window with you too."

As a first reaction Rudek almost answered: Next time. Had she noticed that his hands and legs were still shaking? No, better if there weren't a next time.

It gradually dawned on him what had happened. How lucky they hadn't stayed behind like the rest, waiting in the field by the train. As they were walking away, they saw the crowd gathering by the bombarded bridge.

"The river is all red!" someone shouted, and summoned them with a wave to come and see.

Rudek gave Róża a piggyback and the three of them walked on. She'd seen quite enough today.

"If after life there's death, when the death ends, is there life again?" she asked on the way.

RUDEK

Was all this really happening?

That morning, as they were hastily packing, he had still found it hard to believe. Last night he had calmly come home from work on the tram. And today there were planes in the sky, dropping bombs. The war had ceased to be an abstraction, just some troop movements across a ragged old map spread out on the school blackboard.

Now yesterday's life seemed remote, distant and impossible. Only the weather hadn't changed. It was hot and sunny, a beautiful day.

Róża burst into tears because a wasp had stung her.

He guessed they had roughly twenty or thirty kilometres to go. At this rate, with the child and the luggage, they'd never reach Tarnów before nightfall. Normally he'd have gone through the woods to the highway and hitched a lift. There were always vehicles carrying monopoly goods, such as alcohol, tobacco or matches, running from Kraków to Tarnów and back again. As a student, he hadn't always had the money for the train, and had gone to visit his parents that way. They'd probably bombed the highway too. Or were about to do it. Safer to go by the fields.

But hardly anyone drives this way, he thought, and at that very moment spotted a black dot coming towards them. It was moving slowly up the hill where they had made their second stop. Rudek had time to weigh up the possible scenarios, each one worse than the other.

Incidentally, bicycles were now three or four times more expensive than before the war. There was money to be made.

Rudek waved to the approaching cyclist, who pretended not to see him. Soon after, he turned off the little road to avoid them by riding across the grass.

"Hey!" called Rudek.

Maybe he'd at least take Róża to Tarnów on his luggage rack? He and Ruth would manage somehow. At most they'd spend the night in a hay barn. As in their best times.

The cyclist didn't respond or even slow down.

He must have been about eighteen.

"Wait a moment," Rudek tried again.

The cyclist started pedalling even faster. He rode down the hill, and in less than a minute he was just a black dot again.

"He's probably fleeing too," said Rudek, glancing at Ruth. "Something better will come along."

And indeed it did. Half an hour later they saw a peasant cart on the horizon, one of the kind with high woven sides that Rudek had told Ruth about on the train as something they'd find useful. You could make a covered travelling wagon out of it, pack the whole family inside and transport them out of Tarnów.

"Can you drive one?" Ruth had asked him.

"I don't know yet," he'd said, smiling.

Take the family east. That was his plan.

A year ago they'd agreed that if it started, they'd meet at their parents' place. They did their best to say "if", not "when". Nobody wanted war, like everyone else, they were trying to console each other, but in fact they knew.

Still on the train, he and Ruth had wondered how many seats they'd need in a wagon of that kind. One at a time. Who was where?

After the defeat of the International Brigades and a period of internment Salek had stayed in France. He wrote to say that everything was all right and not to worry about him. What on earth had to happen for him to say things weren't all right? So he didn't count.

Hesio was in Warsaw. Since they'd dissolved his Party, he'd been badly off. Or at least so he claimed, though lately he'd moved to the best district. He was living with an older woman, a widow who had a child. He hadn't introduced her to any of the family yet. He'd been wriggling out of visits home by saying he couldn't afford a ticket.

A month ago, when they'd last seen each other in Warsaw, Rudek had even given him a few zlotys to go and see their parents. Perhaps he still had some of it left?

That day they'd been sitting on a bench in the elegant Swiss Valley park, next door to embassies and ministries, eating halva. Hesio was wearing a snow-white shirt. Made of nice material, silk perhaps. It was the shirt that had set off their conversation about the woman, because he'd got it from her as a gift. He was living with her somewhere in this area, but he didn't invite Rudek to his place.

"She dyes her hair and her stomach's saggy but I love her anyway!" he'd said.

"She's got money too," added Ruth, when Rudek told her about it on his return to Kraków.

Ruth had just arrived and they were having supper together.

"Always better if she's rich," he replied, "than poor."

To which Rena had let out a groan, while also shaking her head, to make sure he fully understood what she thought about capitalists like him.

But who exactly was she these days? She and Zawadowski were living in Zakliczyn, running a firm that sold dairy products; it was called "Health", and Rudek was a joint owner.

Apparently Mieczysław still couldn't forgive her for terminating her pregnancy. If he had known, he'd never have allowed it. As if he'd forgotten that they weren't together at the time.

Rudek gave them the start-up money for their new life, or rather he lent it to them for keeps, because he knew from day one that communists are no good at running businesses, even if it's just selling cheeses and kefir.

On the train, shortly before the bombardment, Rudek had managed to tell Ruth part of the little poem Hesio had written for Rena's birthday.

To help a young couple when on their beam ends
A dairy produce firm was founded by their friends.

Hesio went on to make genial fun of their talent for running a business.

What about the rest of the family? Nusek and his parents were at Goldhammer Street, of course. So was Wela. She probably wouldn't want to leave without Max, but that didn't hurt. He was from the village of Biała – perhaps they'd have a horse and cart to spare there?

As they sat at the clearing, Hesio's doggerel senselessly insisted on rattling away in his head: *To help a young couple...*

The cart was getting closer.

"All right!" said Rudek.

They stood up, brushed themselves off, and headed towards it.

The peasant driving the cart was quite old.

"Excuse me, sir, would you take us to Tarnów?" asked Rudek.

The carter shook his head to say no.

Rudek recognized him from somewhere.

"What about our things?"

In reply the peasant shrugged. Rudek had remembered by now. He'd see him at the Tarnów market. He sold milk, butter and eggs. At reasonable prices.

"How much?" said Rudek, looking him in the eyes.

They were blue. A bit like Lipska's eyes. It was the first time he'd thought of her today. He hadn't had a chance to warn her he was leaving. But she'd probably understand. Hitler hadn't warned him about his upcoming plans either. This morning Rudek had only had time to run to the bank for money.

He'd write to Lipska or phone her from Tarnów.

The peasant smiled wryly. Whoever offers a price first has lost. They both knew that.

But did the peasant know that Rudek had far more to lose than a few zlotys?

"Well, how much?" he asked again.

The peasant literally examined him from head to foot.

"Your jacket."

Luckily not his shoes.

Soon after, in just his shirt Rudek was packing three cases and the bag onto the cart.

"What's the address?" the peasant asked him.

Bloody hell, he looked good in that light summer jacket, although it drooped a bit on the shoulders.

Now Rudek was silent.

"I can't remember the address," he said at last. "But I know where it is."

"Hey, man… What do you mean?" said the peasant, smiling, briefly showing bare gums and three solitary black-and-yellow teeth.

"Take us to Tarnów and I'll show you."

They saw the three black-and-yellow teeth again. This time for longer.

"You'll be the address, eh?"

And he nodded for them to get in the cart.

XXXI

RYWKA

At Goldhammer Street, his parents laughed at them for becoming the address.

"One day that'll be famous," said Nathan. "It'll pass into Stramer family history."

He was unusually jolly, despite what was happening outside.

If only we could shut ourselves in our little flat, thought Rywka, standing by the stove. Close the windows, draw the curtains and forget about the whole world…

Wait it out.

Like Nathan, lately she had been going to synagogue more often. There's a reason why the Catholics say, "When things seem odd, we go to God". Nathan said: "When life becomes a slog, we go to the synagogue". She hadn't seen as many people at shul for a long time.

She had started to dress in black. But only because she'd grown fat. In the face and the belly. The soft belly bothered her more. Next year she'd be sixty. And she had given birth to seven children.

Under the apron she had put on a short time ago to do the cooking, she had a black skirt and a loose black blouse with puffed sleeves and large buttons. She had washed, brushed and pinned up her white hair. There was nothing she could do about her drooping eyelid. In spite of all, she wanted to look good today for her children and granddaughter's arrival.

Still in her clothes, Róża fell asleep on the bed almost as soon as they arrived. Rywka undressed her and tucked her up in the quilt.

"Good night, sleep tight," she said, kissing her granddaughter on the spot where she most liked kissing her children, the bulge between the nose and the brow.

"How's my father?" Rudek asked her.

"Luckily he's not lying down."

They both knew that if he went to bed he wouldn't be able to move, and certainly wouldn't leave.

"Why's he so excited?"

They also knew that after this sort of "high" the gastritis often followed.

"He's written to Ben. To get us all out to America."

Ruth, Rena and Wela wanted to help Rywka with the cooking. She didn't need help; almost every day she cooked for the lunchers by herself, but she assigned them a few small tasks to keep their hands and heads busy. Chop and fry the onions, grate the carrots, lay the table.

Nathan wandered around the flat among Rywka and the children, without a set purpose. He never stopped talking.

Nusek really is like him, thought Rudek. A good thing he'd

gone to stay the night with the son of the caretaker from the next yard, because the two of them at once would be unbearable. Not to mention the fact that we wouldn't all fit.

Only Hesio wasn't in Tarnów yet. But he'd sent a telegram from Warsaw to say he'd be there tomorrow.

Naturally their father refused to hear of leaving for the east.

"First we must wait for Ben's reply."

Rudek noticed that as he said it, he instinctively grabbed hold of his leather belt with the brass buckle. As if to say: solid American workmanship. And indeed. It had survived all those years of wear and of thrashing their backsides.

You can wait for the Messiah, thought Rudek, unfolding the beds for the night.

"We don't know if the post will be working," he said to his father.

He had too much on his mind to be arguing with him as well. Mentally he had already drawn up a list of things he had to do. To start with, gather the whole family, buy a horse and cart, and phone Lipska.

Anyway, we're sure to quarrel on the way. He could already feel the stress and his father's intensity in the pit of his stomach. Could he bear such a long time with him in a single wagon? Wouldn't they kill each other long before reaching Lwów?

Rudek glanced at his mother. As she stood next to Ruth, facing the stove, he gazed at her white hair pinned up in a bun. It was longer and thicker than Ruth's.

"Listen, I know the Germans and Austrians well," said Nathan, refusing to let it drop. "We fought together throughout the last war in the same army. What can they do to me? They won't throw me out of my job because I haven't got one."

Rudek wondered if he should hide the money somewhere, the savings he'd taken out of the bank that morning. He'd had it in his left shoe all day. He didn't answer his father, which didn't mean he wasn't listening when Nathan said he wasn't going to abandon all his belongings, everything he'd acquired in his entire life of more than sixty years. Rudek looked around the flat. He couldn't exactly hide the money among the herbs and spices above the stove.

He knew by now what to say to his father, he had an argument ready, an ace up his sleeve, but he didn't want to play it too soon. He was waiting for the right moment. In other words, for his father to stop gabbling.

He glanced through the open window at the street. In almost every house the lights were still burning. Were they packing too? And where it was dark, had they already gone?

"And you can't transplant an old tree," said his father.

Rudek gazed beseechingly at the sky. All the stars were on show. Tomorrow would be another beautiful day.

Better to cut it down, he thought. Or tear it up by the roots.

At least his father had finally shut up. Rudek waited a while and, still looking at the street, calmly said: "So you'll be staying here at Goldhammer Street alone, will you?"

XXXII

RUDEK

He was the last of the family to go to bed. The same bed he'd shared for years with Nusek. Ruth was already asleep. Just before nodding off he shoved the money under his pillow.

First thing in the morning Rudek put his hand under the pillow. Then he nipped out for breakfast rolls. He put them on the kitchen table and said he was going to the post office to make a call.

"Who are you calling?" asked Ruth.

He took one of the rolls to eat on the way.

"The Syndicate."

The post office was open, but full of people, and Rudek had to stand in line for the telephone. He reassured Lipska. He told her his plan.

Ruth might occasionally say she's proud of me as well, he thought.

He asked Lipska to tell him what she was wearing.

"Grey skirt, little pink blouse, blue high-heeled shoes."

"And underneath?"

Unfortunately he could only hear every other word, because Lipska lowered her voice (she was at work, in the front office), and the people in the queue started knocking on the cabin window to hurry him up.

That evening Hesio arrived from Warsaw.

He'd added a new verse to the poem he'd composed for Rena's birthday:

> *Because of the war economy,*
> *They had to wind up the company,*
> *Those poor capitalist wannabes.*

Everything went according to Rudek's plan. If not better. Wela's Max provided horses and a wagon. In fact, his parents would be on it too, but it was still a huge saving. They'd come from Biała and take the Stramers.

"It'll be a bit of a squeeze," said Max.

Anyway, it wouldn't be so bad. Rena and Zawadowski had decided to go separately. Some friends had two spare seats for them in their car.

Rudek liked this Max fellow. He too preferred to act rather than wait.

Next day, soon after twelve they were sitting in the wagon. Just as they had agreed, each person took just one small suitcase, bag or backpack. But even so the wagon was full. The rest of their things remained in Tarnów.

They set off.

The driver was Max's father, with a grey beard and a yarmulka. Rudek noticed that his son didn't snatch the reins from his hands. Old Kierbel took Róża on his knees for a while and showed her how to drive. They went slowly, wagon behind wagon, car behind car. Not much faster than the people with luggage walking along the verge, who waved at them to hitch a lift. Max's father spread his hands.

"Not a bad mass migration," said Hesio, pointing his chin at the line stretching over the horizon to the east.

Rudek nodded.

He was instantly reminded that the historical Great Migrations had ended in the collapse of antiquity. The era he liked best. There was a reason why he'd done a degree in classical philology.

And now everything was collapsing too. Were the Middle Ages coming back again? He felt like saying it aloud. But what for? They could probably do without that sort of consolation.

Old Kierbel pulled on the reins. A hundred metres ahead of them there was an accident. Everyone wanted to see what had happened. Only the old Kierbels stayed on the wagon with the old Stramers and Róża, who had a stomach ache.

"Maybe from hunger?" asked Nathan, but Róża shook her head.

At least the horses could rest a while.

Rudek saw a girl with red hair lying in front of a car.

"I saw it," said a woman pushing a pram with a suitcase in it. "She threw herself under the wheels on purpose."

He watched as the driver helped the girl to stand up, brush herself off and get into the car.

Nice motor: an Alfa Romeo.

"You can see for yourself!"

"We only have to get moving and instantly I'm hungry," said Nathan once they had set off again.

Rywka had made everyone sandwiches for the journey. First Nathan ate his own sandwich, with cheese and cucumber; then, as Róża had only taken one bite before giving it back to her grandmother, he ate hers. He tried to eat her piece of yeast cake too, but Rywka was in time to stop him.

Rudek lay on his back. He could feel the hay tickling his neck pleasantly. Yesterday he'd been the last to go to bed again. He half-closed his eyes. The road ahead became narrower and he could hardly see the sky. The horses' hoofs clattered at a steady pace and the wagon rocked gently.

He could smell the sweet, pleasing reek of old Kierbel's pipe.

What had he been dreaming about? The moment Nusek tugged at his arm he forgot. In the first instant Rudek thought they'd already reached the border. And those soldiers with eagles on their caps who had surrounded them were the Polish border guards.

They told them to take their things and get out of the wagon, because they wanted to inspect them.

But why were they waving guns around?

"Calmly does it, gentlemen!" he said.

Can't they see there's a child here?

Ruth picked Róża up.

Rudek jumped down from the wagon and took a good look at the soldiers. They were really still children too.

"They're drunk," Max whispered to him.

One sniff of the cork was probably enough, he thought.

How old could they be? Not much older than Nusek, who was hiding behind his father.

"No kidding." Rudek went up to the spottiest soldier, who seemed to be in charge of this play group.

Close up, his face – red with blackheads – reminded Rudek of a ladybird.

Even the pistol he was pointing at him looked like a children's toy.

"Shut up, Yid," said the spotty boy to Rudek and stepped back a pace.

Róża began to cry and cuddled up to Ruth.

"All right," said Rudek, raising his hands a little.

"We're requisitioning this wagon."

They told them all to move aside, and then drove off.

Even old Kierbel, who had lost the most, horses and wagon, said the main thing was that no one had been hurt. The rest were even less inclined to lament or lose heart.

"It's good, but not hopeless," said Nathan, as in the past.

But where exactly were they? They began to look around. They were on a road beside a forest. They sent Nusek to run and find out what was the nearest village. He came back five minutes later. Pustków. It meant nothing to any of them.

Nusek gave Róża a long, green pinecone he'd found on the road.

He noticed that everyone seemed to be in a slightly better mood. While they were waiting for him, Rudek had told them a joke.

The best things always happen without me, thought Nusek.

Rudek picked up two suitcases and rapidly set off first towards Pustków.

"It'd be good to find a place for the night before dark," he said.

He was followed by Wela, carrying Róża. Then Max and Nusek, also carrying two suitcases each. As was Hesio, who walked alongside Ruth. Bringing up the rear of the procession were the older Stramers and the older Kierbels.

Max told Nusek the joke, which was about the guy who goes to see the bank manager, saying he's got advice on how to earn a million dollars in an instant. "You've got a daughter, haven't you, sir?" The manager nods. "And you'd like to marry her off?" "Yes," says the manager, "you're well informed." "And you're going to provide a dowry of two million dollars?" "Yes, that's right." "Well, I'll take her for a million."

Nusek laughed, thinking Rudek was sure to have told it better and more funnily.

It was starting to grow dark. First Rudek saw smoke, then a chimney, a house and a barn. They could hear a dog barking with increasing ferocity.

Ten minutes later they saw it in the farmyard. A little black mongrel. A bit like Fluffy from their courtyard in Tarnów, but even smaller. Now it was just growling at the sight of them.

HESIO

"This isn't Roses Avenue in Warsaw," said Ruth to Hesio as they ducked to follow Rudek into a damp hallway.

How did she know his address? One of the best in Warsaw. Rudek must have told her.

"Well," said Hesio, smiling. "It certainly doesn't smell of roses here."

The interior was quite like at Flounder's parents' house, where he had once hid. How proud and happy they must be now that they'd got their way, their son had fulfilled their dream and become a priest.

The Reverend Flounder, thought Hesio. God does move in mysterious ways.

Even the smell here was like at the Flounders'. The sort of smell that hits you in the face and repels you, but after a couple of days you don't notice it anymore, though other people move away from you.

A dirt floor, a clay oven, a table by the window, a cross on the wall. The woman peeling potatoes in the corner waved them inside.

"God be praised." Hesio knew what to say.

"For ever and ever," she replied.

But her surprised look seemed to say: "Well, I never. A Jew, but a decent human being." (Though maybe after the adventure with the wagon that was just Hesio's impression?)

Three men were sitting at a table by the window, in the light of an oil lamp. Rudek was standing over them, already doing a deal with them.

"Ten and a child," he said.

The oldest, plainly the farmer, shook his head.

"I ain't got enough straw."

"We can bring some from our place," suggested another. "For extra money, of course."

Hesio and Ruth didn't know which man had said this, because both were sitting with their backs towards them. Both stood up from the table simultaneously as soon as Rudek nodded to say that he agreed.

"Minx, in your kennel" one of them shouted once in the farmyard.

Hesio carried their things into the barn. Including his own suitcase, full of new clothes he had brought from Warsaw. Fashionable shirts, trousers and jackets. All made to measure. Unfortunately, he hadn't had a single opportunity to walk through Tarnów in them.

Zofia liked to take him from one tailor's shop to the next. She liked to watch him changing his clothes, or to come into the bathroom while he was taking a shower.

"How beautiful you are," she'd say. "How young."

No woman had ever liked him as much.

She kept saying he was wasting his life. That he should be thinking about marriage and children, which she could no longer give him.

"I'm still a child myself," he told her.

The peasants must have lived nearby, because a few minutes later they were back with the straw. They waited for Rudek to give them the money, and only then began to strew it on the ground. Rudek stood over them to make sure they spread it evenly.

As usual, Hesio was sure things would work out somehow. Anyway, with Rudek we won't perish. He always thinks of everything. Tomorrow we'll sort out a wagon and travel on.

And eventually Hiter's machinery will go to hell and I'll be able to go back to Warsaw, to Roses Avenue.

"Women don't like pessimists," as Zofia would say.

He stared at Max; optimist or pessimist? Never mind, with his American film-star looks women were bound to like him. Tall and slender, with fair locks falling over his blue eyes.

Who'd have expected quiet, timid Wela to find herself such a dreamboat?

What movie had an actor who looked like him? Zofia would know instantly – she never missed a single premiere. In her youth she'd wanted to be an actress, but instead of that she'd married an older man, a former Legionary with a grey goatee beard, and become a general's wife. Hesio only knew him from the photograph in a round frame on the dining-room wall.

Seeing Max's stooping, elderly parents, he never would have believed they could have such a handsome son. He often had similar thoughts when he met the parents of the girls he went out with. Were they really their daughters?

But just a moment. He hadn't seen an actor who looked like Max at the cinema at all. The Kierbels were from Biała, just like Flounder. Suddenly it all fell into place. He knew Max's face not from the cinema screen but from the village pasture. How many years ago was it? Max was still a child then.

Now, come of age, he was standing beside Wela. Hesio went up to him.

"It wasn't you who lent me a book, was it?"

"About the *Titanic*?" said Max, smiling.

So he'd known all along.

From the other end of the barn they suddenly heard a shout: "For fuck's sake!"

Trouble was brewing in the darkness.

One of the peasants got up from the ground, holding his nose.

A second one shouted: "Keep your mitts off!"

Rudek pushed him with his left hand, and held his right, clenched into a fist, like a boxer at the ready by his own face.

Hesio and Max headed towards him.

"Run for it!" cried the peasant who was holding his nose, and raced out of the barn first.

The second fled too, but tripped on the threshold.

To Hesio's inquiring glance Rudek merely replied: "He asked for it."

He refused to say more about what had happened.

He took a cigarette from Hesio and went outside to smoke in the yard. His brothers followed him.

It was completely dark and quiet. Not even Minx was barking at them now.

Rudek blew smoke rings.

"What if they come back?" said Nusek.

"They won't," said Rudek.

"Well, you gave him a good smack!" said Nusek, who had seen it at close hand, and showed Hesio the punch, but stopped his fist just before his brother's nose.

Then he also played the role of the man who'd been hit, and fell to the ground insensible.

As usual, he did it all very fast, as if speeded up. And in the dark too.

He had no idea how much his act annoyed Rudek.

"Knock out!" said Nusek, getting up again. "The guy's lucky he survived."

Cool it, thought Rudek. He just wants me to like him. I should really give him something in return.

"Listen," he said, "whenever you hit someone, have something inside your hand. A pebble, or a small stick, perhaps."

"So you can hit harder?" asked Nusek.

"So you don't break your fingers."

They finished their cigarettes and went back into the barn.

Half an hour later they were all trying to get to sleep. Except Róża, who was already dreaming about the doughnuts from Nanna's sister in the village. They were lying on the kitchen table in their Kraków flat. Wrapped in newspaper, as usual. She was drooling at the very sight of the greasy stains on the paper. But there was no one to unwrap and eat them.

Hesio was wondering if on the way to the village Ruth had brushed against his arm a couple of times on purpose. They were walking side by side. Hesio tried to catch her eye, but she just gazed into the distance. He brushed against her too, but she didn't react. She must have noticed. Well, that he hadn't expected of his sister-in-law!

But why not? She was younger than his Zofia, wasn't she?

Before he met Zofia, he'd been stony broke. On top of that, Stalin had just dissolved the CPP and Hesio had stopped getting his Party activist's monthly salary. He couldn't even afford halva. That really was the last straw. That was how the "economics of love" he'd invented back in Tarnów came to an end. He had to think up something new, and above all cheaper.

He started inviting girls to his little room in Warsaw's Grochów district to see his collection of tram tickets. You can collect anything. Why not tickets? He had to buy them anyway to travel about the city to meetings.

He'd stuck then on the wall of his room at various intervals. So that they formed the shape of a little tram.

Apart from the words *Single tram ticket* and the red letters TR, each one had its own number, a price of 20 groszy and the warning: *Ticket not transferable. To be kept for inspection.*

"And then what do you do?" asked his friends. "Once you've shown it to them?"

He didn't understand the question. If he'd managed to persuade a girl to come to his room at night to see his collection of tram tickets, the hardest part was behind him.

Until one day he invited Zofia. They never got as far as the tickets. She kissed him first, as soon as he opened the door.

Nusek was still excited about Rudek's punch. If only Lolek Szpeda could have seen it. Hit and sunk! He fell asleep squeezing a pebble in his hand, just in case they did come back in the night.

Wela was wondering what the peasant had done to upset Rudek so badly that he refused to tell anyone about it.

Had they spread the straw unevenly? Did they want more money?

"My father heard them say 'you filthy Yid'," Max whispered to her now.

Nathan was thinking about what he and old Kierbel had discussed when the boys went outside to smoke.

"Let's let the young ones go on alone. We'll just slow them down. And who knows what might happen along the way?"

Nathan nodded. He had said from the start that this family expedition was pointless. Like Kierbel, he wanted to go home. Had Ben got his letter by now?

Rywka agreed with this too. They just had to persuade Rudek.

"Son," she said to him.

"Yes?"

"Good night, sleep tight."

XXXIII

RÓŻA

RÓŻA LIKED THE SMELL OF PETROL. She ran outside into Goldhammer Street to see the black car with an open top. It was carrying three smartly dressed officers. She smiled and waved at them.

The car braked.

It turned around and stopped near her.

An officer stepped out of the car; his temples were going grey, and he was wearing a beautiful dark-grey coat with not a single one of its shiny buttons missing. Róża was careful to check. He said something to her, but she couldn't understand German. He reached inside the front of his coat.

And brought out two fruit drops. Yellow ones. Róża politely bowed and curtseyed the way her mother had taught her to say thank you.

She stood in the street a while, inhaling the smell of petrol from the disappearing car. It mixed with the lemony sweetness of the fruit drop.

As soon as she went back into the flat, her mother smacked her on the head. The sweet fell out of her mouth onto the kitchen floor. There was nothing to pick up. It had shattered into tiny, sticky pieces.

"How could you do that to me!" gasped Ruth. "I almost died of fright because of you."

It turned out she had seen everything through the window.

But she had taught her to curtsey herself.

Róża would tell Papa that, and Mama would get what she deserved.

"Don't go in there. You'll wake him up."

The girl tiptoed into the room where Rudek was lying, slowly recovering.

Before now, she had always felt safe beside him. She knew nothing would happen to her when he took her in his arms and they jumped onto a moving tram or swam at the end of the pool. Where not even he could touch the bottom.

His head and face were still covered by bandages. He could hardly see his daughter through them.

"How are you feeling, Papa?"

RUDEK

For several days, since returning to Goldhammer Street, he hadn't got out of bed. Before that he'd spent a week at the Jewish hospital in Tarnów.

Under the bandages he thought through everything that had happened in detail. As if projecting slides onto a white background, or looking at photographs through the peepholes at Tarnów's stereoscopic theatre.

At first light, he, Hesio, Nusek and Max had gone to look around the district. Perhaps they'd be able to rustle up a wagon from somewhere? At once they saw the peasants on a hillock.

The sun was only just rising. It lit up six figures with sticks.

They were waiting for them.

Hesio wanted to turn back.

"You're afraid," said Rudek, "so don't go."

The three of them went to "sort things out".

Even if they had listened to Hesio, the peasants would have attacked them anyway. They couldn't run away, because their parents and the others were still in the barn.

Rudek still ached all over. Worst of all at night, when he kept waking up. He'd been consoled by the doctor at the Jewish hospital who said: "Luckily you'll heal up as quickly as a dog."

They had started looking around for sticks too. The closer the peasants came, the more menacing they looked. Rudek kept going, with head held high, straight towards them.

"I'm feeling better," he replied to Róża.

He could still feel the rage. One to one, none of them would have had a chance with him.

Róża kissed him on his bandaged brow.

It's easiest to hit someone who isn't expecting it. If you hit the right spot, he'll go flying to the ground. These guys were prepared. But Rudek did have time to hit out, and soundly too, because he'd broken a thumb – he'd thrown at least two or three punches before he was whacked in the neck and lost consciousness.

The next thing he remembered was being carried on a cart. He had glanced at his parents, who were leaning over him. As if he were looking at a blurred photograph.

Am I seeing them for the last time?

He felt unwell.

"Son…" said Rywka.

They must have roughed him up good and proper. Kicked him while he was on the ground. Luckily they hadn't broken his arms or legs. They had mainly kicked him in the head. And like Salek, he had a solid one.

How curious that to others it's the head that represents the person. You talk to it, and you hit it, the thought crossed his mind.

When he came round again, he checked if his watch was still on his wrist. Yes, and they hadn't taken the money either. Maybe they hadn't found it? He lost consciousness again.

It was Nathan who had sorted out a horse and cart, and then a doctor, who stitched and bandaged him. Nathan had also got him admitted to the Jewish hospital. Rudek couldn't remember that.

Aren't I too hard on him?

He tried to remember what Salek had once read in an English book. Something very much to the point. How did it go? Perhaps it was: "First we love our parents. Then we judge them. And finally sometimes we forgive them."

Maybe it was time to move on to the third stage. Especially as at tough moments his father could evidently be surprising.

Rudek tried to smile, but it hurt too much.

He asked his father to lie down beside him on the bed.

"Just don't say anything, Dad," he said.

"All right, all right."

They hugged each other awkwardly. They plainly didn't know how to do it. Who should embrace whom? Finally Rudek took hold of his father's bald head and pressed it to his chest. They lay like that for a good few minutes.

The rest of them had come out of the fight without much harm. At least compared with him. Nusek had a black eye, Max had a split lip, and Hesio had several bruises and torn clothing.

Rudek blamed himself for putting a stop to their journey and forcing them to go back to Tarnów.

As his mother told him on their return: "Our whole trip was like trying to cheat destiny. Trouble at every turn."

Now he knew they wouldn't have managed to reach the border anyway. The Germans had surrounded the area and were probably watering their horses in the river Wieprz by now.

He also knew that having promised not to give an inch of ground to the enemy, the Polish government had been luckier than they had – it had successfully escaped to Romania.

Rudek heard the children in the courtyard singing:

The commander-in-chief is now at ease,
He's skedaddled overseas...

He hadn't been out of the house yet. He'd spent days on end lying in his parents' bed with his head in bandages.

"The patriarch of the clan," as Hesio jokingly called him, "receives the family members lying down."

His brothers informed him about what was going on outside. Despite their mother's requests not to disturb him, they didn't wait for him to get better.

Or perhaps they were doing as their mother said and sparing him the worst. But could worse things be happening than the ones they told him about?

Worse than the September defeat? Rounding up Jews in the street for forced labour? Making them wear Star of David armbands?

And burning down all the synagogues in the city?

His father proudly told him that only the New Synagogue had refused to burn down. The Germans had to bring in two sappers to lay dynamite.

He saw it as a sign.

"Of what, I wonder?" asked Rudek. "Beyond the fact that it had solid foundations."

"You'll see. There'll be a letter from Ben soon."

How one thing connected with another in Nathan's head was a mystery to Rudek and the rest of the family.

It's only a sign of the fact that he's not all right, he thought.

A letter came, but from Rena. Ruth read it out to him. Rena and Mieczysław had managed to get set up in Lwów – now Lvov, renamed by the Soviets when they'd annexed eastern Poland. Rena had already found work as a tram driver.

She encouraged them to come. Not in so many words, of course. She wrote: "Do drop in on Uncle Vanya, it's more comfortable than at Auntie Klara's."

In fact their father did have some distant relatives in Lvov, but he was hardly in touch with them at all, because they were Orthodox. However, there was definitely no Auntie Klara among them, even less an Uncle Vanya.

Rena's letter convinced Max and Wela, who was living with him now, to escape to Lvov too. They had been coming to Goldhammer Street at least three times a day, for breakfast, lunch and supper. Just before leaving, with their backpacks on, they called by on bicycles.

"See you at Uncle Vanya's," said Rudek, who was woken up to say farewell.

Another time he was awoken by loud knocking at the door. Was that the same day? The same week? He wasn't sure.

Rywka opened it, and without a word two German officers came in. They looked around the flat, without taking any notice of its residents, as if they weren't there.

The Germans instantly spotted the oak dresser with the carved wooden columns topped with horses' heads, and ordered it to be shown to them. Rudek had to get up for Nusek and Nathan to move his bed aside; otherwise it was impossible to see what was in this most valuable piece of furniture in the flat.

They shook their heads at the sight of its contents – from the outside it promised more than just some old junk: letters from Ben gone yellow with age, a comb, a metal candlestick, a decaying prayerbook and some tefillin.

They had a similar reaction to the interior of the wardrobe.

Róża recognized one of the officers by his greying temples. He was the one who'd given her the fruit drop. But a glance at her mother was enough to stop her from going up to him.

They were however interested in Hesio's suitcase, which they found in the wardrobe.

"See this," said the fruit-drop officer to his colleague, taking out Hesio's snow-white shirt, "what soft fabric."

They cast the Stramers approving looks too.

They took the whole suitcase and left.

Hesio wasn't there at the time, but even if he had been, so what?

At any rate, a day or two later he left Tarnów. Rudek had witnessed Hesio's brief period of mourning for his suitcase.

He had reproached himself, saying that if only he'd put on one of the suits with a white shirt, cufflinks and a tie that day...

But he hadn't done it on purpose, to avoid drawing attention to himself.

"Well, it's a pity," he'd said to himself several times.

"It's a pity to die," Rudek had replied.

For Rudek all these days merged into one. Probably because he saw them all from the perspective of the bed.

He could remember his head spinning because he'd raised it from the pillow too abruptly when he found out the Germans had nabbed Nusek off the street and taken him to the Gestapo.

He wasn't in bandages by then, but the doctor had told him to stay in bed.

"It's lucky I had my Oy-veys on me!" Nusek told them on his return home. "I showed them. I got a couple of slaps around the chops, a kick and they let me go."

"You showed them what? What's an oy-veys?"

"That's what you call an Ausweis."

"You should leave too," said Rudek.

"On my own?" asked Nusek.

"I'm not ready yet."

"I'll wait."

Daniel, the son of the former deputy mayor of Tarnów, came to visit.

"They sure duffed you up badly, you poor guy," he said, shaking his head. "I'd rather it had happened to me."

"I can arrange it for you if you like," said Rudek.

He was feeling better by now, and even sat with Daniel at the kitchen table.

As in the past, his parents said they felt honoured by his visit. But Daniel just let that slide. He was wearing a Star of David armband.

After the Germans paid him a call, he'd decided to leave too.

Rudek had a clear memory of the deputy mayor's flat with innumerable rooms. And wasn't surprised to hear, as Daniel put it, that "it was very much to the Germans' taste".

"They took what they liked from the wardrobe. Meaning just about everything."

Daniel's biggest regret was the dinner jacket his father had brought him from Paris for his thirtieth birthday.

"Right in front of me that German tried it on, admired himself in the mirror, and didn't take it off, can you imagine? What a total bastard. After he left I thought to myself: fuck this. I'm leaving. I went to the bank. And guess what? The cashier, Ignacy, spread his hands. They've blocked my account, can you imagine? But we made a deal…"

"And when are you leaving?"

"I've found some people who get you across the river San."

"Trustworthy?"

"They certainly should be. For that money. A pal they got across sent a message to say it all went smoothly."

Rywka served them tea. And the rarest delicacy they had in the house, which was bread sprinkled with sugar. It was Nanna who had brought the sugar, since spotting saccharine on their table.

"My child won't eat saccharine," she had said.

Roughly once a week she came to Tarnów with buckwheat, flour and eggs. She also brought doughnuts that vanished the same day. She'd be dripping with sweat as she dropped the bundles of food she'd been carrying on her back.

Once she arrived during one of their political debates. Was Hesio yet again telling Rudek that capitalism always leads to nationalism, and nationalism to war? Or was he justifying Stalin's alliance with Hitler? Nanna listened as she wiped her face with a handkerchief.

"I'll tell you one thing!" she interrupted them. "Politics is a whore and a thief."

Then she went to give Róża a doughnut as usual, and see if the child had grown thinner.

"What a perfect appraisal," said Rywka.

BEN

Everything's all right. I got across. You can trust them

That was the message Rudek got from Daniel on a crumpled sheet of paper. The handwriting matched.

It was brought by a waggoner with a moustache, probably one of the men who'd taken Daniel across.

"When there's a group of six," he said, "we'll go again."

Rudek asked him the price; he wanted to make sure they were being charged exactly the same as Daniel. Yes. A total of three hundred zlotys for two people. Quite a solid sum.

It was good business.

Rudek was feeling much better by now. His face was hardly swollen anymore. He'd stopped feeling dizzy. It was just his right thumb that had healed badly, only straightening halfway.

At last he went outside. The very first time he saw them sticking new posters to the advertising pillars and walls of houses. They were aimed at the Jews, but written in Polish and German.

The governor general Hans Frank had given orders for all Jewish bank accounts to be blocked, and had banned Jewish children from going to school.

It was natural for him and Nusek to go first. There was no point in waiting any longer. On top of which it was about to turn cold.

Rudek didn't know how he ended up outside the post office building. But he didn't go inside. It was shut.

"You get yourselves settled first," their parents had said. "Then get Ruth and the little one across, and we'll see about us."

He could only imagine what they felt as they said goodbye to more of their children. Rudek felt like crying at the thought of having to part with Róża. He didn't hide it. She should know how much she meant to him.

And had the others heard him bursting into tears the night before he left? For the first time since he couldn't remember when. And it wasn't crying like Ruth's or Róża's. There was something strange, internal, animal about it. He never cried like that. He shook all over as he did so. Or perhaps it wasn't crying at all? The last time he'd heard anything like it was in childhood, when he'd gone to see his father at the butcher's and watched a chicken being killed the kosher way.

He stopped his mouth with a pillow to avoid waking anyone.

Maybe it was to do with Ben as well?

He'd never met him, but like the whole family, he felt respect for him. After all, for years he had supported them from across the ocean. And expected nothing in return.

Since he was little Rudek had wanted to be that sort of person. Strong and important. He liked to think he was similar to his uncle.

After all, even his father sometimes mistakenly said to him: "Ben, no, please…"

"Dad, may I remind you you're not my younger brother," he'd reply. "In spite of appearances."

"Get off my back!" Nathan would retort.

The day before Rudek and Nusek were due to leave a letter came from America. Had his father's intuition been correct? Had Ben sent them an invitation to join him? Rudek found it hard to believe, but the others were infected by a mood of anticipation for Nathan's return from shopping, because he alone had the right to open the letter.

Can it be possible? And I'm just being too rational?

It seemed to him that ever since the war had begun, people had become more mystical and spiritual. They kept having visions and premonitions, they kept searching for the slightest traces of the hand of God in everything. They believed in fate, in the magic of numbers, they went to see clairvoyants, and Gypsies read their palms.

At least once a day one travelling salesman or another knocked at their door and tried to flog them the Apocalypse of Saint John, the prophesies of Daniel, and of course the predictions of Nostradamus.

Where there's demand, there's supply.

It was just the same in Kraków. When he finally called Lipska, she told him her cats could sense things she couldn't see. Both kept staring at the same point on the wall, in between the ironing board and the stool, where there must be something that a human being wasn't capable of seeing.

"It's true! I'm telling you!"

Let's hope she doesn't end up like old Mrs Fluffy, he thought.

"Apart from that everything's all right," she said, laughing.

The letter from America was waiting for Nathan on the kitchen table.

Rudek had only examined it in the light by the window. It was different, thinner than usual. And typewritten, it looked like official print. It definitely didn't contain any dollars.

Perhaps Ben really had got them some travels documents. Visas to enter America, or an affidavit, in other words an invitation with a guarantee.

At most he and Nusek wouldn't cross the San tomorrow. He'd tell the smugglers something, that they were sick or had had a change of heart. In the worst case they'd lose the deposit – a hundred zlotys.

"Didn't I say?" Nathan held up the letter in a triumphant gesture, like the Statue of Liberty's torch. "I knew it!"

Still in his hat, coat and shoes he walked around the flat with the letter, and then went back to the table, while the amused Róża ran after her grandfather.

Finally he sat down, leaned back slightly in his chair, but changed his mind and stood up again, as if wanting the family, meaning Rywka, Ruth, Rudek and Nusek, sitting at the table, to be able to watch him as he read it.

Or perhaps it was he who wanted to watch them? And count up how many places they'd need on the ship.

He imagined sailing into the port in New York with his family in the bright morning sunlight.

He'd waited so many years for this.

And it had taken another world war for his dream to come true.

He didn't tear off the envelope, but gently slid his index finger under its white edge and slit it open.

He was slowly cranking up the tension, inside himself too; he could feel his heart thumping as he removed the thin sheet of paper folded in half.

Before unfolding it and starting to read, he looked up at his audience again.

The letter was short and official. He read it once, put it back in the envelope, laid it on the table and sat down.

"Well?" asked Rudek.

Nathan shook his head.

The letter summoned Nathan Stramer, as the sole beneficiary, to present himself at the office of the New York notary (Sam Dembitz, Notary Public, 52 W Houston St, NY) on 15 November at 10 a.m., with regard to taking charge of the property left by his brother, Ben Stramer.

"It's a communication from a lawyer." Nathan made a gesture as if wanting to slam his fist against the table, but finally just laid his head on it. "Ben is dead."

He had no children, it was true, but in that case what about Pepi?

In his letters he had rarely asked his brother how they were feeling – he and Pepi. And Ben wrote to him about it even less often.

Rywka laid a hand on Nathan's arm.

Nathan had mainly written to Ben about himself, the children and the successive business ventures he'd tried to launch thanks to his dollars. To encourage Ben to come and visit, he'd tell him what was new in Tarnów. The trams, the fertilizer plant, the most modern prison in Poland.

And so they had corresponded for almost forty years.

Why had he hardly asked his brother any questions? Did he think that since Ben hadn't kept him with him in America at the time he wouldn't... Nathan shrugged. But why exactly hadn't he kept him there? What had actually happened more than forty years ago? All he could remember was how he had felt that day on the quay.

In the past, Ben had never been sick. It wouldn't have occurred to Nathan that something might have been troubling him, since nothing had been troubling Nathan himself. Well, perhaps he had a little less strength than in the past, and lately, when he ran after Róża in the yard, he had to stop because his legs would suddenly start to ache. Sometimes in the city he'd stop in front of a shop window (he'd noticed that now all the Jewish shops had their doors and windows marked with white Stars of David), but when the pain passed, he could walk on.

Had Pepi died first and Ben hadn't written to tell him? And after her death he'd been left alone with no one to take care of him? He was over seventy by now.

If only I could have been there for him, thought Nathan.

It was so many years since he'd seen him – the last time was from the departing ship. But despite only being expressed in letters, his older brother's opinion still mattered the most. He tried to look at himself through Ben's eyes. In his thoughts he still sought his advice. Or, as in the past, he had done his best to get into his good books, by praising the hot dogs Ben liked for example, though Nathan wasn't really all that keen on them.

But also, perhaps most often, he mentally reproached him for never coming to meet his Rywka and the children.

He wouldn't have had the courage to write that to his brother in a letter. He certainly couldn't have said it to him if they'd finally met up. He knew that.

Now it was unimportant.

Apart from the letters and the dollars, what exactly would change? After all, he'd only ever been talking to himself all this time. And those conversations would remain where they had been held before, in other words in his head.

He suddenly thought of the neighbour from Goldhammer Street, whom he had mocked for years.

Will I be like bloody Mrs Fluffy, who went on taking her dog for walks and talking to him long after his death?

She had died soon after the Germans entered Tarnów.

By then she could hardly trudge around the yard, but he still ran into her in the same blue sweater, holding the lead.

"Have you ever seen such lovely tanks?" she had only just asked.

She never got to wear a Star of David armband.

He wasn't surprised that apart from him and Rywka there was no one at her funeral except for a fellow from the local Jewish community, which had paid for the burial. Mrs Fluffy was buried differently from how she lived – without the lead and wrapped in a clean shroud. Nathan had peeped into the coffin on purpose.

She was lucky, because a few days later the Germans dissolved the Jewish community. Would the Judenrat appointed to replace it have paid for her funeral too? So far it only took money off the Jews and handed it over to the Germans.

Or maybe there was an accident? wondered Nathan in the night, when some wailing awoke him. And Ben and Pepi perished in it? A fire, a flood, a hurricane? Such things do happen there. Just as here there's Hitler, Stalin, or other bloody hell.

NATHAN

Next morning they said goodbye to Rudek and Nusek. Before leaving Rudek put some money on the kitchen table.

"It should last you for two or three months."

A Pole or Ukrainian came for them. They got in the back of his wagon. Rywka handed them a bag of sandwiches.

"Dress warmly," she said.

When they set off, Nathan and Rywka followed for a while and waved. Ruth and Róża, with a white bow in her hair, ran along.

"Keep well!" shouted Rudek.

Nathan and Rywka stopped after a few paces. They watched as the last of their children left Tarnów. Their youngest and eldest sons.

Only now did Nathan think of Ben again.

As soon as they got home, he went to bed and stayed there for the rest of the day.

Although his door was closed, he heard Rywka and Ruth going into the yard for firewood. And Róża, alone in the kitchen, playing with her favourite doll, which Nanna had brought her from Kraków.

"Do you think I'm stupid?" she shouted at the doll. "You think I don't know why you're always plodding off to the post office?"

"I never plod."

"You're phoning that blond whore of yours!"

"Stop it. Not in front of the child."

"Maybe you'll get her to join you in Lvov?"

"Give me a break!"

Through the door, Nathan heard something falling to the floor. For a while it was quiet, and he wondered if he should make sure nothing had happened to Róża. But just then Rywka and Ruth came back into the kitchen.

"Pick up your doll," said Ruth.

"Why is Granddad asleep in the day?" asked Róża. "Nobody beat him up."

And in a calm tone Rywka explained to yet another generation that he had "gastritis".

XXXIV

NUSEK

NUSEK COULDN'T WAIT. Work for all, anti-Semitism officially banned, emancipated pioneer girls with red scarves. That was how Hesio had described the Soviet Union to him. He wanted to get to this communist paradise right away. Join the other proletarian boys and girls. He was full of hope that over there, across the eastern border, he'd lose his virginity.

Hesio's arguments spoke more to the human being than Salek's educational arguments. Hesio was not just an effective agitator. It was also said that he had slept with half Tarnów. Clearly, he was just as good a lover as he was a communist.

Rudek was the only Stramer brother not to have let himself be seduced by communism.

"What about your Party leaders Stalin has killed in Moscow?" he asked Hesio.

"We all have a sense of guilt and pangs of conscience..."

"You see!"

"...for failing to help unmask the traitors earlier."

"And have you ever been there?" Rudek continued. "To that Soviet Union?"

Hesio shook his head.

"So how do you know what it's like there?"

And now they were going to be there very soon.

"Capitalism has compromised itself for good and all," said Nusek, repeating word for word to Rudek what he had heard from Hesio. "And after the war it won't ever revive again."

"Shut up and don't compromise yourself," replied Rudek.

Just outside Tarnów four more men had boarded the wagon. They looked like small-town Jews. Much more warmly dressed than Rudek and Nusek, who only had thin jackets. Perhaps they were brothers too? They sat quietly, ready for all seasons of the year – wrapped in those winter coats, scarves and hats of theirs, they looked like rag dolls. But they must have overheard their conversation, and how Rudek responded to his brother.

Nusek decided to say nothing for the rest of the journey, like everyone else. Did they find it as hard to keep quiet as he did?

And what about the driver? He never spoke once, or even turned round towards them.

In silence they reached the river San. When they had jumped down from the wagon, the driver whipped up the horse.

"Where are you going?" said Rudek, grabbing the reins.

"I'll be back with the fisherman. He'll get you across."

"When?"

"Let go and get out of the way!"

Nusek looked inquiringly at Rudek, who shrugged. They hadn't paid the full fee for the crossing yet, so the driver ought to return.

From the direction of the forest, from the road the wagon had gone down shortly before, they heard voices. Four Germans with rifles came running out, straight at them.

"Oh shit," blurted Nusek.

There was no point in fleeing. They weren't going to jump into the water. Rudek was the first to raise his hands.

Before they had had time to figure out what was happening, they had lost their watches.

"Inspection!"

Rudek handed over everything he had. Not much more than they were going to pay to get across the San anyway. Nusek just turned out his pockets. For the first time in his life he was pleased they were empty.

He could see that because of Rudek, who spoke German, they were talking to them in quite a civilized way. Not like at the Gestapo, where in reply to *Guten Tag* you instantly got a fist in the face.

They only beat up the others, who said they hadn't got anything. But the Germans found dollars sewn into their coats and gold coins in their hats. Nusek heard the rifle-butt blows and their screams, but he preferred to look the other way.

He didn't even notice that the driver was back. And he really had brought someone with him. Now the two of them took Rudek aside. What did they want from him? They handed him a piece of paper and a pen. Rudek shook his head. What the fuck was going on?

The driver yanked at Rudek's jacket and pointed a finger at Nusek.

The war is good at curing people of decency, thought Rudek, and began to write:

We got across, everything's all right, we recommend them to others.
Rudolf Stramer

Later, on the riverbank, Rudek and Nusek hugged each other tightly. They were sure it was the last time.

Once Rudek was in the water, the most important moments in his life flashed through his mind. Just as they always describe your final thoughts in books. Mama kissing them in the morning before they left for school. The first time he had his own money from selling cigarettes. The hot chestnuts he got for the siblings.

The deeper he waded, the more recent the memories that came back to him.

Ruth pregnant, saying: "This is a present we'll unwrap in a few months' time." The first time he saw Róża, and she seemed to smile at him and blew bubbles. The old mattress at Lipska's. His promotion to department manager at the Candles Syndicate. Lipska naked, drinking beer in the bathtub. The white bow in Róża's hair this morning.

By now the water was up to his shoulders.

And was covering Nusek's mouth, so he had to stop swearing. From the moment they'd entered the water he hadn't stopped repeating all the curses he knew. When he ran out of Polish ones, he moved on to Yiddish. And so on, over and over, just to keep moving forwards and not turn around. By now he'd rather they shot him in the back. As long as he didn't have to look.

At the same time, he and Rudek were carefully counting their steps.

"Once you've gone fifteen paces, you're to turn left and go four more. Then four more paces straight again, and then eight paces right on the diagonal."

In places the San flowed rapidly, but on the route the fisherman had told them to take they always had their feet on the bottom. They were halfway across. They started to believe they wouldn't drown.

The fisherman had an eye missing. That's to say, he had it, but it was closed. Which gave the ironical impression that he was telling them some sort of bloody joke. That may have been why they couldn't believe he was being serious, and yet they did measure their steps as he had instructed.

"The blind bastard", as Nusek mentally christened him, knew his stuff.

He had also told them what to do once they were on the other side.

"When you're across, hide in the bushes. You must watch out for patrols on horseback. If they catch you, they'll send you to Siberia. Once you're sure there's no patrol, move slowly along the riverbank. You'll see a house with a blue roof and a tumbledown barn, and a painted cottage behind it. Knock at the door and say you're Poles. They'll let you in. And there you have to dry out. Only on the second day can you travel by train. As locals. Since there's a war, nobody checks up."

XXXV

RENA

SHE BRAKED SO HARD she almost caused an accident. The Number 10 tram jerked to a halt. The passengers fell on top of each other. She saw it from the cabin, in her special little mirror.

Minutes earlier, she'd been driving along, humming to herself:

Bay mir bistu sheyn
Bay mir hostu kheyn…

Not very original, but… too bad. Lately that was the most popular song in Lvov. Sung even more often than the revolutionary anthems. And not just by Jews.

How many passengers had it running through their minds right now? she wondered.

Early morning Lvov, as seen through the raindrops on the front window, reminded her of early morning Kraków. Umbrellas on the way to work, to college, to school. Shining cobblestones and house façades. People were jumping across puddles and boarding her tram.

The worn-out wiper creaked loudly but struggled to clean off the water.

Rena liked the morning energy of big cities. It enthused her, giving her hope and strength after the bad dreams she'd had at night.

Constantly thinking about the war would change nothing. It wouldn't stop it. It wouldn't get her parents and siblings out of Tarnów, or send the troops back to their own countries.

"Don't be childish," she told herself. "That's how little Róża might think, not you, a woman of almost thirty."

But maybe the world was being childish? And children can be cruel, as everyone remembers from childhood.

"It's bad for your nerves, go to sleep, darling," said Mieczysław, hugging her.

And he was right. At best her stomach would start to ache, and she should be taking care of herself these days.

Soon they wouldn't be alone. And this time they both wanted it. Rena was hoping for a boy, so when he grew up he'd be tall and handsome like Mieczysław. He probably had the same hope, since he had two daughters already.

She brought the tram to a halt at a stop plastered in faded revolutionary posters and opened the doors.

Of course she supported the left, but nowadays, rather than justice and happiness for all mankind, she was more concerned about her loved ones: Mieczysław and... she touched her belly.

Perhaps I'm getting more like Mama with age, she thought, then closed the doors and moved off.

Compared with Lvov or Kraków, Tarnów as she remembered it seemed sleepy, not to mention the dormant town of

353

Zakliczyn, where she and Mieczysław had lived quietly for the past two years.

Life in the provinces had reminded Rena of waiting. She and Mieczysław often said the people who lived there were waiting for something, but they didn't know what, nor did they really believe it would ever come. You only had to look at the children with their faces glued to the windows in the houses along the road.

But finally the something had come. Poland no longer existed, Tarnów was in the Third Reich, and Lwów was now Lvov in the Soviet Union.

The Lvov newspapers were crowing that the Red Army had liberated their Ukrainian and Belarusian brothers from under the yoke of their Polish capitalist overlords.

"Stalin helped us, he defended us against Hitler," people were saying loudly on the ever more crowded streets. Apparently there were a million refugees already.

While some quietly added: "It's the fourth partition of Poland."

The radio, which Mieczysław sat beside day and night, said something else again. He'd caught a British channel, which for some reason broadcast in German.

Hier spricht London, British Broadcasting Corporation.

At least they could understand something.

Mieczysław had changed since arriving in Lvov. He kept pointing out to her how people in the street were dressed, or that the shelves in the shops were empty.

"Communism," he said, shaking his head. "But poorer than in Zakliczyn."

They walked the length and breadth of the city in search of the missing buttons for her overcoat.

"Fancy not being able to get two stupid buttons in the whole of Lvov!" he told Hesio, who often dropped by in the evenings.

"That's the planned economy," he said, laughing. "Patience. They'll probably toss them in with the next Five Year Plan. Every possible kind."

Sometimes it was hard to tell when he was joking and when he was being serious.

Of course he promised to get them the buttons, but it soon seemed to have slipped his memory.

The window in the driver's cabin kept steaming up. Rena wiped it with a special rag, which became even blacker as a result. Each time, she tried to find a corner to hold without getting her hands dirty. But it was harder and harder. And by the end of the day it was impossible.

As she was putting the rag down beneath the window, she noticed a girl running across the street. Fancy leaving the house in this downpour without an umbrella! She's sure to catch cold. For a second or two the girl turned to face the tram. And if not for her lack of an umbrella, Rena might not have recognized her.

She stopped the tram in the middle of a crossroads and raced out of the cabin.

The passengers squashed in the Number 10 could see her running down Szpitalna Street in her official uniform, with her hair flowing, and then hugging and kissing a woman who looked like her, but younger.

That evening Wela and Max came on their first visit to the one-room flat that Rena and Mieczysław rented in Zamarstynów. With no running water or plumbing and an outside lavatory.

Rena served bread and jam, and instead of tea, an ersatz substitute called "herbatol", diluted with water.

Max told how in Tarnów he had got them false identity papers, and then partly on bikes, partly by train, they had travelled to Przemyśl. They had spent the night there, and next day crossed the border normally, over a bridge. On one side stood the Germans, and on the other the Russians. On both sides they were confused young boys, just the same but in different uniforms.

When the Germans checked their documents, their only concern was the place of residence. The documents included their actual photographs, above fictional Polish names, which they had learned by heart, and a fictional residential address in Lvov.

"And that was how we said goodbye to Auntie Klara," said Max.

Rena had always liked him. Tall and handsome like Mieczysław. But there was something bright and attractive about him too.

"And on the bridge," Wela continued, "the people going in the opposite direction tapped their foreheads to tell us we were bonkers."

"We gave them the same message back," added Max.

Back in Tarnów, Rena had had several dreams about kissing him, and one in which they went to bed together.

"So what are you called now?" she asked them.

"Janina Kwiatkowska," Wela introduced herself.

"And you are…?"

"Bolesław Markowski."

Later, around midnight, Hesio dropped in too. He was the one who had changed the most since arriving in Lvov. Instead of a dandy, now he was an officer.

The military uniform emphasized his slender, muscular figure. He probably wears a size too small on purpose, thought Wela. Like them, he had a new name.

This was the name that appeared underneath his articles, as well as under the photo on his press card bearing the stamp of the *Red Standard*, the newspaper for which he worked at an office on Sokół Street from morning to night, or at least so he claimed. Before he arrived, Rena told the others that nowadays Hesio was spending his nights with an important Polish communist.

"He's consoling her," she said, bending her fingers into quotation marks, "following the death of her husband, who was shot not long ago by unknown culprits."

She had been to see her brother once at the newspaper office (there must have been a Jewish journal there in the past, because there were still some dusty issues with Hebrew font lying on the floor) and had seen the woman. Taller than Hesio, with a sour expression and rings around her eyes. But his taste had changed since the old days in Tarnów. Maybe he'd finally realized looks weren't what mattered most? Lately she had overheard him telling Mieczysław that beautiful women were for men with no imagination.

Maybe it was true. And yet Rena felt insulted.

As she waited for Hesio to emerge from an editorial meeting, she read in the staff wall newspaper that each of the *Red Standard*'s employees was to bring a small box to work with them tomorrow, because they'd be distributing shoe polish.

"Henryk Weber, at your service," said Hesio, smiling, and clicked his heels.

Rena instinctively looked down – at his perfectly polished boots.

XXXVI

RYWKA

NATHAN AND RYWKA wondered how to reply to Nusek's last letter from Lvov.

Have you gone mad? Don't come back here! You're nuts!

That was Nathan's instinctive first response, written on a piece of paper that now lay crumpled under the kitchen stove.

"Letters are censored, have you forgotten?" asked Rywka.

Nusek had written that apart from Rudek, with whom he was living, he rarely saw his siblings, because they never had time for him. He said he felt alone.

Life in Lvov was harder than in Tarnów. He was afraid, and he wanted to go home, to help his parents.

"He doesn't know what he's talking about, the idiot!" said Nathan.

Rywka too was wondering how best to knock it out of his

head. Otherwise he'd end up in the ghetto. And that was in the best case. Or get a bullet in the brain at once.

The Germans were already waiting at the station for those returning from Lvov. Just as he had before the war, the "pig's head" still specialized in catching them, but for different employers. He had a good eye and a good memory. Last week he was the one who spotted Polish Army captain Bezallel Speiser the moment he set foot on the platform. They'd nabbed him, accused him of collaboration with the communists, tortured him at the Gestapo and sent his butchered corpse to the Judenrat in a coal basket.

Rywka was surprised how casually people were talking about it, and how indifferent she felt about it herself. What had happened to her over the past year and a half?

"I know!" said Nathan. "Write in Polish. I'll dictate it to you."

She picked up a pen and began to write. Had the war changed her handwriting? She used to write neatly and clearly. Now her writing was slanting and nervous. The letters overlapped, as if clinging onto each other to avoid falling over. Even words that were written separately were joined together.

No, it must be because of my drooping eyelid, she thought. She'd write a clean copy straight away.

In connection with your letter and your hope for the future, I have one piece of advice. To wit, there's a saying, "A rolling stone gathers no moss".

"Well?" asked Nathan. "Will he understand what I mean?"

Rywka nodded.

And what about Rudek? He always understood what was meant. Shouldn't he talk to his younger brother? Rudek wrote to them regularly from Lvov, unlike Hesio and Rena, who still hadn't sent them a photograph of Władek. Rywka had asked her twice. She hadn't met him yet, but she already loved him. She had written to tell Rena that too. At birth he weighed three and a half kilos. Not too big or too small. Rywka would love to be holding him in her arms already.

The letters from the children that came with the censor's stamp were her only joy. Apart from Róża, of course – her greatest happiness, and at the same time her greatest worry. She would never forgive herself if her granddaughter didn't recover.

Day and night, she and Ruth kept vigil by her bed at the Jewish hospital.

She'd been operated on by Mieczysław's ex-wife. Rywka's heart had missed a beat when she realized who would be her surgeon.

Dr Zawadowska must have recognized her too.

Was that why she turned away and didn't approach them, neither on entering the operating theatre nor on coming out of it an hour later with a sombre look on her face, which Rywka interpreted as a confirmation of all her worst fears? She was sure it was the end, and that she'd never see Róża again.

It was on the day of the operation, maybe the day before or after, that Miss Tecko came to Tarnów for the first time. Rudek had sent her with Aryan papers for Ruth and Róża, and to bring them back to Lvov by train. He must have paid her well for that. But the only person she found at home was Nathan.

How could Rudek have known? They had been careful not to mention the operation in their letters. Didn't he have enough worries?

And so he learned everything from Miss Tecko, who left the papers with Nathan and went back to Lvov alone.

Rywka had to admit that Dr Zawadowska behaved decently, or at any rate the appendectomy was a success.

What luck! For a while she and Ruth forgot about the war.

"It's a sign that everything will work out," Nathan kept saying, when with a smiling Róża they came home from the hospital a week later.

That same day he even taught the child the thanksgiving prayer: *Barukh ata Adonai Eloheinu, melekh ha'olam, hagomel lahayavim tovot, sheg'molani kol tov.*

And for a while he stopped repeating his refrain of the past few months: "If there's a Jew left after this war, they'll take him on tour in a cage and put him on display. There'll be good money in it. But it won't be for us."

Rywka had run into the photographer Chaskiel Bronstein in the street. He was taking pictures of emaciated children begging barefoot on the pavement. He didn't look much better himself. He'd had to close his studio on Krakowska Street. He had no choice, because the Germans had taken almost all the equipment he'd been collecting for years. Everything except for one camera and an old enlarger that had lain in the attic for years.

Rywka asked if he would agree to photograph her with Ruth and Róża. Of course. Next day they dressed in the best clothes they had.

Rywka and Ruth in dark colours. Rywka in a black skirt and a blouse with puffed sleeves and large buttons. Ruth in a black jacket, which covered her threadbare grey dress.

Róża in white – white dress, white sandals, white socks and a white hair ribbon.

"Like for first communion," said Chaskiel, laughing, as he took his time posing them for the picture in their courtyard.

Rywka was to stand behind her granddaughter with her hands resting on her shoulders. And Ruth on their left, with an arm around her mother-in-law.

"Lovely composition. Just a smile, and chins up a bit."

Chaskiel refused to take any money from Rywka.

"I won't take a penny from Rudek's family."

He merely asked for news of Rena.

"How fortunate that she left," he said.

When he brought them the pictures, that same day Rywka ran to the post office and sent them to Rudek along with news of the successful operation and a note to say:

Ruth and Róża are actually much prettier and looking better than this. Róża is always jolly and smiling, though she's making that serious face in the photo because I wanted her to.

In reply Rudek sent Miss Tecko to them a second time. Miss Tecko? She was still a girl. Of Wela's age.

"Joanna," she introduced herself.

A self-confident, smiling blonde with dimpled cheeks. In Lvov she worked at a joiner's shop that made elegant coffins to order. In the bookkeeping department, where Rudek was now the chief accountant.

For three hours she begged Ruth over and over, but in vain.

"You've got good papers. First-rate workmanship. Including Kennkarten."

"I'm known in Tarnów."

"All right, but at night, on the way to the station no one will recognize you."

"Yes, they will!"

"All cats are grey in the dark. Tie up your face with a scarf – 'I've got toothache', yes or no?"

"Don't be a fool, pack your case. That train won't wait," added Nathan in Yiddish to his daughter-in-law.

"Your father-in-law knows what he's saying," Joanna backed him up.

"*Amhu*? One of us?" asked Nathan in surprise, because she "looked good".

The war and the occupation had changed the criteria for judging beauty. One no longer said: she's pretty or ugly, tall or short, shapely or not shapely. Just "she looks good" or "she looks bad".

"I was brought up in Zamarstynów," she said. "Of the sixteen flats in our house four were Catholic, and the rest were Jewish. Every Friday I went to the neighbours for fish and challah. And I played football with the boys in the yard. I was keen. Julek, Dawid and Frycek were my army."

"I won't leave my parents-in-law on their own," Ruth kept saying.

She looked bad, if not very bad.

Rywka hadn't the courage to say it, but she thought it was really about her hair. Every morning she gathered hair off Ruth's pillow, and swept it off the kitchen and living room floor. That was why Ruth was ashamed to go out of the house, even within the ghetto.

"What will people think who haven't seen me for ages?" she once said to Rywka.

She was more afraid of their stares than of the Germans or the blackmailers who hung around at the station to pounce on Jews.

It was a hopeless case, and Joanna went back to Lvov alone again.

Rywka made sure Róża wrote to her father once a week, and that in her letters she reassured him she was well and looking great.

If not for Nanna, they'd have ended up on the street long ago, like the beggars Chaskiel photographed.

Why exactly did he take those pictures of them? For whom?

Nanna came three days after Joanna left, and said that if anything happened she'd take Róża to her sister's place in the countryside.

"We know what the Germans are about and what they're going to do."

This time she had only managed to bring pork fat. On the train from Kraków there was an inspection and the rest of the food had gone. She'd stuffed her bundles in the WC but they'd found them. They'd never fancied poking around in there before. She told Róża about a woman in her compartment who'd produced a juniper-smoked sausage from under her skirt, broken it into pieces and given a bit to each of the passengers.

"With my best wishes. If those brutes are only going to take it off me, let's have a feed."

Then at the station in Tarnów another woman had thumped a whole basket of eggs down on the ground.

"Let 'em choke on these scrambled eggs!" she'd shouted and run off.

Róża laughed and asked Nanna to repeat it: "Let 'em choke on these scrambled eggs!" She also loved Nanna's stories from

Kraków's Kleparz market, where since she had stopped working for Rudek, Nanna was a stallholder.

Rywka could see how much Róża looked forward to Nanna's arrival each Friday, and how she livened up in the old woman's presence. And it wasn't just to do with affection. Nanna didn't have their fear in her.

Despite the fact that recently three Polish women who'd been coming to the ghetto to trade had been shot.

When Ruth wanted to melt the pork fat, Rywka gave her a pan, but she and Nathan left the house to avoid seeing or smelling it. They were due at the neighbours' anyway. Since the synagogues had burned down, Friday evenings with prayers and hymns took place in private houses.

On her return Rywka sterilized the pan and other utensils.

Now she was wondering if Rudek really had left Nanna "a considerable sum", or if she was just telling them that.

Together they went to the church to see Father Flounder.

Before leaving the ghetto, Rywka discreetly took off her armband and put it in her handbag.

They arrived during a break between masses. It was the first time Rywka had been in a church, and she copied Nanna in every way. Touching the water, genuflecting, making the sign of the cross and folding her hands.

She remembered Flounder as a thin, spotty adolescent with a prominent Adam's apple and red cheeks. Two heads taller than Hesio, with whom he had been friends at school. And yet always seemed to be trying to hide behind him.

At first glance she could see that serving God served him well. He had grown handsome and manly. The cassock and dog collar suited him.

A fine gentleman. She would never have recognized him in the street. And to think that once she had considered him bad company for her son.

Now she didn't even know how to address him.

Nanna could sense her confusion, because she got straight to the point.

"If you please, Father, we've come with a request."

The reverend Father calmly heard them out. He wrote slowly and quite clearly, but in childish, oddly large and rounded letters. As he did so, he shielded the document with an elbow, as if ashamed of it. Someone might think from the handwriting that Róża had written out her own birth certificate with Nanna's surname.

"Zegarlińska… and the Christian name?"

Nanna glanced inquiringly at Rywka, who looked around the church and said: "Maria."

Father Flounder finished writing, and with the uncertain expression of a schoolboy handing in his homework gave them the baptism certificate.

"In fact, it's not the first time I've hidden a Stramer," he said.

For a while Rywka couldn't understand what he meant. It had slipped her mind that after escaping from prison Hesio had indeed hidden in the countryside at Flounder's parents' farm. At the time she had gone grey almost entirely, certain this was the worst thing that could ever happen to her, but now she'd forgotten all about it.

"I can have a chat with the sisters and they'll take the child into the convent," he added. "I have good relations with them."

Did she just imagine that he smiled oddly as he made that last remark? Only by that smile did she recognize the old Flounder.

"Go with God," he bid her farewell.

XXXVII

NUSEK

"Want a kick up the shitter?" he heard.

And at once remembered the time he had tried to push his way into a long queue like this one in Tarnów. At the town hall, for gas masks. It was beautiful, hot and sunny. The opposite of now. At the very thought of it Nusek's teeth stopped chattering for a while.

"Fuck off," he replied, and with a proud step went to the back of the queue.

And what had happened to Gizella?

Not even a year had gone by, everything had changed, and once again Nusek was standing among people like himself. Then it had been citizens of Tarnów. Now it was Jews, refugees from Poland, who were standing in line outside the council office in Lvov to sign up to go back home on the German side.

In Tarnów he had looked forward to the winter – Swedish gymnastics with his brothers, sledging on St Marcin's Peak, hot chestnuts from the Hungarian on Sobieski Square.

But in Lvov? Frostbitten hands, feet like blocks of ice, biting cold. Everyone in the queue was talking about the same thing – that dammit all, they were stuck in the worst winter of the century.

Only now, in March, had it stopped snowing.

He was chatting with a boy from Warsaw who was standing behind him, also wearing a hat with ear flaps. His name was Heniek Cukier, under his coat he wore a high-school uniform, and he was talking about some books he'd managed to find in Lvov. Nusek kept nodding just in case, although he had never read Mayakovsky's poetry. Or any other poetry. On the whole, when it came to reading, he'd always agreed with his father and didn't want to end up wearing specs like Salek.

"I've heard Boy-Żeleński is in Lvov and is giving lectures. Do you know if that's true?" Heniek asked him.

"Maybe so," replied Nusek. "I've heard that too."

He didn't know who the hell Heniek was talking about.

Heniek can't have realized, because now he was recommending the best place to buy books in Lvov.

"Batory Street is full of bookshops."

"Seriously?" said Nusek, raising an eyebrow.

"One beside another. Do you know where it is?"

Nusek nodded.

What a boring street, he thought. This Heniek should sooner be talking to Hesio or Salek.

Luckily they changed the subject. And Heniek showed him how he could imitate a jazz trumpet with his lips. It sounded like something off the radio or a record. Nusek was impressed. People in the queue turned to look too. Heniek and his friends in Warsaw had a jazz band, in which each one imitated a different instrument with his lips. Saxophone, double bass, trumpet, percussion. They couldn't afford real ones.

Nusek immediately thought of his father. Old Stramer would have liked that sort of economy.

Two hours later they were frozen solid when they finally got through the tall door into the office, and instantly realized why it took so long to have your name put on a stupid list. The clerk with a pockmarked face (like Stalin, as Heniek whispered into Nusek's ear), calmly drinking tea from a glass in a metal holder, was chatting up almost every young woman.

"So why are you leaving Lvov? Wouldn't you rather stay and get married, to me, for instance?"

It reminded Nusek of the still unsatisfied hope with which he had arrived in this city.

But how, where and with whom was it to be fulfilled? On arrival he and Rudek had stayed with their father's relatives, the Friedmans. On the third floor of a house opposite the synagogue. At night their hosts laid a mattress for them on the kitchen floor. As in the past, in his sleep Rudek took the whole quilt off his brother.

The Friedmans were devout and on the Sabbath they wouldn't let their son Boruch smoke on the balcony.

"Or the rabbi will see."

So he smoked with Rudek and Nusek in the kitchen, with the curtains drawn.

Nor of course was there any question of receiving anyone at the house.

They had only recently moved out. Now they were renting a one-room apartment in Zamarstynów, close not only to Rena and Zawadowski, but also to Wela and Max.

"Let's muck in together. No one will touch muck," they said.

But even so Nusek still hadn't met any girls he could invite home.

And in Lvov there weren't even any prostitutes.

"Prostitution has been banned as a product of capitalism," Hesio explained to him. "And the former prostitutes have been employed as train conductors."

Nusek sometimes spent the night imagining a journey on one of those trains.

He gave the pockmarked clerk his name. And then Rudek's, who had decided that if he couldn't get his wife and child out of Tarnów he'd go back to them.

The clerk dipped his nib in the inkwell, and with purple ink started to enter them into the register. Suddenly he broke off, got up from his desk and disappeared behind a brown curtain dividing the room.

Nusek winked at Heniek, reached a hand through the little window, grabbed the glass holder by its metal handle and drank a sip of tea.

"Have you gone mad?" said Heniek's glance, as he shielded Nusek to prevent others in the queue from noticing what he was up to.

"Not bad," said Nusek, grimacing. "With a dash of booze. Want some?"

Heniek shook his head, looking around to make sure no one had seen.

They heard the sound of the toilet being flushed.

Seconds after Nusek had put the glass back on his desk, the clerk appeared.

"When will it be possible to go back to Tarnów?" he asked him.

"You'll find out at the appropriate time."

Nusek waited for Heniek by the exit.

"What took so long? Did he ask for your hand?"

A few metres ahead of them a beautiful black BMW 326 with German registration plates was parking. A genuine limousine. Four officers got out of it. At once they were surrounded by Jews. In the first instant the Germans took fright, and one of them even opened the car door to hide in it. But then they started to laugh, because they'd realized that the Jews just wanted to ask when the war would be over and they could go home.

At that very moment Nusek and Heniek were walking past the BMW and they peeped inside. Black upholstery, a white steering wheel, 140 on the speedometer! The wide back seat was just begging you to lie down on it.

They reached the end of Kopernik Street, turning around now and then to take another look at the BMW.

Nusek remembered a sentence from his parents' last letter, which had arrived in an envelope stamped with a swastika, a Nazi eagle and the word "Geprüft". *A rolling stone gathers no moss.* The Germans' laughter said the same thing.

He didn't need to know Mayakovsky to understand it.

But did he feel like a stone? At most a pebble that had been kicked from one side of the border to the other.

Not like Rudek. He quickly got used to new cities. Lvov was already the third he'd got to know after Tarnów and Kraków, and that had got to know him. He had a good job at the coffin factory and new acquaintances. Thanks to them he had found Nusek work at the power station.

RUDEK

You could drop that particular stone anywhere in the world, thought Nusek, looking at his older brother. And he'd be fine. He could gather moss in the desert.

All week Nusek looked forward to Saturday. That was when they went shopping at the street market, because there was no food or clothing in the shops. It was there that Rudek had found them padded jackets, felt boots and hats with ear flaps.

Every time they went, he took a careful look at the old coins and stamps too. Meanwhile Nusek inspected broken lamps ("Rudek, I could fix this"), faulty irons and cracked cups that the salesmen must have brought straight from a rubbish tip.

Rudek always did his best to find trinkets for the siblings. A small folding mirror would be useful for Wela, a wooden shirt hanger for Hesio. And a figurine of a child made of tiny stones stuck together? He examined it closely on all sides.

"I'll give it to Rena."

At home he already had a doll from the market that was waiting for Róża's arrival.

Nusek liked to walk around the city with Rudek. Lvov seemed different then from when he went about it on his own. Maybe because he could hardly keep up with his brother and had less time to look at everything.

Once he asked him where he got so much energy.

Rudek cast him a glance, as if wondering whether he could take this eighteen-year-old seriously yet.

For months, every morning he had got up before Nusek in their unheated apartment. They slept in their clothes, hats, scarves and gloves. He did some press-ups, sit-ups and squats. He shaved, had a cup of chicory coffee and went out into the biting cold.

This was the second severe winter in a row in Lvov.

He was the first to arrive at work, he had the keys and opened up the office. For the afternoon break he went to an eatery for beetroot soup and potatoes for thirty-five kopecks. At night he was the last to leave. And at home he was studying Russian.

Looking at him, one might think he'd let himself be carried away by the new ideology and was trying to rival the Stakhanovites from Magnitogorsk or some record-breaking hero of labour from the Lenin collective farm.

Anyway, maybe they were running away from something too?

The manager of the Revolutionary Deed coffin factory said that in spring there would be far more work. As soon as the thaw was over, the offensive would get moving. There was nothing to wait for. They should order more wood now.

If war breaks out, Stalin and the British will chase out the Huns. They'll run off as fast as their legs will carry them. And in the process they'll liberate Poland.

"And you'll go home to your family," he said, patting Rudek on the back. "You'll see."

Rudek nodded at this official optimism. The man was a good manager – he knew what to say to whom. And he also knew who was fond of what. The manager opened his cigarette case.

"Have a smoke."

Back at the Candles Syndicate in Kraków Rudek had always liked chatting to the workers, because they had the best sense of the atmosphere in the street. They made him feel sure that communism had no chance in Poland, since not even those for whom it was designed supported it.

And what were the workers knocking out coffins in Lvov saying? Ruining not just his mood, but also the pleasure of inhaling the lovely scent of freshly cut planks that floated in the air at the factory.

"The whole world is going to war."

"He'll wipe everyone out."

"Nobody can see off Hitler."

They weren't particularly shy about it. They said it out loud and openly in front of Rudek. And some of them added: "And he'll give us a free Ukraine."

They had no doubts about who they were making coffins for.

And what if they were right? What should he do? What plans should he make to avoid ending up in one of them?

Perhaps for the first time ever he had no idea.

There was only one thing he understood about this war, and he'd realized it back in Tarnów. That was why as soon as he arrived in Lvov he had made a deal with a fat, whiskery Ukrainian who sold old coins. Rudek had paid him to supply some other goods. Real Catholic birth certificates and faked Kennkarten.

It was with these that the junior accountant, Joanna Tecko, had gone to Tarnów to fetch Ruth and Róża.

"She's in love with you," was Hesio's instant assessment, on one of his frequent visits to Rudek at work. "Head over heels."

They went outside to smoke.

"Looking ahead, I see," said Hesio, passing the neat rows of coffins.

They sat on a cracked one that everyone used as a bench.

Ever since Hesio had dropped the older communist woman for Lotka, his sweetheart from the old days in Tarnów, he had been transferred to the proofreading department at the *Red Standard*. He had lost his former enthusiasm. He had become pale and anxious, smoking more and sleeping less.

Twice already he had dreamed he'd overlooked a typo. And next day on the front page of the newspaper he saw a picture of the leader captioned: "Joseph Stealin".

He whispered the final word into Rudek's ear.

"That must be every proofreader in the Soviet Union's worst nightmare," said Rudek.

Hesio envied him his nice, quiet job.

"And in such charming company," he said, casting a glance at the desk where Joanna was sitting.

Ever since he had called the Candles Syndicate and instead of finding out what Zula was wearing, he had heard that Miss Lipska had been shot (random passengers had been dragged off a tram and executed in revenge for the murder of a German officer), Rudek had no mind for that sort of thing.

But Joanna really did not want any money from him for her help. She only took enough for the train tickets for herself, Ruth and Róża.

The first time she didn't find them at Goldhammer Street. The second time she couldn't persuade Ruth to leave.

"All that talking – for what and for why?" she said on her return to Rudek who was waiting at the station in Lvov.

How did she know that Yiddish-sounding phrase? Maybe from him?

He asked her lots of questions – how was Róża looking, how

was his mother, how was Ruth, how was his father? He even asked if Róża had grown a lot. But how could she know?

Nor did she know if Nanna was still bringing them food. Rudek had only left her the money for two months. A year and two months ago.

XXXVIII

SALEK

IT'S LIKE A BAD MELODRAMA, thought Salek, when the framed portrait of his mother fell off the wall onto his desk.

Luckily the glass didn't break.

He didn't believe in signs, but even so he was upset.

He examined the photograph of his mother. Regina Stramer looked younger and younger, only her blouse with the puffed sleeves had aged.

Wasn't she a bit like Mickiewicz in profile?

He smiled at her.

It was he who, on leaving Poland, was meant to be in danger, not she, who had stayed in Tarnów.

That was several years ago.

He went back to packing.

What should he do with the photographs of children that he hadn't managed to sell? Pack them too, or throw them away?

After arriving in Paris he had seen a lovely Rolleiflex at a flea market, the same model that Irka once had. Second or third hand, and at half price, but still too expensive for him.

How else, with my French, am I to earn my keep? he thought, returning with the camera under his jacket along Boulevard Barbès to his chambre de bonne, rented by the Party for eight hundred francs a month.

It had probably been stolen before. He hoped at least from the Nazis.

At over thirty, it was the first time in his life that he'd ever stolen. Was robbing a thief stealing too?

The outside of the camera was a bit scratched and dented, but inside it was like new – the shutter wasn't jammed and the Zeiss lens produced nice, sharp images.

For Irka in Kraków photography had been a passion and a pleasure. Now what Salek had learned from her then allowed him to earn a living.

All day long he walked about the Jardin du Luxembourg with the camera around his neck and photographed children. He took their portraits. Then to the surprise of the parents and nannies he didn't ask for a deposit but only an address, and a few days later he turned up with the prints.

He had got an old enlarger from Mo, a Party colleague, who before the war had studied at the Paris Academy of Fine Arts and lived by copying the paintings of the great masters. With his pipe and long beard he looked like one of them too. Since the Germans had marched into Paris he had switched to faking documents and making bags and cases with false bottoms.

Nothing improved Salek's mood like a night in the darkroom. He shielded the windows with black plush, screwed in a red lightbulb and laid out the processing trays. His favourite moment was when the first features of a face began to appear on the paper, after about a minute of soaking in the developer.

Was it the fumes from the photographic chemicals that prompted and kept up his good mood? Leaning over the enlarger, he would smile to himself. And next day he would wake feeling satisfied as he looked at the photographs, now dry, pinned to a string with paperclips.

Every set he sold included one larger portrait, 13 by 18 centimetres, and six small, postcard-format photos. He almost always had to add that yes, of course he could enlarge the postcards too. He set a price for the pictures on the spot, by looking around the flat.

Stucco on the ceiling, Persian rugs on the floor and Japanese porcelain on the mahogany table where he spread out the child's portraits automatically raised their value.

He had only once tried selling anything before. In childhood, when Rudek had sent him to the Tarnów barracks with cigarettes to sell per item. It was no accident that his sales career had ended there. Salek could still remember the look on his brother's face when he got home. He hadn't sold a single cigarette, but some of them had fallen in the mud.

This is perfect proof that progress does exist, he was now thinking.

Of course sometimes he didn't earn anything, or even lost money. For example, last week in the 18th Arrondissement he hadn't taken any money from a family with six children. The flat had damp patches on the walls, the floor was full of holes and he could easily have been in Tarnów's Grabówka district.

But they hadn't let him leave without supper. And the table was even wobblier than the one in Goldhammer Street.

A day later, when some rich people in the 16th were griping over the photos, saying they could pay half price and not a centime more, without a word Salek tore the prints into tiny pieces before their very eyes. In the corridor he looked back, and not without satisfaction saw them scrabbling to put them together.

But usually when he closed an elegant door behind him he ran down the carpeted staircase with a wad of banknotes in his inside jacket pocket, thinking Rudek would have been proud of him.

He hadn't had news for ages, either from Rudek in Lvov or from their parents in Tarnów. The letters had stopped coming at roughly the time when Salek fell in love, which was just after Hitler renounced the Ribbentrop-Molotov Pact and attacked the Soviet Union.

Finally he and his comrades no longer had to explain something they didn't actually understand, which was why the Soviet Union had joined forces with its greatest enemy, the Third Reich. They no longer had to repeat that Stalin was trying to salvage peace in Europe.

Now they said he'd been skilfully playing for time, and they quoted his words: *Hitlers come and go, but the German people and the German state remain.*

And finally the Party had let them start taking action against the fascists, which until now Moscow had forbidden.

Salek had spent the night before his first mission in a rented flat near Place Cambronne.

In fact it was his second mission. He preferred to forget about the first one. He'd been singled out as an "experienced warrior from Spain". He'd been given orders to kill a German officer, who came rolling out of the Folies Bergère, very drunk. Salek zigzagged down the street after him, aware of nothing but his heart pounding and his hands sweating. He forced himself to think of Roman and "Justyn", who were killed in Spain. And his parents, who were being tormented in Tarnów. His brothers and sisters. But it was no use. He wasn't capable of pulling the trigger.

"My finger refused to bend," he told the disappointed commander, an Armenian poet, who finished the job for him.

He heard that he was a common coward.

Now he had a chance to rehabilitate himself by throwing a bomb into a workshop where the Wehrmacht repaired their cars. It was like scattering leaflets, he imagined. It shouldn't be a problem. He lay in bed with his eyes closed, mentally recreating the route he had practised five times the day before – from the flat to the workshop and from the workshop to the metro station.

During the night, Helena, the liaison officer, knocked at his bedroom door. She was holding something. Just in case, Salek reached under his pillow for his pistol, and with his other hand picked up his spectacles from the bedside table. Helena turned out to be aiming a toothbrush at him.

"Solo, lend me some toothpaste," she said in French with a heavy Romanian accent. "Mine's run out."

She was in slightly see-through pyjamas with a red flower pattern.

Salek lowered his pistol.

Was she afraid these were the last hours of their lives, and wanted to go to bed with him?

Because she said something about the warmth we get so little of in our short lives, and then we lie in a cold coffin for all eternity.

Listening to her, he instantly thought of Hesio. It could have been one of those lines his brother used to pick up girls in Tarnów.

"Here you are," said Salek, with an equally strong Polish accent, and simply handed her his toothpaste.

In fact, instead of battling away in French, they probably could have switched to Yiddish. It might well have been her first language too.

Why hadn't he suggested she stay with him at the time? In his place Hesio wouldn't have had a second thought.

Probably because he had to get up in three hours, put the bomb into a special pouch, tie it to his belt and hide it in his trousers. And his mind was filled with praying it wouldn't blow up on the way. That was his greatest fear.

At five in the morning, outside the locked car workshop he lit a cigarette. It made him feel faint; he had never smoked that early in the day, not even in Spain. But he had to light the fuse off something before throwing the bomb through the gate. He had six seconds. He put his hands through the narrow bars and took as big a swing as he could.

As he was running away, he heard the explosion. He slowed down and calmly reached the metro station, where according to plan Helena was waiting. He dropped his pistol into her open handbag. Without a word she closed it, looked him in the eyes (with love? regret? reproach? indifference? – for several months he had returned to that look so many times that he no longer knew) and walked off.

After each mission the liaison officer took the weapon back to the technical division. Which at the same time was a sign that the mission had been successful.

Later they had sometimes seen each other at meetings, but she hadn't taken any special notice of him.

Whereas from that night on, he often thought of Helena and her red-flowered pyjamas.

She wanted to sleep with me, and like an idiot, instead of going to bed with her I fell in love.

Were they roses, or tulips?

He started to volunteer for further missions in the hope of meeting her again. Once he was even held up as a model to other comrades – as someone committed not just to the intellectual work, but also the militant action.

Whenever possible, he discreetly asked his colleagues about Helena. Most of them had heavy accents too. Young tailors, cobblers or workmen who had come here just before the war from small towns in Poland, Romania or Hungary to escape poverty and ever more raucous Nazi slogans. And had volunteered en masse for the resistance movement.

Like Sewek from Kozienice, whose wife and two small children had been killed by the Germans.

"Solo, even if they bloody well catch me," he said, "I don't want to die with a needle and thread in hand!"

"Have you ever been on a mission with Helena?"

Sewek replied that he'd seen Helena in action during a round-up at Place de la Concorde. She'd come out of the metro with a bag in which she had dynamite and two pistols. She saw that the Gestapo had surrounded the entire square and were stopping and searching passers-by. She went straight up to the nearest German officer and asked: "What's going on?"

He went crazy, grabbed her by her coat collar and threw her out of the square.

"Raus!" said Sewek, imitating the German. Sewek had probably been let go because he was a blue-eyed blond.

After their last joint mission – throwing a bomb through a window into a restaurant full of Germans – Salek had noticed that Sewek's trousers were bloodstained.

"Did you get hit?"

"No. I can't feel anything."

By now they were standing safely at the metro station.

"What about your leg? You're bleeding."

Sewek looked at his trousers.

"That's from nerves," he smiled, embarrassed. "Sometimes my haemorrhoids burst."

Salek had finished packing his things. Now they were waiting in a suitcase by the door.

But no one had warned him that Helena was married.

He ran into her one time on the rue de Rivoli. Members of the resistance weren't allowed to sit at home during the day. So they walked about Paris, usually from café to café, simply to avoid arousing the suspicions of their neighbours, who should think they were at work in those hours.

How many cups of coffee can you drink in a single day? They couldn't afford anything else at the counter and afterwards they complained that they couldn't sleep at night.

If they accidentally met in the city, naturally they pretended not to know each other. But on rue de Rivoli Salek broke the rules and greeted Helena.

It was enough for one of them to be followed and both would get caught.

"This is Olivier," she said, introducing a tall man with curly hair. "My husband."

Salek shook his hand. In a shoe-shop window he saw that next to Olivier he looked like David next to Goliath. If not worse.

"I hate husbands," he said as a joke, when Olivier had briefly stepped inside a bakery.

Helena smiled.

Perhaps he'd see her again today? Maybe she'd be the one who knocked at his door? Since several people from their organization had been arrested yesterday, the others had to disappear for a while. The liaison officer was to bring him a ticket and new documents, with which Salek would leave Paris right away.

He didn't know where he was going or who he would be.

XXXIX

RUDEK

ONE DAY WHEN IT WAS getting warmer, Rudek set off to work as usual. Earlier in fact, because he'd woken at three in the morning, thinking about Róża, Ruth and his parents in Tarnów, and failed to get back to sleep. He had also had breakfast faster because he didn't have to chat to Nusek, who'd been sent to Kiev for a few days with the power-station staff. It was fortunate – through him Rudek could send gifts for Wela and Max, who'd been living there for the past six months.

Despite the early hour, there were lots of people at the tram stop. They said three trams in a row had failed to arrive.

Another accident, he thought. Nihil novi sub sole.

He could smell the scent of summer in the air.

Maybe he'd invite Joanna to come home with him that evening? Or if it were warm, first they could go to a café for brandy, and then to his place?

There was no weather forecast on the radio or in the press. So even on such a sunny day as this, plenty of people were standing at the stop with umbrellas.

He decided to go to work on foot.

In the Soviet Union meteorology was a state secret. Nor could you get a city map or a phone book.

"To avoid helping spies with their work," was the explanation.

Not by chance was this the first city where he sometimes lost his way.

And what about Salek? he thought. Did he get lost in Paris too?

Before the war he had read in a newspaper about eighty-two-year-old Mrs Sobelsohn. She had travelled from Tarnów to Warsaw to ask at the Soviet embassy for intervention on behalf of her son, Karl Radek, who was accused in Moscow of belonging to the Trotskyite opposition. The embassy had refused to help. And Mrs Sobelsohn had gone to the post office to send a telegram directly to Stalin. She begged him, as a leader known for his paternal affection, to show mercy to her only son, who, *putting his personal happiness and private matters last, has dedicated his whole life to communism.*

The telegram had cost as much as two hundred zlotys. How curious that the newspaper had provided this detail, and that it had stuck in Rudek's memory. And of course Mrs Sobelsohn's efforts hadn't helped at all.

He had even cut out the article to send to Salek, but to what address? He didn't know where in Paris he was living.

He remembered their father's rage when Salek and Hesio read Marx by the oil lamp. You bloody blind moles!

He wondered what the world would be like today without Marx. What would have happened if Marx had never existed?

If he had simply never been born? Or at least failed to write anything because on the way to the library in London he'd fallen under a droshky? And in what direction would life have gone if neither Hitler nor Stalin had been born, those two pillars of the modern world?

He remembered an old joke. From the days when his father worked as an agent for the Assicurazioni Generali Trieste.

Little Moishe comes to his father and asks: "Daddy, what is insurance?"

"If you're insured and you fall under a tram, for instance, and it cuts off your leg, you'll get, let's say, a thousand zlotys for it."

Moishe thinks a while.

"And what if it cuts off both legs, Daddy?"

"Oy, you dreamer, you dreamer!"

Rudek realized he knew plenty of jokes but he didn't know anyone who made them up.

He thought of Rena. Hair in a mess and always in tears. He hadn't seen her in a better state for the past three months. Maybe he should drop in on her and Mieczysław this evening instead of making a date with Joanna? After work Rena didn't leave the house anymore. Zawadowski drank, and she did nothing but clean. So it was, ever since their little Władek had ended up in hospital with pneumonia. She still blamed herself for not dressing him warmly enough. And said she shouldn't have taken him out for walks.

He had died the day after being admitted to the children's ward.

In the letters she sent to her parents Rena went on writing that everything was fine, that the baby was growing well and had a good appetite. He was given frequent, but not excessive meals. Rena was feeding him according to her mother's instructions, in other words letting him try everything she herself was eating. Władek was starting to crawl. He wore the colourful little sweater her parents had sent them from Tarnów. He was a smiley, cheerful little boy who hardly ever cried. He couldn't wait to meet his grandparents.

In the reply that Rena had recently shown Rudek, their mother had written:

My dearest darling children,

I'm aching with longing to meet Władek, if only in a photograph. Dearest Rena, you wrote to say you'd send me his picture, but it still hasn't arrived. How's he coming along? Will he have teeth soon, or maybe he already has some?

And how are you over there? Are you earning enough for everything you need?

We are well, except that we miss our children very much.

Be healthy and happy. I kiss and hug you tightly. And send lots and lots of big smackers for my darling little Władek. Your loving mother.

Even Nathan, who never wrote to his children, had scrawled at the bottom of the page: *Big kisses for my grandson!*

Rudek crossed a wide street. By now he could see the coffin factory building in the distance.

At first he had tried to console Rena with the story of Kuba. Their parents' first-born son, whose grave he had once found by accident when out with his friends in Tarnów. They had skipped school, and they knew no one would look for them at the cemetery.

"Rudek!" Daniel had called out. "Look, this must be a relative of yours."

That was how he found out about him.

He sat down with his friends beside a wall, on a small gravestone inscribed *Jacob Stramer*, and they drank to his memory.

When he got home, his mother told him that was his brother, Kuba. A strange feeling.

"Rena," he said, embracing his weeping sister. "When he died, she thought she'd never have any more children too."

Maybe he should have waited a bit? And not told Rena that story at once in the hospital.

"I don't want any more children!" she had erupted. "I want my Władek."

Rudek put the key in the lock.

How odd, the office door was open. Had he forgotten to lock it last night?

He pressed the handle. What he saw inside was even odder. The manager was never at work before ten o'clock. What's more, he was tossing papers into the "crematorium", as the employees called the small pot-bellied stove that stood in his office.

"Don't take off your jacket," he said to Rudek. "You're leaving."

"Where am I going?"

"With me. To the east. The lorry's already waiting."

The manager didn't have to say more. It wasn't a business trip.

Half an hour later Rudek had tossed the last of his things into a suitcase. He only packed the most necessary items, in other words almost everything he had here. What about Nusek's clothes? There weren't many. He had left one sweater full of holes, two shirts and a single sock in the wardrobe. Would he be back for it? If only he'd stay in Kiev. But just in case, Rudek left some documents in a Polish name on the kitchen table.

Nusek Stramer would cease to exist.

From work he'd had time to call the *Red Standard*. The cleaner answered.

"I'd like to speak to Comrade Henryk Weber, please," he said.

"All the staff left in the night," she informed him in a weary tone. She must have already had to repeat it many times today.

As soon as he asked: "Where have they gone?" she hung up.

At the top of the suitcase Rudek packed the doll for Róża. He hid his coins, money and documents in his inner jacket pocket.

When he ran downstairs, the driver started the engine and the three-ton lorry shuddered and set off. The manager had agreed to go and fetch Rena and Mieczysław too. He had no family of his own in Lvov.

Rudek prepared himself for every possible situation he might face at Rena's place.

"No, it's impossible," Mieczysław would say, barely able to stand upright. "Hitler wouldn't dare."

He had less and less in common with reality, less and less in common with the lawyer of old, Mieczysław Zawadowski, whom Rudek remembered from Tarnów. Even in appearance. Doubled-up, red in the face, resigned. Time has taken its toll on him, thought Rudek. And on a grand scale.

"But Mieczyś, he already has."

And what if he replied: "But Rudek, I'm not moving from here."

In the state Rudek had seen him in lately it really would be tough for him. Anyway, he could stay. What danger was he in?

But Rena. She had to leave. But what if she refused to go without him?

Rudek would encourage him with a bottle of vodka that was waiting in the lorry.

He had documents ready for his sister, a whole wad of papers in the name of Anna Wojciechowska. Real ones he'd bought, left by a girl who'd died recently. All Rena had to do was paste in her photo and another member of the family would lose the name Stramer.

The next would be gone when Rudek started using the documents he had for himself. He would become Jerzy... He reached into his inside pocket. He had to remind himself what his name would be.

XL

RYWKA

Nanna was their only contact with the outside world. For a year they'd had no news from the children, and they weren't allowed to send letters anymore. Rywka looked at the group photo that had stood on the chest of drawers for all those years. It had moved house with them, but without its frame, which they had sold.

Where were they all now? Were they alive?

It was lucky that through Szymek Hersztejn, who worked outside the ghetto, she had managed to send a telegram to Nanna. Szymek had good looks, he was a charming boy with fair hair and a snub nose. The son of her distant cousin. He'd been living with them since his parents were killed.

"Because they didn't have round stamps in their documents," he said.

Apparently he saw it happen, but Rywka preferred not to ask. It was enough that he woke at night crying.

She had heard that that day on Widok Street a drunken Gestapo officer had used an axe to kill both those with round stamps and those without.

These stamps were an unreliable guarantee of life by now. No one knew which was current today. Round or square, or maybe oval? That was the kind Szymek had in his Meldekarte.

She was woken at night by his crying and Nathan's snoring in turns.

Once again they were all sleeping together. In the marital bed Rywka lay beside Nathan, Ruth and Róża, with Szymek on the couch next to them.

At first the Germans had displaced them to a cottage on the river Watok. It stood among woods and meadows, and Róża could run around.

"Grandmama, look how beautiful it is here!" she said, and Rywka hadn't seen her so happy for ages. "Wonderful!"

The fresh air gave Róża a good appetite. She stopped looking pale. Unfortunately, those three months in the first ghetto had gone by quickly. Then they were ordered to move into the second ghetto, in Grabówka.

Into the single room where they were now. Much more cramped than at Goldhammer Street but also on the ground floor and with an outhouse in the yard.

It was lucky Szymek was with them, and Róża was so sold on him. To her he was an adult. He was fourteen already. He distracted her from what was going on outside. The stinking sewer flowing down the street. The stream of sick, emaciated people in rags. The corpses lying on the pavement under newspapers.

Even when they left the flat, Róża never took her gaze off Szymek, but constantly looked into his bright blue eyes.

Today Rywka had given him the telegram to Nanna, because all morning people had been saying they were going to liquidate the ghetto.

But was it true? Somebody was always saying something. Every day it was different. Rumours flew around the ghetto faster than illnesses. She'd heard that the deportees were instantly burned alive. And also that there were letters from people who'd left on transports and were now working normally.

And every Friday the rabbi repeated that like everything else, Hitler was just a tool in the hands of the Almighty. He only had to blow and Hitler would be gone.

What more would it take for Him to start blowing? thought Rywka on her way home.

The telegram to Nanna was short. All she wrote was: *It's time.* She'd know what it was time for.

But that evening, before receiving the telegram, Nanna arrived of her own accord.

"Something prodded me," she said.

XLI

NATHAN

WHEN NATHAN FOUND OUT they had caught Rywka in the street, he knew what it meant. The neighbour had seen them herding her and Ruth to Magdeburg Square, formerly Wolności – Liberty Square.

Had someone recognized them on the Aryan side, where they'd gone to get something to eat?

Some son of a bitch. Like the one yesterday who'd shouted after Nanna and Róża from a window next door: "A Jewish child is escaping!"

Nanna had hurled colourful abuse at him and he'd closed the window. She'd picked up Róża and run towards the station. What had happened next? Nathan and Rywka didn't know.

All Nathan knew was what he was going to do. He didn't want them to torture him. When they came knocking, he'd go to the outhouse in the yard. The beam would support him. He'd checked, and it was solid. Nor did he weigh as much as in the past. His belt was unlikely to break. It was still a gift from his brother. Quality American workmanship. He tied it on at both ends.

Once again Nathan Stramer could see his brother standing on the quay in New York. But this time the ship was not departing, but sailing towards Ben Stramer.

RYWKA

That morning in the Appellplatz at Stutthof the young officer took out his pistol, but the other, his senior, shook his head at the last moment.

"Waste of bullets."

For Ruth, a few months ago at Auschwitz, they hadn't thought it a waste.

Transport to the sea – that was the decision now.

In his youth Nathan's eyes had shone whenever he spoke of the waves, the high and low tides, and how he would take her to the seaside.

He had promised so many times.

They were going to sit together on the sand, on a beach like the one where the half-dead women had just been unloaded from a lorry onto boats. He was going to put his strong arm around her, and together they would gaze at the waves.

And wait for the sun to set.

"To see the most beautiful sight on earth with the most beautiful woman on earth," he used to say, and kissed her.

He wasn't bad-looking in those days either. He'd promised so many times. Instead of that she'd fallen pregnant. Together they had raised six children.

She had to close her eyes. She saw all the Stramers together again at the kitchen table.

But you never told me the sea water was so bitter.

Never mind, Nathan.

BIBLIOGRAPHY

Roman Brandstaetter, *Bardzo krótkie i nieco dłuższe opowieści* ["Very short and slightly longer tales"], Wydawnictwo Poznańskie, Poznań 1984

Georges Brandstatter, *Résistants Juifs* ["The Jewish Resistance"], Éditions Jourdan, Brussels 2013

Józef Hen, *Najpiękniejsze lata* ["The Finest Years"], Aneks, London 1996

Zagłada tarnowskich Żydów ["The Extermination of Tarnów's Jews"], edited by Stanisław Potępa and Aleksandra Pietrzykowa, Muzeum Okręgowe w Tarnowie (Tarnów District Museum), Tarnów 1990

Martin Pollack, *Kaiser von Amerika: Die große Flucht aus Galizien* ["The Emperor from America: The great flight from Galicia"], Zsolnay, Vienna 2010

Martin Pollack, *Galizien. eine Reise durch die verschwundene Welt Ostgaliziens und der Bukowina* ["Galicia: a journey through the vanished world of East Galicia and the Bukovina"], Insel Verlag, Frankfurt am Main 2001

Stanisław Potępa, *Z życia półświatka* ["The Life of the Demimonde"], Tarnowskie Towarzystwo Kulturalne (Tarnów Cultural Association), Tarnów 2007

Horacy Safrin, *Ucieszne i osobliwe historie mego życia* ["Amusing Personal Stories from My Life"], Wydawnictwo Łódzkie, Łódź 1970

Marci Shore, *The Taste of Ashes: The Afterlife of Totalitarianism in Eastern Europe*, Crown Books/Random House, New York 2013

Julian Stryjkowski, Piotr Szewc, *Ocalony na Wschodzie* ["Survivor in the East"], Les Editions Noir sur Blanc, Montricher 1991

Alexander Szurek, *The Shattered Dream*, translated from the Polish by Jacques and Hilda Grunblatt, East European Monographs, Boulder; distributed by Columbia University Press, New York 1989

Paweł Śpiewak, *Żydokomuna* ["Communist Jews"], Czerwone i Czarne, Warsaw 2012

Marek Tomaszewski, *Tarnów. Żydowskie krajobrazy* ["Tarnów: Jewish Landscapes"], S-CAN, Tarnów 2012

ACKNOWLEDGEMENTS

I would like to thank: Wanda Lacrampe for her invaluable documentary help; Agnieszka Wierzcholska of the Freie Universität Berlin for nine gigabytes of source material on prewar Tarnów; Mariola Góra from Tarnów City Public Library and Adam Bartosz from Tarnów District Museum for their commitment, for looking after me on the spot and all the historical material I requested.

I wish to thank Maria Jakubowicz, Józefowi Hen, Adam Daniel Rotfeld, Aleksander Smolar, Kazimierz Łaski, Marian Turski, Jan Kancewicz, Michał Komar, Katarzyna Stroczan, Nina Wojciechowska, Andrzej Kuhl, Włodzimierz Kwieciński and Małgorzata Melchior for taking the time to answer my often naïve questions.

Thank you to Halina Kralowa, Małgorzata Szczurek and Witek Wrzosiński for reading the manuscript and making helpful critical comments. Many thanks too to my wife and children for their patience and support. And to Jacek Ziemiński for "the economics of love".

AVAILABLE AND COMING SOON
FROM PUSHKIN PRESS

Pushkin Press was founded in 1997, and publishes novels, essays, memoirs, children's books—everything from timeless classics to the urgent and contemporary.

Our books represent exciting, high-quality writing from around the world: we publish some of the twentieth century's most widely acclaimed, brilliant authors such as Stefan Zweig, Yasushi Inoue, Teffi, Antal Szerb, Gerard Reve and Elsa Morante, as well as compelling and award-winning contemporary writers, including Dorthe Nors, Edith Pearlman, Perumal Murugan, Ayelet Gundar-Goshen and Chigozie Obioma.

Pushkin Press publishes the world's best stories, to be read and read again. To discover more, visit www.pushkinpress.com.

THE PASSENGER
ULRICH ALEXANDER BOSCHWITZ

TENDER IS THE FLESH
NINETEEN CLAWS AND A BLACK BIRD
AGUSTINA BAZTERRICA

AT NIGHT ALL BLOOD IS BLACK
BEYOND THE DOOR OF NO RETURN
DAVID DIOP

WHEN WE CEASE TO UNDERSTAND THE WORLD
THE MANIAC
BENJAMÍN LABATUT

NO PLACE TO LAY ONE'S HEAD
FRANÇOISE FRENKEL

FORBIDDEN NOTEBOOK
ALBA DE CÉSPEDES

COLLECTED WORKS: A NOVEL
LYDIA SANDGREN

MY MEN
VICTORIA KIELLAND

AS RICH AS THE KING
ABIGAIL ASSOR

LAND OF SNOW AND ASHES
PETRA RAUTIAINEN

LUCKY BREAKS
YEVGENIA BELORUSETS

THE WOLF HUNT
AYELET GUNDAR-GOSHEN

MISS ICELAND
AUDUR AVA ÓLAFSDÓTTIR

MIRROR, SHOULDER, SIGNAL
DORTHE NORS

THE WONDERS
ELENA MEDEL

MS ICE SANDWICH
MIEKO KAWAKAMI

GROWN UPS
MARIE AUBERT

LEARNING TO TALK TO PLANTS
MARTA ORRIOLS

THE RABBIT BACK LITERATURE SOCIETY
PASI ILMARI JÄÄSKELÄINEN

BINOCULAR VISION
EDITH PEARLMAN

MY BROTHER
KARIN SMIRNOFF

ISLAND
SIRI RANVA HJELM JACOBSEN

ARTURO'S ISLAND
ELSA MORANTE

PYRE
PERUMAL MURUGAN

RED DOG
WILLEM ANKER

THE COLLECTED STORIES OF STEFAN ZWEIG
STEFAN ZWEIG

AN UNTOUCHED HOUSE
WILLEM FREDERIK HERMANS

WILL
JEROEN OLYSLAEGERS

MY CAT YUGOSLAVIA
PAJTIM STATOVCI

BEAUTY IS A WOUND
EKA KURNIAWAN

BONITA AVENUE
PETER BUWALDA

IN THE BEGINNING WAS THE SEA
TOMÁS GONZÁLEZ

TRAVELLER OF THE CENTURY
ANDRÉS NEUMAN